FALLING FROM EDEN, INC.

THE CHRONICLES OF ETHAN STONE

A Novel by

ROSS WRIGHT

ROSS WRIGHT

Falling from Eden, Inc. is a work of fiction. Names, characters, places, and incidents are the products of the author's imagination or are used fictitiously. Any resemblance to actual events, locales, or persons, living or dead, is entirely coincidental.

FALLING FROM EDEN, INC.

*For the
Cunninghams*

ACKNOWLEDGMENTS

Special thanks to the writers of The Purple Page who kept me on track, Annette Monteleone for her continuous support and encouragement, Barbara Wright for her psychological insight to the characters, all the members of The Orchestre Surréal whose names I freely stole, my beat up Mac PowerBook G4 that managed to stay in one piece throughout the writing of this book, and to: John Cunningham, Al Teman, Angela Carole Brown, Dr. Kerry Higgins, Mark Thomas, Barrett Tagliarino, Dominik Hauser, Jamie Lula, Doug Gerry, Halle Eavelyn, Keith James Kennedy, John Hoke, and Robert C. Jones Ph.D. who all gave me invaluable feedback.

Ross Wright

Part One

DEPARTURE

Chapter 1

Fire erupted, engulfing the space pod as it struck through the earth's outer atmosphere. The sudden turbulence slammed Ethan and Ascot as they tightened their seat harnesses. Staring out the TV-sized porthole, they watched as the flames consumed them. The sound and heat felt as if they were sitting in a blast furnace. Neither said a word. Just seconds before, they had been drifting in the cold, silent vacuum of space, praying to the god to whom atheists and agnostics pray when put in such precarious situations.

Abruptly, the fire went out. They were flung once again into the weightless, dead quiet of space.

Ascot broke the silence. "This is bad!"

"What happened?" Ethan strained to see out the small window, trying not to appear nervous.

"We didn't break through the surface tension of the stratosphere. We bounced back into space."

Ethan unbuckled his harness and moved out of his seat to get a better view. The pod was tumbling, the vast blue ball of planet Earth appearing, then disappearing, then appearing again, making him dizzy. "So what do we do?"

"There ain't nothing we can do, but wait."

Ethan closed his eyes. He trusted Ascot's judgment. He had learned a lot from Ascot during the past eight years; one thing in particular was that sometimes patience really is a virtue. It was patience that had gotten them this far, so if there was nothing he could do, he should try to enjoy the moment.

Ascot felt compelled to give Ethan a more complete answer. "We are like a stone being skipped over a lake. As long as we stay within the gravitational pull of the earth, we will eventually stop skipping, break the surface tension of the stratosphere, then fall to Earth like a meteor."

Suddenly the pod lurched and the weightlessness of space ended. Ethan fell back into his seat and strapped himself in. Flames and a loud hissing erupted around them once more, as the pod bounced through the turbulent atmosphere and plummeted towards the earth.

Before they left, it had occurred to Ascot that the escape pod had never been properly tested, much less used, so they had no idea if the thing even worked. It was very possible that this was going to be a one-way ride to nowhere. They could end up a flaming meteor in the night sky, a streak that some young couple will make wishes upon.

The alternative was to stay in a broken space station with no chance that anyone would ever come to their rescue. The choice was simple. If they ever wanted to get home, they had to take the chance. There really was no other option.

As a kid, Ascot read a book about a guy who survived a boating accident. He floated across the Atlantic for seventy-six days in a life raft. Ascot wished he had read more books or knew more about sailors who had been shipwrecked and had survived for years on a desert island. It would have been useful to know what they had done to stay sane and maintain some kind of purpose in their lives. Ascot was just stubborn. He decided he was going to survive this. He was going to get himself and Ethan home, that was it. The temperature of the pod quickly rose. Ascot licked his lips and tasted the sweat dripping off his forehead. It seemed increasingly probable that this would be the last thing he ever did.

Ethan didn't like roller coasters, and boats make him sea sick. Knowing there was nothing he could do, he tried to relax and use the rhythm of the turbulence to accompany his mantra: "I will be fine, I will be fine, I will be fine."

Suddenly the pod became silent. They were back in the cold, weightless vacuum of space.

"Ah, jeez!" Ethan broke the mantra. "This is annoying! Are we going to fall or float away?"

"Getting into the atmosphere is just the beginning," said Ascot, focusing on Ethan's frustration and trying not to appear nervous.

"We are free-falling with very little control where we land, so if we survive the impact, that will be the first miracle. If we don't end up in the middle of the ocean or on top of a frozen mountain, where no one will ever find us, that will be the second miracle. If we end up near civilization where they are friendly, that will be the third miracle. We're talking three miracles. That's a lot to ask for."

Ethan climbed out of his seat again to peer out the window. "That's encouraging. You're just a glass-half-full kind of guy, aren't you?" Ethan was surprised at how sarcastic he sounded. He usually didn't talk to Ascot that way. He took a good look at Earth, trying to figure out what he was looking at, but the real thing wasn't like looking at a globe. There were no lines or different colors. Ethan couldn't tell which side was top or bottom. A thick layer of clouds obscured his view. On top of that, the pod was tumbling so it was hard for him to stay focused on any particular point. Ethan lost concentration. He rubbed his temple to suppress a headache. His body was freezing cold and he felt nauseous from the weightlessness of space.

Ethan floated back to his seat and pulled the belts across his chest and waist. He put his head against his knees and assumed the crash position, the same one demonstrated in those laminated picture cards in the seat pocket of every commercial airline. This relieved his nausea slightly. For the first time since their journey began, Ethan noticed the smell of the vinyl seats. His mind pondered the bizarre circumstance in which he found himself. He was either going to be dead soon or given a chance to start his life over. He thought, "All amazing stories have a moment like this in them." Anyone who was ever considered to be "great" had to have a life-changing moment or he or she wouldn't have been able to earn the title. Ethan suddenly appreciated the opportunity in which he now found himself. "Weird, it's all about how you frame it."

Objects fall to Earth at ten meters per second squared, but due to the friction of the atmosphere, there comes a point where that object reaches terminal velocity, the rate at which the falling object's speed no longer increases. The shape, size, and mass of an object will determine the object's terminal velocity. Ethan recognized that when he got nervous, his mind was consumed with random trivial facts as a means of escape. Images of Professor Huebner, a jolly old man with white hair and a big stomach who taught college Physics, raced through Ethan's mind: "If a pianist played an A 440 on the piano at Carnegie Hall and it took 0.8 seconds to reach the back wall of the auditorium 320 feet away then bounce back to the pianist, what is the temperature of the room?" Ethan had no idea how to calculate that anymore. What does college prepare you for, anyway? Certainly not being stuck in an escape pod in outer space hoping to get a chance to fall to Earth and crash land in some habitable place.

Just then, the pod hit massive turbulence again, as if the hand of gravity grabbed them and pulled them toward Earth. The roar of flames was deafening and the temperature in the pod rose sharply. Ethan kept his head between his knees. He felt his stomach sink down into the chair, and his life started to pass before him. Ethan looked up at Ascot, who tried to pretend he wasn't scared but wasn't doing a very good job of it.

Ethan cleared this throat. "Hey, we made it this far. No one would have expected that!"

Ascot grinned. "True!"

Ascot had been Ethan's default mentor for the past eight years simply because he was twenty years older. It was his nature to be a bit of a know-it-all. Ascot was friends with Ethan's dad and had known Ethan peripherally since he was a boy. He saw Ethan as a precocious young man who lacked direction and a sense of purpose.

When Ascot landed the job as a fitness director with Eden, Inc. and was told he could bring an assistant, he thought of Ethan. The information he had been given was that they were going to a prestigious seven-star resort in a remote location catering to the super-elite. It seemed to be an opportunity where Ethan could expand himself physically, mentally, socially, and financially. That was what Ascot had promised to get Ethan to agree, so when the accident happened, Ascot stubbornly survived to make good on his promise.

The Valhalla space resort was in semisynchronous orbit 6000 miles above the Earth's surface. Ascot was in charge of its massive physical fitness facility. Neither Ascot nor Ethan had any idea what went wrong. When the station was destroyed, they serendipitously managed to be on a piece that had survived. For eight years, the two of them, most likely the sole survivors, had been floating around the solar system like a comet, waiting for an opportune time to jettison from their chunk of the station and get back to Earth. It took years for the alignment and conditions to appear to be right. But were they?

While they were waiting for the optimum time frame, Ascot spent thousands of hours spewing politics, world opinion, sports strategy, and pop psychology onto the fairly willing mind of Ethan Stone. It was his intent to make sure that if they did survive this, their time stuck in outer space would not have been wasted.

Ethan fidgeted in his seat, "What do you think will happen when we arrive?"

"Good question!" said Ascot, still pondering, "I mean that literally. I like the fact that you asked *when*, not *if*, we arrive."

"Hey, I'm a glass-half-full kinda guy. You should know, you're the one who taught me about the Law of Attraction."

"Well, to answer your question," said Ascot, steering the conversation back on track, "I have no idea what awaits us when we land. We could be considered heroes and put on the front page of newspapers and magazines. We could be the headlines on breaking news on all the networks. Our story could become a best-selling book that gets made into a movie then turned into a TV series. In no time we could be rich and famous and have hot chicks chasing us everywhere we go."

Ethan grinned, "Sounds good!"

Just then the pod started somersaulting. The nylon harnesses dug into Ethan's shoulders as his weight slammed against them. This interruption annoyed Ethan. He was enjoying the thought of fame and fortune. Now the uncertainty of his predicament was all too real. For eight years he wanted answers: What the hell happened? Why hadn't anyone come to rescue them or even tried to contact them? What happened to his dad? His girlfriend? What about the half-dozen employees and handful of hardcore gym freaks whom he'd left all those years ago? They all thought he would be back in three months. Did they all think he was dead? Once he's back, are they going to be pleased to see him or pissed off because he put them through the whole grieving process for no reason?

Ethan was certain that, if he made it back to Earth in one piece, his dad would be happy despite all that Ethan had put him through. Once Ethan explained to him what had happened, his dad, being a pragmatic person, would understand and everything would be fine. At least that was what Ethan hoped.

Chapter 2

As a young man, Vince Stone, was a state champion body builder. He was training for the Mr. Universe Contest in order to get his pro card when he met Ethan's mom. He often told the story of how he saw the perfect ass on this Brazilian hottie at a Venice Beach figure competition. He leaned over and said to some random guy standing next to him, "I want that!" The guy looked at him with an expression that said, "Duh! You and everyone else here." Since that day Vince's advice had been, "Be careful what you wish for." After the competition he chased her down and introduced himself. Her name was Delilah, (pronounced De-lee-lah) and it was love at first sight.

They made wild passionate love three, four, five times a day for about two months straight. Every night when they went to bed, every morning when they woke up, before and after workouts; any time one of them took a shower, the other would get naked and jump in. It was the best two months of Vince and Delilah's lives, until she got pregnant. Both of them were making just enough money to pay for their food, supplements, and gym memberships. Delilah was training to become a professional fitness model and pregnancy was not part of her plan. She got very depressed.

Vince wanted her to have an abortion, but she had grown up Catholic. Consequently, the more Vince tried to talk her into having one, the more stubbornly she refused. So in very short time, their two months of bliss were followed by seven months of hell.

Vince competed in the Mr. Universe Competition and blamed his loss on Delilah. Claiming that all the stress she had put him through caused him to retain water and appear puffy. She, with her South American passion, fiercely resented him for blaming her, which only added more stress to their lives.

Soon after that Ethan was born. Vince had another opportunity to get his pro-card. Now with a kid and a bitchy wife living in his little apartment, he was happy to stay at the gym and train instead of going home. He thought, "This is perfect." He had all the motivation a man could need, but then his greed got the better of him. He saw the guys he would soon be competing against, and they were all obviously on steroids. Vince took lots of supplements: amino acids, creatine, vitamins etc., but stopped short of illegal body-enhancing drugs. He didn't want to come up short this time, not now with a kid and a wife to support. He needed to win, so he started shooting up, and the stuff worked. He gained 15 pounds of muscle in 3 months. He was leaner and looked better than ever.

But his competitors weren't stupid and they didn't want to lose, either. Even though they all took steroids they also all knew how to clean out their system before a competition in order to pass a drug test. So they all grumbled about fairness, and the judges agreed that everyone needed to pee in a cup and be drug tested. To no one's surprise, Vince came up positive for anabolic steroids and was immediately disqualified.

Even after that, he still continued to take steroids. He was determined to be a champ, spending eight hours a day in the gym. Within six months, he gained another fifty-five pounds of muscle. Now he was six feet two inches tall, with twenty-four and a half inch biceps, and weighed three-hundred-twenty-six pounds, with five percent body fat. He had become a freak. Everywhere he went, people stared at him. This made him feel very important and empowered. He loved the attention and assumed he would become the next Arnold Schwarzenegger.

Bodybuilding politics being what they are, he was blacklisted and had a hard time qualifying for the important contests. He learned all the tricks that enabled him to clean out his system before a contest and pass all the drug tests, but he could never seem to get a break. When, on the rare occasion, he was able to compete, at best he would get 4th or 5th place, even though his was clearly the best body on the stage. Vince felt betrayed by the sport he loved, but he was stubborn and continued, determined to break through the invisible barrier that was blocking him.

He had a couple of sponsorships that brought in just enough money for him to survive and continue to live in the tiny Venice Beach apartment, but he wasn't winning contests and therefore not bringing in any real money. His hot-tempered wife, who spent her days taking care of their toddler and not pursuing her own dreams, wasn't happy. Vince was getting more and more stressed out, and still blamed her for his failure.

Then Vince did what most men would do, he avoided the difficult issues that were causing his problems, and focused on what he was already good at and felt comfortable doing. This, of course, only made him more isolated and more obsessed; consequently, he took more steroids, spent more time working out, and was getting more and more self-absorbed. Bodybuilding is full of narcissism anyway; it's part of what it takes to be competitive, but Vince was getting out of control.

Delilah pressured Vince to make better money, so he tried to get more endorsements and sponsorships. When that didn't work, he started selling steroids, mostly to guys in their late teens and early twenties whom he saw hanging around the gym. This brought in more money, but it also made him paranoid. The stress of selling illegal drugs, combined with all the steroids he was taking, made him mentally unbalanced. He would have episodes of extreme roid-rage, yelling at people on the street who greeted him, punching and kicking temperamental vending machines, and even throwing dumbbells at people in the gym.

One morning he was walking down the sidewalk on Ocean Avenue in Santa Monica. He was about to cross the street when a guy driving a Mustang made a hasty right turn in front of him and cut him off. Vince snapped. He chased the car on foot for three blocks before the car stopped behind some traffic at a red light. When he caught up to the car, he punched the driver's side window, shattering it. He grabbed the man by the hair, yanked him out through the broken window, and tossed him over a parked Beamer SUV, slamming him into a brick wall. Vince grabbed the guy by the collar, picked him up, and was about to punch him in the face when he was stopped at gunpoint by a half-dozen uniformed and undercover cops.

It turned out that the bleeding and barely-conscious man sprawled on the sidewalk was under FBI surveillance. Apparently he was involved in the making and distribution of kiddy porn, human trafficking, child slavery, and prostitution. The Feds were building a case against Jordan Christoph Madson when Vince stepped in and pulverized the guy.

Sergeant Ron Willinski was in a surveillance van tailing his suspect. A dozen thoughts went through his mind when he saw Madson being pursued down the street by some behemoth. His first fear was that their cover was blown and that the Hulk was tipping their guy off. But when the Hulk bashed and dragged Madson through his window and slammed him into a brick wall, Willinski was fairly sure that wasn't the case.

He gave a worried smile and considered: "If this guy is on the force, there goes our case." Willinski was working on getting transferred to a more prestigious unit in Sacramento. There he would do undercover work in the state capitol where state representatives and corporate lobbyists were busy feasting on taxpayer money. So he wasn't about to have his case get screwed up and lose his promotion.

The first thing Willinski did when he got to the scene was put a police perimeter around the barely conscious perp; he shoo'd off all the lookie-loos, handcuffed Vince, and shoved him into the back of a police car.

He had to figure out how to turn this fiasco into a positive. The upper crust Westside elite were honking their car horns, pissed off that their lattes were being delayed. Madson was bleeding from the head, mumbling, and not making much sense. Clearly he needed some medical attention and was in no condition to drive. That's when a light bulb went off in Willinski's head.

In order to make his idea work, Willinski needed to change a few facts. He slipped into the back of the police cruiser and put on his tough guy voice, and looked straight into Vince's eyes. "My friend, you are in big fucking trouble. You are looking at a long list of charges: assault, attempted murder, breaking and entering. These are serious felonies. When you go to trial, half of Santa Monica will testify that they saw you chase an innocent guy down the street then proceed to beat the living shit out of him. The way I see it, you're going to jail for a long, long time."

"He wasn't innocent!" Vince protested.

"Explain that to the jury when they see that you weigh three times what he does. I doubt they'll be very sympathetic."

Willinski slid a few inches closer to Vince, lowered his voice, and went into his good cop mode. "Look, you're in a bad spot, but I will get the charges dropped if you do exactly as I say, no questions asked!" Vince quickly agreed.

Willinski, an adroit paper warrior, turned in a report stating that Madson had recklessly driven down Ocean Avenue and hit a 348 pound pedestrian, causing damage to the passenger side window and injuring both the pedestrian and Madson. The vehicle was impounded. Madson was taken in an ambulance, where he made statements in a semi-conscious state to the effect of, "Where's my kiddy porn?" A preliminary search of Madson's vehicle found evidence of his involvement in the making and distribution of child pornography.

Madson ratted out his partners in an international child slavery ring and ended up in the Witness Protection Program. Willinski got promoted and moved to Washington, DC, skipping Sacramento altogether.

Delilah heard about the incident almost immediately. That night they got into a big argument. Vince went ballistic, started smashing things, and tossed a sixty-pound dumbbell through their living room window. Delilah stormed out of the house fearing for her life, leaving her two-year-old crying in his crib.

Vince spent two weeks depressed, clueless, single, and broke. He had no idea how he was going to raise a kid. Then out of nowhere, a $15,000 insurance settlement check arrived by registered mail. The Madson case had been pushed through and settled, and Vince had been named a benefactor in a hit-and-run auto accident.

John Silver, the owner of Blood-Sweat-N-Tears Gym, was five foot two, weighed 260 lbs., and looked and acted like a pit bull. The temptation to call him Long John loomed, but no one ever dared to do it. He was Vince's only remaining sponsor and one of the few people left who still liked him. He wanted to sell his second Blood-Sweat-N-Tears Gym in Northridge, about 15 miles North of his gym in Venice. Vince was determined to turn his life around, so they made a deal. Vince bought the gym with the insurance money and moved to the hot and smoggy San Fernando Valley.

Vince breathed new life into the gym, and it quickly became the place in the North San Fernando Valley where all the serious bodybuilders signed up to work out. Among the many improvements that Vince added was a play area, so that parents could bring their kids to the gym. As a young child Ethan spent most of his time and met most of his friends there.

Vince stubbornly waited, expecting that Delilah would show up one day, but she never did. Vince blamed steroids for Delilah leaving him; consequently, he became a born-again natural bodybuilder and never did any sport-enhancing substances again. He ranted endlessly about how steroids had corrupted the sport of bodybuilding and would tell anyone who would listen: "Only a complete frickin' idiot would do them." However, Vince's evangelical enthusiasm and his strident attacks against steroid use didn't win him any friends in the pro circuit because all the pros used them.

The people who run the industry rely on the freak-show heavyweight contestants to bring in the fans and the big revenue, so they need to keep steroid use alive and well, though they could never say so publicly. They preferred that the subject was never brought up, and fervently wished that Vince and his ranting would just go away.

Over the years, Vince became more and more dismayed by the sport of bodybuilding. He stayed busy keeping up the business of running the gym. Before long, he was another bitter single dad who had lost his dream. He was stuck in the rat race, working seven days a week, making just enough money for him and Ethan to survive.

By the time Ethan was nine years old, he would come to the gym after school, do his homework in the corner by the squat rack where it was quiet and the lighting was good, then help his dad by cleaning up, giving tours to new members, and stocking nutritional supplements and sports gear.

Many of the gym employees were rather unreliable, and so was the income that the gym generated. By the time Ethan was eleven, he was working at the gym almost every day. Ethan was cheap and reliable. Vince believed that one of the big problems with kids was that they didn't do anything productive. They sat in front of the TV for hours watching idiotic shows, played video games, and didn't contribute to the household. These kids were going to grow up either feeling entitled or like they were a burden to the family.

Vince wanted Ethan to feel appreciated, respected, and valued. Then there was the issue of safety. The more Ethan was working at the gym, the less Vince had to worry about where his son was and who he was hanging out with. Hard work reduced the chances of him getting into trouble. The last thing Vince needed was a problem child. His philosophy was, "Keep 'em busy."

Chapter 3

Ethan grew up quickly and without much drama. Vince was responsible and well-intentioned, but not the smartest guy, and not someone who would ever rise to be a leader. Ethan wanted to be more than his dad, determined to be the first person in his family to go to college. It helped that they lived less than a mile from Cal State University Northridge and that for the last fifteen years a large percentage of the gym members were either students, faculty, or employees of the University. After high school Ethan took the most logical next step, enrolling at CSUN.

Vince was both proud and wary of Ethan's education. He didn't want his son to become a guy who worked in an office somewhere doing what Vince called "meaningless work." He considered most lawyers, stock traders, salesmen, middle managers, bankers, and office workers to be nothing more than paper-shuffling parasites who fed off a bloated corporate economic system, like ticks on a dog's belly. One of Vince's common rants was, "At the end of the day, do these people make anything? Do they produce anything that has any real value?"

Vince had strong opinions about many things and often his opinions conflicted with each another. On one hand, Vince wanted Ethan to grow up and become someone people looked up to because of his brains and not his brawn. Vince was familiar with the brawn side of life. Many of his washed-out bodybuilder friends were now bouncers, bodyguards, or wrestlers, and to Vince that existence seemed empty and meaningless. At the same time, Vince would chastise Ethan for not working out and not being the same kind of physical specimen Vince had been in his youth. This was confusing and frustrating for Ethan, who always tried to live up to his dad's expectations.

Vince wanted Ethan to do more in life than he himself had done, but was afraid that Ethan might get full of himself and reject their life together at the gym, so when Ethan started college, Vince insisted that Ethan take on more responsibilities. He wanted Ethan to better understand and respect the business and see it as a viable enterprise. Also, money was getting tighter and tighter.

Ethan did his best at juggling school and work. It basically meant he had no social life. His routine was school from 8:00 AM to 3:00 PM, then the gym from 4:00 PM to 11:00 PM, yet despite this schedule, he somehow managed to find himself a girlfriend.

Vanessa was 5'7" and blonde, charming, athletic, smart, and she never dressed like a girl. She always wore jeans, T-shirts, and sneakers or hiking boots. She never wore makeup, and her shoulder-length hair was usually pulled back in a ponytail. They happened to sit next to each other in a political science class. Vanessa noticed that Ethan was staring at her the whole time the professor was talking. Fortunately, she thought he was kind of cute and liked his boyish shyness.

One day after class, she asked him out. He explained that he had to work at the gym every night. Coincidently, her roommate was a member of Blood-Sweat-N-Tears gym, and they looked enough alike that the two of them were able to use each other's IDs. She made a date to meet him at the gym. After that, she came in almost every day, and they would hang out as he took care of business. Ethan made her a VIP member. It was a free membership usually reserved for celebrities and pro bodybuilders, since it was good PR having people like that working out at their gym. It was the first "boyfriend" thing he ever did for a girl.

Vince was happy to see his son happy. He liked Vanessa and often complimented her on her flawless skin, but he liked the fact that she was comfortable hanging out at the gym while Ethan worked. In fact, she often helped him clean up and answer the phone. It was like getting an extra employee for free.

Two semesters of college went by quickly, and Ethan was contemplating whether or not to take some summer classes when Ascot LaRouch, a guy Ethan had seen in the gym almost every day since he was a kid, asked Ethan if he could speak with him. Ascot was an interesting character with a diverse past. He was ethnically diverse—not white, not black—a handsome man in his late thirties.

He could pass for just about anything: Hispanic, Middle Eastern or Mediterranean.

Ascot stood 6 feet and weighed 190 lbs., a former middleweight boxing champion who later became a boxing trainer. He quit training when his prizefighter died from an overdose of diuretics, trying to lose weight two days before his biggest championship fight. Ascot went back to school, got a degree in nutrition and chiropractics, then became a personal trainer for Hollywood celebrities. He married Queie, a famous singer and activist with no last name, so to fit in, he too began to only us one name.

Queie was a celebrity who was constantly in the news for her environmental and political views. She would often get arrested for protesting at environmental and anti-government rallies. Ascot was usually supportive of her and her positions, but lacked the desire to go to jail. He often said, "You're no good to anyone if you're locked up." Finally after seven years of an on-again-off-again relationship, they were getting divorced. Ascot, who was always being lured back to Queie after he said he was leaving, had finally found a way to escape. He approached Ethan and asked if he would be interested in an out-of-town summer job.

Ethan was concerned about leaving his dad. The gym was barely breaking even, and summer was usually bad for business because many college students dropped their memberships and went back home. Ascot explained that he could earn four or five times what he would earn normally, and that would be more than enough to pay for his next year's tuition.

Ethan was intrigued by the idea of traveling since he had never gone anywhere. He wanted to see more of the world than just the San Fernando Valley, but he couldn't abandon his dad. He told Ascot he couldn't do it. Disappointed, Ascot said he'd talk with Vince and explain the situation to him, and maybe Ethan would reconsider.

The same day Ascot offered Ethan a job, Vince was doing a set of squats using the old beat-up squat rack in the corner of the gym. The rubber floor under the rack was worn down to the cement, leaving a two-inch deep hole. Vince, who liked to show off, had put ten 45 lb. plates on each side and had done a set of five squats without a weight belt. As he went to put the bar in the rack, he stepped in the hole, twisting his back slightly. Normally that wouldn't have been a big deal, but with 945 lbs. balanced on his shoulders, it was another matter entirely. A sharp pain shot up Vince's back, nearly making him keel over and drop the bar. Miraculously he managed to catch himself and take the most physically painful step of his life, then slammed the barbell back into the rack. When the weight was secure and off his shoulders, he leaned over and grabbed the side of the squat rack to steady himself. The pain was so intense that he fainted. It turned out that he had squashed his C12 vertebrae and pinched a nerve in his back.

After the accident, Vince had a hard time running the gym. The daily routine of showing new members how to use the equipment, re-racking the weights, un-boxing and stocking the supplements and retail items, cleaning the locker-rooms, even sitting doing paper work, was all very painful. Ethan Naturally and automatically began to take over.

When Ascot returned to inquire if Ethan was willing to reconsider his proposal, Ethan was adamant. "Absolutely not! My dad is in constant pain right now, and he can't run the business without me, plus all the new medical bills are killing us financially."

Ascot reiterated, "You could make enough money this summer to cover Vince's medical expenses and still have enough left over to enroll in the fall semester."

Ethan stood firm, "I can't leave. I would be betraying my father, and he's the only family I have." Ascot nodded understandingly, "I know you have a lot of responsibilities, but your dad is a tough guy, he can handle all this stuff, and I can promise you this, it won't get any easier. The longer you wait, the more responsibilities you will acquire. Before you know it your life will have passed you by, and you will still be working day after day at a decaying gym in the middle of the San Fernando Valley, wondering what the hell happened to your life."

Ascot took a deep breath and was about to lay out another blast of reality, when Ethan cut him off. "I also have a girlfriend that

I really like. If I leave for the summer, I doubt I'll have one when I get back."

Ascot gave a knowing grin, "All the more reason to reconsider."

Chapter 4

The temperature inside the pod was rising quickly. Ethan lifted his head up from his knees and saw flames roaring past the window again. The pod had stopped tumbling, and now they were in a weightless freefall. Ethan remembered a documentary on how the NASA astronauts practiced being in a weightless environment. There were two ways: One was a giant Plexiglas tank full of super-clear water. The astronauts in their space suits would float around and practice doing the things they would eventually do on their space-walks outside the space station or the shuttle.

The other method of achieving weightlessness was a padded airplane affectionately known as the "Vomit Comet." The plane would go up forty or fifty thousand feet then freefall for several minutes. During that time the inside of the aircraft was weightless. Then the astronauts could practice moving and doing things in zero gravity.

Ethan was feeling nauseous and understood very clearly how the "Vomit Comet" got its name. To take his mind off his stomach, he scooted over towards the window to observe their progress. Through the whips of flames he could see the earth, now bigger than before but still quite far away. He looked at the horizon and saw the earth's curvature and considered that this might be the last time he would ever see this. Not many people can say they have seen the planet from this vantage point. Ethan felt proud and special. This provided enough of a distraction to forget about his stomach.

Ethan slid back in his seat and strapped the safety harness tighter against his waist and shoulders. The temperature inside the pod had gotten uncomfortably hot. Inside the bright red jumpsuit he was wearing, Ethan felt a small river of sweat pour down his back then pool under his butt. At the time of the accident the only clothes he had were the sweat pants, polo shirt, and cross trainers he was wearing, but those had worn out long ago. Ethan had found a large box of one-size-fits-all nylon jumpsuits that the janitors and mechanics wore over their work clothes when they did messy jobs.

Ethan thought those jumpsuits were the most unfashionable things he had ever seen, but fashion wasn't a very high priority when you were stranded in outer space. Now that he was going home again, he was actually looking forward to getting new clothes. He forgot what it felt like to wear something that breathed, wasn't scratchy, and looked halfway decent.

Ethan considered the upside: If they survived the landing and needed to be rescued, his bright red suit would be easy to spot. "I just hope being highly visible will be a good thing, and not our undoing."

Chapter 5

Midnight. The Lamborghini Diablo purred as it emerged from the underground garage onto the large circular terra cotta driveway like a dragon crawling from its nest to hunt. In front of the modern beachfront estate was a courtyard, and at its center was a large abstract metal fountain that gave the property an ominously dark industrial feeling. The car steered around it in a practiced manner, never slowing to make the sharp turn. It continued onto the private gravel road leading up the cliff that connected the thirty-two acre Malibu property to Pacific Coast Highway. The marine layer blocked all the stars, leaving only a fuzzy glow from the moon. The only other illumination came from the Diablo's headlights shining through the haze.

Casper Degas drove slowly and deliberately, not wanting to disturb the gravel, possibly putting tiny pits in the Diablo's aubergine metallic glaze. As he approached the end of his private road, the electric gate automatically opened, enabling him to exit without slowing down. It reminded him of the Batmobile coming out of the Batcave in the old TV series. He turned South onto the main road and headed towards Santa Monica. At this hour the road was empty, and he had no hesitation unleashing the Diablo's horsepower.

Casper felt the power and precision of the Diablo as the machine sped and hugged the curves of PCH. This made him feel mighty. According to his gold Rolex, it was seven minutes after midnight. At this pace he would get to his personal hanger at the Santa Monica Airport in about fifteen minutes, earlier than he needed to be. He hated being early and he hated waiting for people to show up, so he slowed down a little and switched on the radio. It was set to KUSC, the only noncommercial classical station in Los Angeles. Mahler's First Symphony had just started, and Casper recognized the opening passage; the sustained A note by the strings sounded to him like the orchestra was tuning up.

He considered that twenty years earlier he had no money, no resources, just a lot of tenacity and ambition. He started the Eden Building Company, a firm that specialized in high-tech custom-built homes, which integrated computers into the structure of the home, making it possible for every aspect of one's environment to be automated—a person's alarm clock, lights, television, coffee pot, toaster, microwave, shower, hair dryer, etc., would be networked together and programmed to go on and off automatically. This allowed his clients to have everything ready for them when they woke up and started their day, and everything ready for them when they returned home. His work became very popular among the very rich, and he was labeled a modern visionary.

Among his rich clientele was Admiral Mason Riddell, a higher-up at the Pentagon. Riddell recognized Casper's ability and ambition, and used his influence to get Casper a no-bid contract with the government doing research and development on various high-tech living environments.

That was when Casper incorporated and became the CEO of Eden, Inc. The company quickly grew. Within five years, he had branched out and created thirty-two separate divisions that involved the research, design, and manufacturing for projects ranging from above-ground to underground, to undersea and off-world living structures, aircraft design, robotics, telecommunications, and medical research.

In a week, he would be turning forty-five. He lived alone and was a very private person. Rarely did he invite people over to his house. His stocky frame and bald head made him look older than he was, but looks can be deceiving. Every morning he did rigorous martial arts training in his custom gym. He did it for physical stamina, agility, and concentration.

The William Tell Overture interrupted the 2nd movement of Mahler's First Symphony. Casper looked at his dashboard to see who was calling, as the radio automatically turned down. Casper tapped the steering wheel to engage the phone. "What is it?"

"Good Evening, Mr. Degas," said a man's voice through the surround sound speakers. His voice was timid as if knew that in any second he would be yelled at for being the messenger of bad news.

"It's Allan from the hanger. The mechanics are recalibrating something on the aircraft, and it won't be ready for another hour, but they say they're confident you will arrive in Washington, DC in plenty of time for your meetings."

Casper felt a surge of rage building in his solar plexus and was about to start yelling at the little piss-ant, but somehow he managed to restrain himself. Instead what came out was calm, not unlike the way Darth Vader talked when he was angry. "Tell the crew I expect everything to be up and running perfectly in one hour. This kind of last-minute oversight is for amateurs, and I don't work with amateurs!" He tapped the steering wheel to hang up the phone, and the Mahler Symphony faded back up to full volume.

The next intersection was Sunset Boulevard. Without hesitation and with no destination in mind, he turned left up the hill and headed East towards Beverly Hills and Hollywood.

Casper's mood had flipped from nostalgic to aggressive. He stomped on the gas pedal. The engine roared and the car leaped forward, throwing his body against the leather seats. He loved speeding down the empty road, feeling the car handle the curves. This is what the car was made to do. Not the bumper-to-bumper bullshit that characterized most of his driving. He unleashed the power of the Diablo, and within seconds he was doing eighty, then ninety miles per hour, swerving through the winding residential section of Sunset Boulevard.

He blasted through Pacific Palisades then Beverly Hills. He was finally forced to slow down at Doheny Drive, the street that divides Beverly Hills from West Hollywood. The contrast is dramatic: one side is a dead-quiet residential neighborhood, the other is the West end of the Sunset Strip, famous for its nightclubs and seedy nighttime activities.

Casper looked at his watch. 12:21AM. He had fifty minutes before he needed to be at the airport. The growl and precision of the V-12 Engine amped up Casper's feeling of power. He felt unstoppable. He crossed the Doheny threshold and drove down the Sunset Strip as if he owned the world.

Standing on the corner of Sunset and La Cienega was a Hispanic woman in her early twenties dressed in tiny skintight shorts, a tiny midriff tank top, and stiletto heels. Casper turned right on La Cienega, pulled over, and pushed the buttons that unlocked the passenger door and rolled down the window. The girl walked in a casual but quick, practiced manner, careful not to trip in her high heels. She got to the window and bent over, exposing ample cleavage. She was a surprisingly pretty girl, big brown eyes, full black hair, a strong jaw, and small straight nose. Casper stuttered, struggling to ask her if she wanted to get into his car. Something in the girl's disposition suddenly changed as though she sensed something was wrong, then with no explanation, she just turned and walked away. Casper watched as a small pickup truck pulled up behind him. She very casually walked over to it and without much hesitation, climbed in. Then they drove away.

A burst of anger shot through Casper's already tense body. "Slut!" he exclaimed with clenched teeth. He didn't like girls all that much anyway, but to be rejected by a common street whore just pissed him off. Who the hell did she think she was? Casper peeled out of his parking spot and tore off down La Cienega. When he passed Santa Monica Boulevard, there was a new group of prostitutes hanging out on the corner.

He pulled over and a young, blond, muscled boy in his late teens, wearing tight jeans and a tank top, jogged over to the car. Casper smiled at the boy. Without invitation, the boy opened the door and climbed in. "Awesome car!" said the boy as his hands caressed the dashboard.

"You should see my collection."

The boy looked at Casper, ran a practiced hand up his leg, and teasingly rubbed his crotch, then asked: "So what are you into?" Casper said nothing. "I'll blow you for a hundred bucks and you don't have to get out of the car." This time Casper wasn't going to let some skanky street hooker get the better of him.

He took a breath, then with confidence and total control he said, "I want to bend you over and do you!" The boy looked at him inquisitively.

"That's two hundred bucks."

Casper pulled two crisp one-hundred dollar bills out of his sport coat pocket like a magician. "Do you have a place?" asked

Casper, putting the money back in his pocket. The boy fidgeted in his seat and scanned the area.

"Sort of. I know a spot where we won't be bothered."

Within five minutes, Casper pulled into a long driveway that went to an abandoned house set far back from the street in the Hollywood hills. He stopped the car, and they both stepped out. The moon was bright in the Hollywood hills. They were just high enough above the city and just far enough away from the ocean that the sky was clear and they could see the stars.

"How do you want to do this?" asked the boy.

Casper, with the voice of a python, said very matter-of-factly, "I want you to take off your pants, spread your legs, and bend over my car."

"Where's my money?"

Casper sneered, reached into is pocket. "Here's one hundred, you'll get the rest when we're done," and tossed a wadded-up one hundred dollar bill at the boy's face. The boy snatched the bill from out of the air and stuffed it into his pocket. Then he pulled out a condom and tossed it to Casper.

"You gotta wear that." Casper silently gritted his teeth; he didn't like being given orders. He stepped back and watched as the boy pulled down his pants and did what he was told. It looked like a perverse police raid from a porno movie.

He thought about the meetings he would be having with the Senators in DC, in just a few hours, and the bizarre contrast and yet shocking similarity it had to this encounter with this clueless boy. This gave him an ear-to-ear grin and a rush of adrenaline surged through his veins.

Casper pulled a pair of black leather gloves from his jacket pocket, and casually tossed the condom on the ground.

"You ready?" growled Casper, as he gently kicked the boy's foot to the side, widening his stance so the boy was spread-eagled against the car. Casper licked his lips lustfully then with a very practiced martial arts move, he punted the boy as hard as he could right between his legs. The boy screamed in agony, turned and looked at Casper with surprise and horror as he fell to the ground.

With the compassion of a tarantula Casper pounced on the boy, driving his knees into his back, feeling the boy's ribs crack and break. He grabbed the boy's shoulder-length blond hair from the back of his head and drove the terrified face into the dirt between the cracks of the old asphalt driveway. Blood began gushing from the boy's nose. Casper jumped to his feet with cat-like reflexes to avoid having any blood get splattered on his clothing. He then grabbed the boy's left foot and dragged him away from the car, scraping his face, stomach, and palms along the broken asphalt. When Casper let go, the boy coughed and convulsed, and Casper kicked him hard in the kidneys.

The boy rolled over onto his side and curled up into a fetal position. Casper leaned over and whispered into the boy's ear,

"No one tells me what to do! Certainly not a lowlife faggot whore! Some fucking barnacle on the ass of society." The boy rolled onto his side. Blood, dirt, and little pebbles from decaying asphalt covered his face and clothes.

He turned his head toward Casper and feebly yelled, "Why? Why are you doing this?" Small specks of blood and saliva flew into Casper's face. Casper jumped back and exploded in rage. Suddenly there was a din of grunts, moans, and cracks as Casper fiercely and relentlessly kicked the boy who lay on the ground. The boy's body began to break. Beads of sweat began forming and dripping from Casper's bald head.

Finally the boy lay coughing and wheezing, barely any life left in him. Casper opened the passenger door and reached behind the seat for a container of Lysol sanitizing wipes. He pulled several out, wiped his face, head, and clothes. The boy moaned and rolled onto his back. Casper took a few steps toward him and kicked dirt and rocks in his face, then pulled out more wipes and began cleaning the handprints off the hood of his car. Casper opened the passenger door, climbed inside, and started wiping the passenger's seat, dashboard, door handles, and anything else the boy might have touched.

He had closed the passenger door and was walking to the driver's side when the boy mumbled, "Don't leave me here." He coughed, and a big wad of blood bubbled out of his mouth covering his lips and cheek. "Please help me!" Casper marched over toward the boy and with no more remorse than a redneck squashing a bug, stomped on the boy's windpipe. There was a dull crack, his neck snapped, and he was dead.

Casper casually looked at his watch. The excursion had taken twenty minutes. He had ten minutes to get to the Santa Monica Airport. He looked around and figured he should at least try to hide the body, although he didn't really care. He could easily create an alibi, and he had the money and the clout to get away with this method of blowing off steam. He was confident that no LA detectives were going to waste their time on this human trash.

He walked around the property and saw that the house was on a hill and at the bottom of the property were overgrown trees and bushes. He walked back to the car, grabbed the body by the hair and dragged it to the edge of the lot, straightened the body, then pushed it like a roll of carpet. The boy rolled down the embankment, picked up speed, bounced a few times, then disappeared into the underbrush.

Casper breathed in the cool, spicy pine air, then surveyed the property. "Not a bad place," he thought. It was quiet and secluded and gave the illusion of being in the mountains. He stood in the abandoned house's driveway, clenching his teeth, and raised his fisted hands above his head like a victorious gladiator facing a cheering crowd. Two men had arrived but now only one remained. He felt exhilarated. Not many people have the nerve to kill another human being and not be rattled. This was why he was superior to the common man.

He smiled, and as he walked towards his car, he discovered a clean patch of asphalt in the jigsaw puzzle driveway. There he kicked the dirt from his shoes, and climbed into his car. The engine roared to life, breaking the silence of the still night. The Diablo pulled out of the driveway like some kind of mythical monster leaving its lair after it had just finished eating.

The windy road led him down the hill back to Sunset and La Cienega. He saw the hot little Latina standing on the same corner. He started giggling to himself. When he said he had forty minutes to kill, he didn't expect that he would take himself literally

Chapter 6

Roaring into the VIP section of the Santa Monica Airport, Casper pulled the Diablo into his personal parking spot inside his private hangar. The ten passenger supersonic Quasar VI corporate jet's heat-resistant nylon phenolic poly-alloy body gleamed under the bright lights as it sat proudly perched in the middle of the hangar. The experimental prototype aircraft used a pulse-detonation wave engine and at 100,000 feet easily cruised at Mach 4. The design engineers and test pilots were convinced that in the right circumstances it could go as fast as Mach 8. It was the latest in corporate aircraft design that Eden, Inc. was working on. They were examining ways to cut some costs so it would come down from absurd to just very expensive. Casper was confident they would find a way and start production within six months.

A man in a pilot's uniform walked with authority up to the Lamborghini. Casper pulled a small garment bag from behind the driver's seat and handed it to the pilot. Without a word the man took it, then headed back toward the plane. Casper tapped on the Diablo's door, suspended 90 degrees vertically above his head, and stepped back as a series of precise electric motors smoothly closed the Diablo's door. His thumb touched the optical scanner on the key, the car chirped, light's flashed, and the Lamborghini Diablo was in a state of suspended animation.

On board the plane, Casper sat in his favorite chair beside a panoramic window in front of the wings. It was large, soft, and reclined almost horizontally. It reminded Casper of the chair his grandfather would sit in and watch TV.

The one-of-a-kind Quasar VI began taxiing out of the hangar and onto the Tarmac. It would take ten minutes to get to cruising altitude and speed, then depending on wind conditions, about fifty to seventy minutes to cross the country. When they arrived it would be an additional twenty to thirty minutes to queue up and get into position to land at Ronald Reagan National Airport.

He thought about opening his laptop and reviewing the strategies he was planning to use for his meetings with the senators in just a few hours. Instead he leaned back and pushed the control buttons on the side of his seat. The chair automatically reclined, configuring itself to a customized preset position. Little motors started to vibrate, gently massaging his entire body. Samuel Barber's "Adagio for Strings" softly emanated from the seat's headrest. Immediately relaxed, swallowed up by his chair, Casper was asleep before the plane even took off.

* * * *

The sun was just coming up, and the yellow early morning glow peered over the horizon. The Crusher leaned against the limo parked on the Tarmac as he watched the queue of planes approach the runway. He was 6'8" and weighed a solid 400 lbs. He may have started life as Elliot Randall Silverstein, a nice Jewish boy from Brooklyn, but those days were long gone. For over twenty-five years he had been working for the government, corporations, and the mob in what he liked to call, "Forced client cooperation."

Because of his intimidating look, fierce demeanor and reputation, he rarely had to beat up or kill anyone anymore. Instead, he would squeeze and crush beer and wine bottles in each hand, rip phone books in half, punch holes in walls and doors, or pick up a TV or refrigerator, then toss it through a window or sliding glass door. These displays of brute strength and sheer nastiness were usually intimidating enough to get the people he visited to reconsider their actions and play ball.

The Crusher had worked for Casper exclusively for the last five years, and had been a reliable employee, fulfilling a variety of job assignments. Today's assignment was to be a scary limo driver, pick Casper up, and take him to see some senators who needed to be persuaded.

The House had just passed an important bill, and it would soon be coming up for a vote in the Senate. It wasn't the most high-profile bill but it was very important to Casper, who desperately wanted it to pass. Often when bills like this came up, the senators, knowing their constituents weren't looking, went fishing for the highest bidder, then voted accordingly. Casper knew the game well and had a unique way of getting what he wanted from these elected officials.

The Crusher had only been awake for a little over an hour and was already starting to sport a five o'clock shadow. His curly black hair was pulled back into a short ponytail, exposing the four-inch scar that started just under his left eye and zigzagged down his cheek. He sipped his coffee, rubbed his stubble, then looked at his reflection in the limo's tinted rear window. His appearance was properly threatening. He hadn't seen Casper in almost two weeks, and he was looking forward to what the day would bring. If he was lucky, he might get to bust someone's head open. The Crusher watched and waited as the Quasar VI landed and taxied towards the VIP section of the airport. The jet's sleek triangular hypersonic shape and the unique sound of its scramjet engine were impossible to ignore.

The airport was crawling with the typical paparazzi, waiting like spiders in their webs for a celebrity to walk by so they could snap an unauthorized photo and sell it to any of a dozen tabloids. Tyler Blackwell Colburn III had just finished his first year of college and was wondering if he should bother going back. He wasn't a college kind of guy. He had grown up the son of a man who had lost the family fortune in a series of bad investments, failed businesses, and several nasty divorces. The Colburn Empire once consisted of over a dozen coal mines, railroads, electrical power plants, dozens of apartment buildings, and seven luxury hotels. Now the family fortune was reduced to an 850-square-foot rundown house with oil stains on the driveway and three-foot high weeds in the yard. Tyler Blackwell Colburn II rarely left his house and was known to his neighbors to be a crazy old man who constantly watched TV and ate microwaved food. Fortunately for Tyler Blackwell Colburn III, known to everyone as Ty-bo, he had never lived the life of wealth and privilege. His father had pissed away the fortune within a year after Ty-bo was born, so Ty-bo didn't miss what he never had.

A mere three months earlier, Ty-bo had acquired a digital camera for $100 from a lady at a yard sale. Her photographer boyfriend had dumped her, so out of spite and malice, she sold everything of his that was in her house, including a professional Nikon D90 camera. The next day Ty-bo got on his motor scooter and began zipping around town looking for celebrities to photograph.

Edward Tilley, an animal rights advocate, was suing his local school district for not providing a vegetarian lunch option at his kid's school. He claimed his children and other vegetarians were being discriminated against. The news media, being sensationalistic, had blown the story out of proportion. Now it had become a First Amendment issue. Supporters on both sides were up in arms. The vegans were fighting for the rights of animals and the preservation of the planet. Their argument was that the farming practices used to raise beef and chicken were destroying the rain forests and contributing to global warming. The beef, poultry, and dairy industries were counter-suing, claiming that the protesters were defaming meat and declaring that the state had no right to mandate how or what Americans eat.

During the apex of this controversy, Ty-bo sat down in a yellow and red plastic chair and began to eat his Quarter-Pounder with cheese. As dumb luck would have it, sitting in the booth next to him was animal rights advocate and poster child for vegetarianism, Edward Tilley, enthusiastically eating a Big Mac. Ty-bo snapped a dozen pictures and ran out of McDonald's, leaving his fries and orange soda untouched on the table. Those photos made it into almost every tabloid, magazine, newspaper, and were featured on several of the cable news channels. Ty-bo made $22,610. After that he was hooked. He went on to sell pictures of Demi Moore picking her nose, Sylvester Stallone with hands in his pants adjusting his private parts, and a few other pictures of famous people looking bad or doing embarrassing things.

Ty-bo was riding his motor scooter into Ronald Reagan International Airport when he saw a cool, unique, and very expensive looking plane coming in for a landing. He knew exactly where to go. He zipped through the airport parking lot to the VIP section. Considering that it was the VIP section, it had surprisingly little security. He had no idea who would be stepping off the plane, but they had to be very wealthy and important people. Photos of such folks were usually good for something.

Ty-bo got off his scooter and stood behind the VIP Check-in center. It was a small building where all the passengers logged in and cleared customs if needed. The high-tech plane taxied, then stopped next to a limo with a brutish guy standing next to it. Ty-bo was about one hundred yards away, but with his zoom lens he could easily get a good shot. The side of the plane opened upward while a motorized ramp telescoped out; it was a scene right out of "The Day The Earth Stood Still," a movie his dad watched on TV every Halloween since he was a little kid. Once the ramp hit the ground, a bald stocky guy, sporting sunglasses, and wearing a black Armani suit walked down and immediately headed towards the limo. Ty-bo started frantically clicking, getting shots of the plane, the limo, the bald guy, and the brute. He stopped and waited for someone else to exit the aircraft. Finally the pilot and copilot stepped down the ramp. Ty-bo knew that the pilot and copilot were always the last to disembark any aircraft. He was surprised; he assumed that more than one guy would be coming out. This stoked his curiosity. "Who the hell was this guy?" He had taken a photo of the pilots exiting the plane when he noticed that the bald guy and big brute were staring at him and they didn't seem amused.

By the time Ty-bo was able to put his camera into its case and the case into his backpack and his backpack onto his back, The Crusher had already managed to travel more than halfway from the limo to where he was standing. For a big dude, The Crusher was an incredibly fast runner. Ty-bo didn't know what to do, and for a few seconds he stood frozen as this charging bull came toward him. Finally the bull grinned, drool shot out of his mouth revealing a solid silver incisor. For whatever reason, that snapped Ty-bo out of his deer-in-the-headlights daze, and his body, without further prompting from his brain, sprang into action. He started running towards his scooter. His habit was to store his helmet by securely strapping it to his seat. He hurried through the tedious process of un-strapping it in order to have a place to sit. He didn't dare take the time to look back; every second counted. He got the helmet unfastened and hastily put it on. Then he leaned over the bike, pulled out the kick-starter and stomped down on it hard. A second later the little engine buzzed to life. With a hard adrenaline twist of the throttle he revved the engine, put the protruding kick-starter back in place, and stomped down on the gears. Instantly the bike took off, but something was seriously wrong.

Suspended in mid-air, Ty-bo watched his only means of transportation zip out of the parking lot without him and into the busy commercial airport traffic. A speeding eighteen-wheeler hit the bike straight on without the driver even noticing. By the time the truck had passed over it, the remains of the scooter looked like wadded-up pieces of tinfoil scattered across the road. Before Ty-bo could absorb the surreal nature of his situation, a gigantic hand covered his face, knocking his helmet off his head. Suddenly he was the rope in a tug-of-war. Something was pulling on the backpack while simultaneously clamping and yanking on his face. It was a sturdy backpack and it wasn't going to break easily. With each pull, the vice-like grip tightened and Ty-bo's nose and jaw were slowly being crushed. It took several yanks before the nylon straps tore from the backpack.

The Crusher stood there with a backpack in one hand and a paparazzo geek in the other. He grunted and tossed Ty-bo against the wall of the check-in building, reached in, and pulled the camera out of the backpack, tossed it on the ground, then stomped on it. What remained was a small pile of broken plastic, glass, and crushed metal. With a little detective work, a clever person could probably have deduced that it had once been a camera.

The Crusher walked over to Ty-bo. "I'm going easy on you this time." Ty-bo looked in the general direction of the gravelly bass voice. He couldn't see anything, his jaw and nose were crushed and the inflammation had already swelled his eyes shut, his head was swimming, and his entire body was in agony. The voice continued, "My client is a powerful person who doesn't appreciate people meddling into his affairs. You got that?" Ty-bo nodded. "If I ever catch you sneaking around trying to take photos of me or any of my clients again -" There was a slight pause. Ty-bo felt the big man's warm coffee breath on his cheek, as The Crusher leaned down to speak directly in his ear, "- I won't be so nice next time."

The Goliath's feet reverberated inside Ty-bo's head as the big man stomped away. Ty-bo was seriously reconsidering the paparazzi lifestyle when the remains of his backpack rebounded off his face and fell onto his lap. An excruciating pain shot through his entire body that was so intense that it was almost euphoric. That was the last thing he remembered before he passed out.

Chapter 7

Running across the parking lot back towards the limo, The Crusher looked like an NFL linebacker who had just sacked the quarterback, scooped up the loose ball and was running for a touchdown. When he arrived, Casper was sitting in the back of the limo, sipping tea, laptop open, talking business on his cell phone. Casper always stayed a step ahead of the Washington beltway news outlets and typically came to Washington twice a month to meet with politicians, lobbyists, and key officials. He often knew more about what was going on behind the scenes than they did. The Washington insiders regarded Casper Degas as a determined man, who knew how to get what he wanted.

There was an aerospace bill in the House about to go to the Senate Floor that would overturn the Kennedy Space Neutrality Act and pave the way for lucrative government contracts for Eden, Inc. In order for this bill to pass, Casper needed to influence a few key senators. Bribery used to be much easier, but there had recently been a slew of charges against senators and congressmen who were on the take. Now all the politicians were very guarded, so all deals had to be disguised and shrouded in subtle favors. The politicians Casper trusted the least were the Bible-thumping, finger-pointing, hyper conservatives. They were the most ruthless and crooked. Having God on their team gave them the cover to be real all-around bastards.

Casper saw the future of big budget government contracts in the ownership and militarization of outer space. He needed this bill to pass in order to put his plan in motion. None of the corporations or their CEOs were thinking that far ahead. Casper wanted to take advantage of their lack of vision and monopolize the market before anyone else got any similar ideas. It was similar to a tactic Bill Gates used when he bought up all the digital rights to thousands of famous paintings. Now anyone wanting to commercially use a digital image of a Picasso, Rembrandt, or Van Gogh had to purchase it from Microsoft. Not many people saw the future of the Internet as clearly as Gates. Similarly, no one realized the potential of owning outer space as clearly as Casper Degas.

Senator Isley Wilson of Texas was dreading his meeting with Casper. Since their last meeting, Wilson had been offered a position on the board of directors of Isis Technologies, a competing aerospace company that was quietly being financed by a Chinese firm. He was considering retiring from the Senate in two years anyway. This position on the board would bring him eight figures a year and set his family up for generations. It was an offer too good to refuse. Also, Wilson was skeptical about the future of American aerospace. The country didn't have the infrastructure to support those kinds of programs any more.

All the New Deal programs created to establish a strong middle class and tax-base had been systematically dismantled since the 1980s. The reason America became a superpower and was able to create NASA and go to the moon during the Cold War of the 1960s and 70s was that it could afford to. Back then there was an infrastructure to support those programs and the will and vision to pursue dreams. That was all gone now, and he didn't see it coming back anytime soon. Wilson was looking ahead.

Over the past several years, he had watched the Chinese build their infrastructure and acquire massive wealth, while the USA continued to run deeper and deeper into debt and allow its own infrastructure to deteriorate. Isley Wilson was the only senator who had dropped out of school after the 7th grade. He knew he wasn't the smartest man on Capitol Hill, but he certainly wasn't dumb. His common sense and gut feelings were very reliable, and they were telling him that if an institution spends more money than it makes, it will inevitably fall apart. He saw the writing on the wall and wanted to get on the right side of it before it toppled.

* * * *

Casper left Senator Isley Wilson's office very unhappy. First of all Casper had sat in the lobby of the Senator's office for over ten minutes. Casper hated waiting for anyone. Then he was rushed through their meeting, and during their time together the Senator's phone rang twice in ten minutes. After the second call the Senator abruptly stood up to leave in order to attend a special committee meeting. As he was getting ready to leave he said very matter-of-factly, "I cannot support this bill because I just read a report claiming that my Texas constituents would lose jobs and money if it were to pass, and to do that in today's economic climate would be political suicide. You understand it's nothing personal. Just business."

This excuse was obviously bogus. That was the standard line politicians used when they wanted to blow someone off. Immediately Casper sensed that something else was afoot, and he was determined to find out what it was. He didn't like being treated like some rank and file lobbyist. Who the hell did that hillbilly Wilson think he was talking to? Everyone in Washington knew that Casper Degas didn't play games and that he always had a plan B.

* * * *

Senator Victor Morales of Florida was very friendly and greeted Casper immediately when he arrived. Casper explained why supporting this bill would be beneficial to the senator and his constituents. Morales was a people reader, he didn't care about the bill and frankly didn't understand most of it, but he saw how important it was for Casper. He understood that if it were important to a man like Casper Degas, then a lot of money was at stake, so clearly there was more here than met the eye.

Victor's current pet project was to stop proposed offshore drilling off the coast of Florida. Part of the recent stump speeches that he had been giving at state fundraisers was, "We have hurricanes almost every year! One spill will muck up our white sandy beaches and destroy our economy. No sane person would want to drill for oil here!"

Casper, who was very familiar with the process of "you scratch my back and I'll scratch yours," was nonetheless caught off-guard when Morales asked, "How can my support of this aerospace bill help my offshore drilling issue?"

Casper was pissed at himself for not seeing this coming and not working that angle. He sat dumbfounded, trying to think of something to say. The Kennedy space center was in Florida. There were thousands of aerospace jobs there. Finally Casper spoke.

"For some time, Eden, Inc. has been considering starting a research and development division in Florida, taking advantage of the infrastructure that's already in place there. This bill could give us the revenue to start that expansion." Morales nodded his head, bit his lower lip, and then swallowed before speaking.

"Not bad, but that's not a good enough offer. That doesn't really help me with my drilling problem." The five foot three, two hundred pound senator sat up in his chair and didn't move, giving Casper a chance to come up with a better offer, but to his surprise, Casper abruptly got up and left the room.

Morales leaned back in his chair, put his stubby arms behind his head, and watched his office door close.

Morales had grown up in Hialeah, a poor Cuban neighborhood in the rough part of South Florida, and in order to survive, he had taken shit from rednecks and rich obnoxious tourists his whole life. Now the tables were turned. Morales really enjoyed the power to say "No" to these assholes who thought they were entitled to everything they surveyed. He knew Casper would be back with a new offer.

Success is both inspiring and energizing. Casper returned to his limo drained and uninspired. The Crusher opened the door. Casper climbed in, sat down, grabbed a bottle of sparkling water from the refrigerator and twisted it open. "Jack!" It sounded more like a grunt than an actual name.

"Yes, boss?" said The Crusher as he started the engine. He had no idea why Casper had given him that nickname, but he went along with it.

"These corrupt politicians are getting out of hand!" He took a sip of his water. "I'm done! No more Mr. Nice Guy!" The Crusher thought there were many ways to describe Casper but "nice" was certainly not one of them. He watched Casper's face in the rear view mirror as he waited for instructions. Casper sat transfixed in the limo's large bench seat. Beads of sweat began to appear on his bald head; then he started clenching his teeth, seething with rage.

"These senators who refuse to cooperate don't know who they are dealing with!" Casper shouted, working himself into a frenzy. "I will not be fucked with, Jack!" The Crusher looked back again and saw that Casper's entire head had turned beet red. "They are going to make me resort to plan B!"

"What's plan B, Boss?"

"You'll find out soon enough!"

"Okay, boss."

Casper wiped his mouth with his sleeve, sat up in his seat, and started stabbing the air with his index finger. "I've dealt with these people before, I know what makes them tick!" He opened the window, and the cool mid-morning fall air blew in. Casper took a big breath. "They will not win, Jack!" he roared. "Vincero! Vincero!"

Chapter 8

Sweat poured off Ethan's face. The pod tumbled and shook as he and Ascot fell to Earth. Ethan felt more nauseated than he had ever felt. He tried calming himself by taking deep breaths, but the air inside the pod was so hot that it burned his lungs. He was forced to take short and shallow breaths, making him light-headed and the experience all the more surreal. He was now starting to get scared. This didn't feel right. Maybe their luck had run out and this really was a one-way trip to oblivion.

Ethan wondered what his dad was up to. What must he be thinking after eight years of no contact? What condition was the gym in? Was it even still there? Growing up, Ethan had lived in his father's shadow. Vince had fans that came to the gym to watch him work out. Even though Vince had never won any big bodybuilding championships, he was a larger-than-life figure, and even twenty years after he had competed he still remained an amazing human specimen—big, strong, ripped, and disciplined. Ascot had explained to Ethan that at some point we all have a defining moment when the bubble of our parents is popped, and we see our parents with new, clear eyes. Instantly they become people with normal abilities and normal problems.

Ethan remembered one time when the gym was just closing, and the last few die-hard members were racing to get their last sets in before being kicked out. Ethan had just torn open a case of Hydroxy-Cut, a fat burning supplement that was very popular, and lucrative. Vince had passed his extensive first-hand knowledge of nutritional supplements onto Ethan since at one time or another Vince had taken them all; consequently, Ethan knew all about every product that was sold at the gym. He could explain the difference between branch chain versus freeform amino acids, he knew which supplements worked, which didn't, and why. Ethan was stacking the bottles inside a glass display case as quickly as possible, so that he could call Vanessa and maybe meet her for some late night hanky panky.

Ethan was just finishing when Vince escorted the last guy out of the gym, locked the big glass doors behind him, then sheepishly came over and sat down on a stool at the nutrition counter. He looked both stressed and perplexed. He didn't look Ethan in the eyes. He just stared at a bottle of hot sauce that was sitting on the lunch counter. Then he confessed that the monthly payment on the adjustable rate sub-prime second loan he had taken out against the business so that Ethan could go to college had recently doubled. Business was slow, memberships were down, and the gym was in disrepair. He hadn't been able to pay the mortgage for a couple of months, and now his credit was ruined. He had no idea how to get out of this financial mess. The big man, who was practically a comic book superhero, broke down and started crying.

That was when the bubble burst. For the first time Ethan saw his dad as a vulnerable, simple guy, who lacked common sense. Ethan appreciated that Vince was a father who wanted to give his son every opportunity that he could, but in the process he had blown it, big time. Now they were on the brink of financial ruin.

Ethan put the last bottle in the case and then locked it. "Isn't there something you can do? Sell something?"

Vince looked up from the hot sauce. "Sell what? Half of this rickety gym equipment I'm still making payments on."

Vince tried to get another sentence out but choked, emitting an incomprehensible mumble. He then sat up straight, sniffled, wiped his eyes, cleared his throat, and with a steady voice stated, "You should take the job that Ascot offered you out of the country."

Ethan was conflicted. He felt simultaneously like an empowered breadwinner and like a hooker who had just been sold off by a pimp. Ethan protested: "It seems that under the circumstances I should stay here and help more than ever."

"No," Vince insisted. "We need income more then ever, and we aren't going to get it here."

"We can do a big membership drive!"

"We've tried that before," Vince interrupted, "and that's not going to do it. I can juggle things here long enough to keep the doors open until you get back. You need to get out, see the world, meet lots of rich people, and bring back a pile of money!"

Vince looked up and smiled. Ethan stared back dumbfounded. Vince wasn't giving him any choice in the matter.

"Ok, I'll call Ascot tomorrow and see if it's still available."

Ascot hadn't bothered to see if anyone else he knew was interested in the out-of-town resort job. The truth of the matter was, he didn't know that much about it, and he didn't feel comfortable asking any of his professional friends who would undoubtedly have questions that he couldn't answer. Ethan was different. Ethan was practically still a kid. He didn't have many responsibilities, he hadn't traveled or done much yet, so for him the out-of-town job was guaranteed to be a step up.

Ascot had gotten the call from the director of the Valhalla resort because Ascot was a doctor and also had the reputation of being the personal trainer to the A-list celebrities. When he married Queie, his client-turned-girlfriend-turned-fiancé-turned-wife, he instantly became famous as Queie's husband and trainer. That led to a series of exercise videos that were advertised on late night TV for several years and were often the topic of many jokes by late night TV comedians. The resort company wanted someone with a title and who had name and face recognition to run the fitness center at their newest, beyond-exclusive resort. It was so exclusive that Ascot didn't even know in which country it was located.

When first offered the job Ascot wasn't particularly interested. It had been a while since he had been in the fitness business. He felt he had more to offer the world than coercing rich people into doing sit-ups. The resort sensed his hesitation and made him a very enticing offer.

The timing was perfect. Ascot had just gotten divorced and wanted to get away. He was feeling overwhelmed with his lot in life and was looking for a change. While he was married to Queie, he had become a community activist and had started several non-profit charities ranging from improving the water quality of the Biona wetlands to battered women's shelters and inner-city community food forests so people could grow organic food and become more self-sufficient.

Being a community activist had burned him out; there was never any relief. He was constantly taking care of people, animals, places, and things. The pressure had affected every aspect of his life, and it was one of the reasons he wasn't married to Queie anymore. Now, Ascot just wanted some relief and for once, have someone take care of him for a change.

The job at the resort gave him an escape. He would have a great place to live, excellent food, and no doubt be in a beautiful environment. It was an adventure he was willing to pursue.

The morning when Ethan called back, Ascot was thrilled. He didn't need to look any further, and he liked Ethan. Ascot had always wished he had had someone who could have educated him in the ways of the real world when he was a young man. It would have saved him lots of time and energy, so he was excited at the prospect of being a mentor and being able to pass along his years of hard-earned knowledge to a young, eager mind.

Ascot explained that he could only recommend him. Ethan would still need to go through a formal job interview process that included a background and security check. Ascot gave him the details and said he'd set up an interview. Ethan hung up the phone feeling anxious; this would be the first time that he had ever left home for an extended period of time. It was both thrilling and scary.

Vanessa's college roommate, Cameron, was a trust fund kid who had no business being in school and had no interest in anything other than partying. The idea that she was in college to pursue an education was laughable. Part of her trust fund, established by her grandparents, required that she attend two years at a university before she could receive her full inheritance. Cameron's parents weren't stupid and knew she was just going through the motions. They had written her off as a lost cause and were now doing the absolute minimum of parenting. She had her trust and, therefore they knew she would be fine, so they had stopped calling or checking up on her. Nonetheless her parents still hoped that maybe the intellectual curiosity that supposedly existed in college might rub off on her, and at the very least, she might make some decent friends. Maybe she would find an acceptable boyfriend as opposed to the usual parasitic riff-raff she typically dated.

One of the perks of being a trust fund, party-girl was that Cameron had access to Club-Med. She could go anytime, and all charges went to her trust, no questions asked. Vanessa and Cameron had it worked out that they would switch IDs so that Ethan and Vanessa could spend a week at Club Med, compliments of Cameron's trust fund. This was going to be their first trip together as a couple and Ethan's first trip with any girl.

When Ethan called Vanessa and told her he might be leaving town for three months and that their trip to Club Med would have to be postponed, she went ballistic. She said that if he left for three months she would break up with him and post herself on a dating website.

Ethan reacted by asking, "Which website?"

"The nastiest ones out there!" she said incredulously: "Hot and Horny Dot Com, One Night Stand Dot Com, Orgasmic Nymphos Dot Org."

The message was clear that she was disappointed and upset. He explained that he had to do this for his dad and for the business. It was only going to be three months. They could go when he got back and had more money, but apparently it didn't matter what he said; she would not listen, and she would not be consoled. This was their first big argument. Ethan was confused; he was starting to grasp the things his dad had said over the years about the unpredictable nature of women. The conversation ended when Vanessa called him an asshole and hung up on Ethan. He put the phone down and asked himself, "Did we just break up? Did I just end my first relationship on bad terms?" He wasn't sure. He felt his stomach knotting in confusion.

Chapter 9

Borrowing his dad's 1965 Ranchero, Ethan drove out of the San Fernando Valley over the Santa Monica Mountains to West LA. The old pickup was the only car Vince had owned since Ethan was born. Vince liked old cars, and when he had bought it, the Ranchero was a classic that needed to be fixed up. Twenty years later, it still needed to be fixed up. The engine ran well, but the paint job resembled a calico cat, with patches of bondo, primer, and rust.

Ethan was headed to one of the more affluent neighborhoods in Los Angeles. When he arrived he pulled into the indoor parking structure of Eden, Inc.'s fifteen story building on Wilshire Blvd in Westwood. The valet parking guys cringed when they saw him. There was a red Ferrari parked right in front of the main entrance, and the rest of the parking lot was filled with Mercedes Benzes, Jaguars, BMWs, and other expensive cars. Ethan was told to keep driving, go to the very bottom of the parking structure and find a spot there; the valet guys made it very clear they didn't want to touch his car.

Ethan had a 2:00 pm appointment with Ms. Vanoushka Gabriela Popov Reyes, known to her friends as Vani. An athletic, five foot ten inch Venus with shoulder-length, curly blond hair, high cheekbones, a strong jaw, and mocha skin, she was the child of a Cuban father and Russian mother, both exiles who had left their countries and defected to Mexico where they became multi-millionaires in the water-filter business. Vani had just graduated in Hotel Management from the University of Las Vegas, where she was seen as an anomaly: A rich Mexican who spoke perfect Russian, English, and of course Spanish.

She was recruited right out of University by Casper Degas to work for Eden, Inc. Within sixteen months she was the operations manager for the Valhalla Resort guest facilities. She was responsible for the physical fitness center, hair salon, spa, casino, meeting rooms, as well as several cafés and restaurants.

Vani had already filled all of the important positions, now she was left with the lower tier jobs to fill. None of the people she had interviewed or hired knew the resort's unique location. All the specifics were top secret, and it was important to keep it that way, so she had to be very careful when interviewing people to not say too much.

At 2:00 pm exactly, Ethan walked into her office. Vani stood up from her desk, walked to the front of the room, and shook his hand.

"So you're the person Ascot recommended?" Ethan nodded.

"Have a seat." She pointed to a chair in front of her desk.

Ethan had no idea what to expect; he was hoping to get enough information to be excited about leaving his dad to run the gym without him, but Ms. Reyes didn't reveal much about where he would be going. She explained that Eden, Inc. catered to a very exclusive and discrete clientele and that Ethan would have to sign a confidentiality agreement if they were going to proceed.

She slid a contract across her desk. Ethan started to read it, but it was all legalese and made no sense to him. Vanoushka saw that Ethan was confused.

"It's just a contract," she explained. "It states that all information pertaining to Eden, Inc. and its subsidiaries cannot be discussed with or communicated to anyone outside the corporation. In other words, you promise to keep your mouth shut."

Ethan nodded, signed the paper, then pushed it back to her.

He had to fill out a stack of papers asking questions about his medical history. Was there a history of allergies or illnesses in the family? Was he afraid of heights? Did he have any phobias, particularly claustrophobia or agoraphobia? There were pages of questions about his family relationships and history. He answered all the questions, then slid the stack across the desk.

She picked up the stack of papers and quickly looked them over. She read his answers and seemed to perk up.

"You have no mother or grandparents and your only family is your dad?"

Ethan nodded; it seemed a very odd thing to get excited about, and he started to get an uneasy feeling. It reminded him of the time when he had purchased a ten-speed from a shady gym member, only to find out afterwards that he had bought a stolen bike. Ethan figured his feeling of uneasiness was just because he was nervous. After all, it was his first job interview and she was an intimidatingly attractive woman. She had an interesting accent; he couldn't tell where she was from and he didn't want to ask. Ethan had grown up around people who were from all over the world. Ever since he was a kid he had been good at placing accents, but Ms. Vanoushka Reyes was hard to pinpoint.

She finished looking over the paperwork then stood up. "Ethan!" He stood up and sprang to attention. "Come with me." She turned not saying another word, and briskly started walking. The only sound was the clip-clop of her hard-soled high heels reverberating down the tiled hallway.

"I have some reaction tests I would like you to perform." At the end of the hall was a large metal door with an electronic keypad. Vani punched in some numbers then held her finger over an electronic eye; a second later the door buzzed open.

The door opened and Ethan felt a cold blast of air smack him in the face. They walked into a large windowless room lit brightly with fluorescent lights. In the middle was a giant metal sphere with electrical cables running all around it. Next to the giant electric soccer ball were two computer terminals side by side.

The electrical equipment hummed, filling the room with the smell of ozone. Ethan was awed by it all. He had no idea what he was looking at specifically, but he could tell it was something unique. Vani broke the silence. "It's a Virtual Reality magnetic chamber, or VRMC. We call it Vermac."

Ethan nodded, noting silently to himself that he hadn't said much to this woman and was feeling like he ought to be friendlier, but saying something now would seem contrived, so he attempted a flirtatious smile.

She seemed a bit confused and took his look to mean he wanted more information. "We use this to simulate hard-to-create environments and situations. We monitor body functions and test people's reactions in these controlled stress conditions."

"Wow," Ethan muttered, not having much more to say on the matter. Ethan followed Vani as she led him to the back of the room to a table with several pieces of fabric on it.

The prototype VRMC suit consisted of several pieces of rubber material like a wetsuit, but heavy like the radiation aprons dentists use when X-raying patients' teeth. Vani picked a vest off the table and helped Ethan put it on securely against his chest with strong Velcro straps. Then she tightly strapped rubber chaps around both his legs, long sleeves around both of his arms, and finally helped him with a pair of boots, gloves and a headpiece. When he was done, every part of his body was covered in VRMC material; he looked like a scuba diver who was about to jump into the frozen waters of the Antarctic and needed all the insulation possible.

Ethan clumsily followed Vani back to the sphere. She pushed a button on the computer keyboard, a door opened, and they walked inside where it was noticeably warmer. The walls were covered in beige foam rubber, making the room smell like a brand new car. Vani handed Ethan a wireless virtual reality helmet, which resembled a motorcycle helmet but had the VRMC material inside. Ethan pressed his head into the helmet. It was a tight fit. Vani carefully checked to make sure the helmet was secure and that Ethan's eyes and ears were properly covered. Once it was on, he couldn't see or hear anything. Then tiny video monitors and headphones popped on, and he was staring at a blank blue screen and could hear Vani in the room.

"Start here." Vani grabbed him by the shoulders and put him in position like a school photographer. "Stay there."

Ethan nodded.

"In a second you'll be stepping into a video game you can feel. Remember it's all virtual, none of it's real, but if you get hit, attacked, stabbed, or shot you will feel it. It will hurt, but it won't be lethal."

Ethan stepped out of position. "What?"

She grabbed his shoulders again and went on.

"If you ever want to stop, just yell, 'stop!' and I'll stop the program. Then don't move. Wait until I come get you."

Ethan nodded again.

"Whatever you do, don't remove the helmet or any of the VRMC material."

Again Ethan nodded.

"You will receive instructions given to you in various ways throughout your journey, either by other people you meet or by signs you see. You'll figure it out, so pay attention to everything! You never know what's going to be important."

Vani walked over and sat down in front of the computer terminal and started the program. Her monitor went on and she could see exactly what Ethan was seeing. She loved watching people go through the program because at every turn there was a new opportunity to do something different, so no two journeys were exactly the same.

Ethan felt like Evel Knievel just before jumping over the Snake River. He heard the door of the chamber close, standing in the middle of the padded ball. Attacked, stabbed, shot? What was he getting himself into? He started to feel himself sweat; then he took several deep breaths and calmed himself down. "It's just a video game," he said to himself. "How bad could it be?"

The blue monitors disappeared and Ethan was standing in an empty room made of stone that looked like the inside of a medieval castle. An old man wearing a hooded black robe stood next to a table lit only by candelabra, his gaunt face flickering in the candlelight. The man motioned Ethan to come closer, held out his bony hand, and handed Ethan an ice cube with a chain through the middle. His voice was soft and gravelly, like a monk with emphysema.

"You must show this to the guards at the city gates in order to leave, and you must leave the city before it melts. Find what is precious, and take it with you. This is your task!"

Ethan nodded, looked down at his own feet, and noticed he was now wearing army boots and baggy green army fatigues. He thought about where to put the ice cube and figured his chest pocket would be the safest place.

Ethan heard a loud grunting voice from behind him. He turned around and saw a 7 foot tall, 500 lb. Sumo wrestler with large bullhorns sprouting out of his head. The beast was crouched down and snarling at him. With amazing speed and agility, the behemoth started charging. Ethan turned back around, and the old man and the table were gone. In front of him was a large empty room. With no idea what to do, Ethan started running. In front of him were three doors: A very small one that looked like he would have to get on his knees and would just barely squeeze through, a middle-sized one that looked like an average bedroom size door, and a very large double door. Ethan looked back. The horned Sumo monster was gaining on him and was only a few yards behind him. The double door was closer, but Ethan considered that maybe the smaller door would slow the beast down more, and in the long run he would buy himself more time.

As fast as he could, Ethan ran past the first door then hit the middle door hard, flung it open, and immediately slammed it shut behind him. He was now outside in the daylight. Behind him the door burst open and the giant was trying to squeeze his way through the doorway. In front of him were a large lake, a small dock, and a rowboat. On his left was a block of tall buildings with a single lane street down the middle, and next to him was an old beat-up ten-speed bicycle. To his right was a large empty field. The giant had squeezed himself halfway through the door and was struggling to get his massive body and horns through.

Ethan ran toward the field. Immediately rocks and fireballs started falling from the sky, exploding and creating large potholes on the ground. He turned around and started running toward the buildings and the bicycle. Several large rats were sitting on the bike's seat and handlebars. The fierce rodents bared their teeth at Ethan as he approached. The falling rocks and fireballs were moving closer, and the Sumo giant was almost through the door. Ethan tried to shoo the rats off the bike, but they were holding their ground.

He grabbed the tire and shook the bike hard trying to knock them off, but they dug in their claws and stayed on. On the ground was a stick. Ethan picked it up and poked the rat that was perched on the handlebars. The big, scruffy rodent fell off, hit the ground, and ran away. The other rat had hunkered down, its claws digging deep into the cheep vinyl seat. Ethan took a step closer, and it flashed its fangs and hissed.

Ethan heard a crash and looked up. The giant sumo beast was through the door and charging towards him. If he didn't get on this bike in the next few seconds, he would have to deal with a much more serious problem than a pissed-off rat. Ethan put the stick in the rat's face to distract it, then reached around with his opposite hand and grabbed its long hairless tail. The rat was big and heavy, its four claws scratching violently in the air as it dangled upside down. The sumo monster was now just a few feet away. Ethan swung the rat under-handed and tossed it, hitting the monster square in the face. The beast stopped in his tracks, roared, and struggled to remove the angry rodent. As quickly as possible, Ethan hopped on the bike. He was still holding the stick and was about to toss it when a thought occurred to him, "This may come in handy later," so he tucked it under his arm, then tore out like a finalist in the Tour de France.

Vani sat and laughed as she watched the monitor. She had seen many variations on this scenario, but Ethan was the first to grab the rat and throw it at his opponent. "This guy was resourceful," she thought. Ethan was now riding as fast as he could through a maze of tall buildings. There were several cameras mounted inside the VRMC Chamber. Vani checked the monitor to see how Ethan was doing. The computerized magnetic chamber, when interacting with the VRMC magnetic suit, was able to create any physical shape using magnetic energy, so all the objects that a person encountered in the virtual world would feel solid and real. Vani described it as a super-duper version of Disneyland's Star Tours.

Ethan was now magnetically suspended in mid-air pedaling an invisible bicycle. She watched him squeeze the invisible brakes, then hop off the bike and walk with difficulty, as if he were on an invisible treadmill.

In Ethan's virtual world he stopped because he had reached the end of the alley. The cross street had no sidewalks. It was a freeway packed with speeding traffic. Crossing it would be more dangerous than crossing a rushing river. He looked around the labyrinth of tall brick buildings. His objective was to leave the city, yet he had no idea which way to go.

He assumed the city must be a circle shape, or something close to it. He looked at his ice cube; it was starting to melt. Before an idea or strategy could formulate in his brain, he heard a rumble in the distance, rapidly getting louder. A gang of hell's Angels on Harleys came riding towards him down the alley. Some of the guys were swinging spiked mace balls over their heads—all of them were screaming like a pack of charging Indians from an old Western movie. He grabbed his stick, thinking, "What are the chances of fighting off a pack of bikers or speeding cars with a stick? None!" He scanned the buildings for an alternative.

There was an old-fashioned metal fire escape on the side of the building. The bottom landing had a retractable ladder that hung one story high over the alley. It was fifty yards from Ethan in the direction of the speeding bikers. This was a now-or-never moment. Ethan surprised the charging pack of hell's Angeles by running towards them. As he approached the fire escape, he realized it was considerably higher than he had thought. It looked higher than a basketball hoop, and he knew he couldn't touch a basketball hoop without a boost. Instead of giving up, Ethan remembered all those Jackie Chan movies in which Jackie would climb up onto a high roof by rebounding off a wall. The fire escape was about five feet away from the side of the building and about twelve feet up in the air.

Ethan ran with all his might towards the building, passed under the hanging fire escape, leaped up taking two large steps straight up the wall, then pushed off. He spun around in midair and dove towards the hanging metal ladder. He was higher than he anticipated and overshot his mark. His chest banged into the side of the bottom landing, and his body slammed into the ladder, knocking the wind out of him. Pain shot through his chest, but he held on as his body dangled above the alley. His fingers had caught hold of the metal grate of the bottom landing, and he was holding on for dear life.

The sound of the Harleys was now deafening. The first battalion of screaming bikers was just a few feet away. Ethan kicked his dangling legs to get momentum so he could swing his body up onto the fire escape landing. Just as he had achieved the necessary momentum to kick himself up, a baseball bat hit him in the foot, throwing him off-balance and nearly knocking him off. Ethan managed to hang on, but his right knee smacked the landing square on the funny bone. Pain shot up his leg; it hurt like hell, but he started to laugh uncontrollably.

Ethan watched through the grate as another biker rode towards his dangling left leg, his large tattooed arms swinging nunchucks around a pile of matted grayish hair held together by a dirty red bandana. With all his strength, Ethan heaved his leg out of the way and onto the fire escape a millisecond before the nunchuck hit the bottom of the landing. Wood fragments splintered off, and there was a clang loud enough to be heard over the roar of Harleys. Ethan got on his feet and hiked up the stairs as fast as he could with a sore foot and banged knee. When he got to the top of the building, he looked down and saw that the bikers were trying to boost each other up onto the fire escape.

Ethan caught his breath, opened his shirt pocket, and looked at his melting ice cube; only sixty percent was left. He surveyed the landscape to see which way to go. He could see a wall in the distance that circled around the buildings and landscape of the city. Where was the exit? He noticed a cluster of proudly waving flags, each a unique single color. That must be the place! Now, how the hell to get off this roof? Ethan looked over the edge of the twenty-story building down to the alley. One side had bikers trying to climb up, another a relentless freeway. He peered over another edge and was staring into the soulless eyes of a fifteen-foot scorpion climbing up the brick wall. Terror and adrenaline shot up his spine.

Ethan ran over to the edge of the fourth wall and peered over it; there was no way down, no fire escape, no balconies, no windows, just sheer wall. Across the alley was a similar building, the same height with the same blank wall. It was at least thirty feet away. There was no way he could jump and expect anything but to fall to the ground and die. Ethan looked around the roof. In the corner was a pile of old pipes of different sizes. There was one large three-inch steel pipe that was as long as the roof, which he estimated to be forty or fifty feet. The smallest pipe was a half-inch and about four feet in length.

He grabbed a thick three-inch pipe about ten feet long and went over to the wall where the scorpion was climbing. The scorpion was now three-quarters of the way up. Ethan aimed and threw the pipe like a javelin as hard as he could straight down at the scorpion. The pipe was heavy and went fast and straight, but the scorpion dodged slightly and pulled its body closer to the wall. The pole missed its head by inches, slid past its armored back, and hit it square on the stinger part of its tail. The impact knocked the scorpion off its balance, and it fell back, its six legs and pinchers grasping the wall to keep from falling. It stumbled and fell a few stories before catching itself. The moment it stopped, another even bigger scorpion climbed up the wall and over the dazed scorpion. Now two of them were climbing, already two thirds of the way up the wall.

Ethan ran back to the pile of pipes. He could hear the bikers climbing the fire escape hooting and hollering. Desperation gave him an idea. He grabbed the long three-inch steel pipe and dragged it to the edge of the fourth wall. He then fed the pipe though the wrought iron railing and started to push it over towards the building across the alley. It didn't take long. He aimed for the wrought iron railing on the opposite building, but the pipe was heavy and he didn't have much leverage, so he couldn't keep it level. The best he could do was to get it to touch the roof below the rail so that it lay there, precariously unstable, at a twenty degree decline. The only thing to grab hold of once he got to the other side was the bottom edge of the roof. Before he could think of anything else, the scorpions were over the wall and on to the roof.

Ethan ran back to the pile of pipes and grabbed a two-inch by four-and-a-half-foot-long pipe. He picked it up and held it like a baseball bat. When he turned around, the scorpion was moving toward him in attack mode, its pinchers up and tail coiled. Ethan crouched down, got a strong footing, and swung as hard as he could, hitting the scorpion in his pincer. Green goop squirted out of the impact spot, getting all over him and the ground around him. The scorpion responded by striking with its tail. Ethan leaped back, and the stinger missed by inches. The scorpion continued towards him more cautiously. Ethan was backing away when he heard the bikers on the roof behind him.

The instant the first bearded, beer-bellied biker set foot on the roof, he charged at Ethan, swinging a heavy chain over his head.

Ethan turned around just in time to block the chain with his pipe. The chain wrapped around the pipe, and Ethan pulled the big, greasy guy towards him, knocking him off-balance. The biker fell forward. Ethan jumped out of his way, spun around, and kicked the tattooed dirt-bag literally in the ass, knocking him into the jaws and pinchers of the giant scorpion. Ethan spun around and faced the next bewildered biker who was distracted by the elephant-sized insect devouring his fellow gang member. As the biker was about to step off the fire escape, Ethan kicked him, knocking him backward down the fire escape steps, causing a domino effect of bikers falling and stumbling over themselves.

This gave Ethan a few seconds to come up with a plan. His only way out was the pipe across the building. He ran towards it. Now the second scorpion was on the roof, and the bikers were picking themselves up and climbing onto the roof as well. Without looking down twenty stories, Ethan climbed over the railing and crouched under the pipe that connected the two buildings. He laid the pipe he had just used as a weapon perpendicularly over the long pipe, grabbed each side, and held on tight.

He pushed as hard as he could and started sliding down the pipe towards the adjacent building. He felt like James West from the TV show "The Wild Wild West." Sparks flew from the scraping metal. The pipe he was holding started to bend slightly from the heat; this had both good and bad results. As it bent, it created a groove, making the pipe more stable, but as the angle of the pipe bent downward his hands began to slip. It only took a few very long, tiring, and anxiety-filled seconds to cross. He avoided slamming into the wall by using his feet to break his fall. Once on the other side, he grabbed the rail and climbed up onto the roof.

On the opposite rooftop, some of the bikers were fighting the scorpions, while others were getting themselves positioned to climb across on the pipe. Ethan kicked the pipe off his side of the roof and watched it fall all twenty stories down into the alley. It hit the ground and bounced around, making a series of clanging noises that reverberated up the canyon between the two buildings.

Now what? Ethan looked around; he had gotten one building closer to his goal, but there was no way down. None of the sides of the building had steps, a fire escape, or even anything to hang onto. Between the building and the next adjacent building was a crane with a wrecking ball. It was swinging between the two buildings, each swing getting closer and closer to each building. Within a few seconds both buildings would be demolished. He had no choice. He had to get off this rooftop, and hopefully the other building's rooftop would offer more opportunity to escape. He positioned himself in front of the swinging wrecking ball.

The giant iron sphere swung toward Ethan, coming within a few feet of the building. He tried to leap on to it but lost his nerve. Ethan watched it swing away and waited. He considered that the next time the ball returned, might be the last chance he'd have before it struck the building, sending it crashing to the ground. The ball swung back, its arc inches from the building. Ethan practically stepped onto the wrecking ball as it changed directions. He ran to its center and tightly grabbed hold of the cable, edging himself to the opposite side of the ball. His stomach clenched as he carefully moved into position, anticipating the moment of jumping off. The ball picked up speed, and Ethan held on like a leech. The swinging ball's apex came within a few feet of the second building.

The idea was to jump off before it headed back, but Ethan didn't get the timing right and didn't jump off. He swung back towards the building he had just left, but this time faster. The ball hit the building at the apex of the pendulum's swing. There was a loud crashing noise like a bowling alley at rush hour. Bricks and dust flew everywhere. Ethan turned his face away from the flying debris and continued to hang on for dear life. The ball changed directions and swung even faster, almost to the point of making him dizzy, but Ethan couldn't afford to screw up. He took a deep breath and concentrated on the task at hand.

This time Ethan stood poised. He felt the ball begin to slow down, coming to the end of its arc. Ethan leaped off, and the remaining momentum of the wrecking ball catapulted him into the air. A second later the ball came to the end of its swing and missed the building by inches. Airborne and out of control, Ethan tried to get his feet underneath himself, but he was leaning too far forward. He flew ten feet before hitting the rooftop, first with his feet, then his knees, then his hands and forearms. Finally his chest hit, and he heard a quiet little crack just before he slid across the rooftop. Once he stopped sliding, he got up onto his feet and brushed off all the dust from the bricks and mortar.

He looked towards the wall. He had successfully gotten one more building closer, and this one had a fire escape stairway down the side. He looked down; no crazed bikers or giant predatory insects. He was feeling pretty good. He had done it. He was going to make it out of the city. He felt his chest pocket for the ice cube, which was considerably smaller. He took one step towards the fire escape when he heard a deafening shriek that startled him, making him jump involuntarily.

He looked up into the sky, and diving down towards the roof was a flock of pterodactyls. He was about to start running down the fire escape when he heard a woman's voice crying for help. She seemed to appear from nowhere, beautiful, long flowing dark brown hair, flawless skin, and proportions that would make any woman jealous. She was running towards him wearing shorts, a skimpy tank top, and she was clearly the target of a hungry pterodactyl.

Ethan contemplated that he could just leave, save his own ass and let her fend for herself, or he could try to help her. Then the wrecking ball hit the building—bricks and dust came flying all around him. Ethan fell to the ground from the impact. He got up quickly, grabbed a brick, ran towards the girl, and tossed it at the pterodactyl with all the strength he could muster. Ethan tackled the girl, knocking her down and jerking her to the side, as the pterodactyl's sharp talons swung past her and back up into the air. Without saying a word Ethan got up, took her by the arm, pulled her to her feet, and they ran down the fire escape stairs. He could hear the building falling apart. It would be only a few more seconds before the wrecking ball would hit again and destroy the building.

They got to the street level, just grass and trees between Ethan and the flags mounted on the city wall. He started walking across the grass towards the exit. He pulled what was left of the melted ice cube out of his pocket. It was a quarter of its original size and it had cracked from the fall and was barely holding together. He looked back at the flags. He was almost there; as long as it held together, he would have something to show the guards to get out.

He looked back and saw that the girl was still standing by the building and hadn't followed him across the grass. "Are you coming?" he shouted.

She stood her ground and shook her head no.

"Are you sure?"

She nodded.

"Are you going to be ok?"

She shrugged her shoulders and gave a sad look.

Ethan sighed; he looked at the grass and patch of trees that lay before him, and he knew he was close to fulfilling his mission. He looked at the fragile remains of his ice cube. He still had a little time.

He walked back to her, holding the delicate cube. When he got there it was the first time he really got a chance to look at her. She was genetically perfect, he thought to himself: "What possible thing could improve this woman? If I could design a woman from scratch, what would I do differently?" Ethan couldn't think of a single thing. One aspect of his job at the gym was to evaluate clients, give them suggestions as to how they could improve their body, and then recommend exercises and diets. That was what Ethan had been doing practically every day of his life since he was fourteen, but this was the first woman that he couldn't find a single thing to improve.

Her voice was soft and seductive, "I need help to get back home," and she pointed in the opposite way.

He looked at the ice cube. The two pieces were teetering. Any sudden movement and they would break. As carefully as he could, he began to put the remains of the cube into his pocket. "Ok, I'll help you."

Out of nowhere a gunshot cracked. The girl fell forward. Instinctively Ethan grabbed her. He felt her body weight increase as her muscles gave way. He held her tightly in his arms. There was another shot, and she was hit again in the back. Blood splattered in all directions as the bullet tore through her flesh. He looked around to find cover.

He could feel her shallow breathing and her pulse weaken. She was still alive. He had to get her out of there. He put one arm under her shoulders the other under her legs and picked her up like a groom carrying his bride across the threshold. As he bent over and reached down, he realized he had forgotten about the ice cube. He watched as the cube fell out of his hand, and dropped onto the ground, and shattered. Instantly the world he was in became silent, the weight of the girl in his arms disappeared, and he was staring into a blue screen.

Ethan was confused and disoriented. For a moment he had forgotten that the world he had been in was fake. He just stood there dazed as someone removed his helmet. The blue screen was stripped away, and now he was looking into Vani's grinning face. "How was that?"

Ethan's body was full of adrenaline, and when he spoke, it burst out of him like a fire hose. "That was probably the most exciting thing I have ever done."

"Really? That's interesting." She was now unfastening the Velcro straps and taking off the VRMC sleeves.

Ethan was very excited, his words came tumbling out loud and fast. "You guys have created a real life matrix-type thing where reality and illusion are indistinguishable."

"Yeah, someday we won't actually have to go anywhere to travel."

"Wow!" Ethan contemplated that. "So how did I do?" They walked out of the VRMC sphere and headed back to the suiting-up area.

"You did well for a first timer." She was now working on removing the chaps. "The program may seem a little over the top, but it's an entertaining way to find a person's priorities, desires, physical abilities, problem-solving skills, mental focus, calmness under stress, and a host of other things. The program is designed on the premise that how a person does one thing is how they do everything."

"Ok?" Ethan was trying to follow the logic.

"The computer analyzes all your moves as well as your heart rate, respiratory rate and a long list of bodily functions. All that data is quantified, giving us a remarkable picture of who you are."

Ethan pulled the hood off of his head. "So do I get to find out what makes me tick?"

"Hmm." Vani removed the final piece of the suit then tossed it onto the table. "That's not for me to decide."

Chapter 10

Giddy from his VRMC experience, Ethan left Eden, Inc. and drove North up the 405 Freeway in the 4:30 afternoon rush hour traffic, that was famous for being so bad that it routinely caused people to snap and start shooting one another. Ethan navigated it in a state of euphoria, spontaneously bursting into fits of uncontrollable chuckling. He realized that this random behavior made him appear crazy to the drivers creeping along all around him, but he was feeling good and didn't care.

He arrived at the gym just as it was getting dark. He opened the door and was assaulted by a warm, humid, sweaty haze. The gym smelled like old socks; apparently Vince had turned the air conditioning off. He usually did that when it started to get cold, but now he was doing it to save money. Vince was sitting behind the counter eating a protein bar; from the way his t-shirt stuck to his skin, it looked like he had just finished working out. Vince had to be extra careful because of his back injury, so he had stopped lifting heavy weights and was doing lots of reps with light weights. He strongly believed that proper exercise was the best way to heal the body.

Vince looked up from the counter, "How did it go?"

Ethan wanted to tell him about the VRMC and how amazing it was, but didn't know what to say. It was frustrating that he wasn't allowed to tell anyone about anything he had seen or done. Then again, who would believe him? He considered telling his dad anyway but changed his mind. He had no idea what the consequences would be. It could prevent him from getting the job. After seeing what they were up to he wanted the job, badly. "It went pretty good." Ethan said nonchalantly.

Vince swallowed the last chunk of his protein bar. "Did you get the job?"

"I don't know. They interviewed me and tested my reactions." Ethan paused, not wanting to have to explain anything in more detail. "Uh, we'll see what happens next."

The phone rang. Vince answered it, sat down at his desk, and immediately started shuffling through a stack of papers. Vince had recently cut back on staff, so now there was always a lot more work to do. It had become Ethan's habit to start working immediately the moment he stepped into the gym. Within seconds Vince and Ethan were off doing their own thing and the conversation was over.

One of Ethan's many responsibilities was closing up the gym. He had just re-racked all the dumbbells, and was starting to vacuum when he got a call from Vani. She was very concise.

"Your application has been approved. Be ready to be dispatched immediately. We will send you an email giving you further instructions." He didn't know how to react, so in a very matter-of-fact manner, he thanked her and then hung up the phone. Afterwards he continued closing up the gym as he would any other day

Ethan considered calling Vanessa and telling her that he had gotten the job and that he hoped when he got back they could start back up where they left off. He imagined making the phone call, playing their conversation over and over in his mind. Every time something would go wrong he would start over and try again, but each variation grossed him out and he saw himself as being weak and needy, two things he absolutely didn't want to be. Nonetheless, an empty feeling drained his spirits anytime he considered that she was gone from his life. She had been a huge part of what made him excited to wake up each morning, go to school, and do his routine at work—his light at the end of the tunnel. He shoved aside any desire to call her, gritted his teeth, grabbed the mop and bucket, and then headed over to clean up the locker rooms.

The last person to leave the gym was Keith, a very fit light-skinned black guy who was usually in the company of beautiful girls, but there was something about him that seemed out of place. He was too meticulous, too well-put-together, too well-coiffed. Ethan unlocked the door for Keith to leave, wondering why it was that the gay guys got to hang out with all the hot chicks.

Ethan was about to lock the door behind him when Vanessa came sheepishly walking up wearing a Foo Fighters t-shirt, cut off shorts, and flip-flops.

"Hi." she said, her eyes shyly scanning the ground.

Ethan looked at her, not knowing how to respond. He was confused, angry, yet extremely excited to see her. He heard himself say, "Hi." They stared at each other for a moment, neither saying a word. When the silence became awkward they both began to speak at the same time, then stopped as if on cue. They waited a moment; when neither spoke, each took the initiative and they both began to speak at the same time again.

"You first!" said Ethan, enjoying the cool night air, a sharp contrast to the stuffy gym.

Vanessa stuttered for a moment, not sure how to start, then finally blurted out, "I'm sorry."

Ethan looked puzzled. "Why are you sorry?"

She adjusted her posture then looked him straight in the eye: "Because I was wrong. You didn't do anything malevolent or even selfish. I recognize you have other commitments and responsibilities, which often means having to make sacrifices. I realize that you would like to stay, spend the summer with me and go on vacation, but right now you have more important things to do."

Ethan stared at her. That was heavy. He'd never had the "serious talk" with a woman before, the kind of talks adults have on Oprah, where people express their feelings, discuss what they want out of life, and make plans for the future. He suddenly felt very grown up. He looked at her with emotion swelling in his heart and said, "I have to clean the bathrooms. You want to come inside?"

Vanessa followed Ethan towards the women's locker room. He told her about the phone call he had just received, that he had gotten the job and would be leaving soon. Inside the locker room Ethan began picking up scattered towels and pieces of paper off the floor.

"You want to know something funny?" asked Ethan, as he picked up last paper towel and threw the in the trashcan.

"What?"

"The women are bigger slobs than the men, and I mean by a lot."

Vanessa gave him a look.

"You don't believe me? You'll see when we go to the men's locker room."

Ethan wiped down the counters, scrubbed the toilets, cleaned the mirrors, all tasks he had done thousands of times since he was a kid. Vanessa helped him, and they continued with small talk. Finally he couldn't take it anymore. He had to tell someone. He had just finished squirting the tile cleaner onto the shower tile, and within a few seconds the chemicals were starting to burn his eyes and lungs. He turned on all the showers so the water would rinse all the chemicals away. It looked like some silly low budget fountain. He looked around as if to make sure no one was watching. "I have to tell you a secret. You can't tell anyone, not even my dad."

"Okay!" she held her breath with anticipation.

"I saw, no, I experienced the most amazing computer program imaginable."

She stood baffled, watching the water steam up the room, and grinned, "You are such a dork!"

She had never called him a dork before. He wasn't sure how to take it.

Ethan's routine was to let the row of showers run for about a minute. That was usually enough to wash down the chemicals so everything would be clean. Carefully, so as not to get wet, he reached for the faucet to begin the turning-off process, when he was unexpectedly jerked away by his shirt collar. Vanessa grabbed him, jumped into his arms, and wrapped her legs around his hips, pulled his face into hers and kissed him. The floor was wet and slippery. Trying not to fall down, he grabbed the nearest shower head to keep his balance; consequently he repositioned the nozzle, soaking the two of them. The water was warm, and neither seemed to object.

Vanessa squeezed her body tightly around Ethan and deeply tongue-kissed him, barely giving him an opportunity to breathe. Ethan felt a surge of testosterone rush through his veins. Every primal DNA cell that caused mankind to flourish and reproduce, regardless of how shitty and inhospitable the conditions were, was chemically activated and ready to start procreating. Vanessa's t-shirt became a skintight gossamer layer revealing each curve of her breasts. When Ethan saw her, what little rational thought he had left circulating through his brain instantly evaporated. He was reduced to a horny protozoan.

He leaned against the shower wall and slid down to the ground, his tongue never leaving her mouth. He rolled onto his back and pulled Vanessa on top of him. She broke their lip-lock, giggled, and then sat up on her knees, straddling his crotch. Ethan reached up and grabbed her breasts. She smiled, pushed her wet hair back behind her ears, then reached down and in one fluid motion pulled her t-shirt off over her head, wadded it up into a ball, and tossed it into the corner, where it made a surprisingly loud splat that echoed off the tile walls. Ethan stared up, transfixed by her unexpectedly large and perfectly-proportioned breasts and erect nipples. She wore clothes that hid them more than revealed them. Ethan was pleasantly surprised by this revelation. She leaned over and put her breasts in his face. He licked and kissed them as he grabbed her ass and tried to wedge his hands under her tight, wet denim cut-offs.

Vince was in his office going over paper work, sorting out which bills he could delay and which ones were urgent. He realized he hadn't had a chance to talk with Ethan since he'd gotten back from his job interview and was feeling a bit guilty. He looked at the clock and figured Ethan should be done closing and cleaning up the gym by now. He went onto the workout floor. All the lights were on and everything seemed to be put away. He walked over towards the men's locker rooms, opened the door, and looked inside. The place was still a mess. This was strange: Why was it taking Ethan so long to clean up? Vince got worried; perhaps something broke and Ethan was cleaning up the mess, or maybe there had been an accident and he was laying injured somewhere.

With urgent concern, Vince opened the door of the women's locker room and was bombarded by a cloud of hot steamy fog. He took a few steps into the room and immediately heard the showers running and loud moaning and grunting. Vince stopped in his tracks. He was always a little wary going into the women's locker room anyway; he always felt like a trespasser and feared he would be mistaken for a pervert, but he needed to know what was going on in his gym. As quietly as he could he walked past the toilet stalls, sinks, and lockers and peeked into the shower area. Wet clothing was scattered about. He recognized Ethan's wet shoes on the opposite side of the room. In the middle, getting sprayed by three showers, were two bodies in the sixty-nine position. Vince didn't really want to look. He thought that would make him a peeping tom. He wasn't sure what to do; this had never happened before, but he needed to know who they were.

He squinted, then as quickly as he could, he peeked through the steam and splashing water. Ethan was on the bottom and Vanessa was on top. "She has a surprisingly nice ass," he thought. He quietly sneaked out of the locker room before they had a chance to notice him. He was reminded of his youth. He didn't have a gym all to himself to take girls to. He had to get blow jobs and have sex in the back seat of cars. Ethan had a pretty good deal. A burst of pride came over Vince; he felt like a dad who had provided his son with something of real value.

Vince stood in the doorway out of sight and listened. In his mind, being an audio voyeur didn't seem as bad as a visual one. He heard loud thumping followed by a crescendo of moaning that rose to a screaming climax. There was panting, splashing, giggling, then showers were turned off. Vince thought about his two weeks of bliss with Delilah and how during that time he felt the stirrings of true love. Hopefully Ethan would have better luck with women than he'd had.

His recollections were interrupted when he heard Vanessa's voice: "Now can we do it in the sauna?"

Without hesitation, Ethan enthusiastically responded, "hell, yeah!"

Vince felt another wave of pride. "That's my boy!"

Chapter 11

At 5:00 a.m. the next morning, Ethan got up and packed for three months. The email explained where to go, when to be there, and that he really didn't need to bring anything. The company provided clothing, toothbrushes, and all the amenities he would need. Nonetheless he packed one bag with two pairs of shoes, a journal that had never been written in, an iPod, a bathing suit, a pair of shorts, a pair of jeans, a half-dozen t-shirts, two pairs of sweat pants, and a sweatshirt with the Blood Sweat and Tears Gym Logo on it.

Vince drove Ethan to Eden, Inc. like a father sending his son off to fight in a foreign war. Vince was proud that Ethan would be able to save their business but embarrassed that he had to. It was Ethan's first real step into manhood. From now on Vince and Ethan would be equals. Ethan seemed unaware of the transitional impact of this defining moment. He was still basking in the afterglow of his night with Vanessa.

The calico, 1965 Ranchero pulled into the garage. There was a loading zone where several cars were dropping people off. Vince pulled in behind a Lincoln Town Car where a chauffeur was opening the door and helping a very well-dressed lady with her things as she went into the building. Vince looked around. All the cars were expensive. He thought, "This will be a good experience for Ethan. It's certainly a step up from the clientele we have at the gym. Hopefully he will have the opportunity to meet wealthy, important people." He knew one thing to be true, "It's not what you know, it's who you know in life that counts!"

Ethan hopped out of the passenger seat and grabbed his bag from the back of the Ranchero. When he looked up, Vince was standing on the opposite side of the car. Neither was sure what to say. There was an awkward silence even with all the noise and activity around them. Finally Ethan heard himself say, "I guess I'll see you when I get back!"

Vince nodded. "I guess you will." It was a very unsatisfying goodbye, but Vince didn't know what else to do. A taxi pulled up behind the Ranchero and honked at him. Instinctively Vince flipped the taxi driver the middle finger. When he turned back around the Town Car that had been in front of him was gone. Quickly he slid back into the driver's seat and then watched his son slip into the crowd that was funneling into the building. With a resigned empty feeling that he should have done more, he put the car in gear and drove away.

Ethan walked into the lobby and was greeted by Ascot.

"Good to see you, Ethan!" He shook Ethan's hand more energetically than was warranted for 6 a.m. "Follow me, I'll show you how to get through this mess quickly."

The large lobby looked like a small airport at rush hour. There were literally hundreds of people checking in at a variety of counters, each according to various departments and job titles. Ethan was surprised to see so many people traveling to the resort at the same time.

Ascot escorted Ethan to the check-in counter behind which Vani was standing.

When they arrived she looked up and smiled. "Nice to see you again, Mr. Stone," and she reached over to shake his hand.

"Thank you." Ethan took her hand, noticing that each finger had a different color nail polish.

Immediately she started typing into her terminal and from then on was all business. She handed him a touch pad that had several documents for him to sign. Then, just like an airline baggage checker, she took his bag and put it on a cart with a pile of other bags. After everything was signed a plastic card popped out the top of the touch pad unit. Vani attached the card to a strap and put it around Ethan's neck. Ascot showed Ethan that he already had his. "This is your ID card. It's also your room key, your credit card when you choose to purchase anything, and right now it's your ticket onto the train and shuttle."

"Wow," Ethan grunted, groggy from not sleeping the previous night.

She pointed to a row of elevators. "Go to the elevator and it will take you to where you need to go."

Neither Ethan nor Ascot knew exactly what to do, but didn't say anything as they walked towards a row of elevators. They searched for a button to push but there were none. Each looked at the other, puzzled but unwilling to appear stupid, so they waited, hoping someone would show up and would know what to do.

A man in a business suit carrying a briefcase walked up to the elevators and waited. A few seconds later an elevator door opened and a very polite female voice with a hint of a British accent said, "Welcome, Mr. Ascot LaRouch and Mr. Ethan Stone." Both Ethan and Ascot simultaneously looked down at the ID cards hanging around their necks.

Ascot looked up holding the card reverently. "I see how this works now."

They stepped into the elevator, and the door closed behind them. There were no buttons to push; it just started moving.

Ascot scanned the room suspiciously. "You do realize something?"

"What?" said Ethan.

"This," Ascot held up the card again, "tells them where we are at all times. Talk about Big Brother watching you."

"Yeah," Ethan grunted. Ethan assumed they would be going up. It was a high-rise building, after all. Instead they seemed to be going down a very long way. After about two minutes, which seemed like an eternity, Ethan's ears popped.

Finally they stopped, the door opened, and they stepped out of the elevator into a cold sterile corridor with a linoleum floor. The same female voice said: "Mr. Ascot LaRouch, Mr. Ethan Stone, please follow the corridor to the left."

An arrow pointing left appeared on the wall. The corridor was very long, and they started walking without knowing where to go. They passed several doors, none with doorknobs.

As they walked down the corridor a door opened and a tall, broad-shouldered, big-boned ebony woman wearing a white lab coat walked briskly out into the corridor. Her hair was tightly pulled back, accentuating her perfectly round head and big eyes.

"Hello, Mr. LaRouch," she said with a proper British accent as she reached out to shake Ascot's hand. She smiled, flashing a row of perfectly straight, blindingly white teeth that contrasted with her coal black skin.

"Please just call me Ascot. I buried my last name a long time ago."

She nodded then turned to Ethan. "Mr. Stone." She had a surprisingly strong grip, her manners were very formal, and she knew exactly who was who. "I'm Mayawa. Please follow me."

They followed her past the automated door and into a bright white room with stark white walls. On one side of the room were four stalls. They looked like changing rooms attached to large cylinders. It reminded Ethan of the stand-up tanning booths they had at fancy salons. On the other side of the room was a luggage conveyor belt and X-Ray machine similar to the ones used at airports.

Standing in the middle of the room was a short, thin man with a full head of perfectly white hair and a white pencil mustache that stood out against his tan face. He was outfitted in a white lab coat and white pants. He had a stethoscope around his neck and a round mirror above his right eye. Mayawa introduced the man as Dr. Conrad. He shook Ethan's and Ascot's hands then got straight to business.

"We will be doing the final preparations for your journey," he said in a surprisingly low husky voice. He explained that they each had one last physical exam. Ethan mentioned that he had been examined earlier that week, and was told he was in fine shape. Dr. Conrad replied that everyone had to go through this.

Mayawa handed Ethan and Ascot each a large clear plastic bag with a zip-lock top and a paper examination gown. Then she led them each to a separate stall that was equipped with an examination table, sink, and drawers full of various medical supplies. Standing at the doorway she robotically explained the process as though she said it two hundred times a day. " Go inside, take off all your clothes and put on the paper gown. Put all your clothes and any other belongings you may have: cell phones, cameras, iPods etc., into the plastic bag.

Leave your ID card on. You'll use it to seal the lock on the bag. Don't worry, you'll get all your stuff later."

Ethan waited for Ascot to make the first move. Ascot looked at Ethan, shrugged his shoulders, and then boldly stepped into the stall. Ethan followed his lead, stepped up to the next stall and went in. He closed the door, took off his sweat pants, t-shirt, cross trainers, underwear, and socks, put them into the bag, then sealed it. The zip-lock unit had a thin credit card swipe lock attached. Ethan leaned over, with the card still around his neck, and swiped it. Immediately he tried to open the bag, but it was locked tight. "Cool unit," he thought. He grabbed the folded gown and shook it so it unfolded open. He held up the ridiculous light blue paper garment and contemplated which way to put in on. He remembered that they essentially went on backwards, with one's butt hanging out the rear. He put his arms through the sleeves and tied the gown in back. A minute later Dr Conrad entered the stall carrying a touch screen computer tablet and began the examination.

He started by looking in Ethan's eyes, down his throat, up his nose. He poked, probed, asked him to cough listening to his lungs, took his blood pressure. Then, in one fluid motion like a magician, he put the barrel of an air gun used to administer shots that don't require a needle against Ethan's shoulder and pulled the trigger. Startled, Ethan jumped out of his seat, and a split second later his arm stung.

"Dude, what was that?"

Conrad chuckled, " I didn't mean to surprise you. It's just an immune boosting cocktail and an inoculation for a variety of diseases. Where you are going, you are going to need it."

Ethan felt a shiver go down his spine. A while back, a gym member claimed that her baby boy had become autistic after receiving a vaccination at the hospital when he was a few weeks old. She was devastated. She tried suing the pharmaceutical company, Merck, but her lawyer soon discovered that there was a provision in the Patriot Act that congress had passed protecting Merck from any such lawsuits. Talk about having friends in high places. Ethan had heard other stories at the gym about how drug companies were more interested in profits than in public health and how the FDA had become the lapdog of the pharmaceutical industry. Ethan had seen first hand some serious side effects from drugs that were much worse than the diseases they were trying to cure. Many of these side effects were accepted, ignored, or covered up. This made Ethan wary of the entire medical industry

Ethan took a deep breath and relaxed. He assured himself that those cases were rare. He knew that if he were going to some exotic, hopefully tropical place, it would be perfectly normal to be required to receive some kind of prophylactic inoculation shot. This thought excited Ethan. He imagined all the cool places he might be headed.

Dr. Conrad finished his exam and punched some figures into the computer, "Okay, everything is good. Now take off your gown and step into the chamber and wait for further instructions." He pointed to a steel door opposite the stall door, tucked his tablet under his arm, and left.

Ethan stood in front of the cylinder, and was trying to figure out how to enter it when the door silently and smoothly slid open. He stepped in, and the door closed behind him. Inside, it was about twice the size of a phone booth. The same female voice from the elevators announced: "Raise your arms and close your eyes tightly, and wait for further instructions."

Ethan did what the computer voice said. A second later there was a loud pop and a bright flash that he could see even with his eyes tightly closed. Immediately his skin felt tight and itchy like having mild sunburn. Then a high-pressure mist sprayed his body from every direction. A few seconds later the mist turned into a tunnel of warm air. Almost immediately he was dry. The door opened, cold air hit him along with a strong smell of disinfectant, and he stepped into a spotless, sterile stall similar to the one on the other side of the cylinder. "Enjoy your journey, Mr. Ethan Stone," said the computer voice.

Hanging on the stall door was an orange and black jumpsuit. A woman's voice, this time from an actual person he couldn't see, spoke from the other side of the stall door.

"Please put on the flight suit, and we will proceed to the next section."

Again, Ethan did as he was told, putting on the suit. It was a fairly unique outfit. It reminded him of the onesies pajamas that toddlers wear. The suit had boots attached, so the first thing he did was to stuff his feet into the boots, which were very loose. On the side of each boot was a button with the word "fit." written below. He pushed the button. There was a hiss, and immediately the boots tightened and his feet felt snug. He thought he must look ridiculous. He was squatting naked over a jumpsuit with boots on. Next step was to pull up the suit and get his arms and body inside. This was fairly easy. The suit must have been a one-size-fits-all type of garment because it was very baggy.

Once he felt properly clothed, he stepped out of the stall. There was an Asian woman with glasses, her hair pulled back in a ponytail, sitting behind a computer screen. She got up and walked over to Ethan. She was wearing a white lab coat, a black skirt, and black medium-heeled shoes. Ethan stood there as she clip-clopped across the spotless shiny white floor towards him. She approached, studying his suit, then with surgical precision began to pull on hidden tabs and flaps that Ethan hadn't noticed. There was the sound of tearing as Velcro was pulled, then reattached. In less than a minute all the bagginess of a one-size-fits-all jumpsuit was transformed into a tailor-made flight-suit worthy of a fashion catalog cover. It was remarkably comfortable, a thin Gortex material with a thin fleece lining—light yet sturdy, insulated yet cool. Ethan felt like he was someone important, all suited up. It was certainly a step up from the sweats he had been wearing just a few minutes before.

She spun him around and did a last minute check to make sure everything was right. Ethan broke the silence. "What was that flash inside that cylinder thing?"

Her eyes continued to inspect his suit while she responded in a slightly bored and annoyed voice. "It's an ultra-violet flash. It kills all the bacteria on your body. The shower washes off the dead tissue, moisturizes the skin, and promotes new cell growth."

Ethan nodded, "I assume the wind tunnel that followed is simply to dry off."

She still never made eye contact, just continued to inspect the suit. "Basically yes, it also helps remove any remaining dead tissue."

"What's the point?" Ethan asked hoping not to sound too stupid.

"To avoid any possible contamination. You are now standing in a pressurized sterile environment and will remain in one until you get to your destination."

Ascot appeared behind Ethan wearing the same black and orange flight suit. He was very excited, like a kid on Christmas morning.

"We're ready now," he said thumping his chest with his fists.

The flight suit inspector stepped back, adjusted her glasses, and took one last look at Ethan. She pointed to a door behind him marked with an exit sign. "You are ready. Your next step is to proceed to the boarding gates."

New people were stepping out of the cylinders and she turned around to help them. Ethan and Ascot watched for a moment as she mechanically began to assist the next wave of inductees. As if choreographed, Ethan and Ascot simultaneously turned and walked quietly towards the exit.

Once they were out of earshot, Ethan whispered, "This systematic process seems so robotic. There is something strange about it all."

"Big Brother is watching," agreed Ascot, grabbing the ID card hanging around his neck.

Ethan wondered aloud: "Why all this hoopla for a job at a gym? How exclusive could any resort possibly be?"

Chapter 12

Disneyland is known for its futuristic vision of the world, so for Ethan and Ascot their journey to the Eden, Inc. seemed more like a ride at Disneyland than reality. They walked toward a faint white light glowing at the end of a sterile, dimly lit tunnel. Ethan noted that there was absolutely no smell of anything. At the halfway point, they could hear the murmur of voices and the bustle of movement echo down the long corridor. With each step, the sounds grew louder.

Buzzing with activity, at the end of the tunnel was a huge subway station lobby. It wasn't a New York or London style subway, all grimy and scrawled with graffiti. The room was spotless; it reminded Ethan of a hospital with shiny, smooth walls and white linoleum floors. Hundreds of people wearing different colored flight suits were scurrying around the lobby, headed full throttle in every direction.

The same computer voice he had heard earlier was making announcements over a PA. In the center of the room, suspended from the ceiling, was a giant 3D TV. Now the voice of the computer had a face to go with it. Ethan had imagined that the voice belonged to a short, brown-haired, frumpy woman, but the woman on the screen was a striking, tall, thin, redhead with bright green eyes, high cheekbones, and porcelain skin. She floated in the air and pointed to the different platforms, giving instructions as to when and where to proceed. Ethan watched transfixed, mesmerized by the 3D screen. The lady explained that each department's flight suit color determined the boarding gate each person was assigned. She repeatedly explained which color went where.

Ethan and Ascot stood in the middle of the room looking for their gate, amazed at how big the operation was.

Ethan shook his head in awe, "Where do you think we are going?"

Ascot was about to answer when a gruff, hurried voice commanded, "Can you please step aside!" Behind them was a queue of several men in red and yellow flight suits, each operating a motorized dolly pushing fifteen-foot high stacks of plastic supply boxes wrapped in cellophane. After the procession passed, Ascot picked up where he had left off.

"I have no idea. I figure if we are going by rail, then the resort must be in Mexico or somewhere close by."

"We'll find out soon enough," said Ethan as they headed towards the train.

They passed multiple colored gates. When they approached the black and orange one, it opened automatically, and the computer voice directed them through. "Mr. Ascot, Mr. Ethan Stone, please board here." They followed the voice's instructions and walked down a ramp onto a small section of a very large train platform. Standing proudly in the middle of the huge room like a gigantic sculpture on display at the Metropolitan Museum of Art, was a gleaming silver and blue magnetic levitation train. It looked like a rocket ship lying on its side. The nose came to a pinpoint. The sides were perfectly smooth, curved, and streamlined. The windows were contoured to match the sides and the doors were so well-engineered that, until they opened, it was almost impossible to see where they were located.

Ethan and Ascot's jaws dropped simultaneously. They stared for a few minutes and marveled at the train's unusual design while people all around them began to board. The train's strangest feature was that it had no wheels, no moving parts; therefore no noise, and no friction.

The computer voice announced: "The train will be departing in two minutes. This is the final call."

Ethan and Ascot snapped out of their daze and, with a renewed bounce in their steps, boarded the train. The compartment was almost completely full. Ethan claimed the last seat next to a window. The seats were nice, reclining lounge chairs arranged two by two, all facing the same direction, like the first-class section of a jumbo jet. Ethan leaned back in his seat, stared out the window, and watched as the last pallets of supplies and remaining people hurried to board the adjoining compartments.

Again the computer voice announced: "The train will be departing in one minute. This is the final call."

Exactly one minute later, without any warning, the doors closed. Ethan grinned; his heart raced with excitement, and he watched the train rise about a foot off the track. Slowly it started moving towards the tunnel at the end of the platform. There wasn't the slightest sound, not a jostle. A few seconds later they entered a tunnel and the compartment turned pitch black. Instantly the interior lights popped on, essentially turning the cabin windows into mirrors.

The train rapidly picked up speed, and the G-force pushed Ethan into his La-Z-Boy lounge chair. Ascot sat back in his chair and smiled. After a few seconds the train achieved its desired speed and the G-force ended. Ethan sat up and looked around. It didn't feel like they were even moving, Ethan cupped his hands around his eyes and looked out the window trying to see through the reflection, hoping to get a glimpse outside so that he could tell how fast they were going, but he couldn't see anything. There was barely three inches of clearance from the train to the tunnel walls.

Ethan noticed that across the aisle was a middle-aged man with a glass of water on his tray-table. On every previous plane or train ride he had ever taken, the water in the glass would have little ripples from the vibration, but the water in this glass was as still as if they were sitting in a living room. The guy across the aisle seemed to be uneasy, confused as to why Ethan was staring at him and his glass of water. Ethan smiled to break the tension then sat back in his chair and stared out the window into the blackness.

Suddenly the train shot out of the tunnel and there was a burst of bright light. Ethan closed his eyes tightly from the pain of the glare. He waited a moment for the sting to subside, after which he slowly and cautiously opened his eyes, allowing them to adjust. Looking out the window all he could see was a blur as the train raced through the desert.

Excited, Ascot pushed Ethan back into his seat, leaning over him so he could get a better look out of the window, then sat back and pointed at the horizon. "My guess is we are traveling about five hundred miles an hour."

Ethan stared out the window. "How can you tell?"

"A pilot explained it to me once. You look sideways until a point appears fixed. The farther away the point is, the faster you're moving."

Ethan looked sideways and had to focus very far in the distance in order to see something that wasn't blurry. "How do you know how far away it is?"

"I don't remember the exact formula, but it's like being able to tell what time it is by looking at the sky. You develop a sense for these things."

Ethan looked out of the window, but had to turn away because the blurriness was making his head spin. As suddenly as the daylight appeared, it disappeared. The speeding train had entered another tunnel. A moment later, to Ethan's surprise, the blackness of the compartment was illuminated with the bluish glow of several dozen TV screens. Ethan was staring into a 3D TV that had been previously hidden inside the headrest of the seat in front of him.

The program began with the Eden, Inc. logo floating and spinning in outer space as heroic music filled his ears from speakers inside his chair's headrest. Ethan sat back and took it all in. It was a first-class production. It had all the features of a super-slick trailer to a big-budget blockbuster. The screen had a shot of space with a tiny dot in the middle that slowly grew in size. Over the music came a macho movie man voice, "Each day our world becomes more and more unstable, polluted, and unsafe. The wealthy are targets for kidnappers, thieves, and terrorists. What is the solution?"

Now the dot floating in the vast emptiness of space was a huge gyroscope-like thing. At its center was a big sphere. Around it spun a horizontal ring. Around that ring was a larger ring spinning vertically. On top of those two rings were two other larger rings spinning diagonally. The four rings spinning in opposite directions at different angles around a sphere reminded Ethan of the atomic energy commission logo that he had seen in old sci-fi movies.

The camera got closer to the spinning rings, and windows inside them became visible. Ethan's eyes widened with amazement as the size and scope of this creation became apparent. Each ring was ten stories high or wide. It was impossible to tell what was right side up. This structure made the International Space Station look like a child's Tinker Toys. The camera zoomed towards a window, then went inside revealing a large, first class, fully-furnished suite. The camera panned an elegant living room that dissolved into a lush bedroom, an opulent bathroom, and a state-of-the-art entertainment center.

The manly movie voice returned. "Valhalla! Land of the gods!" the soundtrack swelled, and there was a loud Star Wars-esqe brass szfortsando chord followed by a flurry of notes. "Eden, Inc., the world leader in exotic vacation resorts, has launched the first ever off-planet resort and living facility." Images of fancy dining rooms, bars, exotic foods, live theater shows, gardens, libraries, pools, Jacuzzis, waterfalls, bowling alleys, pool tables, gambling casinos, miniature golf courses, massage parlors, rock climbing walls, basketball courts, a soccer field, and the fanciest gym Ethan had ever seen. This was "Life Styles of the Rich and Famous" on steroids.

The voice continued, "The Valhalla Off-world Resort offers over two-and-a-half million square feet of livable space which includes the transparent Gene Roddenberry Restaurant, the only place in the galaxy where at anytime you can experience first-class dining with a 360 degree panoramic view of the universe." The camera showed a pretty girl holding two leather-bound menus standing in front of two very large Star Trek- looking doors with the name "Gene" on one door and "Roddenberry" on the other. She turned from the camera, took a step toward the doors, and they slid apart revealing a vast panorama of outer space. The floor, ceiling, and all the walls of the restaurant were made of solid glass. Dozens of tables appeared to be floating in space while fancy waiters scurried around formally dressed people who were sitting, chatting, eating steak and lobster, and sipping wine.

Ethan looked over at Ascot, observing that he was was clearly blown away. Neither of them had expected anything like this. Ethan watched the rest of the Valhalla introduction in a state of disbelief. The announcer explained the Copernicus Observation Deck, where the guests could look through a state of the art telescope and see stars and galaxies billions of light years away. There were fifteen gardens with plants collected from all over the world, and several hydroponic farms that provided most of the fresh produce on board the resort. On and on it went, listing an array of recreational activities with dozens of places to eat and drink.

The video program got his attention when it featured the gym facilities. The camera panned the gym. The room was huge, and it had all the usual things: free weights, the various cable machines, bikes, treadmills, and elliptical trainers of all varieties. There was also all kinds of equipment that he had never seen before. Some of the equipment utilized the same virtual reality technology as the VRMC. There was an aerobics room, boxing ring, and pool, as well as Jacuzzis, saunas, and steam rooms. In the middle of the gym was a nutrition center that provided smoothies, juice, and a large array of workout related foods. It went on and on—the gym was enormous.

Ethan was overwhelmed. How were he and Ascot going to deal with all this stuff? Blood-Sweat-N-Tears was a fraction of its size, and it was a full-time job dealing with all of its issues. It seemed impossible for only two people to run a gym that size. The camera pulled away from the gym and moved across to a family restaurant located next to it. Directly across from the restaurant were a hair salon and a health spa that specialized in massages, facials, aromatherapy, and skin scrubs.

The movie man voice said something about having a staff from over eighty nations. Ethan sat up in his chair and looked around the cabin. The faces he saw covered just about every ethnic group. It did indeed seem like an international effort. That excited him. At the gym Ethan liked talking with people from other parts of the world. He appreciated hearing other people's viewpoints, although the guys at the gym were usually gym dudes, and their perspectives were fairly similar regardless of their nationality.

Another loud dramatic chord sounded and a 3D image of the resort spinning in space suddenly appeared. The voice concluded: "Paradise has a new name. Valhalla, a masterpiece of innovation and technology. Eden, Inc., the leader of resort vacations, has set a new standard for first-class living and has blazed a trail to a new frontier. See you there!"

The Valhalla resort morphed into a 3D Eden, Inc. logo twirling in space. The image faded, and as the lights in the cabin came up, so did the light bulb in Ethan's brain. Everything that had happened leading up to this point started to make sense: all the secrecy, the questions about family and phobias, the high level of security, the sterile environment, the intense physical check-ups, and the rigorous testing in the virtual reality machine.

Ascot turned to look at Ethan and whispered, "Holy crap, I had no idea."

Ethan snickered, "You thought we were headed to Mexico."

The train popped out of the tunnel into a hidden valley surrounded by stark, lifeless rock mountains. There was instant daylight. Once again Ethan squinted as his eyes adjusted to the bright scenery blurring past his window. The train began to slow down and Ethan saw where they were headed. The contrast was surreal. In the distance was a high-tech city in the middle of nowhere.

Ethan turned to Ascot and whispered. "How the hell can they keep all this a secret?" Ascot shrugged.

The train approached the city on an elevated track four stories above the ground. Then it floated past a massive oasis of high-tech glass and steel buildings. The train kept on course past the buildings and towards the launch site about half a mile away. The train passed over a row of hangars where there were rows of planes of all shapes and sizes lined up like vehicles at a used car lot.

As a little kid, Ethan had gone through a stage in which he was infatuated with aircraft. Vince had made him a balsa wood plane for his eighth birthday. That inspired him to read books about the Red Baron and Chuck Yeager. He had collected dozens of die-cast models that included the Kitty Hawk, the SST, and B1 Stealth Bomber. On his bedroom wall he had posters of the Black Bird, the Saturn V Rocket, and the space shuttle. As an adult Ethan didn't think about these things much anymore, but he still admired them. With delight he catalogued all the different aircraft he was seeing as best he could. There were several crafts he had never seen before, but he recognized an F-14 fighter jet, a MIG Fighter, a B-25 bomber, C1 cargo plane, and other small private planes, as well as helicopters of all shapes and sizes.

Standing at the end of the airport's massive runway with nothing around it to distract from its size and grandeur, like the

Statue of Liberty in the middle of the bay, was a massive 200-foot tall spacecraft. It was larger than the space shuttle and much more streamlined. It looked like a cross between the X-15, the first piloted aircraft ever to go into space, and the Stealth Fighter. Its body was long and lean like the X-15 but flat and triangular like the Stealth. Like both the Stealth and X-15 it was painted pitch black. Ethan got the impression that unlike the space shuttle, which had its launches broadcast worldwide, this craft's flights were intended to be surreptitious.

Chapter 13

Slowly and methodically the train edged closer towards the spacecraft. Once it was in place, long spindly corridors sprang out from the launching tower, bridging the gap between the train and the spacecraft. Ethan and Ascot sat still and watched as the doors silently opened. The man sitting closest to the door stood up, gestured for everyone to follow him, then stepped out of the craft into the corridor.

It was no different from disembarking from any commercial airline. Ethan and Ascot just followed the herd. The room connecting the train to the spacecraft was ten degrees colder, airtight, and smelled like the inside of a plastic bag. After the passengers had left the train, the door closed; then, like a giant elevator, the room started to ascend. A moment later there was a loud ding. Everyone in the room turned in unison and looked for the source of the sound. The entire side of the room was now a row of bathroom doors with green lights blinking on and off. The computer voice announced, "We recommend that all passengers take this opportunity to use the toilet before boarding the shuttle." Ethan thought, "Why not," and moved towards the bathrooms to wait his turn.

Once everyone had finished doing their business, the room moved upward again. A fine mist of disinfectant rained down on the passengers. It reminded Ethan of when his dad used to spray Lysol on all the gym equipment during flu season. A minute later the door on the opposite side of the corridor slid open. The same man who had led everyone off the train gestured for them to board the spacecraft.

As the passengers crossed the threshold into the craft they immediately had to go either up or down a few stairs to get to their assigned level. Each section had forty seats configured: four pairs of seats across five rows deep. The computer voice gave each person that stepped onto the spacecraft an assigned seat number.

Ascot turned toward Ethan and grabbed his tag. "Big Brother is watching you," he chuckled.

The computer voice announced: "Mr. Ascot, seat 17H." Simultaneously, a green arrow appeared on the wall in front of him, pointing down to the lower level. Ethan stepped in right behind him. "Mr. Ethan Stone, seat 17G."

Ethan followed Ascot down the stairs and across the cabin. This time Ascot got the window seat. The seats were very soft and equipped with a seatbelt and shoulder strap for each side. Ethan sat down and harnessed himself in. He tried to lean forward to look out of the window, but the harness prevented him. "You see anything out there?"

Ascot shook his head. "Not much, just empty desert."

Ethan continued, "You know, normally around this time I would be leaving school and on my way to the gym to deliver Vince his lunch."

Ascot nodded his head in agreement. "Yeah, I know what you mean. All that seems like a long time ago, and this is only our first day on the job."

Ethan and Ascot sat and waited thirty minutes for all the passengers to board. Ethan was starting to get hungry, and it occurred to him that there had been no sign or mention of food during their entire journey. He wanted to say something about it but was afraid Ascot would think he was a whiner, so he let it go. He could handle not eating for a day.

When all the seats were full and everyone was seated, the cabin door closed. Ethan noticed a sweet smell in the air and immediately began to feel a little woozy. Ethan leaned back into his seat, closed his eyes, and relaxed. The sound of the computer voice spoke softly, and Ethan opened his eyes. The tall, striking redhead's face appeared in 3D on the seat back in front of him. His brain was foggy, and he got the impression that she was saying something about relaxing in his chair and making sure all the straps and harnesses were properly attached. Ethan strained to look around and saw that everyone he could see in the compartment looked very relaxed. Ethan tried to fight the overwhelming desire to fall asleep and focused on the woman's voice, but it became more and more distant, until finally it faded away.

The E-X-5 Transport Spacecraft sat on the launch pad straight up, perpendicular to the ground. Inside the ship all the seats began to rotate, changing the entire inside configuration. Two minutes later the passengers were all sitting as they would if a typical passenger jet were pointed straight up. Of course, none of the passengers on board noticed the change. They had all been knocked unconscious by a combination of increased cabin pressure, lower oxygen levels, and a blast of nitrous oxide.

* * * *

Sepideh Yoonessi was a little girl when she and her family fled Iran during the revolution. They felt awkward being Jewish during a national takeover by a fundamentalist Muslim regime, particularly since anyone who opposed the regime ended up either in jail, tortured, dead, or all three in that order, so the family had packed up and gone to Iraq; not ideal, but secular and safe by comparison.

At 17, Sepideh won the national Iraqi science prize and scholarship for her paper on ionized hydrogen, the conversion of inert matter into charged particles and the potential energy from particle acceleration. She was recognized throughout the nation as a mathematical and science genius and was hailed as a national treasure. Ironically, her national treasure status was given to her just as Iraq and Iran had declared war on one another. Now being an Iranian living in Iraq was awkward, but the government wasn't about to let its national treasure leave.

As a citizen from the opposing side during a time of war, Sepideh had one of two choices: either go to jail, where she would be raped, tortured, and then killed, or work for the government building weapons that would be used against her former homeland. Since Sepideh didn't have much connection with Iran anyway, it wasn't a hard choice; she took the government job. Since she spoke English well, she was assigned to assist and work alongside ballistics expert and visionary, Gerald V. Bull, a Canadian who claimed he could launch a satellite into space with a super cannon. Both the Canadian and American government thought he was nuts, so he went to work for Iraq, where Saddam Hussein funded his crazy ideas. When it appeared that Gerald's whacky notions of blasting large objects around the world or into orbit could actually work and that his super-gun could possibly replace intercontinental ballistic missiles and long-range rockets, it wasn't long before he ended up in a hotel room with a bullet in his head.

After Mr. Bull's demise, Sepideh realized she needed to get out of Iraq ASAP. The international communities had put sanctions on Iraq and were shutting down its weapons program. When NATO weapons inspectors came, she took the opportunity to convince an American officer that she had Iraqi secrets and needed asylum. It worked to the extent that the U.S. Government took her and her family for a ride to Washington, DC to be interviewed by several of the Joint Chiefs Of Staff. She spoke to them as if they were scientists and, not surprisingly, they didn't understand a single thing she said and were ready to send her back.

Fortunately she mentioned that Saddam Hussein had dozens of underground bunkers and that she knew where one of them was located. That was something the Joint Chiefs understood, and for that little tidbit of information, she was allowed to stay in the United States. Casper Degas heard through the Washington grapevine that one of the greatest scientific minds was currently unemployed and living with a family of six in a one-bedroom apartment in Virginia, with no clue as to how to proceed with her life. Casper jumped on the opportunity and put her to work at Eden, Inc. to develop a fuel-efficient hyperspace aircraft that could take large payloads into outer space and back cheaply and efficiently.

After several years of research and design, Sepideh and her team had produced the E-X-5 Transport Spacecraft. A paragon of modern aeronautic technology, it combined three types of propulsion systems. The ship was stuffed inside a nuclear powered electro-magnetic rail-gun four times it's length. The small nuclear reactor generated millions of watts of electricity, creating enough opposing magnetic force to thrust the shuttle's aerodynamic body one hundred thousand feet into the air. Once the craft reached its desired altitude, the scramjet engines were turned on. These engines combined the small amounts of oxygen in the upper atmosphere with onboard liquid hydrogen, thereby propelling the ship to speeds past Mach 10 and launching the craft out of the earth's atmosphere. Once the vehicle reached space where there was no more oxygen, the bottom of the ship opened up and a large ring descended from the belly of the spacecraft. The ring magnetically ionized the hydrogen in space, and the charged particles propelled the spacecraft.

Sepideh described the three stages of the E-X-5's journey as follows: "It starts like a slingshot, turns into a rocket, and ends like an interstellar sailboat. The E-X-5 is the most efficient spacecraft ever built. There are no wasted or jettisoned parts, no giant tanks to retrieve, and very little fuel is used. It's a state-of-the-art vehicle and Eden, Inc. has the only one."

* * * *

Ethan and Ascot sat unconscious in their seats as the ship prepared to launch. It was the craft's 206th voyage into space. All of the previous trips had been cargo runs sending building materials and supplies to the Valhalla space resort. This payload was the resort's staff. They would live on the resort and prepare it for the guests who were scheduled to arrive in a week.

Captain Roger Nagatani was piloting the shuttle. It was his thirty-third flight. He sat in the cockpit trying to calm down and relax as the launch sequence began. The G-force was so strong that the human body needed to be totally relaxed to survive. The simplest and most effective way to make sure that everyone on board was sufficiently relaxed was to put each one of them to sleep except for the pilots, who were required to be awake.

Nagatani, who had been extensively trained and was considered to be an expert shuttle pilot, still got nervous when he heard the countdown sequence begin. The first few seconds of the flight was always an adrenaline rush, and still, after many times, made him a little uneasy.

The countdown concluded, the electromagnet rail-gun catapulted the E-X-5 straight up into the air with a whoosh. Almost immediately there was a sonic boom as the massive craft punched through the air. A few seconds later, the giant ship was just a tiny dot in the sky. Ethan sat strapped into his chair, completely oblivious of the fact that his body had slammed against the seat and was experiencing more Gs than 99.99 percent of the people on planet Earth had ever experienced. He had no idea that he was traveling into the air at four times the speed of a bullet and that, in a few seconds, that speed would double.

*****

Spinning in several directions at the same time, the gigantic rings of the Valhalla Resort dwarfed the approaching shuttle. Nagatani never ceased to be awestruck every time he piloted the craft to the station. On his right, emanating its blue glow into the cockpit, was Earth. Undulating restlessly in front of him like some huge mechanical monster from a 1960s Japanese sci-fi film, was the Valhalla resort. In fact, it was precisely movies and TV shows like Johnny Sokko and his flying Robot, Invasion of Astro-Monster, and Ultraman that had inspired Roger to want to be a pilot and an astronaut.

As a kid he had dreamed of flying into space. Now that he'd been doing it routinely, it had quickly become surprisingly boring. Everything on board the E.X.5 was computerized and automated so that virtually none of his flying skills were being utilized. Also, all the things that Nagatani loved about flying—feeling the speed and G-force when turning, climbing and diving, the bounce from the wind's turbulence, watching the terrain rush past in a speedy blur—none of that existed in the vast, zero gravity of space. For Roger, flying the E.X.5 was slightly more exciting than being a conductor on an automated train, so Roger had devised some things to amuse himself during the journey.

He pulled $2.37 worth of change out of his pocket: seven quarters, four dimes, four nickels and two pennies. The object was to spin the coins in different spots and at different speeds in front of him and have them just hover there and not move or bang into each other. It was much more difficult than it looked. His first attempt set the two quarters spinning in place as planned, but when he tried to get the third one going, he didn't release it right, and it knocked the other two out of their positions. It was like a three dimensional version of billiards played with coins. Nagatani did this with whatever change he had in his pocket. He tried hard not to bring a specific amount or prepare in any way. That would ruin the spontaneity of the game. When done well, he could have as many as twenty coins floating in front of him, spinning and making interesting shapes.

While he was working on getting his $2.37 artistically airborne, the shuttle's on-board computer was maintaining constant communication with the computers on the resort and on the ground. Once the shuttle got within proper range of the resort, the three computers agreed that the shuttle's captured ionized particles should be thrust sideways, maneuvering the shuttle so that it would be synchronized with the movement of the resort's outer ring. From Nagatani's perspective, it appeared as though the ring had stopped moving and the earth and the stars were moving around him. The surface details of the top ring became more clearly visible as the shuttle approached the landing pad.

With $1.87 of change floating around him (somewhere along the line he had lost two quarters) Nagatani sat back and watched the stars and the blue ball of Earth move quickly around him in a circle. The shuttle slid right into its landing pad and immediately gravity was restored. The trick was to catch all the coins and not let any hit the ground. This time a dime and a penny got away. He hadn't moved, yet it felt like he had fallen into his seat. His clothes settled onto his body, and there was a dull thud as all the stowed items in the closet behind him fell back into place. As soon as the shuttle had docked and was locked into position, two building-size structures elevated from below, surrounding the shuttle. Accordion corridors sprang out, sealing all the doors of the ship.

Automatically the cabin pressure in the passenger compartments changed slightly, oxygen levels increased, and an acrid blast of ammonia entered the cabins. The video screens on the seat backs flickered on, and the redhead with the computer voice

ROSS WRIGHT

reappeared, welcoming the passengers to The Valhalla Off-World Resort.

Ethan twitched in his chair and slowly began to regain consciousness. He heard rumbling sounds in the distance. Slowly the sounds started to transform from unintelligible garble to identifiable words. There was a voice that was slightly familiar but he couldn't quite place. For a moment he became aware just enough to be disoriented; he had no idea where he was. Then, like a film projector getting focused, his memory started to fade in and it all came to him. Excited, Ethan tried to force himself awake, but his body protested. He had felt this way once before when he was a teenager, lying in the recovery room after he'd gotten his wisdom teeth pulled. There was another blast of ammonia, and Ethan's body convulsed and his eyes popped open. His head was still spinning, but his body was now wide awake.

Chapter 14

Politics is the art of compromise. A skillful politician has mastered the art of negotiation and knows when and what to concede. Casper Degas had a different approach. If he didn't get exactly what he wanted with Plan A, he would get it with Plan B. For him it was all about strategy, there was no compromising.

Casper had sat down and presented what he considered to be several reasonable offers to both Senator Wilson and Senator Morales and neither of them had given him the help he wanted, so now he had decided that he had had enough. Those arrogant S.O.B.s had been given their chance; it was time to bypass both of them.

Casper picked up his cell phone and simply said, "Valkyrie." Automatically a number dialed. After one ring a woman's voice answered. "Mr. Degas, how may I help you today?" Casper cleared his throat and spoke calmly. She had been expecting his call and was somewhat familiar with this particular case. Casper concluded the conversation with, "This needs to be delicate, no mention of me."

"Got it." She said this crisply, like a soldier who had just gotten her marching orders. Casper imagined her on the phone standing at attention and saluting. "I'll text you all the details." Then he hung up the phone.

Senator Isley Wilson was sitting at his desk, wrapping things up for the day, when his private cell phone rang. The caller ID said "Private Caller." His daughter-in-law was organizing an eighteenth birthday celebration for his grandson that coming Friday and had asked if he could give a speech at the party. For some reason her phone was set to Private Caller. Since very few people knew his private cell number, he assumed it was her. When he answered and a man's voice responded, Wilson instantly became aggravated, a knot forming in the pit of his stomach. He really wanted to go home, and now he had to deal with the jackass on the other end of the line.

A block away, with a clear view of Senator Wilson's office, a limo pulled up and parked. Casper Degas was not in a good mood.

He had just spent the last forty-five minutes stuck in evening rush hour traffic. Despite this fact, he very jovially asked the senator if he had changed his mind about the aerospace bill?

Wilson gave the expected answer, "No, my constituents would kill me if I voted for your bill."

Casper knew that the senator wasn't going to change his mind; he just wanted to keep him on the phone. After their earlier meeting, Casper had done a little research and learned the real reason why the senator from the great state of Texas wasn't supporting his aerospace bill. Casper put on his hardball business voice, "Let's cut the crap. I know about your involvement with Isis Technologies and the offer your corporate cronies made you."

Wilson was flabbergasted. How had Degas found out? Isis Tech was very secretive and no announcement had been made. Wilson thought, "He could be bluffing." The senator sat up in his chair and spoke very carefully and sincerely, as he did every time he gave a speech. "Mr. Degas, I am affronted by your remarks, and I think there is some confusion here. I oppose your bill for the reasons I previously stated and not for any personal gain."

Casper, chuckling maniacally, pushed the button to roll down his dark tinted window. Sitting on the seat next to him was a standard-size briefcase. He opened it. Inside was a pair of high-tech goggles, a very thin touch-screen device, a silver cylinder that looked like a thermos, and a plastic gun that looked like a cross between a super-squirter and a paint sprayer. Casper leaned against the limo's soft back seat, attached the silver cylinder to the gun, and then pointed the contraption at the senator's window. In a fraction of a second there was a barrage of almost inaudible "thoots" as bursts of air erupted from the gun.

Casper continued, "How big a fool do you think I am?" It was a rhetorical question, and Wilson knew better than to answer. Casper needed to keep the senator in his office for a few more minutes and everything would take care of itself. His gun had just released a small army of nanobots, microscopic robots that could be programmed to perform all kinds of functions. Eden, Inc. was developing them for dozens of applications, one of which was medical. The single-cell-size robots could permeate through an opening as small as between the cells of skin, assemble into a camera, take pictures, and then broadcast the data to a touch-screen computer. If radio, microwave or infrared signals weren't able to be broadcast by the bots or received by the computer, then they could disassemble themselves, return, reassemble, and physically deliver the data.

Eden, Inc. had developed nanobot technology that could physically get inside and look at a person's heart, liver, brain, kidneys, and see exactly what was going on. If, for example, there were any obstructions, weaknesses, or disease indicators such as a tiny blood clot, a blob of cholesterol, or some other kind of abnormality inhibiting proper circulation or cellular function, the nanobots could be told remotely to reconfigure from a camera into a drill or some such tool and fix the problem. The application for this technology was endless. To the naked eye the nanobots were invisible, but Casper watched them through a pair of spectroscopic goggles. They slithered through the air, like snakes through water, as they moved towards their target. Within a few seconds, the nanobots arrived at the window and slipped through the tiny cracks of the window frame without slowing down.

Wilson was sitting behind his desk, incredulous at the arrogance of this aerospace tycoon-wannabe. There was a saying: "Washington, D.C., and Hollywood attracted the biggest egos in the world, and if you had any useful talent, you went to Hollywood." He had been in D.C. too long to be intimidated by a punk like Casper Degas. These types of guys came and went constantly, and he knew that if he caved to Casper's demands, he was doomed. Casper would walk all over him the next time he wanted something, and it would never end, so Wilson was standing firm; he was going to nip this in the bud. He turned his chair sideways from the desk so it faced the window with a view that looked out across the park towards the Washington Monument. Then he sat back in his chair and listened to this madman rant on the phone.

"Senator, I will not be toyed with! Had you accepted my offer you would have been hailed as a great patriot, an American hero bringing jobs to our country, but you had to go and crawl in bed with the Chinese! I've run out of options with you!" While Casper was ranting, Wilson had no idea that the nanobots were in his hair, making their way into his windpipe through his ears, nose, and mouth, and assembling themselves in key places in his body. They were so small that it was impossible to feel anything. Wilson could no more feel the nanobots than he could feel dust settle on him. Without any warning or explanation, Wilson felt a sharp jabbing pain in his neck. Suddenly he couldn't move his legs or arms. He had become instantly paralyzed in a seated position, holding the phone to his ear. He started to feel light-headed and was having difficulty breathing. Overwhelmed with panic, he tried to interrupt Casper's incessant ranting, but all he could get out was a feeble grunt.

Casper paused to take a breath before unloading his next blast of insults when he heard the senator start to wheeze and choke. Casper stopped, said nothing, and just listened. He picked up the touch-screen computer lying on the limo seat next to him, to see what data the nanobots were sending. The Senator's body temperature, blood pressure, heart rate, and respiratory rate were online and being monitored. The bots had lodged themselves into the Senator's spine, preventing the nerves in his spinal column from successfully communicating with his limbs. They were also lodged in his windpipe, limiting his air supply, and in his carotid artery, restricting the blood flow to his brain.

Casper got excited. This was so easy! It would be years before forensics would have the technology to figure out what had really happened. A medical examiner would look at this and say he'd had a stroke—simple as that, happens every day. "Surprise! How do you feel, Senator? It's okay, don't answer, and don't take it personally, it's just business!"

Wilson could hear Casper gloating. What the hell was happening and how was this going to end? Wilson looked at the clock on his office wall. It was four minutes past the time he usually left his office; his secretary knew his habits, and he knew hers. If he didn't leave his office by five minutes after the hour, she would come in and essentially tell him she was leaving, so in a minute he would have his chance. She would see him and realize something was wrong and get help. That is, if he could hold out that long. It was getting more and more difficult to breathe.

Barbara Thornton had been Senator Wilson's secretary for fourteen years. She looked at the clock, which read five minutes after the hour. Normally the senator left on the hour, right on the dot; he was a very punctual man. She routinely took the metro, and if she left the office by seven minutes after she would make the earlier train and save thirty minutes on her commute home. Also, it was Friday, and everyone typically left early. She figured that if there were something more to be done on this Friday afternoon, the senator would have mentioned it earlier.

At home, her husband had been moping around the house for the last week. He'd been laid off because of airline security budget cuts. His union was in the middle of negotiating an agreement with no end in sight, so he was unsure of his future and this was starting to make him feel like a eunuch. To cheer him up, she had promised that they would go out to dinner tonight. Barbara got up from her desk, removed the #2 pencil that was lodged behind her ear, and placed it in a vintage red, white, and blue I LIKE IKE coffee cup with all the other pens and pencils that she kept on her desk. She looked to make sure everything was straight and in its proper place. Then she grabbed her purse and quietly went and knocked on the senator's door. She stood with her ears an inch from the door and waited a few seconds, but, because she was in a hurry, it felt like minutes. There was no answer.

She looked at her watch. Six minutes after. This time she knocked a little louder and simultaneously opened the door. The senator was on the phone, his back to the door, his feet up on the window ledge, the position he would take when he talked with family or friends. She remembered that he was in the middle of working out security details for his grandson's birthday party. Apparently, having a sitting senator attend and speak at a party was surprisingly complex. She took two steps past the doorway into the office and listened; she could hear the murmuring of the voice coming through the phone's receiver from across the room.

Clearly he was in the middle of something personal. Normally he would turn, wave good-bye, and that would be her dismissal, but today he didn't move. She could hear his raspy breathing and sensed a tension that made her feel like she was invading his privacy. She looked at her watch: seven minutes after the hour. It was now or never. Either she would interrupt the senator to finalize the day, or she would slip out the door. She thought about her husband hanging out at home all day and the consequences of arriving thirty minutes later. She turned, stepped out of the room, and closed the door silently behind her, then walked briskly across the reception room, out the door, down the corridor, and onto the street towards the metro. Never once did she look back. If she hurried, she would just make her train.

Casper was looking at the senator's vital signs: body temperature, blood pressure, heart rate, and respiratory rate. They were half of normal. Casper could use the touch-screen computer to command the bots to close the senator's windpipe and carotid artery completely and end it quickly, but Casper was enjoying this. It was like an itch; the more he scratched it, the more it spread. Holding the senator's life in his hand had mellowed Casper's temper slightly. He used his soft, soothing, "I want to be your friend" voice: "It's unfortunate that your colleagues won't know what really happened here. Your death could have been my leverage tool. I'll make sure to spread some interesting rumors." Casper looked at the senator's office window. It was the only one with a light left on. "Time to end this," he thought. He touched the screen and watched as the senator's vital signs dropped like a stone. Within a minute Wilson was flat-lining.

For all its ingeniousness, it was irritatingly anti-climatic. Casper liked being face-to-face when he killed someone. He liked to strike the deathblow and feel the pulse flutter to a stop in his hands. He shrugged. Yet another example of the disconnect that modern technology provided. He touched the screen and typed in a few commands. The nanobots in the office left the senator's dead body, floated through the air like a fine dust, assembled in front of the body into a micro-thin camera lens, and broadcast the image of the senator sitting on his chair to Casper's computer screen. He zoomed in to take a closer look. Apparently the senator had a slight nosebleed before he died. "Interesting," thought Casper. He felt the intoxication of power rush through him. He admired the photo. It was clean, untraceable. He put on the spectroscopic goggles and opened the silver canister. He watched the nanobots fly out of the office window frame and propel themselves through the air toward the limo. Then, like homing pigeons coming home to roost, they all flew into the thermos, resembling a backwards movie of champagne spraying from a bottle.

Once the bots were back, Casper rolled up the window and put the cylinder in its case with the gun and the touch-screen computer. "Jack, let's get out of here!"

Chapter 15

Senator Morales liked the perks that his job offered. He was sitting in the back of a limo sipping champagne with representatives from the meatpacking and the tracker engine manufacturing industries. They, along with the senator's bodyguards and four beautiful women in low-cut cocktail dresses, were headed to a Washington cocktail party, compliments of corporate lobbyists. No actual business was being discussed. They were just enjoying themselves, realizing the high life of people in power. They were all unaware that behind them a black stealth electric engine motorcycle was following them. The rider wore a flat-black Kevlar suit and matching crash helmet with a tinted faceplate, rendering the bike and rider almost invisible.

The limo drove through downtown Washington, DC, past broken streetlights, traffic signals, and sawed-off parking meters, then into the wooded suburbs of Virginia. The limo cruised through what were once the forests the founding fathers used to build their houses, past several small farms, a llama ranch, and a bait and tackle shop. Finally they arrived at an oasis of McMansions where the party was taking place.

Surrounding the estate was an eight-foot-high river rock wall with an extra two feet of electrical fencing on top. The limo drove up to a very ornate wrought iron gate, the only entrance to the estate. A security guard stepped out of the shadows, spoke with the driver, scanned his list, then checked IDs. Once everyone was cleared, the electric gate silently opened, the limo drove through, and then the gate immediately closed.

The stealth motorcycle had stopped two hundred yards behind the limo and pulled into the bushes at the edge of the woods, out of sight from the road. The motorcyclist stepped off the bike and opened a high-tech smart-phone type device, then whispered the address of the cookie-cutter mansion. A detailed report on the house, its blueprint, and current owner all popped onto the screen. The motorcyclist read the profile. Apparently a tobacco corporation, through a series of holding companies, owned the mansion and used it for corporate parties and weekend getaways for their top executives and lobbyists.

The motorcyclist put the device away, then punched a code on a small keypad that was hidden on the wrist of the Kevlar suit, causing him to actually disappear. The suit was one of Eden, Inc.'s prototype stealth reconnaissance suits. It used a high-energy field to bend light so that the suit became invisible. There were still a few bugs to work out. The batteries that powered the energy field only lasted about thirty minutes, and the bending of light created visual distortion, so even though the suit technically became invisible, one had to be very careful when using it. It worked best when its wearer stood still, particularly near a window, reflective surface, or something that created its own visual distortion.

When moving in the suit, one always had to be aware of the surrounding environment, and pay attention to where one stepped. The suit may have been invisible, but footprints weren't, and if the suit got in between two people, it would appear as if a fun house mirror had suddenly popped in between them. Confident that most people had no idea that the technology even existed and therefore wouldn't be looking out for it, the stealth motorcyclist silently walked up to the McMansion gate and stood and waited. In less than five minutes another limo pulled up, the guard stepped out of the shadow, did his routine, then opened the gate. The stealth suit followed closely behind the car through the gate and down the long driveway towards the house.

The estate was lit up like a Las Vegas casino. The main house was four stories tall, and every window was shining like a Christmas light on a giant tree. The music wasn't at rock n' roll volume, but it was considerably louder than the typical sophisticated D.C. cocktail party. The dance music's insistent bass drum made the big house pulsate hypnotically.

The stealth suit circled and surveyed the building, assessing the situation. The party had spilled out onto several upstairs balconies, patios, and gardens. Security guards with tiny wireless headsets protruding from their ears and guns concealed in their jackets were standing around trying to look inconspicuous.

The invisible suit stopped in the garden behind a tree near a large open French door that led into the kitchen, crowded with staff and caterers. The suit's helmet had a state-of-the-art listening device that could amplify a very weak signal. Nothing suspicious could be heard outside the house. The helmet was also equipped with an infrared and night vision function, so the motorcyclist could see that no one was hiding in the bushes or monitoring the grounds.

Quickly, with the precision of a surgeon, a series of buttons and snaps were released. The invisible Kevlar cracked open and pulled apart, while the helmet was lifted off, unveiling a cascade of long blond hair. The Valkyrie stepped out of the suit wearing a tight, low-cut, sleeveless, cocktail dress and high heels. She ran her fingers through her hair, fluffing up the curls, then quickly reached in and grabbed a Prada purse from inside the stealth suit. She pushed another button and the suit returned to its visible flat-black self. She concealed it under a nearby bush.

In the night the stealth suit was almost as invisible turned off as it was when on. The Valkryie opened her purse and pulled out a lipstick and compact. Expertly, she drew a thin line of lipstick onto her lower lip, then pressed her lips together. She opened the compact and checked her face. The helmet often smudged the makeup on her high cheekbones. She brushed on a little powder to even out the texture, and then put the makeup back in her purse. As she stepped out from behind the tree, a security guard walked out of the kitchen onto the patio unexpectedly.

Casper had the utmost confidence in The Valkyrie. He had personally trained her and knew that she had myriad ways of being very persuasive or lethal when the situation called for it. She was often assigned to infiltrate political functions and inspire lawmakers to see things in ways that were more favorable to Eden, Inc.

Casper had discovered her ten years earlier while wining and dining a congressman from Houston who had a taste for the seedier side of life. That night they found themselves in an off-the-mainstream venue called The Stallion Ranch. It was an establishment that catered to the Texas high rollers and provided every chemical alteration and sexual fantasy imaginable. The congressman was partying hard, three sheets to the wind, and groping every girl that came his way. Casper was stone cold sober and was cataloging all of the indiscretions with which he could later blackmail the Congressman.

In the midst of their evening escapades, a blonde, tan vixen named "Sabrina" stepped out onto the dance floor. She was wearing a black leather thong, studded with spikes up her crotch, and matching pasties. She began to perform a pole dance routine for a herd of Texas oil tycoons, and would go all the way if the price was right.

The saying, "It takes one to know one," was never truer. Casper instantly saw in her a calculating predator who was all business and would do whatever it took to get what she wanted. She moved like a lioness stalking its prey before pouncing. She was 5'9" and ripped, with zero body fat. Her abs and ass could have been sculpted by Michelangelo, but were not unfeminine. She had big green eyes, a big smile, and exuded a sense of confidence that made her irresistible. With one arm she grabbed the pole, then with incredible strength and gymnastic ability she swung herself all the way around twice, and then kicked her legs up over her head, grabbing the pole with her calves and ankles. As she continued to swing she let go of her hands, straightened her body and arched her back as if doing a swan dive. This move consistently got the crowd riled up, and the room roared with applause. She spun effortlessly several more times around the pole and floated to the ground. When she got back onto her feet she poured on her feminine charms, mesmerizing the crowd like a cobra. Casper watched large bills fly onto the stage as the billionaires emptied their wallets, vying for her attention.

That evening Casper offered her a job. He explained that it would require that she move away and undergo some serious training. She was a young girl from Texas who had run away from her religious, sexually abusive parents only to end up working in a sex club as a stripper, dominatrix, and prostitute. She wouldn't mind giving that up, particularly for an opportunity to make a lot of money, travel around the world, meet lawmakers and the movers and shakers. She was very interested.

Casper took her to LA to study with his Sensei. He had her train twelve hours a day in hand-to-hand combat, including weaponry skills, using knives, swords, and guns as well as making weapons out of improvised materials. It all came very naturally to her, and it didn't take long before she was a lethal, fighting/killing machine. Both Casper and his Sensei had never seen anyone who was so swift, cold-hearted, and calculating. She was a perfect assassin, the very personification of a warrior goddess. That's when she earned the name The Valkyrie.

After two years of training, Casper asked her who in all the world she would like to see dead? Without a second's hesitation, she said her parents. So her first assignment to prove she was a real assassin was to kill her own parents. Afterwards, she claimed that killing them was better than any orgasm, and after she had made her first kill she craved more.

The security guard was eating a plate of hors d'oeuvres, some sort of meat on a stick and a stuffed mushroom thing. The Valkyrie walked out of the bushes and up to the kitchen door like she owned the place, then smiled at the guard like a schoolteacher would a small child. The guard thought about saying something, asking her what she was doing in the garden away from the rest of the party guests, or why he didn't remember seeing her enter the party. She was a woman he would remember, but his mouth was full and he wasn't supposed to be eating on the job. He felt like a kid who got caught with his hand in the cookie jar. Because of the way she carried herself, he assumed she either had to be with someone or that she was someone; otherwise she wouldn't have had such a cocky demeanor. With his mouth stuffed full of chicken teriyaki, the guard tried to smile without losing his food. He watched her step through the French doors and into the house.

No one working in the kitchen paid any attention to the 5'9" blonde supermodel as she walked by in four-inch heels, her maroon dress bordering on lingerie. The staff members were all D.C. event veterans, who were washing dishes, preparing food, and carrying trays in and out of the party. They had seen everything one could imagine and unless someone got assassinated in their kitchen, they couldn't be bothered.

The Valkyrie grabbed a mimosa from a tray as she stepped out of the kitchen and strutted into the middle of the party. She stopped to sip her drink and scan the room. Her assignment was simple. Find Senator Morales, get him to do something that would compromise himself, and send the compromising evidence to Casper so he could use it as leverage. She was equipped with body mics and tiny video cameras hidden in her purse and earrings.

Morales stood in the corner, talking with a committee chairman. This is where the Beltway insiders spent their evenings lining their pockets and advancing their careers; where all the real deals were made.

The Valkyrie looked across the room, caught the senator's eye, and smiled a sexy smile. She could tell that the senator was slightly tipsy. That meant she would approach him with charm and passion, rather than intellect and a fake press ID. Besides, it was Friday night, and the senator didn't look like he was in the mood for business. Morales sipped his Bacardi on the rocks and returned The Valkyrie's smile. Within a few minutes, the two of them were in a quiet room on a sofa next to a fireplace, sipping drinks and talking. The senator liked to talk about himself. She sat and showered him with compliments so that his already inflated ego rocketed into the stratosphere. Eventually she told him her name was Sarah, a country girl from Alabama who had recently moved to D.C. for work.

When the senator asked her what she did for a living, she leaned up against him so he could feel her warm breath against his cheek and her breasts against his shoulder. "I'm invited to parties to make them more interesting." She sat back on the couch, giggled, and played with her hair. A jolt of testosterone surged straight into the senator's groin. He immediately stood up, politely said he would be right back, then walked over to the bar.

When he returned, fresh drinks in hand, The Valkyrie was leaning back on the sofa, sitting cross-legged, and a freshman congressman was introducing himself to her. Senator Morales was extremely competitive. When he wanted something, he had no hesitation in going after it and fighting for it, and nothing made him want something more than if someone else wanted it too.

He walked up to the congressman like a junkyard dog claiming his turf. The congressman didn't recognize him right away and tried to pull rank, a sure-fire way to piss off Victor Morales down to his very core. It brought back deep pathological memories of growing up poor and being ordered around by Florida rednecks. If looks could kill, the congressman would have been stretched out on the floor before he ever had a chance to give the senator his practiced phony politician smile. The congressman was fairly new to the Washington game, and he was just getting used to the enormous egos all around him. The tension was palpable, and the congressman's instincts were telling him to get the hell out of there as fast as possible. As quickly and gracefully as he could, he left, leaving the senator and the hot blonde on the couch to continue with their little game.

Lobbyists aren't stupid. They work like timeshare salespeople. The idea is to get the clients excited, get them to accept the perks, and then sign them up. It's much harder to back out of a deal after accepting the goodies, so for that very reason, the top floors of the corporate party house were all suites that the VIP guests could use whenever they wanted. It doesn't take much imagination to sort out what goes on in a suite at a party house full of drunken, powerful men and beautiful women. When the senator asked The Valkyrie if she would like to accompany him upstairs, she smiled and graciously accepted. This was the moment she had been waiting for. So far there was nothing the senator had said that was even the slightest bit incriminating. She was going to have to get him to do a lot more than just talk.

The two put their drinks on a coffee table and stood; The Valkyrie in heels was a good four inches taller than the senator. He motioned his bodyguards to come out of the shadows. Two men emerged, both wearing the same black suit with matching black shirt and tie. Both were wired up with radio earpieces so they could talk to each other. They could easily have been twins, both stood six feet five inches tall, weighed three hundred pounds, and had their heads shaved. Only difference was, one looked like a photographic negative of the other. Dirk was white and Kirk was black. Morales called them his Irks and he didn't pay too much attention to which one was which. They were both equally intimidating. Since they had been in the senator's employment, no one had dared mess with him.

The Irks escorted the two of them upstairs, Dirk in the lead and Kirk close behind. When they arrived at the room, Kirk went in alone while the trio waited in the hallway. A minute later Kirk returned, assuring them that everything checked out.

The room was simple, but elegantly decorated like a suite at a five star hotel. Morales stepped out of the hall into the room and went straight to the bar. He quickly poured two Bacardis on the rocks and handed one to The Valkyrie. The Irks never drank on duty. Morales offered to show "Sarah" the rest of the suite. He suspected that probably wasn't her real name, but he didn't care. Most call girls use a phony name. He grabbed her hand and the bottle of Bacardi and led her into the bedroom. As he closed the door, he winked at his bodyguards.

The Irks knew the senator's routine. He would get the girl into his room, make her shower, then, in his boxer shorts, t-shirt, and socks, he would engage in some really rough sex. Both Dirk and Kirk didn't fully understand the senator's kinky side, but they had deduced that he had some weird Catholic guilt thing that made him ashamed of his sexual desires, so he compensated by turning it violent. The Irks would often hear the senator screaming and throwing things around the room. When he was done, they would find a girl beaten up, lying on the bed or on the floor. Then to protect the senator's reputation they would either cover the incident up by paying the girl off, or intimidate the hell out of her.

Tonight promised to be more of the same. Dirk opened the entertainment center, grabbed the remote, and turned the TV to ESPN, keeping the volume low. They kept their ears peeled to what was going on in the bedroom while they watched the Chicago Bulls get creamed by the Los Angeles Lakers. As expected, they heard the shower go on, then off. They could hear the senator bark orders, but it wasn't clear enough to understand exactly what he was saying. For a solid twenty minutes there was moaning, screaming, and slapping.

Usually that was about the senator's limit. Then things started to get really rough. The Irks heard bodies being slammed into walls, glass breaking, body blows, and screams. They heard the sound of panting and moaning. Was it pain or pleasure? They looked at each other wondering what to do: step in or wait? Perhaps the senator had finally found a woman who was as kinky as he was and they were engaged in some weird S&M fetish stuff, and he was having the time of his life.

The noise from the bedroom continued. From the din of moans and slaps, the Irks heard the senator scream, "okay, I'll do it, I'll do it! Let me go!" Instantly, alarm bells went off in their heads. Simultaneously, without looking or consulting each other, they sprang off the couch and burst through the bedroom door.

The senator was naked, his hands and legs hogtied with the telephone cord behind his back, and lying face down on the floor. The girl was standing above him naked, hair disheveled, her high heels stepping on his testicles. The Irks saw this and hesitated for a squeamish moment. That was all The Valkyrie needed. She watched the white Irk reach for this firearm. Instantly she kicked her right foot. The high heel that was previously engaged in flattening the senator's right nut flew like a bullet into the forehead of the unsuspecting Dirk.

The high heels were expertly weighted weapons, the toes and heels of which were razor-sharp, and they were as lethal and accurate as a ninja star. Before the big bodyguard was able to get his .38 Special out of its holster, the heel had lodged deep into his forehead, literally splitting his head wide open. He fell like a tree, face first. His skull hit the ground and cracked open like a tomato. Brains and blood splattered all over the floor and onto the helpless face of the hog-tied senator.

Kirk turned and watched his partner fall. By the time he had processed what had happened, the naked Valkyrie had leaped over the senator and, with her razor sharp toe, kicked the big black bodyguard in the trachea. Pain shot through his body. He grabbed his gushing neck and reached for his gun, but before his hand even touched his weapon, a fist slammed him in the jaw, and he was knocked back, stumbling over his partner's dead body. To regain his balance, he let go of his neck, and a stream of blood gushed out like an overflowing Champagne bottle.

To steady himself he grabbed ahold of the wall, leaving a trail of bloody handprints. His mouth was dry and sticky, and he felt dizzy. He tried to catch his breath, but something wasn't right. He hadn't realized yet that she had given him a tracheotomy. Air and blood bubbled around a hole in his neck, and now the blood was leaking down into his lungs, making him cough. Out of nowhere there was a fast, strong kick to his crotch. He doubled over and grabbed his crushed and bleeding testicles. The big man stumbled head first like a gored bull. He tried to maintain control, but his enormous weight and inertia was more than he could manage. He lost control and slammed into the bedroom's desk like a freight train. The Bacardi bottle and lamp that were sitting on top exploded then the desk collapsed into itself like a cardboard box.

The electricity sparked, and the alcohol-soaked desk caught on fire. Instinctively Kirk managed to stumble to his feet and get his gun out. He wasn't seeing straight. He watched as two women put on a maroon dress, and with a shaky hand, he pointed his gun going back and forth between the two images.

The Valkyrie watched as this pathetic oaf picked himself up off the collapsed table and made one last attempt to deal with the situation. She contemplated if she should kill him or let him live in shame. She had just retrieved her shoe from the white bodyguard's forehead and put on her clothes. Now she was standing in the bathroom in front of a large mirror fixing her hair and makeup. The bedroom was on fire, the senator was mumbling and crying into the floor, and the moronic bodyguard was pointing his gun at her, then at her reflection, at her again, at her refection. This needed to end.

She turned and looked straight into the eyes of Kirk. Blood was still pouring out of his neck, and his pupils were dilated. He tried to say something, but air just hissed out of the hole in his windpipe, making blood bubbles. Clearly he was out of it and probably wasn't going to live anyway. She stood still and watched as his gun waved back and forth. When the gun was pointed at the mirror, she zigzagged out of the bathroom with lighting speed, and kicked the man in both knees. The gun went off, shattering the mirror as the big man fell to the ground. With a quick and practiced motion, The Valkyrie wrenched the Colt 45 out of his hand, held the hot, smoking gun by its barrel, and clubbed him behind the right ear, knocking him out cold.

The blood-spattered senator was wiggling on the floor screaming, "You got what you wanted! Now get me out of here!" She ignored his screaming, grabbed him by the hair, and dragged his naked hog-tied body, face down, across the Berber carpet, down into the bathroom, across the tile floor, and over the metal lip into the shower stall. Being careful not to get her silk dress wet, she carefully leaned over the writhing senator, turned the cold water on full, leaped across the room, and turned on the ventilation fan.

She stepped out of the bathroom and grabbed her purse, which had been sitting on a dresser recording all that had happened since she had entered the room. She popped her head into the bathroom. The senator had rolled over onto his side, revealing a first-class rug burn across his chest, thighs, and genitals.

"Don't make me come back!" she barked as she turned off the bathroom light, and closed the door.

The flames on the desk were three feet high, and the room was filled with smoke. She didn't want to be seen leaving the room without the senator, so she went out onto the balcony and saw that she was four stories up. The Valkyrie had just the device for this sort of situation. From her purse, she pulled a pair of maroon opera gloves that matched her dress and a small box of dental floss. Inside the box was a roll of 400 lbs. monofilament test used for big game fishing. She wrapped the test around the railing and tied it in a simple square knot. From her glove came a small ratchet through which she fed the line. Holding the dental floss box in the ratchet hand, she climbed over the balcony rail, leaned back, and rappelled down four stories onto a brick walkway that connected the main house to the pool. She landed gently without making a sound. With a twist of her wrist, The Valkryie cut the nylon test with the side of the box; then she pulled a lighter from her purse and lit the line. Like a firecracker fuse, the flame climbed up the line leaving clear powdery ash blowing in the breeze. Within seconds there was no trace of the 400 lbs. line.

The party was still in full swing. She could feel the pulse of the disco music's bass drum through her feet as she walked around the building to where she had left her suit. She walked unnoticed to the garden off the kitchen. Suddenly, off in the distance, she could hear someone yelling, "Fire!"

She calmly found her black Kevlar motorcycle suit hidden under the bushes exactly where she had left it. All the attention was now focused at the other side of the building, so she quickly climbed into the black suit, put her small purse inside, and zipped it all up. She was about to put her helmet on when a voice yelled, "Freeze!" followed by the crackle and static of a walkie-talkie. She looked up, and standing in front of the kitchen was a clean-cut, boyish security guard. He looked like a kid who had just stepped out of a Young Republicans' meeting. In one movement, she tossed her hair forward, catching it inside the helmet, and slipped the helmet on her head, hiding all her hair.

The guard pulled out his weapon and pointed it at her. "Put your hands in the air!" She did what she was told. "Step away from the tree!" Again she complied, and the tension was eased slightly. Just as she expected, the young, unsuspecting dolt walked closer and took his eyes off her for a split second. That was long enough for her to turn on the light-bending switch and disappear from view.

The guard immediately sprang into action and ran towards the tree in an attempt to figure out what the hell had just happened. The unknowing boy ran straight towards The Valkyrie. As easily as if she were dialing a phone, she grabbed the baffled boy by his neck and, using the suit's built-in Taser function, sent 2000 volts of electricity straight into his brain. He convulsed, then froze into a rigid pillar as the electricity surged through him. When she released him, he fell to the ground in an epileptic seizure. Chances were good, that with a jolt that large, he wouldn't remember a thing. The walkie-talkie fell out of his hand and onto the ground, making a loud squawk. This was followed by a static midrange voice demanding that he answer.

The Valkyrie smiled to herself as she silently walked out of the garden, down the driveway, past the guards, out the gate, and down the road to her motorcycle. When she got on her bike, fire trucks and police cars were screaming up the road towards the burning McMansion. She waited, watching them pass by.

Once the coast was clear, she silently sped off on the stealth bike in the opposite direction. It was a fun night, and The Valkyrie could hardly wait to see how this was going to be spun in the next day's news cycle.

Chapter 16

Groggy from the flight, Ethan and Ascot disembarked from the shuttle. They both felt like they were nursing a hangover as their heavy feet shuffled through a series of long, featureless hallways. As Ethan marched, it occurred to him that he was in outer space; shouldn't that mean he was weightless? He didn't know yet about the intricate physics of the resort's structure and of the constant and precise spinning of its enormous rotating rings, creating artificial gravity. All Ethan knew was that he felt cheated. The whole point of outer space was to be able to float around and do stuff one can't do on Earth.

When they stepped into the lobby, it was like the moment in The Wizard of Oz when Dorothy stepped out of her black and white flying house into the Technicolor Munchkinland. "Wow!" Ethan and Ascot said simultaneously, frozen in their tracks, soaking in the reality of their surroundings. The room was massive, about the size of three or four regular gymnasiums. Two sides were nothing but gigantic glass walls that went up ten stories to a glass ceiling. As the station rotated, the view out into the universe constantly changed. The passengers who had gotten off the shuttle ahead of Ethan and Ascot were staring dumbstruck out into the 180-degree crystal clear panorama of the stars, planets and galaxies. Nowhere on Earth was a view like this remotely possible.

Ethan and Ascot stood and stared with the rest of them. They watched stars float past. It was like standing inside a moving telescope. The Earth came into view like a whale swimming among a school of minnows. The whole room fell silent as mother Earth in its vastness floated by. Its majestic swirls of blue, white, green and brown were a sharp contrast to the monochrome of dotted lights created by the plethora of stars and galaxies. Once the earth had passed, the crowd began to rumble again and people continued about their business. Ethan looked around, admiring the opulence of the room. The space was dimly lit so as to accentuate the stars and the spectacular view of the universe. The floors were illuminated glass that glowed softly and changed colors slowly, giving the room a moody ethereal quality. On opposite sides of the glass walls were terraced glass balconies, surrounded by highly polished brass railings, so every floor had an unobstructed view of the sky.

The middle of the lobby had a sunken section filled with exotic trees, intricate glass, and metal sculptures, as well as several ten-foot high walls that displayed a variety of paintings. It was a cross between a modern art museum and an arboretum. In the center was a glass pond filled with exotic fish and a ten-foot statue of some Wagnerian Nordic God, probably Odin or Wotan; neither Ethan nor Ascot knew for sure.

Ethan had taken an art appreciation class his first semester in college about a year before, and therefore noticed the different types of paintings: there were modern abstracts that looked like paint was randomly tossed on the canvas, some blurry impressionism that seemed to come into focus when he squinted, and a Baroque painting that seemed out of place. It was very busy with lots of trees, horses, and fat pale naked people prancing about, while little naked cherubs and cupids flew around shooting everyone in the butt with arrows. This painting got Ethan's attention. He stared noticing how the light seemed to radiate out of the painting. He looked around the room at all the other paintings, realizing that they all shared this same quality. When he returned his gaze to the Baroque painting, it wasn't there; in its place was a modern realism painting of a sailboat, in a calm blue sea with a tropical island in the distance. Ethan felt a bit silly, realizing that these weren't paintings at all but high-resolution monitors set into museum frames.

Just like a hotel lobby, there was a large front desk with a dozen people working behind it. All the passengers who had just gotten off the shuttle were now checking in. Ethan and Ascot had wandered around the lobby as people stood in line to get their rooms. Now the line was moving quickly, and they decided it was time to check in.

The receptionists behind the counter was an even mix of Indian men and women, all dressed in dark blue matching business suits. A tall bearded man wearing a turban called Ascot to the counter. A few seconds later, Ethan was called up by a tiny woman no more than five feet tall. She was in her mid-twenties and had long black hair pulled back to reveal large hoop earrings.

As Ethan walked to the desk, the computer remotely accessed his profile from the ID tag around his neck, and his info appeared on the small woman's monitor. Ethan stared at her chest trying to read the name that barely fit on her nametag: Aanandamayee Goopavindashiva.

She noticed and giggled. "People call me Anna." She didn't look up, just continued to type into the computer.

Ethan nodded: "Oh, Okay. Hi I'm -" but before he could say anything else, she interrupted.

"Ethan Stone, assistant fitness coordinator." She looked up and handed him a package. "This is a map of the resort, your room number, and a list of safety procedures. Read them and sign where applicable, and after you have done that, put all the signed documents into the box." She pointed to a simple plastic box at the end of the long desk. "In one hour the Captain will be in the auditorium addressing all the new crew members, introducing his staff, and reviewing all the safety features and protocols."

"Great," said Ethan. He turned from the desk with a stack of papers in his hand, not at all sure what to do next.

*   *   *   *

Captain Thomas Krovoza had earned an M.B.A. Degree from Harvard; then, after a year of job hunting and moonlighting as a guard at a beach parking lot, he got fed up and enlisted in the Navy as an officer. Within a year he was promoted to first officer of the atomic-powered submarine, the John F. Kennedy. For his first tour of duty, he was stationed under the North Pole for six months. After two months, the captain got sick and was bedridden for the remainder of the voyage, so Krovoza became the acting captain, and, as dumb luck would have it, NORAD assigned the John F. Kennedy to its first actual covert combat mission.

Chechnyan rebels had hijacked a Russian destroyer armed with nuclear weapons, and they were threatening to launch missiles into Europe. Krovoza didn't know it, but he was a gifted leader and combat strategist. He immediately took charge, ran a tight, disciplined, and respectful ship, and established excellent rapport with the crew. He devised a strategy that disarmed and disabled the destroyer, neutralized the rebels, and got hostages released unhurt. It was brilliantly conceived and executed. Without pomp and circumstance the destroyer was returned to Russia, and the hijacking rebels were tried, found guilty, then executed.

Although the incident was covered up and never released as a national story, Krovoza was recognized as being a natural leader. He was promoted to Captain and assigned to the aircraft carrier Ronald Reagan, on which he spent two years in the Persian Gulf. He considered his assignment there to be no better than providing mafia muscle for well-financed oil companies. His tenure in the military was halted when someone discovered that he was bisexual and was having simultaneous sexual liaisons with his female secretary and his first mate. The irony was that the commanding officer who executed the orders for his dismissal was a notorious cross-dressing closeted queen.

As a result of this scandal, Krovoza quietly slipped out of the military and found himself a job as captain of a cruise ship. There, being bisexual and promiscuous wasn't a problem. After ten years of hauling drunk tourists around the world, he was aching for something new. As fate would have it, Eden, Inc. booked an employee cruise. Casper, being the CEO, was seated at the Captain's table every night at dinner, and the two of them hit if off.

At the end of the week, Casper mentioned to Krovoza that Eden, Inc. had a job that needed a captain and asked him if would be interested. Two-and-a-half years later Krovoza found himself in outer space, looking out a window at the entire planet Earth, and in charge of arguably the most advanced and elaborate piece of machinery ever built.

While the new crew members were filing into the auditorium and getting seated, Krovoza waited in the wings. The resort director was on stage, coaxing everyone to hurry up so he could introduce the Captain. The resort director's job was to run the activities on board, while the captain was responsible for operations and maintenance of the resort itself.

The resort director told some stupid jokes that received polite laughter, and then segued into his introduction of the captain.

Krovoza went on stage and addressed the new crew. He began with a variation of the standard welcome speech he had given hundreds of times before. Only this time things were rather different. It wasn't a ship, and they weren't at sea. "This is the maiden voyage of the first commercial space resort ever made, and we are the first people ever to staff a resort in outer space. We are making history!" Excited applause followed.

Krovoza went on to explain the layout of the resort and how there were built-in redundancies and lots of safety features. The seriousness of their safety could not be overstated. There were many unknown challenges in space, and since there had never been a resort in space before, they had no idea what to expect, so they had to stay vigilant and take all the safety precautions very seriously. A key component of their safety was the life-pod drill: how to get off the ship if it were sinking, so to speak. The first drill was scheduled in four hours. The new arrivals had just enough time to go to their rooms, settle in, find their mess hall, eat dinner, and report to their life-pod station. The instructions were clearly explained in the pamphlet they all had received at check in.

While the captain explained the layout and all the safety stuff, Ethan got distracted and started to daydream, replaying his previous night's encounter with Vanessa in the shower. When the captain was finished, Ethan didn't understand the layout of the resort or what he was supposed to do. Since Ascot was one of the doctors on board and head of his department, he was busy in some sort of administrative meeting. For the first time since they had left, Ethan was on his own.

Ethan opened his pamphlet and tried to sort it out. His room number was D-NE-6-117. He opened the map. Each spinning ring of the resort was assigned a letter A through D. On each ring was a stack of floors 1 through 12, and each floor was divided into four quadrants: North West, North East, South East, South West. Ethan's room number meant that he was on the D-ring, North East quadrant, sixth floor, room 117.

Ethan shuffled out of the auditorium into the lobby, and watched the people around him quickly disperse as if they all had news that a bomb was going to explode. Ethan stood in the middle of the room staring at his map, still not sure where to go. He felt like a little kid lost in Times Square, with no one offering to help.

Out of nowhere, a familiar voice floated in from behind: "You look confused." Ethan turned around to see Vanoushka standing two feet away from him. She was wearing a cross between a military officer's uniform, like the Captain's, and a woman's business suit similar to the female receptionists in the hotel lobby. Her springy blond hair fell to her shoulders, covering the epaulettes that signified her rank. There was something incongruent about seeing this exotically beautiful woman in an officer's uniform.

Ethan smiled and pointed at his room on the map. Vanoushka took the cue and grabbed his information sheet. She pointed across the auditorium. "The lobby, loading docks, control center, and executive suites are all on this ring, the A-ring, it's the outermost one. You need to go to the D-ring, which is the innermost ring. Since the rings are constantly moving, the only way to get from one ring to the next is by the transporter." She pointed to a door across the room.

Ethan turned to look. "Am I going to be disassembled molecularly then put back together?"

"No!" she giggled, "We do have some amazing technology, but we haven't developed that yet."

Ethan nodded, then followed her across the room towards a door marked "**TRANSPORT TO B-RING**" which was next to a row of elevators. Vanoushka looked at her watch and contemplated for a moment. "I can take you to the D-ring. There are some things I need to do down there anyway."

They stepped into a four-meter cylindrical room that had seats around the sides and a brass pole in the middle. Ethan was relieved that the transporter bore no resemblance to the Star Trek unit.

A pleasant ding announced the arrival of the B-ring and the word "South" lit up above the door just before closing and sealing the room airtight. A few seconds later the door opened again, and they were in a completely different location. Surprised and disoriented, Ethan followed Vanoushka out of the transporter onto an outdoor cobblestone shopping mall in mid-afternoon. The mall was fully stocked, and it seemed that the store clerks were finishing up the last details before the grand opening in a few days. The two walked past a shoe store called the "Sanc-Shoe-Airy" towards a row of elevators. When they arrived, Vanoushka pushed the button labeled "Express To Transporter." Within a few seconds, the express elevator arrived.

Inside, the springy-haired goddess continued, "As the rings cross each other, the transporter passes from one ring to another. That's why two stations are always right next to each other."

Ethan was confused but nodded anyway, and she continued. "There are four transport stations on each floor, a North, South, East, and West station, but since the rings are constantly moving, there really isn't any North, South, East or West . It's just a labeling system." Her look implied that it was a stupid labeling system, but there was nothing anyone could do about it. "Each ring is a self-contained unit, so of course, you can travel to any floor or any part of a ring once you're there."

The elevator stopped and announced their arrival with a ding. The doors opened, and they stepped out onto a marble courtyard surrounded by Roman columns and archways. It felt like being outdoors. The air was cool and humid, with a salty ocean breeze. Ethan stepped out, looked up, and saw puffy white cumulous clouds blowing across the blue afternoon sky. The hard plastic soles of Ethan's flight suit were slippery on the polished marble floor, and he almost fell as he tried to walk while staring up. "How do they do that?" he asked, walking carefully so as to not lose his balance.

Vanoushka was a few feet in front of Ethan. She turned to face him. "Do what?" They were standing in the middle of the courtyard. Ethan pointed up to the clouds. She shrugged, "I'm not exactly sure, but it certainly looks amazing. They hired one of the top illusionists from Las Vegas to help design it." She turned and headed towards a large arch that had "**TRANSPORT TO C-RING**" carved in a Roman font on its crest. "There are several simulated outdoor environments onboard. We have gardens, parks, shopping malls, surfing beaches, swimming pools, snow skiing, even a fly fishing pond with fish in it."

Ethan felt like she had suddenly turned into a tour guide.

"Studies have shown that people need to experience nature on a regular basis. If they stay indoors all the time, they start to go stir-crazy. Since there is no outdoors, we have manufactured a variety of natural outdoor environments. We want our clients to be able to forget they are in outer space. After all, this is a seven star hotel resort. People need access to a wide variety of recreational activities. Our clients expect the best. Where else can someone take an elevator to a tropical beach and then get in the same elevator and go to a ski lodge?"

Ethan was flabbergasted; all this was so unexpected and so incredibly amazing. They stepped into the transporter and off they went to the C-ring. The transporter opened onto plush wall-to-wall floral print carpeting that covered the lobby of a Las Vegas-style casino. Immediately, they took an express elevator down to the bottom floor where the transporter to the D-ring was located. When Ethan stepped out of the elevator, he noticed a sign stating that they were on the West side of the C ring. Vanoushka didn't seem fazed by this and headed towards the two adjacent transporter rooms.

A thought burst into Ethan's brain. He began, "Uhh," then stopped; he didn't want to appear dumber than he already thought he was being, but she looked at him inquisitively. "How come we're on the West side if we want to go to the East? Shouldn't the transporters line up?"

She paused for a second and formulated her thought. "The rings are constantly moving in opposite directions so the transporter stations constantly switch sides." She looked to make sure Ethan was following, then went on. "So, in this case," she said pointing to the light above the transporter room, "the next transporter will be here in 54 seconds and it will go to the West side of the D-ring. You have a choice. You can go to the West side and walk to the East side, or you can wait for the ring to swing around and get on the next one, which will be East side station." She stepped into the transporter room that was headed to the West side. "I have business on the West side."

Ethan followed her into the transporter room, "I don't mind walking." He realized he was staring at her, enamored by the way her blond hair framed her mocha neck and how her trapezius muscles curved down, then up into her shoulders. The doors closed, and the transporter crossed from the C to the D ring. There was a ding indicating the change. Ethan tore his eyes off his tour guide and looked up as the door opened.

They stepped out onto large brown Mexican pavers with palm bushes in big, brightly decorated clay pots. In front was a sign indicating they were on the West side of the D-ring. Vanoushka made a beeline to the hallway that circled the entire ring like a row in a large stadium. "I have to go this way." She pointed down the long circular hallway. "Your room is that way," she said pointing in the opposite direction. "Go to the next elevator and take it to the sixth floor. From there you'll figure out how to get to your room. Just follow the signs." Ethan wanted to hang out and follow Vanoushka. He really didn't mind walking. After all, it didn't matter. It was a big circle, so he would eventually get to his room regardless of which way he went.

They looked at each other for a moment, and there was an awkward silence. Vanouska thrust out her hand like a football coach meeting a new player. "Well, Ethan, it was nice to see you again." Ethan, for no particular reason, had a burst of confidence that wasn't typical for him. He grabbed her hand as to shake it but then stepped closer to her, their bodies almost touching. He looked into her eyes and said, "Thank you for showing me around." He leaned a little forward just so his chest lightly touched hers. Instinctively, he swung his left arm around to hug her. She did likewise. He let go of her right hand and hugged her with both arms. He felt her large breasts press against his chest and was aroused by the contrast of her thin muscular back and small waist. They held their embrace for a moment, Ethan soaking it all in; then, at the moment that would have been the appropriate time to stop, he squeezed her a little tighter, this time pressing his groin into hers. He felt her upper body relax, her knees buckle, and she pressed her groin against his. A burst of testosterone shot through his body. He pulled his head back, still holding her tightly, and without any hesitation gently kissed her on the neck. She responded by kissing him on his neck.

They separated and looked deep into each other's eyes. Vani pulled her arms to her side, "I really have to go, I'll see you at dinner." Ethan didn't want it to end and tried to think of some reason to continue, but her body language said loud and clear, "This is where we part company." Then she turned around and walked down the hall.

Ethan turned and went the opposite way. He had only been away from his girlfriend for a single day, and his system was already short-circuiting. As he walked down the hall, all he could think about was being with Vani again. There was absolutely no one around. It felt like he was somewhere he wasn't supposed to be, like in a museum after it closed. He walked past the kinds of things that would typically be found on the lower floors of a fancy hotel: offices, meeting rooms, a library. A moving sidewalk appeared. Ethan looked down the hall. It appeared to be rather bleak, so he got on and went for a ride. It ended at the North East elevator where there was a plaza with more offices and meeting rooms. There he took the elevator up to the sixth floor.

The moment Ethan stepped into the crew area, it was as if he had stepped onto a completely different resort. Behind the scenes everything was bare and basic with absolutely no frills. It was nothing like the area for the guests, which had fancy polished brass doorknobs and glass railings. The crew area floors were plain, unpolished white linoleum. The walls were flat white; the doorknobs and light fixtures were a simple aluminum and plastic.

Ethan walked down the bleak, circular hallway that encompassed the floor. Every ten to fifteen meters there was a perpendicular corridor leading to a row of crew quarters. The plaque on the corridor wall read, "Rooms 200-220." He kept going. The next corridor read "180-200." Relieved that he was going in the right direction, he put a little more bounce in his step. At the "100-120" sign, he turned and walked down the hall until he reached room 117.

He opened the door and stood at the threshold of his new room; it was a little bigger than the sauna at the gym. Plopped in the middle of the room were his luggage and the plastic bag he had put his clothes in when he was issued his flight suit. The room was very narrow. In it was a bunk bed, a little writing desk with a computer monitor and keyboard, a chair, built-in cabinets, a flat screen TV mounted on the wall, and a small nightstand with a phone and a remote control sitting on top. At the head of the bunk bed was a small closet, and in front of that, the bathroom. Ethan opened the bathroom door to have a look. It was a little bigger than a bathroom on an airplane, with the addition of a shower. What had he expected? He hadn't given it any thought, but when he saw all the opulence in every other aspect of the Valhalla Resort, he had thought that perhaps some of it might spill over to the crew quarters. Apparently not.

This situation reminded Ethan of a story his dad would often tell about something that happened long before Ethan was born. A producer named Franco hired Vince and nine other bodybuilders, including Mr. Atlas—Butch McGee, aka the Beast—to pose at a health expo at the Long Beach Convention Center. Franco agreed to pay each man $100 if they did a five-minute solo routine plus a fifteen-minute pose-down. Franco convinced them all that it would be great exposure and that it could lead to more endorsement deals from the supplement companies that were sure to be there. Needless to say, all the bodybuilders agreed to do it, but when they went on stage, it became obvious that none of the supplement companies were present. The health expo turned out to be a shoe trade show, and the audience viewed a bunch of bodybuilders posing in Speedos as a procession of circus freaks. Vince and his buddies all got paid and laughed it off, and that seemed to be the end of that until about a month later when Vince learned, through the grapevine, that Franco had earned $60,000 from an Italian shoe company to deliver Vince and his bodybuilder friends as a promotional stunt. After that, Vince used to say, "I saw trickle-down economics first hand. It's bullshit!"

Ethan wasn't as jaded as his father. He figured these were the facilities one gets for an entry-level position. When he got promoted, he would get better accommodations. Besides, all he really needed was a place to sleep, so for now, his little room was perfectly fine. Ethan stepped over his luggage and then collapsed onto the bottom bunk. He discovered the hard way that his bed was just a single thin foam pad with absolutely no bounce. Ethan put his head on his pillow and looked up at the bottom of the top bunk's mattress poking through the thin slats. A bright red fire alarm and exposed sprinkler pipes mounted across the middle of the drab ceiling caught his attention. He reflected on the video he watched on the train that boasted the opulent amenities, spacious bedrooms, and luxurious bathrooms on board the Valhalla Resort. There certainly was a gigantic divide between the crew and the passengers. Ethan wondered, "What kind of people were these passengers going to be?"

Chapter 17

Safety drills are based on common sense, courtesy and patience. The fact that so few people possess these traits was the reason that Ethan and all crew members on board the Valhalla space resort were required to go through the tedious process repeatedly. Ethan was reminded of all the fire drills in school, and never once was there ever a fire. Supposedly, whenever a school or a building really did catch fire, all organized exiting procedures went right out the window, and it immediately became: "Every man for himself," so what was the point of practicing?

Ethan had no interest in marching around the resort pretending that there was some imminent danger. "Then again," he thought, "A space station isn't a typical environment, so safety drills are warranted." It was not as if he could just run outside if something were to go wrong.

Ethan sat up in his bunk and read the safety instructions assigned to his room. Apparently there were two kinds of emergencies: a standard evacuation and an immediate withdrawal. Depending on the level of emergency, there were two different procedures. Every crew member was assigned to a specific life-pod. A "standard evacuation" meant all crew members were required to go to their specific pod and wait for instructions. An "immediate withdrawal" meant to get to the closest pod and get the hell off the station. The perimeter of the second, sixth, and eleventh floors were equipped with escape pods and could handle many more passengers than would ever be on board at any given time. In the event of an emergency, the elevators and transporters were instantly shut off, and the only way to go from floor to floor was by way of the stairs. The logic behind the layout was that no one on board, at any time, would ever be more than two floors away from an escape pod.

The escape pod to which Ethan was assigned was on the sixth floor of the D ring. According to the map, it was just down the corridor and to the right about fifty yards from his room.

Confident that he knew where to go and what to do, he thought he would relax for about ten or fifteen minutes before the safety drill. Ethan quickly unpacked his luggage and stuffed his belongings into the closet. He took off his flight suit and stood in the middle of the room in his underwear. If he stretched his arms outward from his body, he could almost touch each wall. He remembered that as a little kid he measured his growth by spreading his arms and trying to touch each side of the bathroom stall at the gym. Now that his clothes were put away and he felt more organized, he sat on his bunk, leaned back, and closed his eyes.

*****

Ethan was cutting in and out of a hollow wave on a bright magenta, seven-foot twin fin gun surfboard, getting tubed then pulling out over the lip. As he lay on his stomach, paddling out to catch the next wave, he could feel the warmth of the sun shining on his shoulders. Ethan turned and looked onto the shore. Sitting on the beach in a skimpy Brazilian bikini was Vanouska. He caught the next wave and rode it to shore. Ethan hopped off his board and walked toward the perfectly shaped, bikini-clad hottie. She stood on the pure white sand, eager and excited to see him. He dropped his surfboard and reached one arm around her waist, pulled her towards him, looked deep into her eyes, and then moved in to kiss her.

Off in the distance, a pulsating buzzing noise began. Sirens were going off. All around him, men in military uniforms were scurrying about with their weapons drawn. Out of nowhere, a large fire truck came driving up the beach. The warm sunny day suddenly turned dark and cold. Ethan looked all around for Vanouska, but she was gone.

The buzzing and sirens got louder as Ethan's awareness started to come into focus. "Dammit!" he shouted as he rolled onto his side. It was always that way with his dreams. Just when things were about to get good, something went wrong. He looked around his new closet-sized room. Why were these obnoxious buzzers and sirens going off? Then he remembered what he was supposed to be doing. He quickly put on his sweats and cross-trainers, stepped into the tiny bathroom, splashed water on his face, and looked in the mirror. His hair was a mess. He was about to walk out of the room when a thought occurred to him, "What if I see Vanouska?" He dug out a small bag of toiletry items. Inside were a hairbrush and a toothbrush. He quickly brushed his teeth and stuck his head under the sink in an attempt to soak his hair. It was a very small sink, so he had to splash the water around his head to get it all wet. In the process he got water all over the mirror, countertop, and floor, making a mess in the bathroom.

He quickly brushed his wet hair and was ready to walk out the door when he realized he didn't remember the exact number of the escape pod he was assigned to. There were several in a row on the map. He had difficulty concentrating with the flashing red lights, ear-splitting sirens, and a mechanical voice announcing, "This is a standard evacuation drill. Report to your pod station. This is a standard evacuation drill. Report to your pod station." The voice would stop for a few seconds then repeat a minute or so later.

Frantically, he searched the room looking for the piece of paper that had the map, instructions, and pod number on it. He dug through the clothes he had just put away like a junkie looking for his stash. Finally he saw the folder sitting on the chair; under the folder was the paper. He grabbed it and ran out the door.

He arrived a few minutes later, his fingers shoved in his ears. There were a dozen people standing at attention in front of a dozen different pods. Ethan just followed their lead and did the same. The escape pod was essentially a round room full of seats that ultimately acted as a lifeboat, but unlike a boat there were no life preservers. No one needed to bring anything or prepare in any way because the idea was to show up and help get people on board. Since the computer knew where everyone was at all times, an in-person inspection wasn't necessary. After he stood there for about ten minutes, a loud, sustained horn blew, the lights stopped flashing, and the siren ceased. Ethan pulled his fingers out of his ears and headed to the crew mess.

The mess hall felt like going back in time to junior high school, a big open room with plastic chairs and harsh lighting. Ethan arrived very distracted, his eyes darting all over the room, hoping to spot a mane of springy blond hair. He wandered around the room waiting for Vanouska to show up, hoping he could eat with her. After a while he became self-conscious just hanging around the counter, so he shuffled into line and grabbed a tray and plate. The food was alright, on par with The Sizzler or the standard cheap Vegas buffet. There was lasagna, enchiladas, and chicken. Was it baked or broiled? He couldn't tell and he didn't care. He was starving and generally he wasn't that picky. He had grown up eating oatmeal, egg whites, boiled chicken, and broccoli. Vince never stopped eating like a bodybuilder, so for Ethan, food that even attempted to taste good seemed decadent. He put two pieces of mystery chicken on his plate next to some Waldorf salad and cheese enchiladas.

He found a seat in the corner facing the entrance so that if Vani did arrive, he would see her walk in. Ethan sat alone and ate, keeping one eye on the door. He listened to a group of maintenance guys who were talking at the table next to him. One guy was complaining that he couldn't call home. Apparently all communication to Earth had been shut down on purpose. The people at the front desk had told him that it was a matter of national security. A burly man with a big blond mustache sat up and pounded the table with his fist. "That's bullshit!" The group nodded in agreement; then they all huddled in closer and spoke in lower tones. Ethan had to strain to hear. "This blackout means we can't call home for at least two weeks, and when we do, we can't tell anyone where we are or what we are doing. It's all classified, considered top secret."

Ethan wanted to call his Dad and Vanessa and tell them that he was fine, he missed them, and was looking forward to seeing them when he got back. He couldn't imagine how that would compromise national security. While he was thinking this, he kept his eyes on the door.

A new voice among the huddled men spoke. Ethan stopped chewing so he could hear better. "I tried texting and emailing. Nothin's working now." There was a murmur of grunts and mutterings. Ethan popped the last piece of enchilada in his mouth, took his plate to a bus tray full of dirty dishes and placed it on top of a half-eaten piece of German chocolate cake. Then he left the mess hall, never once having said a single world to anyone.

Ethan later learned that he was ranked at the bottom of the totem pole of the Valhalla resort personnel; consequently, he was assigned to eat in the crappy cafeteria with the maintenance guys, janitorial workers, and various other low-skilled help, while Ascot and Vani ate in the fancy dining room with the officers and passengers. Needless to say, Vani never came.

When Ethan got back to his quarters, he immediately started to get ready to go to sleep. He stepped into the tiny bathroom wearing nothing but a pair of boxer shorts, brushed his teeth, washed his face and was about to hop into bed when he noticed the flashing light on the phone. Surprised, he went to retrieve his message, then had to sort out how to do it. The phone wasn't a normal phone. It had a flat screen and a camera that enabled the callers to see each other, and a touch-screen keyboard for texing. Like all hotels, It was a closed system, so the phone numbers were also the room numbers.

Ethan discovered it was just like retrieving email. He had three messages. There were no names, just numbers. He clicked on the first message. A corny welcome to Valhalla promo ad with the staff and the Captain popped on. Ethan closed it. He didn't need to watch that. He clicked on the second message, and Ascot's face popped onto the screen. His face was really close to the camera, and it was kind of disturbing. Ethan was distracted from what Ascot was saying because the wrinkles, moles and blemishes on Ascot's face were so magnified. The message wasn't serious. He was just saying "Hi" and was letting Ethan know that he expected Ethan to be at the gym the next day at 8:00AM, particularly because some of the equipment still needed to be assembled.

Ethan kept trying to see what Ascot's room looked like. It seemed to be much bigger and it appeared as though he had a window that looked out onto the universe. Ethan's room was a broom closet by comparison. It reminded him of his low status. Feeling a little dejected, he clicked on the final icon. There was a blur on the screen; then there was a woman's voice giggling, and the blur became more focused. It was a pair of spectacular mocha boobs in a black lacey bra being pulled back from the camera so that they came into focus. Then dance music started playing, and the breasts started bouncing to the rhythm as if choreographed. This went on for about a minute.

Abruptly the music stopped, the boobs stopped bouncing, there was a burst of laughter, and then lace-covered flesh squished up into the camera. A giggly woman's voice said, "Have a nice night, Ethan," then hung up. Ethan sat up in his chair dazed. He hadn't blinked or swallowed the entire time and a puddle of drool had formed on the desk. His mind was racing, strategizing about what he would say when he saw Vani next. His nineteen-year-old hormones were popping like firecrackers during Chinese New Year. Not sure what to do next, he stood up fully aroused, then collapsed onto the bed. There was only one way he was going to get any sleep tonight.

Chapter 18

Agitated and groggy, Ethan arrived at the gym the next morning with no idea what to expect. Ascot was there—calm, well-rested, and drinking a cup of coffee. Apparently he hadn't received the same phone message.

Ethan stood at the entrance of the gym and surveyed the main floor. In his mind, gyms were places where hardcore body builders worked out. When people came to Blood-Sweat-N-Tears to tour the facilities and happened to mention one of the local fancy gyms such as Equinox or Evolution, Vince would always say with a growl, "You want to work out or hang out?" Vince considered the soap and towels that he provided to be fluffy amenities. Blood-Sweat-N-Tears was a warehouse of weights where serious people came to lift. There wasn't a lot of attention paid to aesthetics. The walls were scarred and painted random colors. Some of the mirrors were cracked and taped together. Hardly anything matched. The floor was made of old corroded rubber with all kinds of stains, and the bathrooms always had a little hint of a mildew smell no matter how much they were cleaned, yet every champion bodybuilder had worked out there at some point in his or her career.

Ethan was now standing in a room that bore no relationship to Blood-Sweat-N-Tears. The main workout room was large with a light blue and green plush carpet. The walls were painted white and almond. Track lighting was angled in several directions, casting moody shadows on the walls and machines. Multi-colored neon tubes framed smoked glass dividers that separated each machine and workout station. To Ethan it looked more like an art museum or a nightclub than a gym.

They walked around the large cold room, sorting out where to start. In one hand Ascot held a schematic of how the room should be finally assembled. In the other was his cup of coffee. Visible steam drifted out of the cup, mixing its burnt aroma with the smell of metal, plastic, and carpet glue. Ascot sipped, looked at the paper, and then looked around the room again. "Once it's all put together, this will be the most high-tech gym we will ever have been in."

Ethan pointed to an empty part of the room. "So what goes there?"

Ascot pointed to a stack of boxes. "Those." Before assembling anything, Ethan and Ascot took inventory. Ascot was quite meticulous in his approach. Ethan took after his dad, who would never read directions. Vince would tear the box apart, look at the picture on the cover, and then attempt to put whatever it was together. Something would always be wrong so he would have to take it apart and try again. After several attempts, he usually figured it out, but inevitably there would always be a few extra pieces left over.

Ascot looked over the machines on the floor and then to the plans he was holding. "Once we put the rest of this gym together, it's going to be amazing." The completed gym would have hi-tech machines for every body part, for both the fast and slow twitch muscles, as well as free weights. There were several different varieties of aerobic machines, treadmills, stairs, cross country ski stations, rowing machines, as well as normal and recumbent bicycles. All of which were unlike any Ethan or Ascot had ever seen before. There was a boxing ring, gymnastics pit, and a classroom equipped with virtual holographic instructors for floor aerobics and yoga.

The first piece of equipment Ethan and Ascot assembled was an electronic preacher curl machine. It looked similar to the machine at Blood Sweat-N-Tears. It had an adjustable seat and armrest that locked the elbows in place while allowing a full range of vertical motion that isolated the bicep muscles. But instead of having a barbell to lift there were two long padded sleeves and a dual grip EZ curl bar attached to the armrest.

Curious, he sat down on the seat. "So, how does it work?"

"I'm not sure. Why don't you try putting your arms in?" Ascot started looking around on the ground for the instructions.

Ethan cautiously put his arms into the two sleeves. Suddenly the machine came to life—the sleeves tightened around his arms and got heavy, pushing his chest against the bench. The armrest lit up and in front of Ethan's eyes was a holographic projection of the weight and reps.

Ascot found a small booklet and quickly scanned over the instructions. "Are your arms tingly?" Ethan was about to say no when a strange sensation pulsed through his arms and he began to twitch and grab the bar involuntarily. "Something weird is happening," Ethan said nervously.

"Relax! The way this works is: your muscles are being electronically stimulated, enabling them to contract and lift much more weight then normal. The machine automatically adjusts the weight to eighty percent of your maximum and with each rep it will increase and take you to absolute failure." Ascot let the booklet float to the floor. "Pretty cool, huh?"

"Very cool!"

"Now do ten reps!" Ethan did as Ascot commanded. With each rep he watched the holographic display that hovered in front of his eyes graphically show him his range of motion, the number of reps, and the amount of weight he was lifting. Ethan was baffled. The weight he was lifting was four or five times what he could normally do. After ten reps, the machine had tallied up all the weight he had lifted and graded him on his form. Then as suddenly as it had popped on, the machine turned off and his arms were released. Ethan stepped out of the machine, his arms dangled limply at his side.

"How was it?"

Ethan wasn't sure what to think. He wanted to say something clever, but instead looked down at his exhausted arms and heard himself say, "Intense."

****

After assembling twelve hours a day for three days, all the gear and facilities were set up. Neither Ethan or Ascot had ever seen most of the equipment before. Everything was computerized, and all the resistance was magnetic. The same division of Eden, Inc. that had developed the Virtual Reality Magnetic Chamber had also developed the exercise equipment that Ethan and Ascot had just spent several days assembling. Now the trick was to figure out how it all worked.

Ascot sat on one of the computerized stationary bicycles and put on its corresponding virtual reality helmet. He started pedaling and then began pushing buttons, following the prompts. There were hundreds of course choices, from the Tour De France to cruising the boardwalk on Staten Island. "Wow! Somebody had fun designing this thing."

Intrigued, Ethan climbed onto the bicycle next to him. When he put on the headpiece everything suddenly became pitch black and dead quiet. He started pedaling, and a list of questions popped onto the screen. He stated his age and how long he wanted to ride. Then a series of images scrolled before him. He stopped the images at random, and the next thing he knew, he was on a two lane county road surrounded by giant pine trees. Little patches of light made their way through the canopy of pine needles. He started to go downhill, picking up speed. He could feel, smell, and hear the piney wind blow against his face and body. He pedaled through a pristine mountain wilderness, trudging up and down hills for ten minutes working up a sweat. He finally arrived at a sign that read, "Redwood National Forest." When he passed the sign, the forest faded to black, and the wind fell silent. The experience was so real that he literally forgot for a moment that it was an illusion. Ethan tore off the headpiece. "Wow!"

Ascot was standing next to him with a knowing grin on his face. "Pretty frickin' great!" He started walking towards the opposite end of the gym. "Wait 'til you see this boxing system at work."

Standing in the corner was a generic-looking mannequin wearing boxing gloves and red satin trunks. He had no legs; his waist continued down to the floor where it flared out like a saltshaker. Ascot sat down on the side of ring next to a touch-screen computer interface. "I got it working last night." Ascot reached into a box and tossed a plastic bag the size of a basketball at Ethan. "Put these on." Startled, Ethan caught the package awkwardly, then donned the gloves, head gear, and mouth piece it contained. He looked at the mannequin, which had a convincing scowl on its face.

Ethan had never stepped into a boxing ring before, let alone fought anyone.

Ascot started typing on the touchscreen. "The Ultimate Sparring Partner is floating on a computer-controlled magnetic field and can be programmed to fight like any boxer in history."

A feeling of dread oozed over Ethan like prickly molasses. He thought, "My first time in the ring and I have to fight Mike Tyson?" He looked up with one glove on and gave Ascot a sarcastic smile.

Ascot sat back down at the touchscreen. "Also the Ultimate Sparring Partner's height and arm reach can be adjusted."

Ethan was struggling to get the second glove on. "Well then, adjust it so it's the size of someone whose ass I can kick."

Ascot grinned, "Nah! Your opponent is going to be your exact size." Ethan watched as the mannequin's height and arms grew an inch or two.

"Don't worry, I'll make him go easy on you."

Before Ethan had a chance to talk his way out of it, he was dancing around the ring, face-to-face with an angry mannequin who was punching at him. The Ultimate Sparring Partner did a left jab fake and then a right hook that caught Ethan just above the ear. "Not fun!" Ethan yelled.

"Pay attention!" Ascot excitedly pointed at the opponent. Ethan turned to face the mannequin just as the Ultimate Sparring Partner executed a left uppercut and smacked him firmly under the chin. "Never let your guard down!" Ascot yelled with a practiced coaching voice, bobbing and weaving ringside. Ethan had never boxed before and wasn't feeling properly prepared. He put his hands up in front of his face like he'd seen every boxer in the world do and just as his floating mechanical opponent was doing. The boxing robot jabbed, and Ethan blocked the blow. "You're doing great, kid," yelled Ascot. "You're a natural. Keep moving. Use your feet and work that left jab."

Ethan started to get focused. He was warming up. The punching and blocking was beginning to feel less foreign. He sucked in a large burst of air through his nose and adjusted his mouthpiece. He made two fast left jabs and noticed beads of sweat forming on the forehead of the ugly scowling mannequin. This unexpected detail to realism distracted him for a moment and he lost his focus. Ethan looked the mannequin in the eyes and realized there was no one there. He wasn't fighting a person, so no matter what he did, he wasn't going to hurt anyone. With a newfound determination and focus, Ethan lashed out with unbridled rage. This ugly mannequin face was the embodiment of all his childhood teasing, all the humiliation of being a teenager with zits on his face and teeth too big for his mouth. Ethan was exorcising the pain of growing up without a mother and having an eccentric father who could barely function outside the confines of his own gym, the frustration of not being able to hang out with friends and do kid things because he had to work at the gym every day.

At that moment, he wanted to pulverize this stupid machine. All the sounds of the room faded. Ethan saw nothing but the ugly bald head of the Ultimate Sparring Partner. His physical stress, strain, and pain instantly evaporated. He bounced across the ring, keeping up his guard. He watched as the eyes of his opponent tracked him and the Sparring Partner's arms went into a defensive position. Ethan lunged forward and gave two quick left jabs to the face, but his opponent's hands shot up and blocked the blows. Ethan landed a strong uppercut into its chest. The sparring partner's hands went down, and Ethan landed two furious blows to the head, causing the mannequin to teeter. Still focused on destroying this machine, Ethan bounced over to the stumbling, life-size doll and got in four more solid blows to the head, the last one spinning the boxing dummy around and bouncing it off the ropes.

When the Ultimate Sparring Partner hit the ropes, it came back faster and with more determination. It jabbed and slid sideways across the floor. Ethan jabbed back but missed. The mannequin was wearing Ethan out. After about a half-dozen jabs and slides, Ethan noticed a pattern and instantly devised a strategy. Ethan faked a jab, and when the mannequin slid to avoid it, Ethan nailed it with a strong right cross. But the move opened Ethan up, and his opponent hit him with a strong uppercut to the chin.

Ethan was swimming in a pool. The water was warm. He felt weightless as he floated on his back. As he looked up, he could see billions of stars in a purple-black sky. On the side of the pool, Vani in a small orange bikini, stood with her mane of yellow hair accentuating her brown body. He turned over to swim toward her. The stars disappeared, the water turned cold, his head hurt, and Ethan found himself on his back looking up at a blurry, grinning Ascot.

"Hey, slugger, how you feel?"

Ethan tried to get up, but his head was spinning and his equilibrium wasn't reset yet. "Great." Ethan's voice was gravelly and sarcastic.

Ascot energetically grabbed his arm and helped him up onto his feet. "Hey! You made it to Level Two on your first time. That's damn good." Ethan stumbled over and leaned against the ropes. Ascot handed him a plastic bottle of water and continued. "You looked pretty good. A few times you even resembled an actual boxer."

Ethan nodded, sure that Ascot was trying to make him feel better after a mechanical doll had just kicked his butt.

"Now check this out." Ascot climbed under the ropes and sat down at the touchscreen computer terminal and typed in a few things. The ring got dark, and two three-dimensional holographic images appeared. It was Ethan and the Ultimate Sparring partner standing in the middle of the ring. "Isn't this cool? You can now analyze everything you did in the ring and learn from your performance."

Ethan watched in amazement as his doppelganger bounced around silently in front of him.

Ascot explained. "The Holographic Playback Unit can freeze any frame, go in slow or fast motion, and present the fight from any angle, including the perspective of each fighter."

Ethan climbed out of the ring and sat in a ringside seat. "Normally I would be riveted, but right now I feel like puking."

Ascot got up from the touchscreen, "I'll give you some aspirin." Ethan followed Ascot across the gym floor to the nutrition center. Boxes were stacked up all over the room on tables, countertops and the floor. "I started unpacking some of this stuff last night." A large glass refrigerator stood behind the counter, stocked with a wide variety of drinks Ethan had never seen before. Ascot went behind the counter and rummaged around while Ethan sat at the counter stool. "Here you go," Ascot handed Ethan a pack of pills and then pulled out a drink from the fridge.

Ethan examined the drink in his hand. It was a black and yellow octagon cardboard container with large red letters that said, "Liquid Fire, extreme energy drink." Ethan read the ingredients like he always did before drinking or eating anything, a habit he had learned early on from his dad. He continued to examine the container, trying to figure out how to open the unique pop-top. "What are all these proprietary blends of branch chain amino acids and medium chain triglycerides?"

Ascot pulled another drink out of the refrigerator and examined it. "Hmm. There's a lot of unrecognizable stuff. I know Eden, Inc. makes all its own supplements, very expensive and very exclusive. 'Proprietary blends' means it's one of their secret formulas."

Ethan washed down his vitamin pack and aspirin with a swig of "Liquid Fire." "This stuff tastes pretty good."

Ascot stepped out from behind the counter and tossed Ethan a peanut-butter-banana high protein nutrition bar. "You have to see this."

Ethan hopped off the stool and tagged along down a hallway to a series of storage rooms. Ascot opened the door grinning, waiting to see Ethan's reaction. "Holy crap!" Ethan exclaimed, "It would take fifty people ten years to eat all this!"

The room was packed from floor to ceiling with boxes of nutritional supplements. "Everything you can imagine is here: pre-workout energy, post-workout protein, muscle builders, fat burners, even supplements to make your hair grow."

Ethan walked around the small remaining space in the middle of the large storeroom and surveyed the boxes while he ate his bar. He turned and looked at Ascot, who was staring into a box he had just opened. "What's up?"

Ascot looked frightened. "I think I just found some stuff I wasn't supposed to." Out of the box he pulled a six-inch-thick stack of what looked like individually wrapped Band-Aids. Ethan stared at

Ascot, waiting for an explanation. It certainly didn't look like any big deal. Ascot looked Ethan in the eye and spoke calmly and clearly. "These are growth hormone patches made from the pituitary glands of human beings. In order to make these, you've got to crack open someone's head and slice up their brain."

"Ooo, that's gross..." Ethan was both disgusted and intrigued, and without thinking he reached out and grabbed a patch.

"They're extremely expensive and very illegal," Ascot continued. "A few years ago a bio-lab company was taking bodies from war torn areas of Africa and the Middle East, then selling the parts on the black market. I heard about the development of the pituitary patch as a means to try to reverse the aging process."

" Wow." Ethan looked at the patch in his hand like it was radioactive.

"The company responsible was never revealed because they are so protected and politically connected. I think that company might be Eden, Inc."

Ethan handed the patch back to Ascot like it was contaminated. He was about to put the last bit of peanut-butter-banana bar in his mouth, but stopped to reconsider. "Hmm.... Why would they do that?"

"Think about it. It makes sense because, among other things, Eden, Inc. is a large military contractor. It profits from war, it lobbies to start them, it arms them, and it supplies mercenaries to fight them, so why wouldn't it harvest the bodies of soldiers and civilians who die in them?"

Ethan decided after all to pop the last piece of the peanut-butter-banana bar into his mouth. "Huh? It's possible I suppose." He said skeptically while chewing.

Ascot looked very worried. I doubt Eden, Inc. would be keen on us knowing that they are behind this."

Ethan thought about it a moment. "Even if it is them, dude, we're in space. Who the hell are we going to tell? And I really doubt they're worried about two guys who work in a gym."

Ascot stared hard at Ethan. He didn't like his conspiracy ideas being so easily dismissed. "Hey, whistle blowers end up mysteriously dead every day. Never underestimate the paranoia and power of a crooked company and the lengths they will go to shut someone up."

Chapter 19

"Entrepreneur, philanthropist, and visionary, Casper Degas, gave a moving speech yesterday at the First Baptist Church in Dallas at the funeral of his long-time friend Senator Isley Wilson of Texas. 'Isley was a forward thinker whose leadership and advice I respected and admired. I will miss him tremendously,' said a tearful Degas, who, along with the Senator's family, friends, and Washington elite, honored the 72-year-old senator who suffered a stroke and died in his Washington, DC office last Friday evening."

-J.D. Grab, Correspondent to the Washington Times.

A big smile came over Casper's face as he read the morning paper and sipped his coffee. "Page three. He didn't even make the front page." Casper walked out onto his balcony overlooking the Pacific Ocean. Flocks of seagulls were diving into the white caps then gulping down their breakfast of smelt and anchovies. Casper sat in a padded outdoor chair protected from the onshore wind by a large glass partition, admiring the breathtaking view.

"Nanobots," he thought. "How easy was that?" He was feeling good. He had successfully eliminated two key opposition votes. Senator Morales, after his humiliation and close call with death, had decided to change his mind and support the bill after all. Casper felt very empowered. There had been an obstacle in his path, and he had acted effectively and had taken care of it. That was what defined leadership: never giving up, never saying "no," never saying that "it can't be done." Casper felt unstoppable. He was on a short list of great men: men with vision, resources, and the tenacity to conquer anything that stood in their way.

When Casper went into business, he studied the lives and systems of the super rich: Ford, Rockefeller, Getty, Gates, etc. He concluded that they all had similar things in common. They all had insatiable ambition, they were all warriors in business, and they all controlled some aspect of an emerging technology. Now it was

Casper's turn. He was in position to become the exclusive real estate mogul of outer space, and he who controlled outer space would eventually control the world. Real estate was real wealth. Most of the super rich made their money in real estate or, at the very least, used their wealth from their business to invest heavily in it because they understood that real estate was a real asset that would always be in demand.

The way Casper saw it, borders were determined by weapons. Lines were drawn where one nation's weapons were pointed in one direction and the adjacent neighbor's weapons were pointed in the in other direction. Historically, wherever these two opposing forces settled were the imaginary lines that divided nations, economies, cultures, languages, etc. It only made sense that if one were able to point a weapon straight down on anyone, anywhere, anytime, for any reason, then those hard-won borders would instantly become irrelevant. Also, since most of the world used satellites for communication, whoever controlled space controlled the communication of the world. It was an innovative approach and one that was certain to pay off big. Space was uncharted territory, and its potential was unrecognized by just about everyone in the world, and of those few who were creative enough to see it, only Casper had the means to capitalize on it.

The Senate was scheduled to vote on Senate Bill 1425 later that evening. The icing on the cake was a series of earmarks added by Senator McDuff for a bunch of anti-terrorist provisions using space weapons and surveillance to help fight the War On Terror. He had explicitly stated that in order to compete in the new age of advanced technology, a new way of thinking and new tools to fight a war without borders and boundaries were needed.

This added bonus gave Eden, Inc.'s space weapons division even more power and opportunity to monopolize space. Casper was in the habit of buying favors from lawmakers and was well known for his lobbying efforts, working both sides of the aisle by giving targeted senators lavish trips, state-of-the-art equipment, and bundling together large campaign contributions. In return he got votes and earmarks that directly helped his business. More business meant more money, and with that money, he could buy more favors, so everyone involved saw it as a win-win situation.

While the Senate was in session discussing all the aspects of Senate Bill 1425, Casper was at the Eden, Inc. desert air base tracking communications satellites with a radio telescope. Even with Senators Wilson and Morales out of the way, he knew the vote was going to be close and he wanted to create an incentive for the senators to vote in his favor.

Casper closed his office door and made sure he was alone; his secretary was on her lunch break, as was most of the office. Now was the best time. He didn't want to be interrupted, and he certainly didn't want anyone to have a clue as to what he was up to.

He looked at his computer screen and decided on a target: a ten-year-old telecommunications satellite owned and operated by Eden, Inc. and fully insured. From his office computer terminal, Casper aimed the microwave laser cannon that was stationed outside at the far end of the compound, opposite the shuttle launch sight. The computer locked on, and within a fraction of a second, it calculated the exact distance, the speed at which the satellite was traveling, and the exact trajectory needed to make a hit. The calculations involved in hitting a fast-moving target in outer space from a fixed point on the spinning surface of the earth were immense. Casper smiled at how effortless it was going to be to pull this off.

His plan was really quite simple. That was the beauty of it. Casper was known as a visionary, a philanthropist, and an expander of technology. He had all the cover a guy could ever hope for. No one would suspect him and his company, particularly since it was one of his own satellites, and no one would suspect insurance fraud. It just wasn't done with satellites, even though the insurance payout would be more than enough to launch a brand-new satellite that ultimately would be more efficient and make him more money. Casper pushed the button, and the microwave laser cannon sitting alone in the desert sun blasted its silent and invisible payload into space. On his computer monitor Casper watched the satellite whiz through space at tens of thousands of miles per hour. Then in a blink of an eye, it vanished. A balloon message popped on the screen,
"TARGET DESTROYED!"

Casper smiled. That ought to inspire enough senators to vote for the bill. Within an hour there was buzz on Capitol Hill that there had been a terrorist attack on an American satellite and that cell phone service was severely disrupted. There had been no warning, and no group was taking credit for it, but speculation abounded. One rumor was that China had shot it down with a rocket to show America that they could. Therefore if any country tried to put a weapon satellite in space over Chinese soil, China could and would easily shoot it down. All Chinese official spokesmen strongly denied that they had had anything to do with it. Other speculators said it was Muslim extremists living in Afghanistan or Pakistan who wanted to cripple the West. Of course, they used more cell phones per capita than the West, so for any thinking person, that hypothesis was dumb.

Fox News led the midday news cycle with how this assault against America was tantamount to an act of war. It proceeded to show the devastating effects the satellite terrorist attack had on the lives of college students who were on Spring Break and partying in bathing suits in Miami Beach.

The Senate had taken a thirty-minute recess, and Senator John Fitzgerald was getting up from his desk in his office. He had just gotten off the phone with the Kentucky Senator's dickhead assistant who had demanded that Fitzgerald support his boss' ridiculous congressional committee findings or the committee would block Fitzgerald's bill, which was coming to the Senate floor for a vote the following week. Immediately after slamming the phone down, one of his aides told him the news about the satellite. In Fitzgerald's hand was a docket of bills the Senate was scheduled to vote on that day. At the top of the list was Bill 1425. Surrounding the bill's synopsis were his handwritten notes that he had taken during the Senate's discussion. He reviewed his notes: "Terrorist attack, global surveillance, them or us, a new frontier, sounds like bullshit."

He found it very suspicious that this should have happened on the exact day of the vote. "Qui bono?" he thought. "Who benefits? Probably whoever made the thing, so why aren't they looking there?" His mind was racing. "It wouldn't be the first time a country staged a terrorist attack on itself in order to push through a political agenda. It worked every time!" Fitzgerald knew he wasn't going to solve this mystery before the Senate took a vote, so he turned on the TV and flipped through the channels. Fox had a large-breasted coed in a bikini complaining that she had gotten lost in the city because her cell phone didn't work and now she had missed competing in the wet t-shirt contest and wasn't sure if she would have enough money to stay in Miami for the weekend. Senator Fitzgerald rolled his eyes and mumbled just loud enough for the 20-something office aide to hear. "My God, this generation is dumb!" but he had gotten his answer. The public knew about the attack, so if he voted against the stupid bill he would be labeled as, "Weak on Terror." His opponents would certainly use that against him, and consequently he would have to prove his anti-terrorist credentials constantly for the next five years. If it were a set-up, it had worked; the bastards had just put his balls in a vise.

That evening Casper got a call from Senator McDuff congratulating him on the outcome of the vote. McDuff's thick Southern accent and booming baritone voice sounded like the cartoon character Foghorn Leghorn. "My friend, you just hit the jack-pot!" croaked McDuff. Of course there was a quid pro quo angle to the call, so Casper quickly invited the Senator, his staff and their families to stay a week at any of the Eden, Inc. resorts anywhere in the world, all expenses paid. Casper hung up the phone and smirked, always amused by how things really worked in Washington. Casper sat back and mused, with a little manipulation and with very little public attention, Senate Bill 1425 passed 49 to 48 with three votes absent.

The Senate unknowingly had just created a tollbooth to outer space, putting Casper Degas in the position to own, control, and monopolize all the space surrounding the earth. The idea of owning space, to most people and to most of the lawmakers, seemed ridiculous, so no one really understood the consequences of the bill or took it that seriously; however, Casper was convinced his plan was foolproof. Before the airplane, no one had any concept or ever considered the idea of air space, but now it was a given. The same was true for outer space and satellite space. The more the immeasurable vastness of outer space became occupied and measured, the greater the need to take control of space. Casper was sowing the seeds of space domination and control. He knew he was holding the keys to the kingdom of the post-modern era.

Newton's Third Law of Motion states: "For every action there is an equal and opposite reaction." The blast from the microwave laser cannon had blown the satellite's solar panels apart and overheated the high output nuclear battery inside the satellite's main casing, creating a massive explosion that sent shrapnel soaring through space in all directions. Casper's concern about where that debris might end up wasn't a consideration whatsoever. Why would it be? There wasn't anything near it for thousands of miles. If any debris were to fall to Earth it would most likely burn up as it entered the atmosphere. If a piece or two did manage to survive, it would most likely land in the ocean and go unnoticed, so while Casper went out to celebrate his new status as the real estate mogul of outer space, a more poetic, even karmic, interpretation of Newton's Third law was playing out.

Chapter 20

At 10:00 AM, Captain Krovoza was awakened by an obnoxious ring. By the time he realized it was his phone, and then able to find it on the floor under some discarded clothing, it had already gone to voicemail.

Normally he was up at 6:00 AM, showered and coffeed by 6:30, and on the bridge by 7:00. He had spent the previous evening with Ricardo, the head chef, and had woken up with a headache and a vague memory of the previous night's events. He was alone in his bedroom, but there were several used condoms scattered around the floor. He stumbled out of bed and shuffled barefoot across the soft Peruvian wool carpet and into the extremely plush bathroom: with two sinks, a large infinity-style Jacuzzi tub, a separate nine-head shower stall with Italian mosaic tiles, a full body dryer that blew warm air all across his body, and a dressing area with a full-length mirror.

He got to the sink, splashed cold water on his face, and then grabbed a perfectly folded towel hanging on a rack next to the sink. Now that he was a bit more awake, he dried himself off, turned and stood naked in front of the full-length mirror, and looked at himself objectively. His love handles had grown some, and his upper body had lost some muscle mass, but not bad for a guy his age. He was still in pretty good shape. He was beginning to feel a little better about himself until he noticed some new strands of white hair, a new wrinkle on his forehead, deeper crow's feet, and pronounced bags under his eyes from staying up late and partying all night. His throat was scratchy, and his breath was horrific. "I'm too old for this bullshit!" he muttered. He went to the sink, put his mouth under the faucet, turned the handle, and felt the cool water pour down his throat. Feeling newly hydrated and invigorated, he turned on the shower. Instantly there was a loud rush of water from all the showerheads, and the room began to steam up. Before stepping into the multiple streams of water, he poked his head out of the bathroom and shouted towards the sitting room, "Coffee...Now!" The automated coffee maker switched on and began brewing.

By 10:45AM Krovoza was on deck in a newly-pressed Captain's uniform and polished shoes. No one would ever have suspected that he had been up all night drinking and fornicating. It was his routine to start his day on the bridge, to check in with all the department heads and to go though all the operating processes making sure everything was working properly. This typically took less than an hour; then he usually gave command of the bridge to his 1st officer, then spent the rest of his time on duty eating lunch, working out, and roaming around the resort.

From a navigation standpoint there was really nothing to do. The station was locked in a semisynchronous orbit, circling the Earth twice every sidereal day. It wasn't like being on a ship at sea where a captain had to steer the vessel and deal with unpredictable weather patterns and constantly changing currents. By comparison, a simple harbor boat cruise was a hundred times more involved than hanging out in this fully automated orbiting hotel. He missed the unpredictability of the ocean. Who knew that running the most advanced machine ever made would be so boring?

The first mate was exhausted. He had waited almost an extra four hours for the captain to arrive on the bridge. When Krovoza finally came, his first order relieved the first mate, who eagerly left to go get some sleep. The first officer wasn't due for another hour, so Krovoza had the bridge to himself for a while. The view on the bridge was spectacular. It was almost like stepping outside into space. The walls and ceiling were all polarized glass that changed its tint depending on the amount of sunlight. At the moment, the resort was in the shadow of the earth and received no direct sunlight, so the glass was completely transparent. As the resort travels around the Earth, and into the sunlight, the polarized glass becomes darker until its almost solid black, shielding the bridge from the Sun's light, heat, and deadly solar radiation.

Krovoza still felt wrecked from the previous night's events and wasn't sure where to start. He paced around the empty bridge staring out into space. This always made him feel ridiculously small and insignificant, which was a bit more than he could deal with in his current condition. His only logical means of escape was to distract his fragile mind by immediately getting to work. He sat down at the computer and logged onto the network. He glanced over all the ship's operating systems, checked all the updates, and then ran a few tests. Everything checked out normal. The ship was running perfectly.

The crew was preparing for the first batch of guests, who would arrive in thirty hours. So far everything was on schedule. Krovoza sat back in his chair and looked up at the glass ceiling at the Big Dipper. In his hyper-automated world, today was going to be yet another normal, uneventful, even boring day. He looked at his watch. In fifty-five minutes his first officer would arrive, and he could go wander around the ship. He logged off the network, and the screen went back to the desktop displaying a screensaver of the Valhalla Resort with the earth in the background and the Eden, Inc. logo underneath. He stared for a moment at the picture of the resort and admired the engineering genius that had gone into making the elaborate structure.

A second later the main computer screen at the front of the bridge started flashing bright red lights and an alarm went off. Krovoza's head was still a bit fuzzy. Loud noises and flashing lights had the same affect on him that Kryptonite had on Superman. He covered his ears and stumbled over to the main bridge terminal, which was dedicated to all of the ship's safety functions. Flashing on the screen was:

UNKNOWN INCOMING OBJECT!

Krovoza stared in disbelief. What the hell could be coming at them? He took a deep breath. Probably nothing. Besides, the resort was built to withstand the impact of small asteroids. It was probably just some outer space snowballs, and whatever damage they did, if any, would be minimal, and his crew could easily fix it, but he knew he had to be careful. NASA was having problems with tiny flakes of paint in space because even though the objects were almost insignificant in size, they could travel so fast that they could literally tear a hole through a space ship. He punched a button on the computer keyboard, and the alarm ceased. He looked out into the sky all around him, and he couldn't see anything moving. He didn't expect to see anything, but instincts were instincts, and he trusted his gut. The computer displayed the coordinates, size, and description of the objects and their arrival time.

He punched in the code to bring up a visual image of the objects as seen through a very high-resolution telescope. It looked like a spray of buckshot coming their way. This made no sense. For starters, asteroid showers almost always approached Earth straight on. This stuff was flying alongside the planet accelerating in an orbital freefall like a marble spiraling down a funnel. Dumbfounded, he tried to make sense of it. Mechanically he typed in the code to make the telescope zoom in. Instantly the debris came into focus. He noticed that it wasn't organic rock spinning and tumbling toward them, but rather irregular shapes of machined metal.

The speed, distance, and time of arrival were changing so rapidly that they looked like the numbers on a Norwegian gas pump. He tried to make sense of the blur. Frustrated, he froze the screen image. It said the debris was 11,287 miles away traveling at 58,071 miles per hour arriving in 11 minutes and 39 seconds. He stood and took a deep breath.

He would have to try to move the resort out of the way, but which way? Eleven minutes would be plenty of time. The computer screen automatically went back to the calculation window, and the numbers were a blur again, but now they were spinning even faster. Curious, Krovoza froze the numbers again. This time it read: 8, 662 miles away 71, 373 miles per hour arriving in 7 minutes and 28 seconds. Krovoza felt his stomach sink to his feet. The debris was rapidly accelerating. The images of the debris were now much closer and much clearer. He saw that the shower of softball sized shrapnel included a couple of large chunks about the size of a toilet bowl. He figured a satellite must have blown up, in which case, the metal was either titanium or depleted uranium. Either would tear through the Valhalla resort like bullets through a wet paper towel.

The screen showed that not only was the debris accelerating, it was also expanding like buckshot out of a 12-gauge shotgun barrel. He concluded that it didn't really matter in which direction he went. He just had to get the hell out of the way. Krovoza ran over to the Captain's chair, grabbed the joystick that controlled the main thruster in his right hand, and squeezed. There was a loud roar that resonated throughout the ship, and everything shook like an earthquake.

The only loose objects on the bridge were a small pile of magazines on the opposite side of the room and a coffee cup. They flew off a desk and scattered all over the ground. The rocket's G force pinned Krovoza against the back of his chair. He studied the screen. It seemed to be working. The objects were just a few seconds away, and he had just a little further to go. There was no time to waste. He squeezed the thruster, and again he felt his body slam into the chair from the sudden acceleration. He could only imagine what the rest of the resort looked like. "Everything on every floor of every ring must be a disaster," he thought. This sudden acceleration from a static orbit was not something the resort or anyone on board was prepared for. He would have to do a lot of explaining to smooth this over.

He sat and watched the debris on the screen rapidly grow. The numbers that displayed the speed and distance of the incoming objects were spinning much faster now. He gritted his teeth; he was going to do it. He was going to pull this off and get the resort out of harm's way. A spray of solar panels pieces passed over the glass roof just above Krovoza's head. He held on continuing to move the massive resort forward, assuming that there may be more debris to come. Before he could breath a sigh of relief the ceiling peeled open like a sardine can. All the chairs, couches, and computer equipment were sucked out like dust bunnies being vacuumed up from under a couch. Instantly all the air was gone and the pressure in his body expanded, making it impossible to breathe, then, as if grabbed by a giant hand, his body was sucked out into space. Krovoza's last thought was: "This was our maiden voyage. From now on, I will be remembered like Edward John Smith, Captain of the Titanic."

Once Krovoza was forcibly separated from the thruster, the rockets shut off, and the computer automatically corrected the speed of the resort to restore geosynchronous orbit and normal gravity. As it was correcting itself, another wave of debris came, blasting holes into the outer two rings like a grenade in an outhouse. The spinning rings instantly lost their structural integrity and started tearing and twisting apart. Within a few seconds, they broke into a dozen pieces, cracking off the main structure and flying off in every direction.

The third ring was now exposed and vulnerable. One of the large satellite chunks slammed, dead on like two billiard balls in a game of pool, into a liquid oxygen fuel tank. The explosion caused the entire twelve floors of the third ring to blow apart and turn into mulch. The small bottom ring that encircled the nuclear reactor was miraculously un-punctured. The shock wave shot the spinning and tumbling ring off into the depths of space.

Chapter 21

Massages were part of the amenities offered at the Valhalla resort gym. This seemed somewhat redundant since there was a fully dedicated spa that did nothing but massages, body scrubs, milk baths and all that froufrou shit that Ethan thought was ridiculous. None of the masseuses had arrived yet, so it was no surprise that Ethan and Ascot waited until the very end to outfit the massage and aromatherapy rooms. Everything was finally in place. All the gym equipment was set up, and the merchandise was properly displayed. All the VR (virtual reality) programs were operational. The previous night Ascot and Ethan had taken a moment at the end of the day to admire their work. They had spent three long days setting up what was, without a doubt, the most high-tech, amazing gym they, and possibly anyone, had ever seen.

The next morning Ethan arrived later than usual since there wasn't much left to do. Ascot had just arrived a few minutes before him and had just started doing some paper and computer work. Ethan went and grabbed a foam rubber mattress from the pool area and carried it into one of the rooms used for aromatherapy and massages. The rooms were oval shaped and just large enough to accommodate a massage table and a reasonably skinny person to maneuver around it. The walls were dark-brown, curved, and smooth, with built in notches for holding incense and candles. There were no lights. Other than the kitchen, the aromatherapy rooms were the only rooms on the space resort to authorize the use of an open flame. The rooms were intended to create a sense of peace, tranquility, and serenity, while every muscle in one's body was systematically pulverized.

Ethan had just stepped into the room when he realized that he really should have brought the massage table in first; since the mattress went on top. He looked around the oval room for a place on the wall on which to lean the mattress; since the room had no corners, he decided it really didn't matter.

Out of nowhere there was a deafening bang that shook the room then left if vibrating. It felt as if Ethan were standing inside a giant bass drum. Instinctively Ethan fell to the ground and covered his head. Being from California, the first thing that came to his mind was, "Earthquake! Maybe this was the Big One," the one that seismologists kept predicting was going to shake California off its continental shelf. Then Ethan remembered he was standing inside a space station thousands of miles away from Earth, let alone California.

The room shook again more violently, and the room lurched, the mattress fell on top of him, and he was thrown up against the wall. A fraction of a second later he heard another loud boom, followed by the screeching sound of twisting and tearing metal. There were more bangs, and the room jolted and violently shook in different directions. Suddenly airborne, Ethan tried to comprehend what was happening, but his mind was a jumble. His instincts were to try to keep from getting pounded as he tumbled around the room like a rag doll in a dryer. Inside the small dark room, he had no way of knowing what was up and what was down. For a moment he had stopped tumbling, and now it felt like someone was standing on his back. Ethan was stuck like a bug on a windshield against a rough textured surface. He guessed it was probably the ceiling. Unable to move, he felt the skin on his cheek begin to mold around the tiny bumps.

Suddenly, there was another loud boom. The room tumbled and Ethan was tossed spinning head over heals. Suddenly the artificial gravity ceased, he was instantly weightless, and his body bounced off the walls like a ping-pong ball in a bingo machine. Ethan tried to get his bearings, but it was pitch black and he had no idea which way was up. In the chaos, the mattress floated by and banged into him. He grabbed and hugged it tightly. The soft polished leather surface was cool against his cheek and it made him feel more protected.

He floated around in the dark, gently bouncing off the oval walls. Almost instantly, the weightlessness made him nauseous. He squeezed the mattress more tightly against himself and took a deep breath. The air in the room was getting stuffy, making his nausea worse; he wished the sickening feeling would go away. Then, as if he willed it, there was another explosion. The room rattled, and the concussion from the shock wave made his ears sting. Instantly, the gravity was back. Ethan fell to the ground hard, then bounced around like a human pinball. This time, he tried to use the mattress to help cushion the blows. He bounced from one wall to another, his exposed knuckles bumping against the floor and the walls. He banged his shoulder, then rebounded slamming into the opposite wall with the mattress taking most of the blow.

Finally he stopped moving. He was lying face down on the ground with the mattress on top of him. The mattress felt surprisingly heavy, so much that he assumed that there must be something more piled on top of him, but the room was empty. The only thing he could imagine was that the massage room walls had collapsed upon him.

He lay in the dark for several long seconds, recovering, trying to make sense out of it all. He took a series of deep breaths trying to calm himself down as his heart pounded deafeningly in his chest. Instinctively he rolled over, looked up, and saw a sliver of light coming from the ceiling. He realized that it was the crack between the door and the floor, so he was lying on the ceiling. With great effort, he felt around the rough surface. The ceiling had a small vent a foot and a half from his head; he grabbed it. Holding something solid made him feel more in control and less lost. Now he could start to feel the cuts and bruises he had acquired.

Just as he was getting adjusted to being squished against the ceiling, a loud blast erupted, a sound similar to a rocket taking off. The room started to turn up-side-down, or was it right side up? Ethan felt his body begin to slide. He held tightly to the vent. Now the ceiling had become the wall, and he was hanging on the side of it. His mind was so revved up that he had no concept of time. A fraction of a second seemed like minutes. He continued to hang onto the vent while the room rotated; the mattress fell away from his body and landed below him. He couldn't tell how far down it was and he wasn't sure if he should let go, but the room continued move. His body began to slowly peel away from the wall until he was dangling from the ceiling.

He hung there for what seemed like minutes, the gravity growing stronger and stronger. It felt like he was holding the weight of two people, then three. Finally his arms and fingers gave out, and he fell from the ceiling onto the floor, a distance of only two feet, but when he hit the ground, it stung his feet as if he had jumped off a roof. He immediately collapsed and fell against the mattress. He felt extremely heavy and could barely move. With great effort, he spread his arms and felt the cool, smooth surface of the floor. Trying to orient himself in the dark, he looked around the room as best he could with his face pressed against the mattress. He gazed down toward his feet and saw the crack of light. The door was now behind him.

A panic started to run through his body, something similar to claustrophobia. He remembered freaking out as a kid during a game of hide-and-seek. He had hidden inside a clothes hamper; his sadistic friend, knowing he was inside, had sat on the lid and wouldn't let him out. Now Ethan was experiencing that same boxed-in feeling. Knowing that panic wasn't a valuable option, he had no choice but to relax and clear his mind. Exhausted, Ethan closed his eyes and passed out.

Chapter 22

Gurgling in a puddle of drool, was the first thing Ethan noticed when he woke up immobile and delirious. He could have been unconscious for minutes or days. His body hadn't moved an inch and he was still squished against the leather mattress, his knees and knuckles swollen and throbbing. Ethan took inventory and concluded that the majority of his body was in pain. There was the distinct acrid smell of blood in the room. "Not a very therapeutic aroma," Ethan thought. The irony made him laugh. In the hierarchy of survival, massages, milk baths, and aromatherapy were low on the list.

The puddle of drool had increased and was bubbling during each labored breath, making breathing more difficult. Ethan turned his head upward and felt the warm liquid run down his cheek. The second it touched his ear, it grossed him out and he was motivated to get the hell off the floor. He slid his hands next to his chest as if he were going to do a push up, when he tried to push up it felt like five people were sitting on him. He couldn't budge. His hands just sank into the mattress.

As a kid, Vince once took him to the pier in Santa Cruz California, one of the last ocean-side amusement parks in the state. There was a ride there called the Cyclone, where the passengers stood against the wall of a cylinder that spun around. As it picked up speed, the centrifugal force pushed the riders up against the wall, then the floor dropped down leaving all the riders suspended against the wall, like a bug. As a kid, Ethan was amazed by it and thought it was the coolest ride ever. He wasn't sure what was happening to the resort, but it felt like he was on that same ride; however, instead of being stuck to the side of a wall in a twirling cylinder, laughing with his friends, he was stuck to the floor in a dark room alone somewhere in outer space.

Ethan took a deep breath, and tried to clear his head. He needed to get up and figure out what happened and what to do about it. He tried lifting his head and couldn't; clearly something was wrong. How could he be so weak? This frustration gave him a surge of adrenalin, which coursed through his body raising him to a new level of determination. He began to rock from side to side, building up momentum, and then with a big push, he rolled off of his stomach, out of the foam, and onto his back. The hard floor banged his shoulder blades, but it was the pain of progress and Ethan welcomed it. Again Ethan rocked back and forth a few times, pulled up his legs, and rolled onto his knees. He really felt the bony part of his knees hit the floor, which seemed unusually hard. His eyes had adjusted to the dark. The tiny crack of light that came in through the bottom of the door made the dark walls shimmer ever so slightly.

Ethan looked around to assess where he was in the small room. He determined that he was basically in the middle and crawled a few feet towards the door, knowing that there was a door handle that he could use to help him get up onto his feet. Each move shot a pain up his legs. When he got to the door he reached up and felt around for the door handle. He grabbed it. His hand was sticky from the half-dried blood that covered his fingers and palm, blood that had oozed from his knuckles.

He tried to pull himself up but the handle came down and the door was pushed outward. It felt like a flashbulb went off in his face. He couldn't see anything for a few seconds as his eyes adjusted to the light in the room. The swinging door had bounced against the wall and was now coming back to close him in. Not wanting to be stuck in the room again, Ethan crawled forward, head-butted the flimsy door as it swung back, and made his escape.

He continued to build momentum on his hands and knees as he moved down the hallway towards the main workout room. As his vision came into focus, he tried to wrap his mind around what he was seeing. He had to do a double take. The last thing Ethan saw before he stepped into the small massage room was a very impressive gym that he and Ascot had spent the last week assembling. Now the gym was a surreal abstract sculpture. Equipment was scattered around the room as if they were bowling pins after a strike. All the virtual reality bikes, rowing machines, and everything else that wasn't bolted to the floor, were nowhere near their original locations. The walls of the gym were gashed and dented. The fancy smoked Plexiglas partitions were all either shattered or cracked, and small bits of safety glass littered the floor like confetti after a parade.

He stopped crawling short of the carpet full of glass, his hands and knees hurt, he lay on the floor for a minute to relax and catch his breath. "Ascot!" Ethan tried to yell, but only a weak wheezy voice coughed out of him. He waited, listened, and heard nothing.

He rolled onto his back, staring up at the pummeled ceiling. He cleared his throat, "Ascot! What the hell's going on?" Again he waited and listened. No answer. After several minutes, Ethan got tired of lying on the floor. A few feet away was a banister separating the gym from the hallway to the pool area. Ethan got back up on his hands and knees. This time it was a bit easier. He crawled over and braced himself against the banister.

Ethan always admired the level of concentration his dad had when he would try to squat his max and break his record. Before tackling some enormous weight, Vince sometimes would take several minutes to get into "the zone." Ethan took a deep breath and concentrated, focusing on using as much explosive power as he could muster. He was about to try to stand up, but he lost focus. The situation seemed ridiculous, he wasn't squatting a thousand pounds, he was just trying to stand up. What was the big deal? He blocked that out of his mind, and quickly got back into the zone. Grabbing the banister, he pulled himself up onto one knee, then with a loud grunt he pushed up as hard as he could. Once he got both feet under him, he felt his balance and pushed up. It felt like the last rep in a heavy set of squats. His legs shook, but he got up, got balanced, and felt the weight against his feet.

"Now what?" He licked his lips. His tongue was dry and he tasted blood, he couldn't tell how banged up he was. The first thing he wanted to do is drink some water and get cleaned up. He looked around the room. Down the hall and past the pool were the locker rooms. Across the room in the opposite direction, considerably closer, was the nutrition center. Scattered all around were hundreds of nutrition bars, bottles of drinks, and packages of vitamin supplements. It was as if a giant piñata had exploded on one side of the room. He headed towards it.

Thirty-five laborious steps later, Ethan arrived at the nutrition center, covered in sweat. Without breaking stride he slipped onto one of the barstools that was bolted to the floor in front of a counter. He felt the weight of his torso press against the bottom of his spine; it forced him to sit up straight. Strewn across the lunch counter were various food items. Ethan grabbed the closest two he could reach. An energy bar and a protein drink. The plastic drink bottle lay on its side and bulged like a water balloon. He assumed that the strangely deformed container had gotten tossed around and squished in the accident. He picked it up. It was much heavier than usual. On further inspection, he noticed that the container couldn't handle the weight of the liquid inside it, and it seemed as if it was going to burst any second. Fascinated, he turned the bottle around and watched the plastic expand and contract as the liquid moved around the container.

"That's not normal," Ethan thought, as he opened the protein drink and took a sip. It tasted the same as it did the day before, but felt thicker going down. He opened the energy bar. It was compressed to just a bit more than half the thickness it was normally. He took a large bite. It was much tougher and harder to chew, but tasted the same. Ethan wolfed down four bars and two drinks as he surveyed the wreckage that used to be the most sophisticated and coolest gym on or off the planet, and wondered, "What the hell do I do?"

He wasn't sure what exactly happened, but it was obvious that however the artificial gravity on the station worked, it was on overdrive, making everything much heavier than normal. Which means a blow from something that would normally be inconsequential could be fatal. He needed to find Ascot and anyone else who might know what had happened, and what to do next.

Ethan looked around, not sure where to start. Not many people typically occupied the lowest and smallest ring of the resort, so if there were any, he hoped that they would still be alive.

Chapter 23

Minutes after eating the Eden, Inc. energy bars Ethan was hyped up and ready to explore the wreckage. He twisted his body to get off the stool, and a sharp pain shot up his side. His whole body ached, his hands were still covered in drying blood, his clothes were torn and grungy, but he had no idea how badly he might be hurt.

Once, a guy at the original Venice Beach Blood-Sweat-N-Tears gym dropped a 50 lb. dumbbell on his head while doing flys. He laughed it off and drove home with nothing more than a lump on his forehead. That night, he went to bed early and never woke up.

Ethan considered that he really ought to see what kind of shape he was in. He decided he would first clean himself up and make sure he was ok before he went looking for anyone. He stuffed his pockets with some more bars and grabbed a bottle of some red colored drink, then slid off the stool. Extra gravity was no longer a surprise, so now it didn't seem as difficult to move across the floor. He looked down the hall and realized that the shortest way to the locker rooms was through the swimming pool and spa area. Mechanically, he headed down the hall.

The door was heavy and hard to move—he really had to lean into it like a football lineman in order to get it open. Inside the pool deck area, everything was soaking wet, and all the lounge chairs were stuck together in a big pile in the back of the room, like an abstract Tinker Toys sculpture. All the tossing had obviously sloshed all the water around, consequently the pool was now only a little more than half-full.

Ethan was instantly more relaxed the moment he set foot into the room. The room was warm, steamy, and had the clean smell of ozone. He walked past the pool and headed towards the men's locker room. A cushion from one of the lounge chairs, that was now a part of the sculpture, lay in his path. Each step he took was labored. He didn't dare deviate from the direction he was headed, so he stepped into the cushion kicking it into the pool. When it hit the water it made a weird splat and the normal ripple effect didn't happen, instead the water wiggled like half-cured Jell-O.

When Ethan arrived at the steps that led into the pool, it was like the Sirens calling to Ulysses. Before he knew what he was doing, he was slipping off his shoes, pulling his shirt over his head, and unbuttoning his pants, letting them fall to the ground. Still wearing his underwear and socks, he stepped out of his pants, grabbed the handrail, and stepped down to the first, then to the second step leading into the warm water. The surface tension of the water felt as though there were a plastic film on it. When Ethan first put his foot into the water it bent awhile before it gave way. He was so sore that he just wanted to relax in the warm water. He didn't notice that the water failed to splash as high as it would have normally. He just knew that it felt good, and it seemed thicker, kind of like swimming in a warm milkshake.

The water took the weight off his body. He pulled off his socks and underwear, wrung them out and tossed them onto the deck next to his clothes. He examined himself: he was covered in scrapes and bruises, a few cuts that were already beginning to congeal, but nothing serious. No gashes or anything that would require stitches. He washed away all the dried blood. The good news, if there was any, was that he was in a germ-and-dirt-free environment so he probably didn't have to worry about infections.

Ethan grabbed the clothes from the side of the pool and rinsed them out. Blood leached out of them and made small, slowly-moving swirls of red in the water. Once the clothes stopped oozing blood, he wrung them out and tossed them on the deck. He swam around in the oddly thick water, watching in fascination how the water didn't splash or move normally. Finally, he stepped out of the pool feeling very refreshed.

Inside the locker room were a pair of swimsuit dryers, Ethan stuffed all his clothes in the two little machines, and then ran a half-dozen spin cycles. Eventually his clothes were 95% dry. He put on the damp clothes and stepped into the full body wind tunnel dryer. Within a few minutes he and all his clothes were warm and dry. He stepped out feeling a little guilty, like perhaps he shouldn't be feeling so good. Who knew what condition the other people on board were in?

He remembered what airline flight attendants always said: "Put your own oxygen mask on first before you help others." Wasn't that all he was doing? Making sure he was in good enough shape to help others? That's not selfish, that's just practical. He opened the red drink with the intention of taking a sip and guzzled half the bottle. After swimming and drying, Ethan's body was surprisingly dehydrated, so the cherry-flavored drink with a big jolt of sugar and electrolytes soothed his body and tasted great. "Okay," he decided, "it's time to find Ascot."

Ethan walked back to the nutrition center and thought about his situation. The only way he was going to survive was if he got strong enough and fast enough to adapt to this crazy situation. He thought of all the supplements that his dad sold at the gym; some worked really well, while others didn't work at all. Scattered all around the floor were bottles of all kinds of muscle building and dietary supplements. He remembered when he had stocked them all and had read all the labels. Eden, Inc. had a huge variety of supplements, some with ingredients that Ethan had never seen or even heard of before, he couldn't tell if they were synthetic steroids or natural herbs bundled together in a "proprietary blend," then called something else for marketing purposes. That was very common. For example, almost every sports nutrition company has their own proprietary version of protein: some micro-clustered, triple-filtered, branch chain, assimilated, free-form version of milk, egg whites, or soy.

Vince was always saying that these things were fairly meaningless. After all, the human body has been assimilating and converting food into energy and new cell growth for millions of years. He repeatedly said, "So long as you provide the lumber, your body will build the house." Vince didn't think anyone should worry about those types of nutritional products. "They were all just food!" but drugs were different. One needed to be very careful when doing any kind of sports-enhancing drugs.

Ethan thought about his situation; he had to admit it was pretty unique. He remembered a movie where a girl and a guy were hitchhiking across the country, it was the middle of the night and they were stuck in a rainstorm with no money and no food. The girl says, "I have a credit card, but I can only use it for an emergency." The guy points out: "I think this qualifies."

Ethan picked up a bottle of Dyno-Flex Super Muscle Growth formula. They were probably nothing more than amino acids but if they were synthetic steroids he didn't care. If there was ever a time to take them, now was it. The pills suggested two in the morning and two at night. Ethan had no idea if it was morning or night, so he took four, then put the bottle in his pocket.

Ethan laboriously walked across the gym to Ascot's office. If he was in there during the accident, the desk and all of the office furniture would most likely have crushed him. With trepidation, Ethan opened the door. The room looked ransacked. The built-in filing cabinet's doors were open, the floor was covered in papers, the desk and chairs were on their sides, the computer and all the pictures that had been hanging on the walls were on the floor, but there was no sign of Ascot. Relieved, Ethan closed the door and scanned the floor. Rubble was everywhere.

"Ascot!" His voice echoed down the hallway. He waited and heard nothing in return. Every step was a huge effort. He took a few, and then leaned against the wall to rest. He wiped the sweat off his forehead, took a few more steps, then mustered the energy to continue the search. It was taking him hours to cover an area that should only have taken fifteen to twenty minutes. "Ascot!" Nothing. The only sound was the reverberation of his voice through the ramshackled rooms.

Frustrated, he knew Ascot had to be here. In the morning he and Ascot were often the only people on the bottom level. The restaurant and spa people didn't show up until after lunch, if they showed up at all; their facilities were set up and ready to go and they had little to do until the guests arrived. Occasionally a maintenance guy would come down to get something out of one of the storage areas where they kept plumbing, heating, and various kinds of maintenance equipment. Ethan didn't particularly like those guys; they were very cliquish and, for whatever reason, he didn't fit in. But now, Ethan was eager to see anyone.

Ethan lumbered into the hallway that led to a row of storage rooms. It was littered knee-high with pamphlets, spa products, nutritional supplements, cleaning equipment, restaurant gear, PVC pipes, plumbing tools, and broken furniture. Overwhelmed by the daunting mess, Ethan leaned against the hallway wall and took a deep breath.

"Ascot?" This time there was a ripple in a pile of massage brochures and individual shampoo bottles in the middle of the hallway. A burst of adrenaline shot through Ethan. He took large strenuous steps towards the pile, trying to navigate through the debris. After a few yards, he lost his balance and crashed into the wall. He grabbed hold of a door jam and managed to stay on his feet. The pile moved again slightly. Ethan took another deep breath, regained his balance, and then attacked the pile.

Ethan methodically began to remove the debris. Everything was much heaver than normal and his hands quickly became tired. When he finally uncovered Ascot's battered body, Ethan had lost all the strength in his fingers and could barely pick up anything more.

Ascot's face was bruised and beaten. His pants and shirt were spotted with blood. Blood flowed out of his nose and his left ear. His left arm was twisted and bloody, and his legs were facing the opposite direction of his torso. Ethan clenched his jaw and tried not to show any emotion. He wiped the sweat from his forehead and leaned towards Ascot. "Hey! Can you hear me?"

Glazed and disoriented, Ascot turned his head toward the sound of Ethan's voice. He moaned, then turned his head back to its original position, coughed, and then mumbled, "I can't feel my legs."

Still struggling to keep his cool, Ethan figured now was not the time to tell him that it looked like his lower spine had been twisted and broken, and that he probably would never walk again. "We gotta get you off the floor," said Ethan, as he finished removing the remaining debris from Ascot's legs.

He grabbed Ascot's feet, and with a grunting heave, he flipped and pulled Ascot's legs so they faced the same direction as his torso. The instant Ascot's legs fell into place and his body was aligned, he simultaneously burped and farted. It was so unexpected that Ethan started to laugh.

Ascot cracked a weak smile. "Hey, relax" he said, through bloody lips. "It's Newton's third law: For every action there's an equal and opposite reaction."

Ethan burst into uncontrollable laughter, breaking the nervous awkwardness between them.

Ethan remembered that down the hall in Ascot's office was an office chair with wheels. That could serve as Ascot's transportation until they could find something better. Ethan leaned back off his knees and into a squatting position, then with great effort, he pressed himself up onto his feet. "I'll be right back."

Ascot was now lying on his back; he watched in surprise as Ethan struggled to stand up. "What the hell happened?"

Ethan looked down at Ascot, who only hours before was a vital figure but now seemed fragile. "I don't know exactly, but we are living in a whole new reality."

Chapter 24

Moving Ascot out of the cluttered hallway was the first challenge, where to put him was the second. The best thing Ethan could think of was to use the women's locker room as a makeshift hospital; it had running water, toilets, sinks, and a large dressing room with chairs and a couch, but most importantly, it was closer and bigger than the men's.

Ethan dragged the massage mattress, complete with his drool and blood stains, out from the little massage room and into the women's locker room. It was considerably heavier and much more difficult to move this time around. The locker room wasn't in too bad a shape—other than a few empty trashcans and a dozen towels scattered around the room, there wasn't much that wasn't bolted down. Ethan cleaned the room, found a place for the mattress and made a sort of bedroom for Ascot. "It's fortunate," Ethan thought as he worked, "that we are living in an environment where the temperature is constantly 78 degrees Fahrenheit, so there isn't much chance of us suffering from hypothermia."

Once everything in the locker room was in place, Ethan went back to Ascot's office to find the office chair with wheels and a first aid kit. Fortunately the chair was sitting on top of the pile of debris, and just as Ethan began to dig through the clutter to look for the first aid kit, he heard a moan echo from down the hall. He stopped his search and dragged the chair out of the room. It was banged up, but the arms, seat and wheels worked fine.

Ethan rolled the chair down the hall as far as he could, and then started clearing a path. It took a long time to move the clutter. In this new environment, the simple act of bending over and picking something up was exhausting. Having the chair to lean on and to use as both a wheelbarrow and walker helped a lot.

Finally there was a path through the clutter. The next challenge: how to get Ascot onto the chair and then wheel him to the locker room? Ethan had constructed a staircase from stacks of paper and boxes that led up on to the chair. Ethan would have to: sit Ascot up, bear-hug him, then heave his paralyzed body up in stages. Even without the extra gravity it would have been a challenge. Everything was in place and Ethan was gearing up to lift Ascot, but Ascot's clothes were soaked in blood and smelled really foul. Ethan realized he had just washed all the blood out of his clothes and didn't want his only clothes to get dirty so soon.

Ethan was considering taking his clothes off when he spotted a box of coveralls that the maintenance guys wore over their uniforms when they did any kind of grimy job. Inside was a one-size-fits-all type of attire—white, baggy, lightweight and warm, it functioned like a body condom. The box was taped tightly shut. Ethan rummaged around for something to cut it open with. Fortunately, within seconds, he found a pair of scissors and a box cutter. After getting the box opened, he pulled out a pair of coveralls. Keeping all of his clothes on, he climbed in, zipped it up, put the scissors and box cutter in the coveralls' side pocket, then went back to help Ascot.

Ascot was barely conscious, which was probably a good thing considering it wasn't going to be a comfortable ride. Ethan squatted, pushed, pulled and slowly edged Ascot up the makeshift staircase. Finally, after much strenuous heaving, a limp, delirious Ascot sat slumped over in an office chair in the middle of the debris-filled hallway. The coveralls Ethan had on didn't breathe and he was roasting hot, soaking wet from sweat and covered in Ascot's blood. Ethan leaned against the barely conscious Ascot, in order to catch his breath and gear up for the next challenge.

After much effort, Ethan finally had pushed Ascot to the locker room. Ethan was getting used to seeing objects fall to the ground much faster and harder than usual, and was concerned about getting Ascot off the chair without dropping him. Ethan wheeled the chair next to the mat and tried to ease Ascot off as best he could, but Ascot was extra heavy and hard to control. He fell out of the chair and hit the mat hard on his back. Speckles of blood flew out of his mouth. Ethan was glad Ascot was delirious; most likely, he wouldn't remember much.

The lighting in the middle of the women's locker room was much better and Ethan could see Ascot's wounds much more clearly. Ascot looked and smelled really bad. Ethan knew he needed to take action, but didn't know where to start. He went back to the office and dug through the rubble until he found the first aid kit. Inside were bandages, hydrogen peroxide, antiseptic cream, needles, sutures, antibiotics, and painkillers.

A few years earlier, Ethan had been walking home late at night from Blood-Sweat-N-Tears and stumbled into a scene where a kid, who was a Mexican gang-banger with a shaved head and covered in tattoos, had been shot several times in the stomach. The kid was bleeding, confused and stumbling around an empty lot. When the paramedics arrived they grabbed the kid, strapped him on a gurney, and started slapping him on the face to keep him awake. They were asking him all kinds of questions, and without hesitation they cut off all his clothes with a pair of scissors and tossed them in the gutter. Ethan was startled at how brutal and matter-of-fact the paramedics were. In an attempt to emulate them as best as he could, he grabbed some towels, pulled out the scissors he had put in his pocket and began cutting off all of Ascot's clothes.

Several wet towels and lots of scrubbing later, a naked Ascot lay on the mat. All the blood and feces had been cleaned off of him and hydrogen peroxide had been poured on all the cuts and abrasions. Most of his scrapes and gashes were small and, for the most part, had stopped bleeding; except for one very deep cut on his left thigh just above the quadriceps. Ethan figured he'd gone this far, what the hell? He might as well stitch him up.

The needle and sutures were sealed in a disposable sanitary pouch. He opened it and was assaulted by the strong smell of alcohol. Ethan was surprised at how tough skin was and how hard it was to push the needle through it. Ascot's leg twitched as Ethan tried to sew him up, making the job all the more difficult.

Ethan had once removed stitches from his dog, Brutus, when Vince couldn't afford to go back to the vet to have them removed professionally. He and his dad had put the dog on the kitchen table, cut the sutures, and then pulled them out with tweezers. A surprisingly valuable lesson now, Ethan remembered that each stitch was a separate suture with its own tied knot. Ethan gave Ascot seven stitches about an eighth of an inch apart. When he was finished the gash was sewn shut and the wound had stopped bleeding. Ethan pulled gauze and tape out of the first aid kit and smeared antiseptic cream on all the wounds, covering up all the larger ones with bandages. When he was done, he covered Ascot with two thick fancy spa towels, and then put a folded one under his head as a pillow. At this point, there wasn't much more that he could do. Ascot was asleep.

Ethan was sore and covered in sweat; he leaned forward with his arms locked on his bent knees and stretched his back muscles. He watched sweat fall off his forehead at double speed and splatter onto the white tile floor, then he stood up straight, grabbed a towel, wiped his face, and slipped out of the bloody coveralls. He had no idea how much time had passed since he'd last eaten, but he was hungry again. The thought of eating another protein bar had no appeal. He started walking and before he knew it, he had an energy drink and a protein bar in his hand and was headed towards the diner next door.

Ethan's legs were shaky from the strain of the extra gravity, but he had gotten his balance and was walking a bit more easily. He walked past the beauty salon and looked in the window. It looked like a tornado had landed in the room. Ethan had no interest in exploring it. That was for another day. Right now he was interested in food.

The diner's décor was a retro 1950s space-age look: red and white vinyl built-in booths, linoleum tables, chrome stools and counter tops. The good news was everything was still in its proper place as if the accident never happened. Ethan walked past the rows of booths and counter tops and through a pair of swinging doors into the kitchen.

Everything was brand new: the large walk-in refrigerator, freezer, oven, stove, griddle, sink and counter tops were all shining virgin stainless steel. In the middle of the kitchen was a pile of pots, pans, blenders, slicers, mixers, utensils and all kinds of commercial kitchen stuff that wasn't locked down. Under the pile was a pool of blood. When Ethan saw it, he instantly became aware of a foul smell and a shiver ran up his spine.

Ethan was surprised that a dead body wasn't particularly scary. Ethan stared, fascinated, as it just lay there. Ethan recognized the guy. He had seen him in the crew mess a few nights before. He was probably in his mid twenties, short, stocky, with straight hair. Ethan wondered if it was racist to assume he was Mexican because he worked in a kitchen. Ethan thought for a moment. He couldn't remember the last time he had seen a busboy anywhere in Los Angeles who wasn't Hispanic. It was part of the class system in America that was taboo to mention.

Ethan felt bad that he never spoke to the guy and knew nothing about him, not even his name. He stared at the dead body for a while. He had never seen a real dead person before and was surprised at how mundane it was, even with all the cuts and broken bones, he looked like an ordinary guy lying there.

After all the work of digging him out, there was no acknowledgement or appreciation, just a lifeless corpse that needed to be dealt with. The shirt on the corpse was all twisted. Ethan grabbed the back of the dead man's neck and lifted the torso up so he could try to straighten out the shirt. The corpse was very heavy. Consequently Ethan couldn't hold him up very long, and was therefore only able to straighten the shirt slightly, but in the process, he saw that the dead man had a tattoo on the back of his shoulder that said "Arturo" in fancy letters. That reassured Ethan. The chances of the corpse being a Mexican had increased significantly.

Early in Ethan's excavation he found a large box of plastic trash bags and some packing tape. He doubled up two trash bags and stuffed the body in headfirst. That covered a little more than half the body, and he covered the other half with another pair of trash bags, then taped them together. It looked like a body bag he'd seen on TV. The blood on the floor made the floor slippery, making it easier but messier to drag the plastic covered body over to the walk-in freezer.

The freezer was once neatly packed full of meat, ice cream, and potatoes, but was now in complete disarray. Ethan moved the randomly scattered food and stacked it neatly, creating a space in the corner for the body. There was no good place for a dead body on a space station and there was no way to jettison a body into space, so if he found any more dead people, they would have to go into the freezer with Arturo. Ethan wanted to think of the dead body as a guy with a name and not just a faceless corpse.

Ethan mopped up the blood then got the kitchen working well enough to fry up some cheeseburgers. He carried the burgers in a plastic basket to one of the diner's soft cushioned wrap-around red vinyl booths. He sat down and the bottle of Dyno-Flex super muscle growth formula bulged in a pocket making it very uncomfortable to sit down. He pulled the bottle out of his pocket and decided he might as well take some more. He needed all the damned strength he could come up with. The hot greasy burgers were heavenly. He didn't realize how hungry he had gotten. Every move he made in this mega-gravity environment was strenuous and he had burned many more calories than usual.

Within seconds after finishing his two burgers Ethan was deliriously tired, he had been operating on pure adrenaline. This was the first time he had sat down on a comfortable surface and had the opportunity to relax. Before he could ponder the question, "What am I going to do now?" He was lying on the booth's bench sound asleep.

Chapter 25

Casper Degas stepped into the tee box of the executive nine-hole golf course behind the main office building of the Eden, Inc. desert air base. It was 7:30 AM and the temperature was already approaching 95 degrees. Casper had the entire course to himself so he could work out business strategies in his head while he played.

The next day guests would be arriving from all over the world to be part of the inaugural opening of the seven-star Valhalla Space Resort. This was a turning point for Casper and a turning point for Eden, Inc., the culmination of over ten years' work and billions of research and construction dollars. Casper wanted to be prepared and in good spirits tomorrow, so while he was working on his golf game he outlined his speech.

The guests were the super elite, the top one-tenth of one percent of the world's wealthiest people. They expected, insisted, and were used to being catered to, in every aspect of their lives. Casper knew the importance of making a good first impression, so his speech would be both an investor's pitch and a presentation to make the guests feel special— the first to experience Valhalla's cutting-edge technology. Casper teed off and hit his first ball, straight down the fairway and onto the putting green. It was an outstanding shot and it put Casper in a good mood; then an idea popped into his mind about the next day's presentation. Casper grabbed his journal and jotted down some of the impressive innovations that went into creating the space station, but what really got the attention of the super elite, more than fancy gadgets, was security. He would be including a large section on the safety angle.

Casper put his bag of clubs on his shoulder and headed down the fairway to his ball. As he walked, he imagined speaking to the audience, which included members of the Saudi Royal Family as well as several of the internet and telecommunication tycoons. In his mind he reviewed the points he wanted to make, cleared his throat, and put on his most sincere smile to the audience of palm trees and sand traps.

"Ladies and Gentlemen, welcome to the most innovative and exciting experience of our lifetime. We are living in a new paradigm. No longer are we confined to exotic places of the world as our only destination for vacations and living. Our planet is overcrowded, unsafe, and financially and socially unstable. People of our status are constant targets and so much of our time, energy, and resources are spent dealing with security and safety. No more! We have now achieved what the Greeks saw in their gods. We can live among the stars, in unprecedented luxury. Valhalla is the first of our seven-star space resorts, where we can conduct business and live in a completely healthy and safe environment, away from all pollution, disease, and personal threats."

Casper looked around the course, practicing his eye contact. "Technology is blazing at an unprecedented pace and so is the growth rate of our world's population. There is no way to stop it or even slow it down. Overpopulation, natural disasters, poverty and crime are making the world worse each day. The only real solution is to create a new one. Yes, a new world. We have a ten-year plan to–"

An unusual buzz from his smart phone interrupted his speech; neither a ring, an announcement of a text message, nor a low battery warning. He was less then ten yards from his ball. He had just had a fantastic first shot and was eager to sink an eagle. Casper got to his ball, put down the golf bag, and grabbed his favorite putter, a gift from his grandfather. Then he shuffled alongside the ball, working himself into a putting stance. He decided he would first finish the hole, and then check his phone. Casper was feeling good, his concentration was high, and he was confident that he could sink the ten-yard shot. Just as he was about to hit the ball, his phone buzzed again, breaking his focus.

Casper swore, tossed the club to the ground, and grabbed his phone. He had an app that connected his phone to his computer; in case there was an emergency, the computer would call his phone. There had never been an emergency, so the app had never been used. He was pushing a few buttons, trying to remember how the program worked, when the phone's screen began showing a satellite video of space. Casper was confused. He zoomed in on the picture and realized that the debris from the big explosion days before had been orbiting the earth, continued to pick up speed, and was now headed straight towards the Valhalla space resort. He watched in frozen horror, his mind racing. Of all the times to be on a fucking golf course!

There was no time to react; impact would occur in a matter of seconds. The debris was traveling at thousands of miles per hour and there was no way to stop it. He watched the screen as the space station's rockets ignited in an attempt to move out of the way. This was good. Captain Krovoza was on top of it. Casper relaxed slightly. Krovoza was the best and this was why. Casper watched without breathing as the giant station moved from its orbit, as the debris came racing toward it.

Using his phone, Casper linked up immediately with the resort's onboard computer. He typed in his password, granting him access to instant-message whomever was monitoring the computer. "What's going on? Give me your status, NOW!"

Immediately there was a response. "Captain just ignited booster rockets, no...."

The computer went off line. Casper stared at the little screen, stunned, then went back to the app that displayed the satellite images. His heart sank. The screen looked like a cue ball had just broke a rack balls in a new game of pool.

The resort was designed to withstand a good bit of banging, but there wasn't much out there to prepare engineers to predict what might hit a space station. They anticipated the possibility of small meteors, but the statistical chances of getting hit by anything in the vast vacuum of space is over a billion to one, so this just wasn't supposed to happen.

Stunned, Casper forgot all about sinking the eagle. He mechanically put his putter back into the bag and started walking back to his office while he watched the accident over and over again, hoping for something to click and help him decide what to do next. The eighth time through, he noticed that while the first bit of debris was small and probably wouldn't have had a devastating affect on the station, by attempting to move out of its way to avoid any impact, Krovoza inadvertently put the resort right in the line of fire of the largest chunks of debris. Casper returned to the live satellite images and watched the pieces of the resort scatter and tumble off into the vastness of space.

Billions of dollars gone in a few seconds! Raising the Titanic would be a piece of cake compared to trying to rescue the Valhalla. He watched as chunks of the resort drifted further and further apart in every direction. There was no way to salvage any of it. The one upside was, better that it had happened today before all the high-profile guests had arrived. Chances were everyone on board was now dead, and even if they weren't, they weren't coming back. He was going to have to sweep this under the rug in a big way. He could cover up the deaths of a couple thousand nobodies. Had the movers and shakers had been on board, that would have been a different story.

Casper imagined being a fisherman, spending hours reeling in a prize-winning marlin, and just as the giant fish is about to be pulled on deck, a huge shark comes and bites it in half. In some situations there is just nothing you can do but move on. Casper entertained the idea that exploring and inhabiting space was a silly notion, but that idea only lasted for a brief moment. His gut was telling him that the future was in space. He just knew it. Wasn't it obvious? He could feel it deep in his bones. The ridiculousness of his doubtful thought only strengthened his resolve. He knew that he would find a way to turn this tragedy into a success, and that in the end he would succeed.

Casper walked off the golf course and onto the Tarmac. He looked over to the opposite side of the compound towards the shuttle on the launch pad. It stood proud and magnificent, a paragon of technology. There was no way he was going to let something this amazing go to waste. He had gotten so close; this was just a setback that he would have to deal with. All good stories have setbacks, but overcoming them was what made a person great, and there was no one greater then he.

To recapitalize and build a new resort would cost billions. Raising that kind of money in the private sector quickly was tough. He had to keep the accident quiet. If the public got wind of it his stock price would plummet, and that just wouldn't do. There was no time to waste. He had to think quickly.

First thing was to postpone the flight for guests. Upon reaching his office, he notified his staff to send out an announcement to all passengers, explaining that due to some technical and weather concerns, the shuttle launch to the resort would be postponed until the matter was resolved.

Safety first! That was always appreciated. The story's real purpose was to change the focus and put the attention on the shuttle, not the resort. After all of NASA's shuttle accidents, people would understand, and that would temporarily hold them off for a while; so long as he stayed in communication with his clients and gave them service with a smile, he knew he could get away with almost anything.

The next thing was to blame someone else. It worked before—every tragedy created an opportunity. Casper needed to find a convincing way to spin this one. Plus, he needed a good scapegoat and an angle to lobby Congress with.

Governments like to have an enemy; it's an easy way to control the population. After the last satellite incident that Casper had successfully blamed on the Chinese, US-Chinese relations were currently strained over all matters involving space. The irony was that the more China denied any involvement in the destruction of the satellite, the more the right wing spin machine twisted their denial to make them appear more guilty, creating more mistrust than before. The American corporate media was relentlessly making the argument that only America should be allowed to occupy space, for the safety and security of the world. Space should be a private American territory.

Casper had met with many of the Joint Chiefs of Staff and they had always liked the idea of putting weapons in space and claiming space as their own. Now that Senate Bill 1425 had passed and successfully overturned the JFK neutrality act that proclaimed space as a place where no nation could claim ownership or advance military plans, Casper and the Joint Chiefs were looking for ways to quickly take advantage of the grab bag they had just created. Casper was on top of his game.

This twist of fate made it possible for Casper to corner the market on the development of space. With the help of the Joint Chiefs, and the power of the United States Government preventing any other nation from claiming and occupying space, he could get the new Valhalla resort funded as a black budget operation, tap into the incredible Washington waste, and no one, not even the President, would even know about it. Casper had more than enough resources at his disposal. Building a second resort would be much easier and faster than building the first one.

He had everything he needed to appeal to Congress. He had enough congressmen and senators in his pocket and now was the time to cash in those favors and, if necessary, play more hardball.

Back in his office, Casper paced around the room thinking, grabbed his cup off his desk, and took a sip of his tea. It was cold. He reluctantly swallowed. He could pull out the terrorist attack card if he needed to, but that would make the station appear vulnerable and he didn't like that image at all. The Valhalla Resort should be a pillar of strength, security and elegance, not some cheap little prefab structure that can be blown apart by random space trash.

Casper sent a memo to his entire staff explaining their setback and outlining the directions they needed to take to get the space station and the company back on track. As far as covering up the disappearance of all the missing workers, Casper had a special crew for that job. They were the sort that didn't officially work for him. Casper pulled up a file with all the Valhalla Resort personnel, and sent instructions that all these people needed to disappear cleanly, quickly, and with no loose ends. If any friends or family members started poking around questioning their demise, he'd have to make sure they, and all records of them, vanished as well.

Thousands of people died every day, and many of those deaths were impossible to verify. Since none of the crew knew where they were going, they couldn't have told any of their friends and family where they were. So they could have died anywhere. The key was to make sure they died in a different country than their residence. That made it much harder for the family to investigate. They could make up several tragic accidents: a plane crash, bus or boat accident—perhaps even a terrorist attack, just so long as it didn't happen on any Eden, Inc. property.

Casper sat back in his chair. Little more than an hour had passed since the resort had blown apart, and the machinery of getting it all back on track was already in full swing. This is what separated the men from the boys: perseverance and determination. He was feeling confident that it would all work out and he would rise stronger and more powerful than ever. He turned and looked into the mirror and ran his hand over his bald head, wiping off a small amount of perspiration. He stood up, adjusted his collar and tie, and spoke to himself: "When you play in the big leagues, the stakes are high, decisions are hard, and you can't be squeamish."

Chapter 26

Human bodies have an amazing way of adapting. Ascot rolled across the gym strapped in an office chair, using a sponge mop like an oar. The backside of the mop had an abrasive fabric that gave him some traction when pushed against the floor. Enough time had gone by that the new extra-heavy gravity environment seemed normal to Ethan and Ascot. They could now move about all day without getting exhausted.

Ascot was constantly spouting off facts: "You know Harvard, or one of those universities that do research, put glasses on people and when they wore them everything was upside down, and it only took a few days before their brains put things right side up."

"Hmm." Ethan knew better than to respond and say something that would interrupt Ascot's flow, but Ascot needed acknowledging grunts to keep him going and to ensure that he was being heard.

"The brain can cope with almost any challenge. That's probably why human beings have adapted and have inhabited every continent and climate on Earth."

"Yeah!"

"Who in their right mind would live on the North pole? But the Eskimos do it. If that's not determination and innovation I don't know what is."

"Sure."

"We are adapting to a climate of being squished, and it's not just our brains adapting—every cell, all our muscles and organs, are under tremendous pressure. Our heart has to work much harder than normal to pump blood through our body."

"Makes sense." Ethan had no idea if Ascot knew what he was talking about, but he knew better than to challenge him on it. If he wasn't knowledgeable about these things, he was certainly passionate, and Ethan, who really didn't care, was no match for him. Ethan's concerns were to get things done so they could survive.

Ethan had searched all accessible areas for more survivors and found no one, alive or dead. The ring had ten levels. Each level was separated with pressurized doors in case there was a pressure leak. Then all the air would be sucked out into space and everyone on that floor would be instantly killed. The computer, as well as several other redundant systems, monitored the pressure and all the other aspects of the environment for safety. If there were any kind of breach in the system, the doors would immediately shut, quarantining any damaged areas.

All other nine floors had pressure leaks, so Ethan and Ascot were the only survivors, confined to the bottom level of the bottom ring of the once magnificent Valhalla Space Resort. Miraculously, everything on their level was still working.

In one respect, they were lucky that the bottom level was almost empty when the accident occurred. This meant they didn't have to share their finite amount of food and medicine with anyone, but it was also very lonely.

Ethan made himself busy by constantly cleaning and putting things back in order. It was also a way for him to distract himself from their uncertain future. They had no idea where they were. They were the first humans to actually be lost in space. The chances of them ever being rescued were highly improbable. Ascot's opinion was that it would be very difficult for them to actually leave the solar system. He figured they were probably still within the earth's gravitational pull and were orbiting the planet like a satellite.

The bottom ring had one row of small observation windows, like portholes on a ship. As far as Ethan could tell they were nowhere near the earth. They were spinning through space and seemed to be moving extremely fast.

Ethan put Ascot's office back together. Remarkably, the computer terminal worked. Ascot was able to tap into the resorts mainframe server, which operated all the automated functions on all the floors of the ring. He tried to find a way to restore normal gravity, but the ring had no rocket thrusters, so there was no way to change course or stop the remains of the space station's momentum. Ethan and Ascot were being hurled on an uncontrollable freefall through space, and there was nothing they could do about it.

According to the computer's calculations, the gravity on board was 2.9 times greater than Earth's, and was increasing by .0024 Gs each day. The longer they stayed on board the more likely they would eventually become a puddle of skin and bones. Ascot wasn't sure if he should tell Ethan that they were going to be slowly crushed to death.

The only thing they could do was to stay ahead of the curve, and get stronger faster than the gravity increased. They were living in a true Darwinian world. Strength and adaptation meant their survival.

The only working clock was on the computer, Ascot monitored their sleeping schedule and discovered that on average they were awake for ten hours, then slept for ten hours, and about every three hours they ate something. They were living a twenty-hour day. Ascot was very wary of the two of them losing their minds and he knew that they needed structure if they were going to survive.

Ascot jumped into his old role as a personal trainer. He assembled all the Eden, Inc. bodybuilding products and created a regimen of supplements and diet for both of them. Ascot recommended that they take twice the daily dosage of the super-supplements, even with the shorter days. He constructed a workout routine using weights and the VR equipment to make sure that they got stronger as the gravity increased.

Having their days organized gave them a goal to accomplish, and it made the days go by quicker. Vince used to tell his fans, "Diet is the key to bodybuilding, but it's surprisingly hard to be consistent." With Ascot in charge, Ethan would have no excuses.

About a week before he had left, Ethan had been watching a program on the Discovery Channel about prisoners and how they adapted to penitentiary life. The irony was that the serious criminals, who had committed the most atrocious crimes and were sentenced for life, were generally more cooperative in prison. They had better attitudes and were much more skillful in adjusting to life in the penitentiary, simply because they knew they would never be leaving. This bit of trivia inspired Ethan to maintain a positive attitude; If he was going to make it through this, he knew he needed one. So, Ethan decided to do some of the same things that the prisoners had done.

He wanted to write a diary to keep track of all the days, and record their progress. The hallway walls were bright white and offered a large canvas, so the last thing Ethan did before he went to sleep was write what he had done that day on the wall. Ethan thought he was being resourceful, since there wasn't much writing paper and he didn't trust a computer that he couldn't back up. Ascot was trying to figure out where they were and how to get home. If the day finally came for them to leave, Ethan's plan was to just take photos of the diary wall so their story would be preserved.

Ethan enjoyed the routine of cleaning up and making the place more comfortable. It gave him a project to keep focused on, and something to write about on the wall. Typically, after spending most of the day cleaning up and moving extremely heavy objects around, he often didn't have much energy left. Ascot, having been a personal trainer for years, insisted that Ethan take list of supplements and follow a specific workout routine religiously, irrespective of anything he may have already had done that day. To appease Ascot, Ethan did as he was told, and the two of them would go through their daily exercise routine together. Ethan thought that Ascot just liked to yell at people and watch them sweat. Consequently, Ethan felt his strength improve and his body quickly adapt to the increasing gravity.

Ethan needed all the strength he could get, since there was no end to the mess. The place looked like the aftermath of a tornado and everywhere there was something to clean up. When a section seemed to be put back together, Ethan would discover a new level of clutter. Things he hadn't even notice before were suddenly obvious. It wasn't until he got the gym floor organized that he became aware of all the broken safety glass in the carpet. Just that alone took an entire day to clean up, even with the help of an industrial vacuum cleaner.

Each day as he organized the mess, Ethan would search through the rubble looking to find something that he could utilize in their quest to stay alive. This possibility of discovery kept his mind engaged, and gave him something to look forward to. As far as he and Ascot knew, no one had ever been lost in space before, so they had no idea what they would need to survive.

Ethan considered the idea that he and Ascot were creating a fascinating story, and if they ever did make it back to Earth they would become instant celebrities. Their story would be made into a movie, and everything they did and wrote on the wall that allowed them to survive would become known and would affect humankind. Ethan concluded that it was absolutely necessary to remain vigilant and optimistic, because what they were doing was important.

The first room to be put back in working order was the gym. Ethan was very excited when the gym floor was finally inhabitable. Now Ascot could roll around the floor among the weight machines more easily and participate in the process of organizing the place.

At first, Ascot spent most of his time on the mat in the bathroom, just dragging himself around the room any time he needed water or had to use the toilet. As he got stronger and started to adapt, he would climb into the office chair and push himself around with the sponge mop. Ascot was someone who had a hard time asking for help. Even paralyzed, he wasn't comfortable being dependent. Above everything else, Ascot wanted dignity and freedom. He wasn't going to get that living in a woman's bathroom.

As Ascot became more restless, it became apparent that they needed to find ways to make him mobile. Eventually they came up with a plan. Ethan gave Ascot a closet full of sheets. Ascot tore them up into two-inch strips, and then spent a few days weaving them together to make rope.

Ethan would check on him and watch him sitting on his chair, tying one end of the strips to a locker and weaving. He was remarkably adept at it.

"You look like you've done this before," Ethan commented.

"When I was a kid, we would have hair day once a week."

"Hair day?"

"It's something white people can't relate to."

"I wasn't sure you were black."

"Enough to have sisters who had lots of springy hair, so washing it and combing it is an all-day process. We would have hair day, especially when we were little. As we got older, my sisters all had braids and they would spend the day watching movies and braiding hair. I'm talking twelve hours straight of braiding hair. At some point a person, even one as determined as my mother, would have to take a break, so I got recruited more than once to be a designated braider."

"So is this bringing back old memories?"

"I just need some Mother's Pride Orange Soda, popcorn, and a shitty TV set with aluminum foil wrapped around the rabbit ears, and it'd be like going back in time."

Chapter 27

Once Ascot finished making a pile of rope, Ethan tied them to various objects throughout the bottom floor, making Ascot a pathway through and around the gym, into his office, out onto the hallway and to the diner next door. Ethan was able to cover all the usual destinations Ascot needed to visit. This was a big help. It was a lot easier for Ascot to pull himself around with the rope than to push himself around with a mop.

Ascot tried every possible thing he could think of to contact Earth. He sat in his office for hours scouring the onboard database from his computer, looking for some way to send a signal to a satellite and broadcast a message to Earth. Sometimes he would go so long that he would miss meals or not sleep. Ethan didn't want to interrupt him because when Ascot got frustrated, he would get angry. Ethan began to doubt Ascot's computer skills because nothing like a rescue signal was ever successfully sent. One time, Ethan checked in on Ascot and caught him playing video games, which he had downloaded off the mainframe. Apparently, Ascot had some advanced computer skills, but Ethan didn't see how playing Call Of Duty 4 was going to help them get home.

The escape pods, which were the space equivalent of lifeboats, were supposedly operational. They were designed to travel from the orbiting space station to Earth and not through the depths of space. It appeared that this was their one hope of getting home. The question was, where was Earth?

After much trial and error, Ascot was able to receive a satellite signal just long enough to determine the resort's trajectory. Essentially, they were floating through the solar system like a comet being pulled and tugged by the sun and all the planets—way out of lifeboat range. As best Ascot could calculate, it was going to take a few years before they would be close enough to Earth to attempt an escape on the life pods.

As it was, there wasn't much they could do but wait. Ascot calculated that they were continuously picking up speed as they flew through the solar system, so the window of opportunity to jettison might be only a few minutes. If they were asleep, they could miss it. The onboard computer was programmed, once it was within range, to automatically link to any of Earth's satellites like a laptop to a router. Ascot rigged the computer to set off all the fire alarms the moment the computer was linked to a satellite. That would let them know that they were within jettisoning distance from the Earth.

By the time Ethan had cleaned up and organized all the stuff that was scattered around their floor, the diary wall was a third full. By then Ascot was pulling himself around with no problems and they had adapted so well that they had forgotten what it was like living with normal gravity. By now the gravity had increased to almost six times the earth's gravitational pull.

They had successfully entered what Ascot called the maintenance phase of their survival on board. This was a time when things could get very monotonous, and that could be dangerous. Ascot would make sure they had goals set every day. Ethan started doing his exercise routine religiously, now that there wasn't anything major to clean up. Ascot was able to put his personal trainer hat on and spend two to three hours a day pushing Ethan to work harder. The fact that Ethan would exhaust his body kept him from being restless and with the extra strain he would naturally sleep ten hours straight.

Ascot encouraged lots of rest. He didn't want them to be tired and make stupid decisions. It was also important to have a strict eating schedule and balanced meals. They divided up their meals between the gym food and the diner food. They rationed it so they would have enough food for ten years. After that, they were screwed. Ascot was fairly certain that they would be within jettison range well before ten years.

For Ethan, this was the most consistent eating, sleeping, and workout schedule he had ever followed in his life. Vince always said that the hardest thing about bodybuilding was "Clearing out your schedule so you can do what it takes."

Ethan thought it was ironic that being shipwrecked, so to speak, was what finally got him away from the stress of his day-to-day life so he could finally focus on himself. Ethan felt mentally and physically better than he had ever felt before.

During their workouts, Ascot would often get on a subject and start ranting. He particularly would go off on medicine, society, and politics. Having been an activist for years, he was full of conspiracy theories and was very cynical about the political establishment.

Ethan really didn't have political opinions. He was one of those people who paid attention peripherally but didn't think about it too much. His life didn't seem to be affected by what happened in Washington, so like most people his age, he didn't care, but it was fun to listen to Ascot rant; also, it was the only entertainment on board. The gym was full of video monitors for the guests to watch while they worked out, but all the monitors received their signal from space station's outer ring. Needless to say nothing was being broadcast these days.

The only other things that resembled entertainment were the Virtual Reality exercise machines. The sheer need for human interaction was a motivation for Ethan to work out. He began to look forward to seeing new faces in the VR machines. There he could race people in exotic places all around the world on bicycles, rowboats, and cross-country skis. Ethan would get so caught up in VR world that he would spend hours at a time mountain climbing or bicycling.

Then there was the Ultimate Sparring Partner. It was something that he and Ascot could do together and interact with. Ethan wasn't particularly interested in boxing, but since there wasn't much else to do, it quickly became the most fun he had.

Ascot showed him some various combinations and with just that he was able to move up through the different amateur levels quickly. The punches of the Ultimate Sparring Partner seemed to be getting slower and weaker. In reality, Ethan and Ascot's brains were adapting to the faster speed in which things moved with extra gravity, and their bodies were getting stronger. Now Ethan could easily see the punches coming whereas before he couldn't see them at all, and when he got hit, it didn't hurt as much as before. The floating mannequin never used to budge when Ethan hit it. Now it wavered and was being knocked around from his blows. Ascot was impressed. "You keep this up, when we get back, you'll be a contender!"

After four years of training, Ethan had sparred with the greatest names in boxing history—everyone from Joe Louis to the Klitschko brothers. He got to fight Rocky Balboa and Apollo Creed, who weren't even real people. There were over a thousand names programmed into the Ultimate Sparring Partner, all of whom the floating mannequin could emulate, most of whom Ethan had never heard of. He wasn't a boxing fan, and only knew Joe Frazier, Muhammad Ali, George Forman, and Mike Tyson because they were household names and had movies made about them. Ascot repeatedly reminded him, "It's a good thing you don't know who these people are because if you did you'd be scared shitless."

Ethan had just knocked out a nameless fighter in the fifth round and was feeling good about himself. "I want to fight each person programmed in the machine, and beat him."

Ascot snickered, "That's impossible! You would have to become the greatest boxer who ever lived to achieve that goal."

Ascot's remark triggered a side of Ethan that even Ethan didn't know he had. He was determined to prove him wrong. It may have been a result of having a steady diet of pharmaceutical-grade proprietary-blend, pro-hormone, muscle-building supplements that pushed his testosterone level, and therefore is aggressive tendencies, to a new high.

Whatever the cause of his ambition, Ethan reacted by starting each day by lifting weights, then preparing and eating his first meal and taking the prescribed supplements. An hour or two later, he would either ride the VR bike, race someone on the VR rowing machine, or go VR mountain climbing. After that, it would be time to eat again, so he would prepare the second meal. Usually by then, Ascot would be restless and would want to burn off some of his frustration, after having spent most of his day supposedly working on the computer.

Ascot would start Ethan's boxing training by showing him some new moves and combinations. They would work on that for a while, then for fun Ascot would pick some unknown name on the Ultimate Sparring Partner roster and see what would happen.

Chapter 28

Ethan was starting to develop his boxing style. He had a very strong right hook, and he liked to go in low and close, and deliver a quick series of body blows. That gave him a bunch of points. He was good at faking left, then moving right, then sending a left jab to the chin, and delivering a strong right hook to the back of the head. With some opponents, he was able to achieve a knockout with this combo.

"You can only fool an opponent once with that move," said Ascot repeatedly, until it became almost his mantra, but it was one of Ethan's best tricks; since each opponent was new, it worked. Ascot was constantly telling Ethan to use proper boxing technique, keep his guard up, stand toe-to-toe with his opponent, dodge and block the jabs, and practice his combinations. Then try to recognize which combinations his opponent was using. For Ascot, it was more honorable to box well then it was to pull a few shady moves and win.

Ethan didn't share that opinion. His goal was to win, and all he cared about was watching his points increase. The computer kept track of every aspect of every fight and cataloged all the statistics, so after a few years of fighting an opponent every day, Ethan had an impressive record. Ascot would remind Ethan, "You can't compare your record to anyone else. No real boxer has a championship bout every day," but Ethan just wanted to make the numbers go up and he didn't care how he did it.

Ethan was fighting a light heavyweight named Asphalt Tucker who was knocking the shit out of him. Neither Ascot nor Ethan had ever heard of Asphalt, and they weren't sure if he was even a real guy. Asphalt was fast, hard to hit, hit hard, and he never let his guard down. Ethan couldn't get in close enough to do his signature body blow move and none of his other usual strategies were working, so he wasn't scoring any points.

Ascot started yelling at Ethan from ringside, reminding him to use proper technique. Ethan stood toe-to-toe with Asphalt and sparred with him, trying to block his relentless, fast, and hard-hitting jabs. Ethan was quickly tiring. After a couple of rounds, Ethan realized he needed to change his strategy. When round six began, the bell rang and Ethan sprang out of his corner, trying to make the first move to get Asphalt on the defensive, and on the ropes. Ethan started with a series of fast left jabs; Asphalt ducked, blocked and landed a blow to Ethan's stomach. Involuntarily, Ethan doubled over and Asphalt hit him with a right hook, knocking him to the floor. Ethan lay on the ground trying to catch his breath. The clock was counting down 10, 9, 8, 7, Ethan looked over at Ascot, who shook his head. "Stay there — don't hurt yourself."

Something deep within Ethan was enraged. He hated the idea of just giving up. Maybe it was a piece of Vince's stubbornness, or his mother's passionate Latin genes, but Ascot's words made him furious. Ethan had survived the impossible. He was living, adapting, and thriving in an environment that no other human had ever experienced before. He knew that he could do more. Growing up, Vince had often said to him, "Winners go the extra mile."

Lying face down in the middle of the ring, he felt his body start to recover and burn with adrenaline. Ethan was pissed off, he wanted to show Ascot what real determination looked like. He wasn't about to let some unknown yahoo, named after a street surface, get the better of him. 6...5...4, Ethan rolled onto his side, took in a deep breath and held it, giving his cells new oxygen. 3...2, just as Ascot relaxed, knowing that the fight was over, Ethan sprang up and clobbered Asphalt on his left ear, knocking him off-balance, surprising even the computer. With newfound strength and determination, Ethan started unleashing the combinations he had practiced every day for the last six years. Now he was beating the crap out of Asphalt Tucker. Ethan got in close and landed eight fast, hard blows to the stomach. Almost any real person wouldn't be able to stand after a barrage like that.

Asphalt did a rope-a-dope and immediately Ethan backed off and waited in the middle of the ring for his opponent to come after him. He wasn't going to exhaust himself while his opponent relaxed on the side. Seconds later, Asphalt bounced off the rope and came after Ethan. Ethan stood his ground and waited near the ropes until the charging bull was two arm lengths away, then Ethan charged back.

The unorthodox move even confused the computer, programmed to fight in the styles of over a thousand boxers. Ethan buried his head down and put both gloves straight out in front of him as if he were diving off a high dive. Then he leaped forward and rammed Asphalt straight in the jaw. The next thing Ethan realized, he was lying on his back and the Ultimate Sparring Partner was lying down beside him. The board was counting down. 10, 9, 8, this time Ethan got up as fast as he could, then stood and watched the board continue to count 4...3...2...1. A siren went off and K.O. popped on the screen in big red letters.

"What the fuck was that?" Ascot looked bewildered." That's not boxing! That's scrapping with a toy!"

"Hey, I won, didn't I? You wanted me to stay down and lose!"

"It's not just about winning, it's how you win that also counts."

"I've heard you say a thousand times, 'Politicians don't care how they win, and no matter how ugly the win is, at the end of the day, they're the ones sitting in the office. So, how is this any different?"

"This is a sport, and sports are about honor."

"Did I break any rules?"

"Technically, I don't think you did."

Ethan got down on one knee then opened his arms wide like Al Jolson in the last verse of "Mammy." "Well... Then I won fair and square. Isn't that the friggin' point."

Ascot pushed himself away from the ring and towards the Ultimate Sparring Partner's control panel. "Let's review your performance before I pass any more judgment."

Ethan crawled out of the ring as Ascot reached over to push the replay button. Whatever the outcome, Ascot would review the fight on the 3D playback, showing Ethan what he did wrong and what worked. Ascot gave Ethan his usual pointers. When the sixth round came and Ethan was lying on the canvas, then sprang up at the last second, Ascot laughed. "That's a move you can only do once in a great while. I have to admit I didn't see it coming and you surprised the hell out of me." He looked at Ethan and gave him a thumbs-up gesture.

Ethan finished taking off his shoes. "That's a good thing, right?"

Ascot nodded. "The element of surprise is always good. Keeping your move a surprise is tough—your opponents will start to expect it."

Ethan and Ascot did this routine every day; it kept them both busy and happy. They both felt like they were growing and getting something valuable out of the situation. After their boxing session, Ethan would write on the wall, usually describing what he had learned in the ring, and then he would go to sleep.

The clothes that Ethan had been wearing when the resort blew apart had fallen apart years earlier. Most of the sports apparel that the gym had for sale was for women and were all too small, so Ethan started wearing the jumpsuits that were used by the maintenance people. There were several boxes full of them, clean and reasonably comfortable. When he first tried to work out in one, it had gotten too hot, so he made some modifications, starting by cutting off the legs and arms to make a jumpsuit with cutoffs and short sleeves. It was comfortable but looked ridiculous. It was something he imagined a guy marching in West Hollywood Pride Parade would wear. He tried all kinds of variations. He cut them in half like a karate dojo, made some with long pants and short sleeves, and vice versa. After a while, he didn't care what they looked like, no one was looking, so long as he could stay warm when he felt cold and stay cool when he got hot, he was happy.

Chapter 29

Buzzing and ringing jolted Ethan out of a deep sleep. The deafeningly loud fire alarm was announcing something important. His room was pitch black. Groggy, he tried to turn on the light, and knocked over his bedside table and lamp. The obnoxious noise was painful and disorienting. While fishing around in the dark, trying to find the light switch, he stumbled: banged his toe on something hard, lost his balance, and fell into the wall. He got up, fumbled around the room until he finally reached the door to the dimly-lit adjacent room.

About four years earlier, Ethan had turned part of the spa next to the gym into his private bedroom area. He liked the fact that the lights in the spa's main room had a dimmer switch. It was much more relaxing then the harsh bright lights of the gym. He had turned a massage room into his sleeping area. The room was very dark and had an air vent that ran constantly, so the room stayed cool and never got stuffy. He slept on a large massage mat, wearing his designated sleeping jumpsuit, under a pile of large spa towels.

When Ethan arrived at the gym, Ascot was quickly pulling himself across the floor into his office. A second later, the loud clanging bells of the alarm stopped and Ascot came rolling out into the hallway, very excited. "Shit! We don't have much time! We've been picking up speed and our proximity to the earth may only last a few minutes, so we need to hurry!" Ethan was up, but didn't feel awake. He was very used to his routine of sleeping for ten hours and there was never any reason to wake up early.

His last day on board! It didn't feel right. He assumed that he would have time to get his things together for the journey home. He walked over to the nutrition center and pulled a bulging, yellow, octagon-shaped bottle out of the refrigerator. "What about the wall?" Ethan asked. "We need to take a picture of it!"

Ascot stopped pulling himself across the room and looked at Ethan incredulously. "Forget it, we may not have enough time. Let's go look!"

Ascot and Ethan hurried to the porthole windows in the observation deck on the opposite side of the ring. The rope didn't go that far so Ethan pushed Ascot down the hall. Ascot didn't like being helped, but he didn't have time to argue. Looking out the window made Ethan dizzy. The ship was tumbling so fast that the stars were out of focus. Ethan took a deep breath, stared out the porthole and forced himself not to get dizzy. Every few seconds a blue ball whizzed past their view. Ascot grinned. "That's it! We're back! We're back!"

Ethan couldn't say anything; he was on the verge of throwing up. The Earth was about the size of a silver dollar in the porthole and was getting larger quickly. Ethan swallowed, a sour taste in his mouth. "It looks so far away. Is it safe? Can we make it?"

Ascot looked at Ethan sternly. "We are getting closer by the second. I calculated our trajectory a long time ago. Apparently I was a little off. We must have really picked up speed, because I wasn't expecting to get into this position for almost another year. Our increased speed would mean that we've interacted with the other orbiting bodies and were pulled slightly differently than I predicted. Now it looks like we might be headed straight into Earth's orbit."

"Isn't that good?" asked Ethan, "Then we won't have to go so far in the escape pod."

"You don't get it!" Ascot's voice registered panic. "If our chunk of the ring hits the earth's atmosphere at the speed we are going, it will be like a 747 nose diving into the ocean at supersonic speed."

Ethan looked out the spinning porthole again and sure enough the spinning planet was closer.

Ascot continued. "If we eject from the pod too late, we'll be traveling too fast and we run the risk of smashing into the atmosphere and disintegrating."

Ascot pushed himself away from the wall and rolled down the hall back towards the gym. Ethan immediately followed and started pushing his chair, keeping up the momentum and getting him back to the main floor where he could pull himself around with the ropes. "Grab whatever you need and let's get to the escape pod in five minutes."

Ethan looked at his bare feet. What did he really need, some shoes and a bag of food? "Okay, see you in five minutes." It seemed like an anti-climatic ending to their life of eight years in space.

As Ethan gathered his things, he was surprised at his reluctance. He had been fantasizing about leaving every day since the day of the accident, yet now he was finding it kind of difficult. This stupid place, which was like being in a glorified prison, had become his home. He was happy and comfortable, and he knew what to expect when he woke up each day. Now he was stepping out into the unknown.

He turned on the light in his bedroom and looked around the room. What did he need? He changed into a brand-new red jumpsuit with a Valhalla Resort logo on the chest, the last one in the box. It was a special day, so he might was well be as dressed up as he could. The only shoes that Ethan had that were still in decent shape were a pair of bright blue boxing shoes with a red stripe on the side, so he put them on.

He stepped out of the bathroom and into the dimly lit lobby and looked around for the last time. He had spent so much time and energy cleaning up the place that he had gotten attached to it. He grabbed a shiny silver Mylar shopping bag that the spa used, and quickly stuffed it with drinks and nutritional bars. "That should get us home," he thought, not really sure, since he had no idea how long it would take to get back to Earth.

"Lets go!" Ascot shouted, as he pulled himself towards the escape pod. "We don't have much time. We are on a collision course." The image of burning alive, then falling to a fiery death, motivated Ethan to pick up his pace. He opened the hatch and stepped into the pod.

One of the first things he had done when they were putting the place back together was to outfit the escape pod. Ascot wanted Boy Scout preparedness in case they had to bail out unexpectedly. Now Ethan double-checked the water and food supply that had been sitting and waiting for this day, and put his Mylar bag of goodies next to it. There were some blankets and a long jacket— made specifically for working in the walk-in freezer. They seemed to have enough supplies to last a while in case they landed somewhere away from civilization.

This was it, the real deal. Ascot sat in the pod doorway with a sponge mop in his hand and a briefcase on his lap. "How the hell do I get in, and where the hell do I sit?"

Ethan laughed, only to be interrupted by the fire alarm, which put an abrupt stop to it.

"We have to jettison now," Ascot said calmly but firmly. "I set the alarm to go off five minutes before we get sucked into the earth's gravitational pull and go down in flames."

Ethan grabbed Ascot under his shoulder and hoisted him off the chair. Having no options, Ascot allowed Ethan to carry him down the five steps into the pod and plop him into the first seat. The two sat motionless, the buzzing alarm reverberating throughout the hall and into the pod. Ethan leaned over to quickly catch his breath, his head resting on the seat next to Ascot, then like a well-trained machine, he jumped up and shut the hatch.

Instantly the sound of the buzzer disappeared behind the composite metal and glass door. Ethan went through the exiting procedures that he had practiced a hundred times before. Like a robot programmed to do one particular function, he pushed a series of buttons and pulled levers that powered up the pod, turned on the computer, and disengaged the pod from the station.

Ethan and Ascot watched and waited, but nothing happened. Ascot slid across a row of seats to look out a porthole, "What's not working? Why aren't we jettisoning?"

Ethan went over the procedures quickly, retracing his steps. "I did everything right. I don't know what's going on."

The Earth was now large in the porthole and the resort was traveling fast towards the stratosphere where in few minutes the friction from the outer atmosphere would tear them apart and shower the planet with fiery fragments.

Ethan stared at the control panel, "I don't know what else to do—I did everything right! We should disengage and float away."

Ascot looked at Ethan, who was perplexedly going over his process, trying to sort it out. "Maybe the accident bent something and now the pod is stuck." Ethan nodded and stopped. "Then we have to try another pod."

As if on cue, they both looked out the window and saw Earth, now very large, spin past them. Ascot slid across several seats towards the exit. "Let's go! We don't have much time!"

Chapter 30

Ethan's ears popped from the pressure change as he opened the door; it was like going from the mountains to sea level instantaneously. Ascot's office chair was parked in front of the door. Ethan grabbed Ascot under his arms, and dragged him up the five stairs, his lifeless legs banging against each step as Ethan struggled. Once they were out, Ethan plopped him into his chair. The second Ascot's butt hit the seat, he grabbed his mop and pushed himself down the hall towards the nearest escape pod.

Ethan looked in the pod at all the supplies he had packed years before. Without time to restock the next pod, he quickly grabbed the Mylar bag, and then sprinted after Ascot.

It took less than a minute to open the door and drag Ascot into the new pod. Both of them were ramped up and everything seemed to be going in slow motion.

Ascot watched Ethan close the hatch and go through the exact exit routine. The pod hummed to life, the lights went on, and everything seemed to be going according to plan. The final step was for the door to close, sealing the station from the hatch, and then the two pieces would separate. They watched as the door closed with an audible click. But then nothing happened. Ethan scrunched his face into the hatch's porthole to look at the door's latch mechanism.

Ethan sat down, his heart pounding. "What the hell is wrong? It's doing everything it's supposed to do, but we just aren't pushing away."

Ascot slid across the seat, looking out the porthole at the quickly approaching Earth. "Maybe because we're tumbling, it's getting hung up on the side? Something to do with the increased gravity."

Ethan looked at Ascot. "So what do we do?"

"We need something to give us a big push."

"Like what? Explosives?"

"I don't think we need any; we just have to rig a way to keep the door open once the hatch is closed, then the inside pressure will push the pod out."

"But the pod won't disengage until the door closes!"

Ascot forced himself not to panic and just sat still. Ten seconds later he sat up and looked straight at Ethan. "This is what we need to do!"

Ethan, having trusted Ascot for many things that led to their survival, listened intensely.

"Go to my office and get the oxygen bottle out of the first aid closet, then get a dozen of those aromatherapy candles and a lighter out of the locker next to the massage rooms."

The tumbling pod's portholes were filled with a close-up view of Earth. They were dangerously close. With no time to question Ascot's plan, Ethan jumped up, pushed some buttons, and then began to manually unlatch the pod's hatch.

"Wait a second!" Ascot yelled. Ethan looked back at Ascot. "Does the health spa have any hairspray?"

"Tons of it." Ethan snapped back smartly.

"Get a couple of large canisters. Also we need something heavy, bring two 20-kilogram plates from the free weight area."

As the hatch opened, Ethan sprinted out of the door towards Ascot's office. In less than two minutes he was back with a green oxygen bottle about the size of a fire extinguisher, two white fluffy towels twisted into a knapsack holding a dozen candles, a couple of lighters, and two large canisters of hairspray. Ascot had crawled up the stairs and was sitting in the doorway. Ethan dropped the swag in front of him.

"Excellent!" Ascot immediately started organizing the stuff. "Now go get the weights!"

Ethan ran towards the gym floor and got two 20-kilogram weights from the bench press. When he came back, the oxygen bottle was lying on its side wrapped in a towel, with the canisters of hairspray tied above and below its nozzle. They were positioned in the middle of the doorway, right where the doors would come together. All around the stacked bottles were lit aromatherapy candles, giving the room a spicy, woody smell that, despite the imminent danger, made Ethan feel a bit more relaxed.

Ascot started to scoot his body down the stairs into the pod.

"Now, put the weights on the towel on the back and the side so it's secure." Ethan was still not sure what the plan was, but did as he was told. The bottle and canisters were packed tightly inside the towels with the necks sticking out, and the weights locked them in place preventing them from moving sideways and backwards.

Ascot crawled into his seat. "Let's try this again!"

Ethan was right behind him, pushing buttons and securing the hatch the second he got into the pod.

Both Ethan and Ascot held their breath as they watched the thick, solid door close, hitting the oxygen bottle nozzle and canisters. The door crushed the hair spray bottles slightly, but not enough to break them and the oxygen bottle nozzle held. The door just stopped squeezing. The pod didn't disengage and the seals weren't broken.

"Open it and close it again!" Ascot shouted.

The room started to get bumpy, which meant they were beginning to enter the earth's atmosphere.

Ethan opened the door, then closed it, trying to get as much power behind the door as he could.

Again the same thing; it closed and the nozzle held. The pod started shaking. They were being pulled in by Earth's gravity. If they didn't jettison soon, they would become a fiery meteor.

Ethan kept repeating the process. The room was getting hot and bumpy. After a dozen tries, he pushed the close button again, and turned to look at Ascot to tell him it wasn't working. As Ethan opened his mouth to speak, there was a click, the door closed, and a second later there was a loud bang. The nozzle on the oxygen bottle had broken off and both the hair spray canisters were easily crushed open. The fluorocarbons and pure oxygen instantly ignited, blowing the safety door open. The shock wave from the explosion finally pushed the pod away from the remains of the tumbling space station.

Instantly they were weightless. Ethan's ears rang from the blast. Disoriented, he floated away from the door and bumped into a nearby seat. He grabbed the headrest, his fingers squeezing deep into the foam, and anchored himself. Ascot was staring out of the window. Curious to see for himself, Ethan followed Ascot's lead and let go of the chair. He drifted over to the opposite window and stared in disbelief out of the porthole.

It was the first time either of them had ever seen the damage to the resort from the outside. What was once a magnificent machine was now a horrific pile of twisted scrap metal. They watched the tumbling mess float away, quickly getting smaller until it hit the atmosphere and broke into pieces. The tiny nuclear reactor that was in the center broke free from the ring and bounced like a beach ball before penetrating the earth's atmosphere. Ethan and Ascot watched in wonder and amazement as the reactor fell towards the planet, quickly becoming a glowing red-hot fireball. A few seconds later there was a gigantic blinding flash of light.

Ethan instinctively pushed away from the porthole to protect his eyes. He floated across the pod, banging into the top of the seats like a bingo ball. Blindly he groped, trying to grab hold of something so he would stop ricocheting. Finally, he caught hold of a seat back with his feet and stopped his momentum. Then he pulled himself down into the chair.

"That must have been noticed by someone," Ascot said, rubbing his eyes. "It's not every day a nuclear reactor explodes in the sky and a destroyed space resort rains down on Earth."

"So you think there will be people on the lookout for us?" asked Ethan.

"I'd say there is a very good chance of that."

Ethan was suddenly nauseous. Zero Gs didn't agree with him at all. He took several deep breaths, trying to calm his stomach. He floated over to a seat opposite Ascot, who was sitting in the driver's seat and had already secured himself by fastening his seatbelt and shoulder harness. They both turned and watched as the Mylar bag floated into the middle of the pod. Ascot unstrapped his harnesses, pushed himself into the air with his hands and with surprising grace floated across the room, grabbed the bag with one arm, pushed off the ceiling, and floated back to his seat. "Hey! I might as well take advantage and move about freely while I can."

Ethan, who was on the verge of throwing up, his head between his legs, cautiously looked up. "Absolutely!"

The pod had a manual thruster control in case the onboard computer didn't link up with the mainframe on the ground. Ascot assumed that since they had been lost in space for over eight years, the chances of the computer linking were not good, so he had been practicing this maneuver in his mind for years. The screen monitored their position in relationship to the earth. It showed that they were somersaulting, orbiting the planet in a Southwest arc until they came around and crossed some invisible line and then headed Northwest.

Ascot carefully grabbed the throttle. He watched the screen as they tumbled and began to count the tempo of each somersault. He squeezed the throttle and the pod's thruster rockets kicked on. Immediately the screen showed that the pod had stabilized and changed course. Their Southwest trajectory had moved North slightly, altering the angle of their orbit. Ascot fixated on the screen like a tiger stalking its prey. Ethan heard him mumble under his breath as he went through the steps: "That looks good.... We can stay on this course.... If I move the thrusters we should hit the stratosphere at a ninety degree angle...."

Ethan found himself praying. He wasn't religious or even sure he believed in God. He was praying that Ascot had a clue as to what he was doing. He knew that if the angle was wrong they could bounce off or break into pieces. When it came to re-entry they only had one chance and Ethan had to trust that Ascot would get it right, so if they could receive any help from some cosmic divine source, he was all for it.

Ascot had stuffed the Mylar bag of food under his seat. Now the bag was slightly open and a peanut butter crunch protein bar caught Ethan's eye. His stomach was in knots and the thought of food had no appeal. He thought about being back on Earth seeing his dad, Vanessa, the gym. "They must all think I'm dead. Will they be happy to see me?"

Or what about people in general? What was it going to be like to see and talk with other people again? The thought made him a little nervous. He was fairly sure that he wasn't crazy, but how do you know if you are crazy or not? He hadn't seen or spoken to anyone except Ascot for over eight years. They could both be out of their minds and how could they tell? He thought maybe he wouldn't know how to act around people. It is possible to be that out of touch with reality? He was comforted by the fact that if he thought he might be crazy, then he probably wasn't, because real crazy people think everyone else is crazy and they're the sane ones.

He had no idea what had been happening on Earth for the last eight years, so he was going to be ignorant of any current events or new technology. Of course all this worrying could be for nothing. They still had to make it through the atmosphere and safely land somewhere hospitable. If they landed in the middle of the ocean or on the top of the Himalayas, they'd be screwed.

Because they had to change pods, they no longer had any of the extra supplies and survival gear. This gave Ethan a nagging feeling. If Murphy's Law were to apply, now they would certainly end up landing somewhere where all that stuff would be absolutely necessary. He tried to block these thoughts from his mind and think positively. The Power Of Positive Thinking, wasn't that a book? Ethan tried to overlook the list of screw-ups and potential disasters that lay ahead and started mumbling positive affirmations.

A sudden violent rumble interrupted his affirmations, as the pod's rocket thrusters kicked on and shot the pod on a direct course towards Earth. Ascot tightened his seatbelt. "Let's hope this works, I just aimed us towards California. I was careful not to be too optimistic, so I aimed for the middle of the state. I didn't want to overshoot it and end up in the ocean."

Ethan sat up and looked out the window. "That was wise of you."

"In a few seconds we should—" Ascot's words were interrupted as the little pod shook like a paint can in a Home Depot mixer.

"—feel some turbulence?" Ethan finished Ascot's sentence.

Ascot sat back in his seat and let out a deep breath. "Let's hope this tin can is able to handle the journey! 'Cuz there's nothing more we can do but wait and ride it home!" Just then, the pod started tumbling. Both men grabbed the sides of their seats and hung on for dear life. Ethan felt dizzy and the pod started to get hot. He watched as flames blasted past his window. They clutched their seats, not saying a word, sweating profusely inside their jumpsuits. It was the most uncomfortable moment either had ever experienced. Ethan did everything in his power not to throw up, both from fear and nausea. Silently, he went back to praying.

Chapter 31

Staring at a computer screen, Julian Childs sat in an air-conditioned office in the middle of the desert. He had been working for Casper Degas for just over two years. Before that, he worked for Dimetell Systems Corp as a hacker. His actual job title was System Security Software Analyst. Dimetell Systems Corp made a wide array of electronic and computer equipment, but what made them unique was that most of their designs were stolen. The company would buy the latest and greatest doodad on the market, have their engineers tear it apart, and rebuild something just like it, only it would look different and be cheaper. The higher-ups at Dimetell started to get impatient and didn't want to wait for the products to come out onto the market before they could build and release their knockoffs, so Julian was hired to break into other companies computer systems and steal their design plans.

Julian was a super nerd. He was thirty years old but looked and moved like an old man. He was 5'9" with slumped shoulders, thinning hair, and a large, protruding Adam's apple. With bulky clothes on, he barely weighed 125 lbs. and had absolutely no muscle tone. The most strenuous thing he did on a daily basis was tie his shoes.

Julian was first introduced to Casper Degas when he was working in his private room at Dimetell, when out of nowhere, the heavy metal security door was kicked off its hinges. An extremely large and angry man who could have been a stand-in for Bigfoot filled the empty doorway.

He was delivering the message that Bigfoot's boss didn't appreciate people breaking into his company's computer system and stealing their schematics.

The Dimetell security guards and CEO who had tried to stop The Crusher from personally delivering this message had all been beaten within an inch of their lives. A similar fate was about to be bestowed upon Julian when a fit, well-dressed, bald man intervened and offered him an option. He could either be crushed like an egg by the gentleman filling up the doorway, who looked eager to oblige, or he could come with them and tell him everything he had done and explain how he had done it.

With a spine as ridged as an overcooked fettuccini noodle, his decision took less than a microsecond. Julian couldn't even stand up to the nerds in school who used to tease him about his name. They would call him Julia Child and ask him for recipes, so, without an ounce of resistance, Julian followed Casper and The Crusher out of the building, past a pile of barely conscious guards, and into the parking lot where they watched the Dimetell Systems Corporation building begin to burn to the ground.

Julian went to work for Casper. Casper liked him because he was efficient and detailed. His absolute lack of loyalty to anything meant Casper knew where he stood, so long as he paid Julian well, he would be reliable. Casper used Julian to break into various types of security systems to steal designs or get all sorts of private personal information on celebrities, politicians, and corporate CEOs. Julian gave Casper all kinds of ammunition and leverage he could use against his competitors and politicians. Besides digging up dirt, Julian was also responsible for monitoring the satellites and keeping them in tip-top working order. That was exactly what he was doing when he noticed something peculiar.

Julian wanted to believe in UFOs, but was skeptical by nature. It seemed that every UFO story eventually got debunked as being either a hoax or some misunderstood natural phenomenon. So, when a large object not following a prescribed orbit appeared on his monitor, he was both excited and suspicious. Clearly this wasn't a hoax.

He had special classified access to spy equipment. Most of the Eden, Inc. satellites were relays for cell phones and television transmissions as well as spy satellites that could read a license plate from outer space. Julian quickly accessed the closest satellite camera and focused it on the moving object.

He knew about the Valhalla resort; it was now just a sore spot in Eden, Inc.'s history. Its replacement was Asgard, named after the home of the gods. It had been in construction for over seven years now and was almost finished. This new resort was bigger and better than the first one. Photos, models and mockups of Asgard's elaborate furnishings and magnificent structure decorated Casper's office. Casper didn't allow anyone to call it Valhalla II, because it reminded him of the now-shrouded mishap that had destroyed his first baby. Julian looked to see if Asgard was online; thankfully it was.

Julian immediately recognized what he was seeing—the very specific construction had to be Valhalla's bottom ring. Dumbfounded, he stared at the screen. How was it possible that it could have been floating around in space for so long undetected? He watched in disbelief as the ring, with its nuclear reactor, hurtled through space. It looked like it was on a crash course to Earth. He reacted immediately. "Oh my God, Casper's going to be furious!" No one liked to be the one to give Casper bad news.

If the Valhalla Resort were suddenly to appear unannounced, that would have seriously bad consequences. However the chances that someone was monitoring that part of space, at that exact moment, were pretty unlikely. This wasn't something a person could see with their naked eye, but if they had to cover up their cover-up, that could get messy.

Julian double-checked to make sure that the satellite images he was receiving were being encrypted. He definitely didn't want any unauthorized person to stumble upon them. Then he pressed the record button to ensure Casper saw everything.

Julian reached for the phone. There were two numbers to reach Casper: the important number and the "drop everything you are doing and get over here" number. Julian hesitated. Did this warrant dialing the super-urgent number? He had only dialed it once before, when he got some new dirt on a senator just before Casper was going to have a meeting with the man. Casper didn't act like that particular incident was really worth using the "drop everything" number, so ever since, Julian was a bit skittish about using it.

Just as he was about to dial, he saw an escape pod jettison from the remains of the resort. Julian was flabbergasted, survivors on board? How could that be possible? It had been over eight years and God knows where in space they'd been traveling, but how else could a pod jettison? There could be no other explanation. Julian got a sinking feeling in his stomach. Casper was definitely going to be very angry.

In a trance, phone still in his hand, Julian watched as the two objects on the screen flew away from each other. The large ring was quickly pulled in by the earth's gravity— colliding with the upper atmosphere and breaking into pieces. The crash was spectacular and Julian sat mesmerized as a colorful rainbow of debris scattered across the sky.

Julian mumbled to himself. "This is very bad." He was so flustered that he stood up to look for the phone. He scanned the desk and around the room, then realized he was holding it. He knew exactly which number to use.

The phone rang and Julian's heart rate doubled. On the second ring it doubled again. Fortunately, Casper answered before Julian's scrawny body went into cardiac arrest. "This better be important!" Casper barked.

"Ah, well, yeah." Julian didn't know where to start. His eyes were fixated on the screen, the nuclear reactor was now a flaming meteor falling towards the earth. If it were to hit the ground and explode, the amount of damage could be astronomical, and any investigation would reveal that the reactor and the radiation came from Eden, Inc. Just as Julian was about to try to utter a coherent sentence, the nuclear reactor indeed exploded and the satellite went dead. "Oh, shit!"

As much of a hardass as Casper was, he knew Julian well enough to know that if he had the balls to call him on this number and couldn't get a sentence out, then something seriously fucked up must be happening. He hissed into the phone: "Stay put. I'm on my way." Then Casper calmly excused himself from the meeting he was in, and headed straight to Julian's office.

When Casper arrived, Julian was scrambling to get the satellites online. He was now in "fix-it mode" and that was when he was at his best. Without missing a beat, Julian succinctly updated Casper, leaving out none of the details.

Casper sat in a chair opposite Julian and watched the replay of the pod jettison. "That's impossible, how could anyone survive eight years?" His face hardened as he continued to watch the screen. "If that pod hits the earth, with or without anyone in it we need to be the first ones who find it!" He stood up and paced around the room. "Even if it's empty and the media gets a hold of it, we're screwed. It's got our name all over it. We can't deny its existence."

"You can say it was being tested and the pod went off-course." Casper nodded in agreement. "But what if there are people still alive and they make it back to Earth in one piece? If word gets out, that could create a media mess that would destroy Eden, Inc." Casper pointed to the pod on the screen. "We have to figure out what the hell happened and get to the pod before any of this is even suspected!" Casper replayed the video and watched the pod jettison from the remains of the station. The more he watched it, the worse his mood became. When the nuclear reactor exploded, he shook his head and snorted. "How much of the ozone layer did that just take out? Maybe it's time to get into the sun-block business."

The only good news was that the explosion happened about a hundred miles South of the North Pole, over the ocean. It was not likely many people saw it. Any radioactive fallout would most likely land in the ocean and go undetected.

Casper flopped down in front of an empty computer terminal, one of the many backups in Julian's office, and typed in his super-secret, all-access password. "Each pod is equipped with a homing device. We never really expected to use them. If the pod were ever deployed, the mainframe computer would guide the pods safely back to earth." He was flipping through the file system as fast as he could. "We need to find those codes, turn on the homing device, and then we can guide and monitor the landing of the pod, so instead of chasing it down and risking someone finding it first, we'll just have it come to us!"

Julian liked to watch Casper handle a crisis. He had a knack for getting to the heart of the problem and being unemotional about the decisions he made. He did whatever was necessary to get the job done fast and efficiently. Casper stood up from his computer with the look of satisfaction on his face. "Found it! I was afraid that with the construction of Asgard the old Valhalla files might have gotten trashed, since we reused and reworked so many of the designs."

Julian just watched. He knew to stay out of Casper's way. Casper pulled a cell phone out of his back pocket and punched a number on the speed dial. He looked at Julian: "It's time to call in some backup. I want this handled properly."

The Crusher picked up the phone after the second ring. "Yeah, boss?"

"Get up here!" That was all Casper needed to say. He hung up the phone and shot Julian a look. Julian got the message and went into action, rushing to his computer and digging up all the old personnel files from the Valhalla resort.

A minute later, the pony-tailed Hulk filled the doorway. "What's up, boss?"

Casper sat in front of the backup computer and quickly explained the assignment. His tone was deadly serious and he clearly stated that he would have no tolerance for mistakes. "No one can know what's going on, and not one fucking word of this is going to be whispered in the press."

"Got it!" said The Crusher as he grabbed a chair, sat down next to Casper and looked at the monitor.

Casper tapped on the keyboard and the pod came into focus.

"We have a trace on the pod. It's not under our guidance, but we can follow its every move."

"No problem!" The Crusher pulled a small GPS device out of his jacket pocket, and then typed in some codes that he read off Casper's computer screen. A second later, like magic, the escape pod appeared on The Crusher's little GPS screen.

Casper stood up and paced around the room. "I don't care what lengths you have to go to cover this up. We are months away from Asgard being finished and literally changing the world as we know it. I don't care who you have to kill, what buildings you have to blow up, or if you have to erase an entire city from the map. I want that pod back and if there is anybody in it, I want them brought back here alive!"

The Crusher stood up and punched his right fist into the palm of his left hand. "I'm ready! Any idea who might be in that pod?"

Julian handed Casper a list of names. "I went through the records and determined who were the most likely people to be on the lower ring during the time of the accident—maintenance, restaurant, spa, or gym workers."

Casper handed a copy of the list to The Crusher. There were eight names with a picture and short bio on each person: Two restaurant workers, two spa workers, two maintenance workers, and Ascot and Ethan.

Julian continued, "The pod holds twenty, but I think at the most there could be eight to twelve people on board. That's about how many people could have been on the lower level at the time of the collision, assuming they all survived the accident as well as the eight years of floating through space, which would be a miracle. The number's probably lower."

The Crusher looked through the list. He was used to hunting down trained professional assassins. Was this a joke? Then a thought occurred to him. "I remember some of these names. Didn't we take care of their relatives and associates, and erase the histories of all these people?"

Casper opened a classified file. "All family members and close friends of these eight people have died, in either car accidents, or various other types of everyday tragedies."

The Crusher folded his massive hairy arms. "Yeah, I remember doing that! So they got no friends or family, nowhere to go, and no one's looking for them."

"Yes, but they don't know that," said Julian.

"What's the point?" barked Casper, interrupting. "We'll get to them before they leave the pod! Right?"

The Crusher looked at his GPS, then his watch. "Absolutely, boss, we'll bring them in before anyone suspects a thing."

Twenty minutes later, The Crusher was standing on the Eden, Inc. desert base Tarmac with a small squad of Kevlar-covered commandos. A fuel truck drove up and two guys in coveralls jumped out like an Indianapolis racetrack pit crew, quickly fueling the Eden, Inc. ZX-549. In less than five minutes, the small stealth reconnaissance jet was fueled and ready. The crew got back into the truck and moved on to a sky crane helicopter, and then finally the

Eden, Inc. prototype SP-330 a stealth troop-cargo-transport-jet-copter. This machine was an experimental helicopter that traveled at jet speeds, was dead quiet, and could not be detected by radar.

The ZX-549 recon-jet pilot carried a handheld GPS as he walked towards the plane. He stopped en route, saluted The Crusher, and held up the device. "We have them locked in. It looks like the renegade pod will be landing in the Nevada Desert about 300 miles East of the Mojave."

With a wave of his arm, he ordered the commandos to board the cargo-troop-transport-jet-copter. The pilot stood, waiting for his orders.

The Crusher spoke loud enough to be heard over the aircraft engines. "We'll be right behind you. Fly high so as not to attract attention—we'll be in constant contact. All cell phone coverage in that area will be shut down. We want to prevent anyone from telling anyone about the pod. You have orders to do whatever you need to do to make that happen. Understood?"

"Yes, sir!" The pilot saluted and jogged over to his jet.

The Crusher was the last to board the jet-copter. He ordered the pilot to take off. The pilot gave him a thumbs-up, grabbed the stick and began flipping switches.

The co-pilot motioned him to look at the GPS screen that showed the position of the pod. "Sir, it looks like the pod is going to be landing on sovereign Indian Territory. If we go in there, we'll be in violation of several treaties."

The Crusher looked at him. Where the hell did this Boy Scout come from? He shouted over the roar of the engine, "That's why we have stealth technology, you idiot!"

The crafts rose into the air, as the shimmering afternoon sun reflected on the Tarmac and bounced off the planes.

Part Two

A RADICAL RETURN

Chapter 32

Las Vegas has consequences. At least that's what they say. Johnny Slow-Hawk Atahalne, a Navajo Indian, had just lost six thousand dollars playing blackjack at Circus Circus. He was now driving home, trying to think of a way to tell his wife that he'd just lost all of their vacation money and that they wouldn't be able to go to Cancun this summer as planned. She was going to kill him.

Driving his dusty, four-wheel-drive Dodge flatbed pickup truck, he pulled off the road and took a shortcut through the desert. It was late afternoon. The landscape offered a calming feeling for Johnny. In just a few miles he would be on his native land. There, he was centered, more a part of the earth. There, he had roots and traditions and felt like a whole human being. The big city was the polar opposite. It made him feel like a sponge, being squeezed of his money and humanity.

His previous night's experience was eating him up inside. He had never felt so enslaved before. In one night he had lost his financial freedom. It would take him at least a year to make that money back and pay off his credit cards. What pissed him off the most was that he did it voluntarily. He wasn't captured and sold to traders and forced to pick cotton. No, he walked right into it, a free man with no serious debt who had gotten greedy. Now he'd be working to pay off his creditors with nothing to show for it. Hell, he could have bought something ridiculous like a sixty-inch flat screen 3D HDTV and a surround sound home theater system. He would still have been in debt, but at least he'd have something to show for it. As it was, he barely had enough gas to get home.

Johnny was trying to think of things he owned that he could sell to try to make up some of the money he'd lost. He had a couple of motorcycles, but a dirt bike on the reservation was almost a necessity. His TV was too old to be worth much. His wife's jewelry... well, even the thought was off-limits. As all of this was going through his mind, he noticed something odd moving across the sky. There were rumors that the government and private corporations tested all kinds of experimental aircraft over the desert where no one would see them. He had spent quite a lot of time in the desert and he never saw anything, so he had assumed the rumors were bogus.

As it got closer he saw a big fireball, with large flames trailing off its shiny, metallic body. Curious, he stopped the car to get a better look. "What the hell is that?" Johnny mumbled to himself as he shaded his eyes with his hand. Maybe this was some kind of omen, the beginning of the end of the world, fire raining from the sky? He looked around. There was just this one object. If God was going to rain fire and brimstone from the sky to punish the world for its sins, like creating Las Vegas, or implementing a financial system that turned people into greedy rattlesnakes, then he would certainly have sent more than one ball of fire.

Johnny stood and stared, not moving a muscle, watching the object get larger and closer. When it looked as if it was going to fall right on top of him he started to get nervous. He thought of Kokopelli, the Native American God of mischief. This was the kind of thing he would do; send down a giant fireball to make a point. Put things in perspective. Show him how bad things could actually get so he didn't feel so lousy about his personal predicament.

Perhaps it was his destiny to find this falling object from the sky. He continued to watch as the orange flares shooting and trailing got larger and clearer. Johnny didn't know if he should stay put or take off, since he couldn't tell where it was going to land. He had a way of second-guessing himself only to find himself in worse shape than if he had just done nothing. Like not walking away from the blackjack table when he lost his first thousand dollars.

He decided to stand his ground. If it were his fate to have an object fall from the sky and land on his head, then running wouldn't change anything.

Now he was thinking it must be a meteorite. It was a big ball of fire, there were no wings, and an aircraft would have flames blowing out of its tail. Plus if it were a plane on fire, it would be spewing black smoke, not red and orange. No, this was what objects looked like when they fell into the atmosphere from space.

Old George Clever-Trout Bidzil was the closest thing the Navajo community had to a medicine man. He wasn't a real doctor, but he knew a lot about a lot of things and often gave sage advice to anyone in his community who needed it. Johnny had spent time with George and he once mentioned that black smoke only comes when carbon is being emitted from a burning object. Hot metal and hot rocks don't make smoke, only things like wood or coal do.

Johnny suddenly started to feel empowered. Perhaps this was a great opportunity. Perhaps he needed to lose all that money so he could be here at the right place at the right time and in the right state of mind to see it. This cosmic debris falling towards him might be his ticket out of debt. A giant meteorite is probably worth hundreds of thousands, maybe even millions, of dollars.

Just as he was thinking about what he could do with a million dollars, a giant parachute popped out of the fireball. Instantly the flames stopped and what appeared looked like a giant burned-up metal coffee can, floating down through the sky. So much for getting a pile of money. This was so typical of his life. Just as something good was about to happen, there was always a change of plan. Like the night before, when he had two Kings and the dealer had a Jack and a three, then he dealt himself a two. The dealer was just one number under the hold rule, so he pulled one last card and got a six. In an instant, Johnny's life changed. He watched his future turn to shit as his pile of chips moved across to the opposite corner of the table.

The wind in the desert typically picked up in the late afternoon as the sands cooled. Johnny stood and stared in fascination as the object silently drifted overhead. What the hell was it?

He stood speculating on what it could be, probably some kind of military device. What the hell looks like a meteorite and then sprouts a parachute? Some kind of experimental aircraft: a spy satellite or perhaps a spy plane cockpit canopy? Whatever it was, it was off-course and if he could get a hold of it first, maybe he could get some reward money for it. The wind was picking up so the pod was now drifting considerably further than Johnny first anticipated. He jumped back into his Dodge pickup and began to follow it.

Johnny drove over the bumpy desert, paying more attention to the pod floating in the sky than to the terrain. On several occasions, he almost crashed into Joshua trees, cacti, and a few boulders. The pod was close to landing and he was getting excited. He was on sovereign Indian land and therefore out of US jurisdiction. He could probably hold it for ransom and squeeze some money out of whoever came to collect it. That way he wouldn't have to tell his wife about losing all their money in Vegas. Maybe then the saying, "What happens in Vegas stays in Vegas," would come true for him, too.

As the pod got closer, he realized it was larger than he imagined. Even with his winch and all the tie-downs he used to haul wood and furniture, something that big might not fit in the back of his truck. He had to find a way, because he would have to confiscate it if he were going to hold it for ransom. Otherwise whoever lost it would just come grab it and he would get diddly squat.

Johnny watched the pod hit the ground and tumble end-over-end like an Indy car crash. The parachute was still open and catching the wind, so instead of stopping, the pod bounced and started skimming across the desert, tossed around randomly as if a cat were playing with a ball of yarn. Johnny watched as it slid and skidded out of control, banging into rocks. He was convinced that at any moment the can would crack open and whatever was inside would spill out and get scattered all over the desert.

Johnny drove more cautiously now. He had no problem following the pod's trail of devastation. Anyone else, with half a brain, who was looking for it would have no problem, either. The desert might be bare, but there was life and things did grow. The big can left a trail of scarred earth, crushed and broken Joshua trees, cacti, and parachute shreds. There would be no way to hide its arrival.

By the time he got to the object, he had driven over two miles from where it had first touched ground. The thing was dented, burned up, and half buried in the red desert sand. He glanced around to get his bearings. He was miles from any road and he hadn't been paying attention to where he had been going.

As a kid Johnny used to go off-roading and knew the terrain and the landmarks, but the desert could be very deceptive. He started to get a little worried. Most of what he relied on to navigate across the desert was only visible during the day. It got dark quickly in the desert, so he knew he needed to hurry.

Johnny got out of the truck. The back of his jeans and T-shirt were damp from sweating inside the cab. He put on his cowboy hat and circled the entrenched capsule, noticing that his steel-toed cowboy boots made clear traceable footprints in the red earth. Should he try to erase the evidence of his being there?

He still had no idea what the pod was. Up close, it was too big to be a satellite. It looked a little bit like the Apollo space capsules that the astronauts splashed down in, but even bigger. He figured fifteen or twenty people could fit inside. There was some writing on it but it had been burned up; there was a V and maybe an A, but he couldn't even make out the language.

He expected to see the thing cracked open, but it wasn't, just battered and beaten. He touched it tentatively, then jumped back as it burned his hand. He put his fingers in his mouth. That must have been why the Apollo astronauts landed in the water, to cool the damn thing off.

Johnny walked back to the truck and pulled out a pair of thick leather gloves from under the driver's seat. He leaned against the truck's oversized cab and contemplated how on Earth to get this thing onto the back of his two-ton Dodge flatbed using his little cable winch? He had hauled small cars before and had even gotten a big Boston Whaler on the back once, but then he had had more equipment: a metal ramp, a dolly, a big bag of bungee cords, and a dozen 2"X4"s to slide the boat up on.

He looked into the truck's bed. He found a metal ramp, a crowbar, and one, weathered eight-foot 2"x4" that had been sitting in the back of the truck for years, but not much else. He had been hired by Old George to deliver four classic Harleys to Vegas from the reservation. That's what had gotten him into this mess.

George was a gifted mechanic with an encyclopedic knowledge of old cars and motorcycles. As theme restaurants became more popular, George began to get all kinds of work turning old junkyard scrap into restaurant artwork. However, as smart as Old George was, he wasn't a savvy businessman, so he never really made any money. It seemed that each project paid just enough so that he would barely break even. Johnny figured if there were a reward for returning this spacecraft, he would give some of the money to Old George. He deserved it.

Johnny knew he could use some help loading the spacecraft, but then he would have to split the reward money. Was it worth it? He would deal with that later. He pulled his cell phone out of his back pocket and wasn't terribly surprised to see that he had no reception. After all, he was in the middle of nowhere.

The sun was going down and he didn't have much time. He sat and thought for a minute, staring at the spacecraft then at his truck. The proverbial light bulb went off, and in an instant, he saw how to mount this gigantic tin can onto his truck by himself.

He was quite impressed. It wasn't like him to be particularly clever. The craft had crashed nose first and burrowed into the ground with its butt sticking up in the air at a 45-degree angle. Around the nose was a rather high ring of dirt. Instead of digging the craft out, as he had first planned to do, he would take advantage of the dirt.

He backed the truck up to the tallest part of the pile, where the nose of the craft had plowed into the ground. With the truck running, he put on his gloves, climbed out and manually unwound the winch, then pulled the cable to the rear of the craft. He managed to wind the cable around the pod several times, creating a big noose, before securing the hooks. He grabbed the old eight-foot 2x4 and pushed the noose as high as he could up the back of the pod. The idea was to flip the pod end-over-end, and have it somersault onto the back of the truck.

When the cable was firmly in place he walked back to the cab and turned on the winch. The motor whined and began to roll. The cable bounced and slapped against the pod until it was tight. The weight of the craft started to force the motor to slow. Johnny didn't know how much torque the winch had and he started to get nervous. He watched with apprehension as the motor started to grind. The truck started sagging, bottoming out the shocks. Just as Johnny was about to give up, the pod suddenly budged, breaking free from it's dirt tomb. The whine of the winch relaxed as the pod was smoothly reeled in.

Johnny stopped the winch when the craft was perpendicular to the ground. It stood at least twenty-five or thirty feet in the air and was almost the same size around. His oversized flat-bed truck was now dwarfed by the craft. How the hell was this going to work? He got into the cab and put the truck in reverse, simultaneously inching backwards while reeling in the winch, keeping the tension on the pod so it stayed upright. Once the truck bed was butted up to the craft, Johnny chanted a little Navajo prayer. He wasn't exactly sure what it meant. It was something his grandmother used to say and it made him feel better. He eased the winch just a little, pushing it past the tipping point, and the pod began to fall.

Johnny watched from his side and rear view mirrors. The pod fell slowly at first, then suddenly came crashing down, banging onto the cab's top and the truck bed. The shock was so sudden that Johnny flinched and accidentally jerked the vehicle in reverse, which serendipitously worked to get the truck further under the pod as it bounced into the back.

Johnny jumped out of the cab and looked at the result. His truck looked like one of those carpenter ants carrying a leaf ten times its size. At least half of the pod was sticking out over the now-dented cab. Johnny examined the dent. A surge of anger blasted through his body. He spit, then kicked the rear tire. His truck was always in pristine condition and now this escapade had damaged it. At least it hadn't broken the windshield or rear window. He walked around and examined the truck. The shocks had popped back up. From the looks of them, the pod was big but not that heavy.

Curious, he looked again, trying to see if there were any markings on the craft that would give him a clue as to where it came from. Most of the paint had been burned off and the rest was covered in dirt. Now the sun was starting to set and it was getting more difficult to see anything. He needed to hurry. He could deal with everything else when he got home.

Once he had circled the truck, he figured the pod was positioned well enough to tie down. Fortunately, many of the parachute cables were still attached to top of the pod, though the parachute was shredded in the crash.

He grabbed a pair of bolt cutters from the toolbox behind the driver's seat and started cutting the cables into usable lengths, which he attached to his bumpers and other parts of the truck. He used the remaining cable as ropes to secure the pod as best as he could.

By the time he was finished, the sun was just a small orange bump on the horizon. He was confident that he knew which direction to go, and was now glad it was going to be dark. Driving into town with this big load would cause attention and suspicion; now there was a much better chance that no one would see him. His purpose in all of this, he reminded himself, was to get this thing home and hide it, find out what it was and to whom it belonged, and then get them to pay him to return it.

Without trying to see what might be inside or if the craft had a homing device, Johnny hopped in the cab, turned on his headlights and started heading home through the windy, bumpy desert.

Chapter 33

Pulling into his driveway, Johnny's truck was running on the last few fumes of gas. He wasn't about to stop at an Arco with a spaceship strapped to his truck, so he took as many back roads as possible to avoid being seen. The whole time he chanted his grandmother's Navajo prayer to distract himself; he thought it helped reduce his stomach acid in times of stress.

A few years earlier, he'd built an RV hangar off the side of his garage. His wife wanted to travel so he bought a Winnebago. It just sat in the driveway for months. The sun, sand, and wind began destroying the paint, so he built a shelter for it, but the cost put him in debt and he ended up having to sell the Winnebago. They never once took a trip in it. The RV hangar was a sore subject in the Atahalne family, but today it would serve a purpose: the hangar was just large enough to hide the spacecraft.

It wasn't until he got a mile from the house that Johnny began to wonder where he left the gas can. He was going to have to take his wife's car and get gas for his truck. Then a thought occurred to him. "Maybe there's gas in the spacecraft? What do they run on anyway?" He realized he never bothered to find out what was inside, but it was probably better that way. Had he opened it up in the middle of the desert, something could have fallen out and gotten lost in the sand. No, better that he waited! Now he could see what he was doing and carefully catalogue everything he found.

The clock in the truck had long ago stopped working and Johnny's only timepiece was his cell phone, which still wasn't getting any reception. He didn't know what time it was when he rolled into his driveway, but he knew it couldn't be that late because, thank God, his wife wasn't home yet.

He jumped out of his truck, opened up the hangar door and then went into the house to get a beer. There was a half-eaten burrito in the fridge as well. He tossed it into the microwave. It was 10:29. His wife would be home in less than an hour.

He thought, "It sure would be good to know what is inside the craft before she gets home." If he could have good news to tell her, maybe the fact that he pissed away their savings would go unnoticed.

After scarfing down the remains of the burrito and chugging half the bottle of beer, Johnny grabbed a flashlight and went back out to investigate the pod. It was so dirty and burned up that he hadn't noticed the half-dozen porthole windows around it. He tried wiping the dirt off with his hands but the dirt was baked on and he couldn't see through it. He went and tuned on the hose, then grabbed the bucket and a brush that he used to wash his cars. He squeezed the nozzle. There was enough soap residue in the bucket that it created suds when he filled it with water. He scrubbed a window for a solid five minutes before it was clear enough to see through, then pulled the flashlight out of his back pocket and put it up against the shiny window.

"Aw, shit!" Johnny yelled, his stomach acid shooting off the charts. He did a double take just to make sure he wasn't imagining something. "Shit!" this time kicking the pod with his steel-toed cowboy boot, making a loud clang. There were people in there. With his luck they would be dead. He had watched the pod crash and had followed it as it tumbled and banged for two miles. How the hell could anyone survive that?

Now he didn't know what to do. Should he call the police? No, not yet. He should open it. He shined the light into the pod again. He could see two bodies, strapped in upside down, wearing some kind of jumpsuit.

Then another thought occurred to him. What if these guys weren't humans? Maybe they were aliens, but that didn't make sense—why would an alien need a parachute? Then again maybe for some reason they had to eject from their mother ship. He stared at the bodies. The one in the red jumpsuit was kind of facing his direction and he could see his hair was all messed up and he had a scruffy beard. Probably not aliens. Johnny fiercely started hosing and scrubbing in hopes of finding a door to open, and finally he located something on the side near the bottom.

He hopped into the truck's cab and said a good luck chant, hoping there was enough fuel to start it. When the engine turned over, he said a quick thanks and backed the truck into the hangar. The roof cleared the pod by a mere six inches. Once the truck was three-quarters of the way inside the hangar, he climbed out, grabbed his tin shears, unhooked the winch cables, and started cutting the parachute cables. With a clang, the pod slid off the back about three feet.

He crossed his fingers and the truck started up again. He revved the engine. With as much torque and force as possible he popped the clutch and the two-ton flatbed leapt forward. There was a horrible screeching sound as the pod slid off the cab's roof, across the truck's bed, and onto the floor of the hangar. He looked into the rear view mirror and saw that the pod was sticking out of the hangar about four feet. That wasn't going to do. He put the truck in reverse and slowly backed into the pod, pushing and scraping it across the concrete floor until it cleared the doorway.

He parked his truck and closed up the hangar door. Inside, the room had two six-foot fluorescent light fixtures with two long bulbs. Johnny flipped on the light switch. Only one of the four tubes worked; it flickered on and off like a spastic strobe light and made a horrible buzzing noise.

The pod had rolled to the side slightly, making the hatch more accessible. The thing was beaten up and dented and though he tried to unlatch the hatch, it was stuck. He grabbed a couple of crowbars of different lengths and a few hammers, and got to work hitting the hatch.

Johnny had worked construction and in a body shop. Over the years he had dismantled all kinds of things and knew what it usually took to tear something apart. But this friggin' thing wasn't budging. It was like cracking open a bank vault. Eventually, using a chisel, he was able to make a wide enough space in the doorjamb to insert a big crowbar. He yanked and pulled, applying all of his body weight, using the leverage from the long metal pole. When that didn't work, he began hitting it with a sledgehammer. Finally the hatch popped open, leaving Johnny exhausted and covered in sweat.

He wiped his forehead with his shirt and then stuck his head into the craft. It was extremely hot inside and smelled like a locker room, but it was surprisingly roomy. Johnny stared, trying to figure out what kind of craft it was. He didn't see a cockpit or any controls, just a bunch of seats. He looked at the guys strapped into their chairs and wondered what nationality they might be. They were both ethnically hard to pinpoint, what with the long hair and the jumpsuits and all.

His flashlight reflected on something shiny under a seat near him. It was a fancy shopping bag full of drinks and candy bars. They were brands he had never seen or heard of, but they were written in English. Johnny reminded himself that didn't automatically mean they were American; there are several countries that speak English. However, that did narrow things down quite a bit. He looked around for more clues, but didn't find any.

Now was the moment of dread. He climbed inside and went over to see if either of the two guys was still breathing. He reluctantly crawled over towards the one in the red jumpsuit and touched his forehead. It was warm. Of course it was warm! It was practically two hundred degrees inside this can. He shined the flashlight to see if the guy was breathing, but the jumpsuit was too baggy and he couldn't tell. Johnny put his ear against the guy's mouth and was shocked. "The dude's alive!"

A burst of energy shot through Johnny. He crawled over to the other one in the white jumpsuit and did the same thing. "They're both alive!" He let out a sigh of huge relief. His stomach calmed down and he turned to the problem at hand: he had to get these guys out of the pod and... do what? Call a hospital? He didn't want to do that, since he would inevitably have to explain who they were and where they came from. He unbuckled the stranger in the red jumpsuit's harness, then grabbed him under his arms, and attempted to drag him out of the pod. The guy didn't budge. Johnny checked again to make sure he hadn't missed a strap. He pushed the body an inch off the chair to make sure the guy wasn't stuck to his seat with Velcro. Why the hell was this guy so heavy? He looked like he was 190 lbs. max, yet it felt like he weighed over 400 lbs.

Johnny pulled and tugged. There was no way he was getting either of these guys out by himself. He climbed out and went to the kitchen. He found a relatively clean dishtowel and soaked it with cold water. He climbed into the pod and went back and put the cold towel on the stranger's face. Then he began to gently thump the unconscious man on the side of his head while shinning a flashlight into his eyes. After a few moments, the stranger's eyelids began to flutter, and he licked his lips. Johnny squeezed the towel, wringing the water into the man's mouth.

The stranger violently coughed, his body going into a spasm, spewing water and saliva onto his red jumpsuit. Johnny wasn't sure if that was a good or bad thing. He nervously climbed out of the pod to get this strangely heavy man and his companion some more water. Then he needed to figure out how the hell he was going to explain this to his wife, who would be arriving home at any minute.

Chapter 34

Drifting in a twilight state where dreams and reality are seamlessly blended, Ethan's head was throbbing. He started to become aware of something smacking his face. He heard an unfamiliar voice asking him, "Are you all right?" He felt something cold and wet touch his face, but he still wasn't able to make the transition into consciousness.

The last thing he remembered was falling. They had bounced around, finally broken into the stratosphere, and were falling to Earth. Ascot said that he essentially had no control and that the computers were in charge. There were flames outside the window; it had gotten very hot and he became nauseous. He thought their situation couldn't get any worse, then they hit turbulence and it felt like they were inside a Bingo Ball machine. He got dizzy and thankfully must have passed out.

Now he wasn't falling, so they must be back on Earth and they must have survived the landing. Even in his semi-conscious state Ethan grinned. "We did it! What were the frickin' chances of pulling that off?"

Ethan continued to lie on his back, strapped to the seat. His eyes weren't working well and everything was a blur. He was disoriented. His mouth was dry and his breath was bad. He could tell that the inside of the pod was dark, so the lights weren't on, or working. A dark shadow passed in front of him and water was poured into his mouth. The cold liquid shocked his parched lips and tongue. He coughed and a moment later a cold plastic water bottle was placed in his hand, but he couldn't hold it. He wasn't awake yet.

Ethan was just aware enough to do an inventory on himself; he wiggled his right foot, then his left, so they both still worked. He checked every part of his body. As he did so, he began to wake up, and by the time he had finished he was reasonably coherent. It seemed that none of his bones were broken, he didn't have any agonizing pain anywhere, and he wasn't bleeding. He became conscious of his breathing and he took several slow, deep, energizing breaths.

He fished around, felt the cool, perspiring water bottle near his hand and grabbed it. Ethan lifted it towards his lips. It was light and felt empty. Expecting nothing more than a few drops to dribble out, he was startled to find the bottle was full, and accidentally dumped water all over his face. This woke him up.

Ethan wiped the water across his face and through his hair, then massaged his eyes with the back of his hand. Yellow and red spots danced across his vision. When he stopped and opened his eyes, he could see clearly: the pod was lying on its side and the hatch was open. He could feel the cool air as it came in from the outside. There was a kind of oily smell, like the smell of an auto mechanic's shop.

Ethan unstrapped himself from his seat. Ascot was still strapped in and unconscious. Ethan crawled over to him. As he got closer, he could hear him breathing. He poured some of the remaining water out of his bottle onto Ascot's face. Ascot's eyes fluttered and his lips wiggled, then he let out a groan.

"Hey, guess what?" Ethan's voice was soft and raspy. "We made it! We're alive, and somewhere on Earth. At least that's where I think were are.... Where else could we be?"

Ascot's head turned towards the voice, his eyes still dilated and not yet focused. His mouth moved, but nothing came out right away, then in a groggy voice almost an octave lower than usual, he said, "What'd I tell you? You should never doubt me."

Ethan turned and looked out the hatch into the dimly lit room. "I'm going to find out where we are."

Ascot rubbed his eyes and looked at Ethan. "Be careful!" It came out like a croaky order. "Assume you aren't welcome anywhere. There may be people who don't want us to reappear after an accident of this magnitude."

For eight years, Ascot had been filling Ethan's head with conspiracy theories and strange happenings that suggested that people in power would do anything to get what they wanted. They had no problem killing people, destroying things and blaming others for it. Ethan remained skeptical. He didn't see how all that was possible, but Ascot had been right about a lot of things, so he would take his advice and be cautious.

Ethan crawled across the side of the pod, the water bottle still in his hand. He felt a little light-headed. Everything seemed bouncy and almost weightless; it was disorienting. He got to the edge and popped his head out of the pod, noticing an open door. There was a hallway, from which drifted faint and inarticulate voices. Ethan froze and listened, but it was impossible to tell what language they were speaking.

The hatch was five or six feet above the ground. Ethan dangled his legs out of the pod and looked down. There was a stepladder off to the side. Whoever had climbed in had moved the ladder out of the way, making it harder to get out.

Ethan pushed off with his hands and jumped to the ground. The feeling was surreal, like he was floating slowly down, and what should have been a heavy thump on the ground was a gentle landing.

He stood on the ground in reverence. He never thought that being on planet Earth would make him so happy. "It's the simple things," he thought. As he stood there, the ground seemed to sway under his feet. It reminded him of when he got to shore after spending the day throwing up on a whale-watching boat with his high school senior class.

Ethan's first few steps were like those of a newborn fawn. He bounced around, stumbling. Ethan felt like he was walking on a trampoline. He tossed the water bottle from one hand to the other; it seemed to drift through the air as if in slow motion. Ethan's head was swimming. This was fun. Perhaps they weren't on Earth after all, but rather some planet that looked like Earth. He thought of comic book stories of parallel universes—at this point, anything was possible.

Ethan took a deep breath, stretched his arms and looked around the garage in the flickering light. He walked towards the lit hallway. Parked next to the pod were two motorcycles. Ethan was curious. From the look of them they appeared to be well-used dirt bikes. He brushed the dirt off the side of the gas tank to reveal the word, "HONDA." What were the chances that two planets made Honda motorcycles? No, he was on Earth.

Lying on a bucket next to the motorcycles was a slightly wet flashlight. Ethan flicked it on and looked around the room. He was in a double-high garage and the pod filled the room. Around the walls were piles of typical garage stuff: boxes, shovels, and buckets. There were several piles covered by ratty old drop cloths. Out of curiosity, Ethan went to the closest pile and uncovered a short stack of bricks and three 90 lb. bags of concrete mix.

Ascot had speculated that since they had been living in a world where the gravity had been steadily increasing, their brains and bodies had adapted to it. Now, for them, being on Earth would be like walking on the moon. Ethan wanted to test it out and see what all those years of working out in space had done to him.

He picked up a brick, which felt like it was made of Styrofoam, and tossed it from one hand to the other. It appeared to float back and forth before him. He gave the brick a little squeeze. There was a pop and it disintegrated into a burst of red powder. Ethan dusted himself off and with one hand picked up the 90 lb. bag of concrete mix, which felt like a 5 lb. sack of oranges. He stared at the bag as he effortlessly lifted it up and down. He grinned, then burst out laughing. He had never been this excited before in his entire life. He was a friggin' freak. He could hardly wait to get back to the Blood-Sweat-N-Tears gym and show his dad what he could do.

Chapter 35

Wind in the desert can be strong enough to shake a house off its foundation. Johnny's neighbor, Freddy, was outside looking for his cat, Buddha, a 15 lb. Siamese, who had a habit of bringing small half-dead animals into the house. Freddy's wife and his two daughters were always the first to wake up and discover an injured lizard or kangaroo rat flopping around the blood-smeared kitchen floor, or a mauled snake tucked between the pillows of their couch. The girls were seven and ten and they would scream and make a big fuss. One would have thought that the Manson family had paid them a visit. Freddy, who was not a morning person, would be rousted out of bed to clean up the carnage, and then he would spend the rest of the day spaced out from lack of sleep. So Freddy made it a habit to bring the big cat indoors before he went to bed.

It was a cool, calm night. His wife and daughters were asleep, so Freddy was being quiet. He was tired; he wanted to find the cat then get to bed. He thought he saw the cat in the distance, near a Joshua tree and a pile of rocks. He went to go check when a sandstorm, followed by a low rumbling hum, came out of nowhere. Dust, dirt and small rocks started pummeling Freddy, who was dressed only in a pair of shorts, a wife-beater T-shirt, and a pair of sandals. He had abandoned the quest for the cat and was retreating to his back porch when he saw the source of the wind.

There was a large black helicopter landing in Johnny's driveway next door. The helicopter made almost no noise. Had he not been outside he would have assumed it was just the desert wind blowing sand and dust against the windows.

Freddy had lived next door to Johnny for six years. For the first couple years they didn't talk to each other much; they were neighborly but not friends. As their kids got a little older and started playing together, Freddy and Johnny had gotten more acquainted, and for the last two years Freddy would go so far as to call Johnny his friend. Freddy had confided in Johnny about his past as a drug dealer and had told him about the four years he had spent in prison. Johnny wasn't surprised; there were a few clues: Freddy was built like a weight lifter, covered in tattoos, dressed like a gangster, rode a Harley, and hung out with druggies.

Freddy's first thought was that the Feds were coming to bust Johnny for something. The government had been pushing the boundaries of authoritarianism and moving towards a fascist state slowly and surely for years, so anything was possible, but the more Johnny thought about it: "If Johnny was mixed up in something that could get him into real serious trouble with the authorities, I would know about it." He thought. Also this was Indian land. The Feds couldn't just come in with tactical weapons and pull a stunt like this, so who else had these kinds of resources?

Amazed and curious, Freddy watched from the shadows of a Mexican palm tree as the pitch-black stealth helicopter disappeared behind his house and landed in Johnny's front yard. Freddy was confused. What the hell was going on? He wasn't going to sit back and let this kind of strong-arming go down without a fight. He'd spent too much time trapped in the system to let the system screw them over. He knew that Johnny was working for old George, who had just made a bunch of money from the Vegas casinos. Was it a coincidence that every time an Indian started making money the government came in and tried to shut him down or take a cut?

The helicopter landed and instantly the wind disappeared. Staying in the shadows, Freddy crept over to Johnny's house to investigate.

From his hiding spot (the brush near the driveway, next to the mailbox), Freddy watched a large man in a tailored black suit step out of the helicopter, walk up to Johnny's front door, and without breaking stride kick it open and walk in. Freddy knew something was seriously wrong. These weren't Feds. He looked at the helicopter and the pilot. This was a private outfit, some bullshit mercenaries working for God-knows-who.

Freddy looked around to see if anyone was stationed as a lookout. It didn't appear that there were any; apparently they weren't that concerned about any outside interference. Freddy quietly sprinted back to his house and picked up the telephone. There was no dial tone. He tried his cell. No signal. Clearly these motherfuckers had disabled the phone lines.

Pissed off and full of testosterone, Freddy grabbed the first thing he saw that could be used as a weapon—1980 Louisville Slugger he got when he was a kid. He grabbed the bat and went over towards the house. It wasn't like him to go out of his way to rescue someone. His general attitude was, "if you're stupid enough to get yourself into a mess, then it's up to you to get yourself out of it," but this was different somehow; this violated their Indian sovereignty and crossed the line in a big way. Every fiber of his body knew that these guys were up to no good, so now he was going to straighten them out.

Freddy stayed in the shadows and crept closer to Johnny's house. He was so fixated on the house and trying to find a way to get inside that he didn't notice the armored, stealth, all-terrain vehicle silently pull up in front of the house and park behind the helicopter. Two heavily armed men wearing black Kevlar military combat uniforms silently and rapidly emerged from the vehicle.

The rear kitchen door, next to the row of trashcans, was almost always open. As quietly as possible, Freddy snuck inside and made his way towards the living room, where he could hear Johnny's heated voice barking, "What do you want?"

A deep, resonant, male voice calmly responded. "You know why I came."

Freddy was on his hands and knees, peeking through a crack in the doorway between the kitchen and living room. What he saw surprised him. Apparently Johnny had anticipated this guy breaking in and had been prepared. Johnny was sitting on his La-Z-Boy lounge chair pointing a shotgun at the big burly intruder.

Needless to say, this wasn't the scenario that the intruder had planned, but the man looked perfectly calm, as if having a shotgun pointed at his chest from six feet away was something he did every day for a living. Johnny gestured to a smaller chair and told the man to sit. The brute nodded. Then, with perfect ease, as if he were familiar with the room and the furniture in it, he pulled up the chair, sat down, and smiled.

Freddy now felt a little funny. He came over to help Johnny, but it seemed that Johnny had things handled just fine, and now he had broken into Johnny's house and was spying on his neighbor and perhaps was about to witness something he'd rather not see. But curiosity got the better of him. Discovering someone's secrets was a hard thing for Freddy to turn away from, so he patiently waited and quietly listened to see how it was going to play out.

Johnny looked at the brute and waved the gun. "You know I can shoot you and call it self-defense. A simple case of an intruder trespassing in my home."

The man in the suit nodded. "So whadda you want?" He had an East Coast accent that sounded like a Mafia caricature.

Johnny sat up and cleared his throat. "The first thing I want to know is, what the hell's in my garage, why the hell are you here, and who's behind all this?"

The suited man grinned, "That's not what you want." His eyebrows rose, and he leaned back into his chair. "You're lookin' fer hush money. You figured any outfit that can build somethin' that floats down from outer space has got some deep pockets, and a million bucks or two don't make a dent in their bottom line."

When Johnny heard the cave man in the suit casually mention a million dollars like it was pocket change, he almost wet his pants. He was thinking he would try to squeeze a hundred grand out of these guys and if he got fifty he would be thrilled. At the sound of a million, he got a little tingle in his groin. Immediately he started spinning fantasies about what his life would be like if he had a million dollars. Physically he was still sitting on his La-Z-Boy pointing a shotgun at this stranger, but his mind was transported to a tropical beach in Tahiti. The hairy suit guy was still talking, but to Johnny, it was just ambient noise mixed in with the waves crashing on the pristine white sand beaches.

Johnny's trance was broken when the man's Brooklyn drone said, "So, who's da guy hiding behind the door?"

Johnny carefully turned his head for a split second and saw a frightened eyeball through a crack in the door about a foot-and-a-half above the ground, framed by long straight black hair with a few grey streaks, looking up at him. Before Johnny could say, "Freddy?"

The Crusher was lunging for the shotgun. Freddy was still a biker and gang-banger in his soul, and was as loyal as a Labrador. To help a friend, he would never turn away from a fight. He leaped onto his feet and sprang through the door with his Louisville slugger in his hand, swinging at The Crusher's head.

With a gesture that said enough is enough, The Crusher grabbed the barrel of the shotgun and turned the gun sideways, twisting Johnny's hand so that it forced the gun to go off. Johnny's wife's collection of useless commemorative plates and snow globes exploded, scattering shards of colored pottery and wet glitter, along with their cheap Ikea shelf stand. The brute pulled Johnny into him so that their faces were a mere inch apart. With a maniacal snarl The Crusher, now standing up straight and towering over Johnny, said with garlic-tinged breath, "It's show time!"

Then like a rattlesnake striking, the big man's forehead crashed into Johnny's nose. Excruciating pain shot through Johnny's face. Immediately his eyes were watering, blurring his vision, and weakening his grip on the shotgun. Less than a second later, The Crusher's heel pounded onto Johnny's toe like a jackhammer and a wrecking-ball fist slammed into his solar plexus. The next thing Johnny knew, he was lying on the ground next to his La-Z-Boy, unable to breathe, and his shotgun was no longer in his hands.

Freddy ran towards the behemoth as The Crusher leaped up from the chair. Freddy was only four steps away, and ready to hit a home run with the big brute's head, but by the time the vintage baseball bat was swinging full force, The Crusher had grabbed the shotgun and blocked the blow. The bat bounced off the barrel, making a dull clang and knocking Freddy off-balance.

The Crusher, with childlike enthusiasm, grabbed Freddy by the throat, positioned his thumb against Freddy's windpipe, then with a quick squeeze crushed Freddy's trachea. With the other hand, he flipped the shotgun around and slammed its butt into Freddy's forehead. There was a hollow, squishy thunk and a sharp crack similar to the sound of a watermelon cracking open. Blood and phlegm covered Freddy's nose and lips. In disgust, The Crusher let go and Freddy's limp body fell to the floor.

The Crusher was tired of playing games. He had allowed this ignorant yahoo to waste enough of his time. He was curious if Numb-Nuts or anyone else knew or had seen anything. Apparently they hadn't, so it was time to grab the pod and get the hell out of here. Johnny feebly wiggled on the living room floor, writhing and wheezing. The Crusher pushed a button on his wristwatch, opening a walkie-talkie communication line to the commander of the armed forces waiting outside. "I need this place cleaned up!"

There was a high-pitched blast of hiss, followed by a thin, tinny voice. "Roger that! What's the damage?"

The Crusher looked down at Johnny, who was trying to roll off his back and onto his side: "We have two dead bodies and some potential witnesses. We need a total clean sweep of the entire neighborhood."

"Roger that, we're on it."

Johnny looked up and could only see a fuzzy outline of the beast. He heard the conversation and thought, "Wait a minute, I'm not dead!" The next thing he was aware of was that his head hurt, because he was being lifted off the ground and suspended by his hair. He smelled the garlic breath again, and Johnny's last thought was that the East Coast accent sounded pissed off.

"You're making too much goddamned noise!" With a practiced twist of his powerful wrist, The Crusher snapped Johnny's neck like a farmer does a chicken, and then dropped him onto the ground. A second later, two Kevlar-covered combat fighters came through the door, weapons drawn. The Crusher pointed down the hall towards the garage. "The pod is inside the garage. There can be no witnesses, no survivors, no evidence of us ever having been here."

The Kevlar guys nodded and ran off down the hallway.

Chapter 36

Pretending to be Kwai-Chang Caine from "Kung Fu," walking across rice paper without leaving a mark, Ethan stepped out of the garage into the house. Ethan was moving with a new level of grace and fluidity that he had never experienced before. Once inside the house, he could tell that the voices were speaking English, and they were talking about the pod. The voices led him down the hallway and into the kitchen where he stopped and listened, so as not to be seen. He could hear two men having a conversation in the adjacent room, and so far there had been no mention of either Ascot or him. Suddenly there was some commotion; a gun was fired, and a guy was barking orders to kill everything and everybody.

For about a minute, Ethan had felt on top of the world, the earth was soft and pliable like a giant foam party tent that he could bounce around on. He was excited to go back to Blood-Sweat-N-Tears and see how much he would be able to bench press, hoping to set a gym record, and impress his dad.

All that excitement and forward thinking came to a grinding halt when he witnessed a hairy hulk snap a guy's neck with one hand, followed by gun-wielding storm troopers busting down the door. Better safe than sorry. Ethan didn't wait to find out whose side these guys were on. He needed to get back to Ascot and both of them needed to get the hell out of there.

Ethan leaped down the hall, each step covering ten normal steps. When he arrived, the escape pod was surrounded by goons. They looked like Star Wars storm troopers, only instead of white plastic suits they were covered head-to-toe in flat black Kevlar and their guns were real. For Ethan and Ascot this signaled a definite change in plans. Ethan hid in the shadows of the garage and watched as the armed men executed their moves with military efficiency. A storm trooper had climbed in and was yelling at Ascot to get up. Obviously, he hadn't figured out that Ascot was paraplegic.

From where Ethan was hiding in the shadows, he could see halfway into the pod. He watched a Kevlar goon press a machine gun barrel to Ascot's temple so as to motivate him to drag himself across the pod's empty seats.

The large garage door rolled open and The Crusher stood outside looking in, the sky crane helicopter parked behind him. "Let's cable this up and get it the hell out of here!" The giant stood and looked at Ascot, who had pulled himself to the edge of the pod hatch. "Get him up and into the chopper!"

"He can't walk, sir!" said a voice from behind a facemask, pointing his gun at Ascot's head.

"I don't care, drag his ass to the chopper!"

The storm trooper took his rifle and pried it under Ascot's butt, then kicked him out of the hatch. Ascot fell to the ground, landing on his side, making a loud thud, then bounced and a softer thud echoed. The whole time he didn't make a sound.

A storm trooper on the ground grabbed Ascot's feet and tried to drag him, but he wouldn't budge. After several tries, he stood back, puzzled. "I need help! He weighs too much."

The soldier in the pod jumped down and grabbed Ascot's opposite leg. Together they pulled, and slowly Ascot slid across the garage floor.

Ethan hid in the shadows and watched as the men struggled to move Ascot. Two other storm troopers came out of the helicopter, cables in their hands, and ran towards the pod. They began to quickly and methodically hook the cables onto notches in the pod, ignoring the fact that the pod was still inside the garage.

Ethan wanted to do something to help Ascot, but he knew that to reveal himself would be suicidal. He restrained himself as best he could as he watched his friend get dragged away.

The two commandos were now struggling to drag Ascot across the dirt driveway towards the large helicopter, just as it began to slowly ratchet up the cables to its crane. The metal ropes bounced, shook, and banged into the pod, producing low thunderous bass drum sounds. Little dust devils stirred in the driveway where the cables slapped the ground. The storm troopers jumped out of the way, hopping over cables like kids playing double-Dutch, until each cable was as tight as a contrabass piano string. Then they stood perfectly at attention on opposite sides of the crane, waiting for orders. Ethan thought, "If I had a gun I could so easily shoot them," but of course he didn't, and the noise would have given away his position. Staying in the shadows of the garage, Ethan sidestepped across the wall towards the large open door. Less than ten feet later, he crouched down next to a pile of something covered in a blue plastic tarp. As quietly as he could, he felt underneath and found a pile of river rock.

An idea flashed in Ethan's mind. Ascot was almost at the door of the helicopter. Ethan had one shot at a surprise attack. He grabbed a handful of the smooth, baseball-sized river rocks.

When Ethan was a kid he watched all the Rambo movies and thought it was cool when Rambo would sneak in the shadows, and attack the bad guys with his knife or bow and arrow. Now was Ethan's chance.

The guards continued to stand at attention waiting for their next set of instructions. Ethan rose and with as much force as he could muster, threw a river rock at the closest guard. It hit the guy straight in his faceplate, so hard that he was thrown back and knocked over. The other guard looked over in confusion. Ethan aimed and flung another rock with all his strength at the other guard, who was yelling at his partner to get up. The rock whizzed past his ear. Instantly the commando went into combat mode.

The guard shouted something that Ethan didn't understand at the guards who were struggling to get Ascot on board. They grabbed their weapons and the three guards snapped into a seek-and-destroy-formation; their downed comrade was still out cold.

Ethan tossed a rock at the helicopter, making a loud thud. Two of the guards turned to look towards the noise. Ethan pitched a rock at the one who didn't look, hitting him square on the thigh knocking him sideways. Hopping on his one good leg, he spun around and immediately started shooting blindly into the garage.

Ethan's fighting instincts, sharpened after eight years of training on the Ultimate-Sparring-Partner, caused him to jump out of the line of fire before he even realized he had reacted. Still not used to the lack of gravity, he overshot, barely maintaining control.

Bullets were flying in all directions as all three guards emptied their weapons into the garage. Ethan jumped up and landed on top of the pod. He lay on his stomach and shimmied up to the edge, where he was able to look down on the storm troopers who were shooting at everything except the pod; obviously they had strict orders not to damage it.

After a half-minute of unending machine gun fire, the shooting stopped. The commandos cautiously walked into the garage, guns still drawn. Ethan waited like a python in a tree until the last soldier stepped past him, then he jumped down and landed on top of unsuspecting soldier. There was a squishy sound with the crunch of broken bones, as the guard crumpled like a paper doll. Ethan was surprised; he did much more damage than he had expected. The two other soldiers turned to look and one charged Ethan, using his rifle as a baton.

Ethan sprang into a practiced boxing stance; he noticed his awareness was heightened and everything was moving in slow motion. As the commando ran towards Ethan at turtle speed, a feeling of fearlessness washed over Ethan's body. He was ready. The storm trooper, seeing that Ethan was unarmed, raised his rifle butt over his head, leaving his entire body open. For a boxer, this was almost as easy as hitting a heavy bag hanging from chain.

Ethan faked left and then slid right. The charging commando reacted predictably. Then the reptilian part of Ethan's brain, the bundle of neurons that kept his lungs breathing, his heart pumping, and his reflexes reacting, automatically went into a series of preprogrammed boxing combinations. He shot a left body blow straight into the storm trooper's stomach. The entire weight and inertia of the charging soldier felt like someone had gently tossed Ethan a pillow. The storm trooper doubled over, losing his grip on the rifle. Before the rifle hit the ground, Ethan landed a solid right hook onto his jaw that knocked his legs out from underneath him. The commando's head smacked the concrete floor with a Kevlar clunk.

The remaining storm trooper had just snapped the magazine into his rifle when Ethan leaped across the length of the garage and grabbed the weapon out of his hand. Then, in one fluid motion, just as the first bullet slid and locked into the chamber, Ethan snapped the weapon in half, making a loud crack.

The storm trooper was dumbfounded. He was a trained professional who had dealt with all kinds of scenarios, but never had he seen anything like this. The next thing he realized, he had been grabbed by the collar and tossed like a horseshoe across the yard. He was now airborne and flying straight towards the side of the helicopter, and there was nothing he could do.

The moment Ascot was dropped, he was ignored; since he was crippled they presumed he was no threat. He sat up and watched Ethan face off with the soldiers. Thinking of what he could do to help, he climbed into the helicopter, dragged himself into the cockpit, grabbed the pilot by the throat, and then spoke his first words since the soldiers had shown up: "You move and I snap your neck like a chicken." Though Ascot tried to put as much menace in his voice as he could, it still came out a bit airy and feeble.

A second later, a big burly guy dressed in a suit and tie showed up, brandishing a gigantic pistol. He shot several rounds into the air, grabbed Ascot by the hair, and pulled him out of the cockpit. Unlike the commandos, The Crusher had no problem dragging Ascot around. He put his big gun onto Ascot's temple, interrupting whatever plan Ascot might have had.

"Enough of this bullshit!" The big man snarled (nothing airy or feeble about him). "Come out and I won't shoot your friend!"

The Kevlar-armored goons moaned. They crawled out from the shadows of the pod, helping each other stumble their way towards the helicopter. A minute later, Ethan stepped out of the far side of the garage. The Crusher was surprised. All this commotion was just one kid in a ridiculous red jumpsuit. "Smart boy!" said the big man. The pilot turned on a headlight. The Crusher dragged Ascot by the hair a few feet so they were in the spotlight. Ethan could clearly see the big brute's gun and that he meant business. "I don't want any last minute funny stuff. Get your ass in the chopper. You two are coming with me. Got it?"

Ethan hesitated, then nodded.

At that moment, Ascot summoned all his strength and punched The Crusher in the balls. Ethan cringed as he watched The

Crusher let go of Ascot's hair, double over and grab his groin. Ascot turned to Ethan. "Get the hell out of here! Don't worry about me. If you come with me, we're both dead!"

Before Ascot could say another word, The Crusher recovered, stood up, and kicked Ascot between the shoulder blades. Ascot caught himself with his arms, then spun around to face The Crusher. He kicked again, this time aiming for Ascot's head, but Ascot easily blocked it. Now The Crusher was really pissed off. First his men get their asses kicked by a boy, now he had to actually fight a cripple? What an absurd scenario.

Ascot scooted across the dirt driveway, dodging and blocking The Crusher's blows. "Get out of here now, Ethan!" Ascot's voice was strong and forceful, just like when he would coach Ethan in the boxing ring. After all the years of training, it had a Pavlovian effect. Ethan's body responded first; as he jumped into gear, he instantly became alert and intuitively understood why Ascot was sending him away.

Ascot realized that their only means of survival was to separate. Once these people, whoever they were, had them both, there would be no reason to keep them alive. Now if the goons wanted them, they would need to keep them alive and use each other as bait.

Ethan retreated into the garage, then turned back to see a whole new level of anger in the big man's face. Realizing that Ethan wasn't going to jump in and help his friend, The Crusher pulled a Taser gun from under his suit jacket and at almost point-blank range shot Ascot in the head. The Crusher stood over Ascot's writhing and convulsing body for several seconds as the Taser's wires crackled and sparked in the dark. Once Ascot was clearly unconscious, he shut the device off, pulled out his big gun, and started shooting into the shadows of the garage.

Several gunshots blasted holes in the drywall near Ethan's head. He needed a way out fast. He grabbed the first thing that he saw: a dirt bike. It had been a while since he had ridden a motorcycle, but he figured it would come back to him quickly. It seemed to be his best option; a dirt bike was fast and could travel over almost any terrain, so he could go places that would be hard to follow.

He pushed the bike to the edge of the pod, alongside the slew of taut cables and just a few feet from the garage door. There was another blast of gunfire that hit the side of the hangar, terrifyingly close. The big blades of the helicopter started to slowly rotate, swinging dangerously low. Ethan hopped on the bike. The shocks bottomed out because of his extreme weight. He could see a straight shot out of the garage, up the driveway, and to God-knows-where. It was now or never. The bike started on the first kick. Ethan revved the engine.

The helicopter blades began picking up speed, slicing though the air, increasing their pitch, and kicking up a storm of dust and dirt. Ethan looked straight ahead at his escape route with the same focus and determination he had every time he fought a new opponent in the ring. Using the dust from the helicopter as cover, he popped the clutch and shot out of the hangar, up the driveway, and onto the road. The Crusher fired into the dust cloud.

The dirt bike, with no head or taillights, was swallowed up by the debris. The only thing The Crusher could aim at was the high-pitched buzz of the engine that began to fade into the distance, like a swarm of bees. Ethan felt a sharp stinging pain on his back and thigh that he assumed were from the rocks and pebbles kicked up from the helicopter's turbulence, but it was nothing and he wasn't looking back.

Completely furious, he climbed into the helicopter and grabbed a large metal suitcase. The storm troopers were back on their feet and stumbling around. He ordered them to get in the chopper. Then the moment the last commando had gotten on board, he motioned it to take off.

He would clean up the rest of this mess by himself and then take the all-terrain stealth vehicle and hunt down the fugitive.

Chapter 37

Marcie Atahalne, Johnny's wife, had spent the weekend with her friend Sylvia, whom she had known since childhood. They had gotten very nostalgic talking about high school and how their lives were shaped by the experience. Sylvia had married her high school boyfriend and was now divorced with four kids. The two oldest were in jail and the younger two were on their way. Her husband Herb had left five years ago and hadn't been seen or heard from since. She was trying to raise her kids, clearly unsuccessfully, and was working as a waitress at Chuck's, a diner off the historic Route 66.

After their weekend together, Marcie was feeling pretty good about her lot in life. She wasn't rich or famous, but for a girl growing up on a Navajo reservation that was never something she aspired to. Johnny wasn't perfect, but he was a good man. He said what he meant and did what he said, and he took pride in providing for his family. Their fifteen-year-old daughter, Abigail, was a good student and was involved in many extra-curricular school activities. She had also taken to Navajo culture and liked to spend most of her weekends with Johnny's mom. She liked helping her grandmother make jewelry and weave carpets, then sell them at the local tourist shops and swap meets. Abigail wanted to earn some money for their summer vacation to Cancun.

Since Abigail wouldn't be home from her grandmother's until tomorrow, Marcie was daydreaming about spending some alone time with Johnny as she drove down the dark country road a half-mile from her house. Out of nowhere, a dirt bike with no lights, going like a bat out of hell, came straight at her. She slammed on her brakes and skidded off the road. Her heart was racing, her good mood gone. She sat paralyzed in her old Ford Focus, not moving a muscle. She waited, wondering if more were coming. Within a few seconds, the whine of the motorcycle's engine faded into the night, but no more came.

Agitated, she put the car in low gear and carefully drove out of the thick sand and gravel shoulder, and got back on the road. Who could that have been, and where was he coming from? She figured it was probably one of Freddy's friends. She would tell Johnny, and he would tell Freddy and see to it that that sort of thing never happened again. She rounded the final bend to her house and gasped.

A gigantic black helicopter was taking off and a large man in a black suit carrying an oversized briefcase was walking towards her. "Who was this guy?" she thought. "Nobody from the reservation wears tailored suits unless there's a wedding or a funeral." She had a bad feeling. She reached under her seat and fumbled around for a few seconds until she found her .22 pistol. Johnny insisted that she keep a gun in her car for protection. She never had to use it, and she had only fired it at soda cans, but it did make her feel more secure when she was by herself.

As she rolled her window down to talk to the man, the helicopter took off, making a big cloud of dust and sand. There was something attached to the helicopter and it was inside the giant garage. Suddenly the hangar blew apart—2x4s, drywall, and stucco exploded in all directions. She watched in stunned horror, unaware that the man in the black suit was reaching into her car.

The Crusher had anticipated that a woman living on a reservation might be packing a gun. Sure enough she was, but she was also distracted by the garage being ripped open. The Crusher seized the moment and grabbed her gun, then snapped her neck. Marcie's body flopped against the steering wheel, making the horn go off. That noise wasn't acceptable, so he pushed her limp body to the side, but the seatbelt shoulder strap kept the body upright and she kept falling forward onto the horn. The Crusher unlocked and opened the door, then unsnapped the seatbelt harness. Marcie's dead body fell out onto the ground.

The helicopter was gone, just a faint pulsing thwop-thwop-thowp in the distance. The Crusher looked at his watch, and then grabbed the suitcase. He walked to the front of the property near the parked all-terrain stealth vehicle. He opened the case and pulled out a three-inch round metal stake and shoved it in the ground, then pushed a few buttons. A small red LED light popped on. He then pulled a flashlight out of the case and surveyed the area. He grabbed two more metal stakes, walked briskly to the opposite side of Johnny's property, and repeated the procedure. The house next door seemed quiet, but he could sense that there were people there, so moving quietly and staying out of sight, he went over and planted the final stake in the neighbor's backyard.

By the time he was finished, he had planted and armed three devices in the ground, triangulating both Johnny's and Freddy's properties. Satisfied with his work, The Crusher headed back to the all-terrain vehicle, and tossed the suitcase into the passenger seat. Suddenly, as if on cue, a light flickered on in the house next door. His suspicions were correct; there was someone home.

Eden, Inc. had developed and patented a high-tech and lethal device using microwave flash technology. Three nuclear-powered microwave-emanating flash sticks could be placed in the ground as far as a third of a mile apart. With surprising efficiency, the sticks would project high-voltage beams to each other like a gigantic microwave oven. Everything inside the triangle would become white-hot in a matter of minutes. Once the inside temperature exceeded the melting point of silicate material, such as dirt and rock, a big flash would appear. The sticks would create an implosion inside the triangulated area, and everything inside would turn to ash. Instant moonscape.

The Crusher drove the stealth vehicle off the property and onto the road. Once he had pulled around a bend and was no longer able to see the property directly, he pushed the button that triggered the flash sticks. He looked at his watch and drove for about two and a half minutes, then stopped. The night was pitch black; no streetlights, the moon just a sliver, and the stars speckled the desert sky. The Crusher put on a pair of very dark sunglasses, sat and waited. Within a minute there was a pop and a bright flash lit up the entire valley. Even with sunglasses on, it was as if a dozen camera flashes went off simultaneously three inches from his eyes. For a second he couldn't see and he waited for his eyes to adjust again.

The Crusher stepped out of the vehicle, walked back up to the bend, and admired the blizzard of sparkling dust where the two houses once stood. Everything had been incinerated, no trace of anything. Throughout the night the wind would scatter the ash and by morning it would be as if the houses had never existed. The neighbors, who knew the area well and had have lived their entire lives on the reservation, would question whether or not two houses had ever stood there.

A mile away, Buddha the cat turned and headed away from home, some instinct making him realize home was no longer there.

Chapter 38

Fumbling his way through the dark dirt streets of the reservation on an unfamiliar vehicle filled Ethan with anxiety. He looked around in all directions, afraid that at any turn the goon squad would find him. He had never been shot at before; his mind and body were reeling from the adrenaline rush. He was going as fast as he could on an old, well-worn dirt bike that, while well-maintained, had clearly seen better days, and Ethan was concerned that it might not handle either his weight or the speed at which he was pushing it. He had no idea which way to go, but figured he should avoid public roads, so when he arrived at an actual paved street he turned off and headed into the desert.

Ethan did know he wanted to go as far away as possible, so what mattered was that he keep moving in the same direction. The sky was clear—literally billions of stars with nothing to obstruct his view. The San Fernando Valley didn't have stars like this; growing up in the city he was lucky to see a dozen stars at night. He chose to follow a group of three stars in a straight line—they were easy to find and he figured he would aim for the middle one. Also, in the distance was the silhouette of a mountain. He revved the bike's engine and headed straight for those two points.

Suddenly, behind Ethan, a bright flash of light lit up the desert for a split second. He could see all the bushes as if it were high noon. This allowed Ethan to ascertain that the terrain ahead was fairly flat and clear of debris, so he sped up, comfortable that there was nothing in front of him to hit or fall off of. The flash was followed by a distant pop, then a metallic-smelling breeze, as if a giant open oven door was blowing its unnaturally hot, dry air across the desert. Ethan wasn't exactly sure what had just happened, but he knew whatever it was, it was bad news.

Ethan drove full-throttle across the dark desert. The whine of the engine filled his ears as he concentrated on the dark terrain racing by. The desert sand felt like a big pillow and his mind perceived the bumps and jumps as if he were floating in slow motion. He had gotten into a rhythmic trance, with no perception of time, when the bike began to sputter. A few minutes later, the dirt bike that had been his lifesaver died. Twilight was arriving and the stars were quickly beginning to fade.

The rising sun cast an orange-yellow glow over the horizon. Ethan stood straddling the exhausted bike, processing the fact that he was back on Earth. He could see for miles in all directions but there was nothing that resembled civilization anywhere. Just his luck; he went from being lost in space to being lost on Earth. He had driven himself into the middle of nowhere, but at least he had gotten away from the people who were trying to kill him. He hopped off the bike, its engine sizzling from being worked hard throughout the night. He leaned the bike against a lone cactus bush— it had no kick stand and he wanted to show it some respect.

The ground still felt like he was walking on a trampoline. Curious, he wanted to test his new physical limits. Body still reeling from the chase, Ethan took in a deep breath and let it out slowly, trying to relax. No one was shooting at him and he wasn't free-falling inside a fiery tin can. He could relax finally, for the first time since he had left the station.

He walked away from the bike and cactus to a flat sandy patch that could have served as a gymnastic floor mat. The only problem was that there was a big rock in the middle. Ethan's first thought was to look elsewhere, but instead he pushed the rock, which rolled easily. Now there was a hole in the sand where the rock had probably rested for the last several thousand years. Though the rock was large and therefore difficult to grab, Ethan wanted to see if he could lift it. He stretched his arms around it, got into a squat position, then squeezed his arms and pushed with his legs. To his surprise, not only could he lift it, the weight was also manageable.

He carried the stone, which was easily twice the size of his body, about twenty or thirty feet, then dropped it on the ground, amazed. With a new sense of excitement, he jumped into his newly created recreational space, which was like jumping on a trampoline. He jumped as high as he could. When he landed on the ground he felt the sand and earth give way under his feet. Then he sprang back up, trying to reach higher. Each time he jumped, he was shocked at how high he could reach, then how slowly and softly he appeared to fall to the ground. He was easily jumping forty feet into the air, feeling unstoppable as the warm wind blew against his face and through his hair. He added a single forward flip, then a double, then a triple, finally a backwards flip. Each jump felt exciting and euphoric. As he bounced up and down, he could feel the tension leave his body.

He stopped just as he was beginning to break a sweat. Ethan walked back to the cactus and stood in its shade; the sun was barely up and it was already getting hot. He was going to have to find shade throughout the day or the desert sun would fry him. He looked at the motorcycle, admiring its dark blue color, which he hadn't noticed in the dark. He also observed that on the front left shock was a laminated piece of paper. He leaned over the bike to read it. It was a class C motorcycle registration to a John Atahalne. The address was a P.O. Box in some city in Nevada.

Ascot had said that he had aimed for the East side of California so as to not overshoot it and end up in the ocean. He definitely didn't overshoot. Ethan grabbed the bike and inspected it for more clues. When he picked it up, it was surprisingly light. For kicks, and in the spirit of testing his strength, he grabbed the bike's frame and lifted it over his head. It was as easy as hoisting a folding chair. He then shifted his weight and held the bike with one hand, then put the bike down gently with a single arm. He reexamined the bike to see if it listed its weight anywhere, but he didn't find anything. He rolled it back and leaned it against the cactus, where it cast a shadow that looked like an Aboriginal statue of a strange, mythical Centaur.

Ethan's physical transformation was starting to sink in. What he was capable of doing now was incredible—the possibilities were endless. He was now even more eager to get back home to the gym and measure his strength. He was easily going to break all the gym's records, probably even world records, but first he had to get out of the desert in one piece.

Moving on foot, Ethan headed towards what looked to be the closest hill with an outcropping of rocks on top. It turned out that it wasn't as close as it had looked, it was more like a mountain than a hill, and the pile of rocks on top were each a couple stories high. By the time Ethan got to the top of the mountain, the sun was almost directly overhead, beating down on him. Ethan enjoyed the hike, since he was able to jump over the gigantic boulders and effortlessly climb the steep terrain.

At the top, Ethan found what he was looking for. In the distance, in what seemed to be traveling in an East-West direction, were train tracks. The logical thing to do would be to follow the tracks.

He was getting very hot and thirsty but had nothing to drink. Images of waterfalls and cool springs floated through his mind, heightening his desire. The crappy-tasting octagon-shaped energy drinks, that he had been consuming for the last eight years, filled his mind like an erotic fantasy. He forced himself to block it all out and focus on getting to the tracks. Ethan remembered movies where guys were trapped in the desert. They would only travel at night when it was cooler so they wouldn't burn up or get sunstroke, but where the hell was he going to hang out for eight hours while waiting for the sun to set?

There was some potential shade in the rocks, but the sun would have to pass over before any shadows would be created, and that would be hours from now. By then several trains could have passed by, and the idea was to some how get a ride on a train? He wouldn't care which direction it was headed; wherever it would be going was better than staying here. Ethan plotted his course.

Judging distance in the desert is very deceptive. Ethan started hopping off the rocks and heading towards the tracks. They were much farther away than he had anticipated and finding them took longer than he hoped. When he finally arrived, they seemed remarkably small and unimpressive. The sun was just arching downward. He followed the sun's lead and walked West along the tracks.

Growing up in the Valley, he would occasionally see the commuter and freight trains pass through. When he was little, Ethan would count the freight train cars and get excited when there were over a hundred. When he got older and was driving, having to wait twenty minutes for the friggin' trains to pass wasn't fun at all. His recollection was that the commuter trains traveled quite fast, while freight trains were comparatively slow. Considering he was in the middle of nowhere, he anticipated that he would encounter a freight train. What commuting goes on out here?

As luck would have it, the first train came about an hour later and it was headed East. As expected, it was a freight train. Ethan thought, "Now what? The train isn't just going to stop and let me board. Also it's going in the wrong direction." Home was West.

Ethan stepped out of the tracks and watched the train pass. The dead quiet of the desert was interrupted by the clang and rumble of bouncing and shaking metal. He watched carefully as cars of different shapes and sizes roared past. The train wasn't going particularly fast. He judged that he could easily run and match its speed and hop aboard like he had seen hobos do in old movies. However, in those old movies there were always open, empty cars. So far all the cars were stacked shipping containers that didn't have any side openings or anything to grab onto. Even with his newly acquired strength, speed, and agility, jumping onboard seemed precarious. He had visions of himself slipping, falling under the train, getting run over and being sliced apart by the big metal wheels.

He shook the morbid images out of his mind. That wasn't helping. He continued to watch the train pass. Finally there were a few empty flat cars where the containers hadn't been stacked yet. They had chains, hooks and other things he could grab a hold of. From the looks of it he could easily hop aboard, but he hesitated, unsure if he wanted to go the wrong way.

He watched, as the train continued to pass. He wasn't counting, but it had to be several hundred cars long. Then a tinge of doubt crept over him. What if there wasn't a westward traveling train? Or what if there was one and there were no flat cars to get on? A rush of panic passed through Ethan's body. "I should really take advantage of this opportunity," he thought. He stepped back to judge how much more train was coming. He could see the last car moving toward him and there weren't any other flat cars. He had missed his chance.

Now Ethan was really starting to panic, suddenly aware of how hot, tired, and thirsty he was. If he stayed out here in the desert he would burn up and die. Then there were several auto carriers, each transporting twelve automobiles stacked three high and four across in a zigzag pattern. There were plenty of places to grab, so without a second thought Ethan began running alongside the train, quickly matching its speed. Then, with a dynamic leap, he caught hold of a chain that secured a truck to the carrier and pulled himself up. The next thing he knew he was sitting in the middle of an auto carrier, chugging down the tracks, headed in the wrong direction. He expected that the rushing air would cool him off. Instead it felt like a blast from a gigantic hair dryer, making him thirstier and more uncomfortable then he already was.

Not sure what to do, Ethan rode the train for about forty minutes, scanning the desert for any sign of where he should get off. He didn't want to be caught riding illegally; he didn't know what would happen to him, but he was fairly certain it would be a major hassle to deal with. The tracks seemed to go perfectly straight for miles, so when it suddenly made a turn for first time, it felt dramatic. The tracks were now in the shadow of a small rocky mountain and the temperature was easily twenty degrees cooler. He could hop off here and wait in the shade for the train going in the opposite direction.

A half-mile further, Ethan saw a main road and a rest stop—an oasis in the middle of the desert. Ethan immediately crawled to the edge of the train car and hung off the side. He saw an area up ahead free from any big rocks and large cactus plants. When he got to the clearing, he jumped off. To his surprise, he didn't even fall down when he landed. He ran about fifty yards to slow himself down, then stopped in the shade and watched as the last car went by. Once the train was out of sight, he headed towards the highway, not sure if he had made the correct decision.

It took only a few minutes to get up to the neglected rest stop. There were no vending machines, no maps or information. There was a bathroom with a urinal, a toilet, a sink, and no toilet paper or paper towels. The mirror wasn't even a real mirror, just a polished slab of metal that for the last twenty years people had scratched their names in. There was only a tiny spot in the center that offered any reflection. Ethan stared at himself for a moment. He was covered in dust, his hair was a mess and he hadn't shaved in days. He hoped the cloudy, smudged, scratched metal mirror made him look worse then he really was. He was considering the idea of hitchhiking, but now, looking at himself, he realized, "Why bother, I look like a filthy, crazy man that no right-minded person would want to go near."

Ethan wondered about Ascot. What is the right thing to do when a well-equipped militia captures your friend and you have no idea where they have taken him? Ascot said they were safer separated than they were together. Since Ascot was smart and could take care of himself, the only thing Ethan felt he could do was head home.

Looking in the grungy mirror, he brushed the dust out of his hair, then unzipped his jumpsuit and pulled his arms out. The thin material fell down and piled over his ankles. With only his half-boxer briefs on, Ethan shuffled a little closer to the sink. He leaned over and pushed down on the single button valve. The water pressure was disappointing. He cupped his hands and waited for it to dribble out. When it filled half of his hands the valve popped off, stopping the flow of water. Trying not to spill, he used his elbow to push the button again and start the flow of water. When it popped off the second time, his hands were full of water that he eagerly slurped it down.

He repeated the process a dozen times. After he had drunk enough, he poured the cupped water over his head. The cool water felt great. He continued, splashing water onto his face, chest and back until it dribbled down and covered his entire body. Ethan wiped the water around his body like it was suntan oil until a thin even layer of cool water covered his body. He noticed that his legs had several perfectly round uniform welts. It looked as if someone had poked him with a light purple ink pen. He rubbed one and discovered that it was slightly tender. "Weird," he thought, then he pulled the jumpsuit up and put his arms back through the sleeves, then zipped up the suit to the middle of his chest. It was just high enough to keep it from falling open. Then he stepped out of the bathroom. The warm, dry desert wind blew over him and the thin layer of water on his body quickly lost its cooling properties.

Ethan walked from the restroom bungalow to the road. Not a single car was visible as far as the eye could see in either direction, and that was very far. He went back to the ledge that overlooked the vista and the train tracks. To his pleasant surprise the westbound train was passing by. He was a half-mile away and he thought he could run and just catch it.

Determined to get onboard, Ethan enthusiastically leaped off the forty-foot rest area vista and onto the sandy slope, then sprinted down towards the tracks. He hadn't sprinted like this yet, marveling at his speed and how each stride carried him at least five times his normal distance. It felt like he was floating over the ground.

When he caught up to the train, he figured at least three quarters of it had passed him already. He stopped alongside the train to catch his breath and waited for an empty flat car. He stood for what seemed like a long time. All the cars were stacked shipping containers, with little or nothing to grab. "Where were the flat cars?" It was possible that there weren't any left so he had better find another way to hop on—he was running out of train to catch.

The space between the train cars was about four feet. He just needed to propel himself up above the wheels, and then could suspend himself between two cars. Once onboard, he could shimmy up and sit on the roof like he had seen people do on a program about India.

Now that he had a plan, he jumped into gear alongside the train. Once again, he was easily able to match the train's speed. He knew he could propel himself high enough to get onboard, but the clanking and grinding of the train's big metal wheels was intimidating. The earlier vision of being run over and turned into hamburger started flooding his mind again, but he knew he had no choice. He had to get onboard, so he focused on the fact that he had already accomplished it once.

Ethan made a few practiced hops to build his confidence and to make sure that he could get enough altitude while running at train speed. Aiming for the handle between the cars, he mustered up the courage and jumped. When he pushed off the ground, he hit a soft sandy spot, causing him to fall a little short of his target.

Groping to try to find something to cling to, Ethan pressed his hands and feet against the sides of two adjacent container cars, but they were slippery from all the industrial grease and grime. He lost control and fell backwards. Now his shoulders and feet were wedged against the container walls and he was slowing sliding down towards the grinding metal wheels. In a panic, he pushed hard against the locked steel door like it was a leg press. The door buckled, and then popped open. Suddenly there was nothing to press against and he was falling.

Ethan spun around to face the ground moving beneath him. With just the tips of his fingers, he pushed against the slippery container, hurling himself like a pole-vaulter. Ethan was almost through the door when his stomach hit the lip of the container, stopping his momentum and shifting his weight forward. Ethan started falling headfirst, down towards the crack between the cars. With an iron grip he reached behind and grabbed the container's metal lip just under his hips. He squeezed and it crushed like a soda can, but it held his weight and stopped him from falling.

For a moment he lay on his stomach suspended between the two train cars, looking down, watching the sweat from his forehead fall like snowflakes onto the moving tracks beneath him. He tightened his grip and pulled himself into the freight container car.

Once inside, he stood up. The first thing he noticed was the smell of cardboard and fresh ink. The only light came from the crack in the door. As his eyes adjusted, he saw that there wasn't much room inside—most of the container was stacked floor-to-ceiling with cardboard boxes. He moved a few around to make a space to lie down. Once he no longer needed to see what he was doing, he closed the door. Immediately the car went dark. Only a small sliver of light came in from the bend in the door, and the rattle of wheels seemed further away. Since he was in the bottom of two stacked containers, the roof received no direct sunlight and the inside was cool.

The fact that Ethan was not sure where he was heading, or what to expect when the train arrived at its destination, all seemed trivial. He was in a quiet, dark place with no one chasing him. Relief washed over him as he lay down on his bed of boxes, the most relaxed he had been since he landed back on Earth. The vibration of the train felt like a Magic Fingers massage bed, and within seconds Ethan fell sound asleep.

Chapter 39

When the Magic Fingers stopped vibrating, Ethan woke up. The sound of metal cars banging into one another faded into the background as the last of the long train's inertia was dispelled. Ethan sprang to attention. He didn't want to be caught as a stowaway who had broken a door. He slowly cracked open the bent steel door, making a horrific scraping noise. Ethan instinctively held his breath so as not to create more attention.

He slipped past the crinkled opening, stood on its ledge, and looked side-to-side for a place to jump off. The air outside was cool and salty. The sun had just set and the sky was a dark orange. There was the sound of industrial vehicles, cranes, and men working. Ethan jumped towards a stack of containers and parked train cars. It felt like he was floating as he leaped over three rows of tracks. He landed softly on the gravel, and then ran towards the shadows of the yard.

The workers went about their business and Ethan managed to stay unnoticed as he snuck out of the shipping area. He had arrive in San Pedro, California, where the trains meet the ships and trucks. It was an abused area with no trees, dilapidated buildings, and the smell of diesel fuel mixed with the stagnant seawater.

He looked around for a pay phone or some kind of way to call his dad, but there weren't any. Besides, he didn't have any money. Ideally, he wanted to show up at the gym unexpected and surprise Vince. Once he had lost contact and began this impossible journey, he nursed a fantasy of showing up unannounced and surprising everyone. It was a silly idea, but it would be a memorable entrance—one of those things they would talk about for years.

When he got out of the docks and onto the city streets, he was shocked to see how much things had changed. Everything looked rundown and dreary. There was heavy traffic and the smoggy sky gargled from the constant drone of surveillance helicopters flying overhead. Digital billboards flashed lawyer ads and wanted posters with photos and video clips of scary-looking criminals who were shooting, robbing and mugging people.

"Maybe it had always been like this," he thought; perhaps over the years of being away he had idealized "home" and made it out to be much better than it really ever was. Then he saw army tanks positioned in the street and men in uniforms randomly stopping cars and pedestrians at checkpoint kiosks. Ethan stopped and watched. Their vehicles were emblazoned with "Department of Homeland Security," it looked like they were asking for ID. Ethan didn't have any ID. The last ID he had was his Valhalla Resort room key, and he had gotten rid of that right after the accident.

Feigning nonchalance, he turned and went a different way up a side street and onto another main road. There he saw prisoners wearing bright orange jumpsuits all chained together working on the side of the road, and picking up trash. He got a little nervous. His red jumpsuit was a little too similar to their orange ones for comfort, so he turned again.

He found himself walking North on the sidewalk of Pacific Coast Highway, passing a sea of homeless people who were squatting in a cascade of abandoned storefronts. In opposition to this down and out lot was a gaggle of young Christian militants, wearing uniforms and carrying signs with hateful slogans that shouted: "God Hates Fags and Drug Addicts!" "You're Poor Because God Hates You!" and, "Believe In Jesus Or Burn In hell!" No, this was not the America he had left eight years before, and nothing had changed for the better.

Ethan continued to walk, doing his best to ignore all the crazy people. Fortunately no one seemed to be paying any attention to him. This surprised him considering what he was wearing, but apparently it took a lot more than a silly outfit to stand out around here. Which suited him just fine.

A ten-wheel industrial dump truck passed Ethan as he walked up the PCH. Like a dog possessed to chase a moving car, he ran towards the truck and with a single impossible leap, jumped up into the dump bed, landing on a pile of sand out of view from the street. He did it so fast and fluidly that if anyone had seen it, they would have assumed that their eyes were playing tricks on them.

Ethan burrowed into the sand, like kids do at the beach, so that only his face was exposed. The sand was warm and relaxing. The dump truck passed through all the inspection stops without incident. Ethan watched the street signs go by and was pleased to find that the truck was heading North on the 405 Freeway. The traffic was heavy, so Ethan was confident that if he had to, he could jump out at anytime.

Eventually, Ethan recognized the distinctive smell of the Anheuser Busch beer brewery at the corner of the freeway and Roscoe Blvd. Nordhoff Street would be the next exit. He unburied himself and peeked over the rim of the dump bed. Traffic wasn't as heavy so the truck was now moving faster than before, but to Ethan's senses everything still seemed very slow. The truck was in the lane closest to the shoulder and for a moment it looked as if it was going to exit. If so, he would have hit the jackpot, but the truck stayed in the slow lane and passed his exit.

Ethan climbed down a ladder welded on the side of the dump bed just behind the cab. Large side view mirrors showed a red-faced, red-bearded man with glasses staring at him, his face a mix of both surprise and terror. Not sure what to do, Ethan gave him a contrived smile and an insincere wave as if he were riding on a float in a parade.

Feeling ridiculed the driver's face turned red with anger, and then he leaned over and opened the glove box. Papers, screwdrivers, and cigarette packets fell out and onto the floor, and then, like a magic trick, the driver was holding a gun. Now it was Ethan's turn to be surprised.

Chapter 40

Without hesitation, Ethan leaped off the moving truck onto the side of the freeway and tumbled down the embankment leading to a side street. The driver honked his horn in triumph, continuing on his way. Ethan got up and brushed himself off. Perhaps it was not the most graceful method, but he got here. He was now about five miles from home and could easily walk the rest of the way.

Ethan started walking West on Nordhoff. Many of the same burger and taco joints were still there as if nothing had changed. Ethan approached the university near the gym. He could take a shortcut through the campus. It was night, so most of the buildings were closed. A few students and maintenance people were just leaving. He felt extremely out of touch with humanity. He had been on Earth for a day now and all he had done was run for his life.

He hadn't had a chance to talk to anyone or find out what had been going on in the world for the last eight years, and he now felt completely disconnected from everything around him. He didn't even know what day it was, or month, for that matter. Ascot had supposedly kept track and he thought it might be August, but he couldn't be certain.

Ethan was hungry, thirsty, tired, and dirty. He found a drinking fountain and drank so much that he had to stop to catch his breath, then continued. When he looked up, a maintenance guy pushing a trolley of cleaning supplies stopped in the building across from him. Wanting to talk to someone and wash up, Ethan jogged across the lawn towards the building. The janitor had just gone into the women's bathroom, so Ethan stepped into the adjacent men's.

His face was sunburned and had week-old stubble and his hair was filthy, still matted from lying in the sand. His red jumpsuit was scraped up but not torn. Ethan filled his hands with liquid soap and turned on the water. A river of black dirt ran off his hands into the porcelain sink. He rolled up his sleeves and washed his forearms. When that was done, he lathered up his face and hair, and then stuck his head under the faucet to rinse it off. He was able to get most of the suds off, but there wasn't enough room in the sink to get water to the back of his head. So he splashed it off as best he could.

When he was done, he stood up. His dripping wet head was making a puddle on the floor. Somehow he had managed to pour water in his ear. He shook his head like a Labrador who had just climbed out of a swimming pool. Water drops sprayed the mirror and the countertops. He walked towards the paper towel dispenser and a paper towel automatically emerged from its mouth. Ethan tore off half-dozen towels and dried his face, then rubbed his head until the towels were soggy. He ran his fingers through his hair, then tossed the soggy wad towards the trashcan and missed. It hit the wall with a splat and stuck there, reminding Ethan that he was still getting used to his new strength. He reached for another wad of paper towels.

Ethan heard the squeak of the janitor's cleaning cart and looked up. A stubby man no more than 5-feet tall, with thick, shoulder-length black hair haphazardly streaked with grey, and a nose two sizes too large for his face, was staring at him. Ethan looked at the wadded paper blob spattered above the trash can, then shrugged with guilt. The little man's eyes squinted in rage, then he puffed up, like a gorilla ready to pound his chest, and howled in an incomprehensible language. Embarrassed, Ethan slipped out of the bathroom with the janitor brandishing his mop behind him.

His first encounter only added to Ethan's feeling of disconnected insecurity. Blood-Sweat-N-Tears Gym was less than a mile from the university. With a new burst of determination and the hope of soon being with people who would be happy to see him, he ignored his hungry, tired body and started jogging towards the gym.

The asphalt felt like foam rubber as he bounced across its surface. He was at the gym's parking lot in less than five minutes. Only, there was no gym. The Valley's icon of bodybuilding was now divided into several shops, including "Toto's Barkery," a bakery for pets. Ethan cupped his hands and pressed his eyes against the glass to look inside. Sure enough, where rows of free weights once stood were now barrels full of dog biscuits. Where the juice bar used to be, stood a glass bakery counter full of cookies and donuts for dogs.

Ethan was flabbergasted. Had everyone lost their minds? "What could be more absurd than a pet bakery?" The answer came almost instantly. Next door in the window was a large glossy poster of an Irish Setter wearing a pair of glasses; an optometrist for dogs.

The businesses in the strip mall were closed except for a liquor store and a pizza joint. Ethan headed towards them. He wanted to find out how long the gym had been gone. He stepped into the liquor store. The place smelled like an old ashtray and buzzed from cheap florescent lights. He asked everyone in the store, both employees and customers, if they had even heard of Blood-Sweat-N-Tears Gym. None of them had, but then again, none of them looked like they had ever set foot in a gym either.

Ethan headed towards the pizza joint. The restaurant was getting ready to close and the last few customers were getting into their cars. When Ethan opened the door and stepped inside, he was assaulted with the smell of garlic, pepperoni, and melted cheese. Ethan couldn't remember the last time he smelled anything so mouthwatering. Ignoring his body's physical cravings, he asked everyone inside if they knew anything about Blood-Sweat-N-Tears Gym. All the workers were eighteen-years-old. The manager was probably twenty, and as long as any of them could remember, the dog bakery had always been there. Well, so much for his detective work.

Discouraged, Ethan stepped out of the store, not sure of where to go, as an old El Camino in showroom condition pulled into a handicapped spot. A burly guy with a big beer belly wearing a Dodgers baseball cap stepped out. Clearly, he was not handicapped. Ethan stepped towards the man, who closed the door and clicked the alarm on with a chirp. "Go away, I don't have any change." The man's voice was low and raspy.

Ethan stopped, confused. "I'm not asking for money."

"Yeah, right!" the man responded sarcastically.

"No, I'm looking for information on the old Blood-Sweat-N-Tears Gym."

The man in the hat was opening the door to the pizza place, then suddenly changed gears, looking curiously at Ethan. "Sure, I remember the place. I knew Vince. He had an old Ranchero." He pointed to his car. "He kept saying he was going to fix it up one day, but never did."

Ethan was so excited that he had found someone that knew something that the words burst out of him before he could stop himself: "Yeah, I'm Ethan. Vince is my dad!"

The man's face looked like he'd just seen a ghost. He didn't say anything, just walked through the door to the pizza counter to place his order. Ethan followed him.

The kid behind the counter looked up at the clock, disappointed. It was seven minutes before closing time, and he was hoping to go home early. He sighed, and in a snotty voice said, "Whatever you order is going to have to be to go!"

The man in the hat nodded and ordered two large pizzas and a large antipasto salad. Looking at Ethan, he added, "and a slice." He swiped his ATM card, punched in his numbers, and then grabbed the receipt and the slice of pizza.

Ethan waited patiently, hoping to get more of the story, but the man looked scared, even paranoid when he turned and waddled over to the closest fake wood bench, gesturing to Ethan that he should follow. Ethan slid into the seat opposite the big man, who pushed the slice of pizza over at him. Ethan's eyebrows shot up.

"Eat, eat, you look like you need it." Without another word, Ethan dove into the slice, and as his tongue touched the mozzarella, he was transported back in time to when his dad would take him to Chuck E. Cheese's for his birthdays. After Ethan's thirteen's birthday Vince wouldn't allow him to eat pizza anymore, the fat-to-protein ratio was unacceptable. The fat man adjusted his Dodgers cap, and then put out his hand. "I'm Skip." Ethan wiped his own hand off on his jumpsuit and returned Skip's gesture, never pausing as he chewed. Skip continued, "I own and run a little legal firm up the street for the last thirty years. I pretty much know all the business owners in the area, particularly the smaller non-chain establishments, which are getting fewer and farther between. Each year some big national chain comes in and wipes out the local small businesses."

Ethan paused between swallows. "What happened to the gym, and where's my dad?"

Skip looked side-to-side, leaned across the table and whispered. Ethan leaned in smelling his stale beer breath. "Uh, you are supposed to be dead, so what the hell happened?"

"It's a long story."

Skip leaned back on the bench expectantly. For a moment, the two men stared and waited, then Ethan made the first move. "I got a job out of the country and there was an accident. Everyone but me and another guy were killed. We were isolated and finally managed to escape, and it's taken us several years to get home. I think there was a cover-up to hide what really happened."

Now it was Skip's turn to raise his eyebrows. "Hmm, shit like that happens all the time, but most people don't escape. I would watch your back if I were you."

"So, do you know where my dad is?"

"Unfortunately." The man pulled out a sleek new iPhone and brought up a webpage, then handed it to Ethan. It was a website of old newspaper articles dedicated to unsolved mysteries. There were hundreds of examples where people mysteriously died, and then their businesses and property were taken over by a competing corporation, which benefited handsomely from the tragedy.

"Is my dad in here somewhere?"

"He was, but it was a long time ago and his story is old. New stories like these come out almost every day."

Ethan stared at the lettering on the man's baseball cap and waited for him to continue, trying to keep his focus. There was an awkward silence. Finally the man cleared his throat. "Eight years ago he had an accident."

"What kind of accident?" Ethan's voice rose unintentionally.

"He was found on a bench press. A barbell crushed his chest."

Ethan's eyes started to swell with tears. Embarrassed, he rubbed them dry and wiped his nose. "Was there an investigation?"

"No, it was considered an accident and that was that."

Ethan looked confused. "Anyone who knew Vince would know that makes as much sense as a fish drowning. Surely there must have been some suspicions."

Skip leaned back and patted his bulging stomach. "I wouldn't know. I'm not much of an exercise guy."

A blob of watery snot fell out of Ethan's nose and onto the table. He immediately grabbed a napkin and wiped it up.

Skip looked at Ethan kindly. "I got suspicious when the property changed ownership without the usual probate. It was never advertised, no signs in the window, no online listings. First, a corporation took over the gym, and then they moved to a bigger location a few blocks West. After that, they subdivided the space into three shops and charged a boatload of rent. How those businesses manage to stay afloat selling dog biscuits is beyond me. Something seems fishy."

Ethan grabbed a napkin, wiped his nose again, and with a crack in his voice: "I shouldn't have left!"

Skip grabbed Ethan's arm and looked at him sincerely. "Don't blame yourself, kid! It's not your fault your dad died and you probably couldn't have stopped it even if you were here."

Ethan nodded. "What happened to all his personal stuff?

"I watched the Ranchero get towed after the registration expired, and I heard the landlord who owned Vince's house had everything hauled away. I don't know where to. It all happened very fast. It was as if someone purposely didn't want to leave any unfinished business behind, and that normally never happens in a probate case. I can't prove anything but it feels like something's rotten."

A busboy wheeled a mop and bucket past the table, then started mopping the back of the restaurant. The kid behind the counter held up a brown bag. "Here's your salad, oh and, what kind of dressing do you want?"

Skip nodded, excused himself, and headed to the counter. Ethan still had the iPhone in his hand. The gadget hadn't changed much from the original version, though it was much faster and the screen was clearer. He Googled: "Vanessa Montel, Northridge, CA." Ethan's stomach sank as an article from a local news blog with a photo of Vanessa popped up. It was dated eight years earlier, and it was an obituary. Ethan looked up. The pizza boy had just handed Skip one of his pizzas and was now slicing up the second one.

As fast as he could, Ethan skimmed over the article. Apparently there had been a hit-and-run accident. She had been drunk and was walking home alone late, after a night of partying. That didn't sound like Vanessa at all. She wasn't a party girl.

Ethan clenched his teeth, seething with anger. What were the chances of the only two people in his life, that he really cared about, suddenly dying within a few months of him leaving? If he only did one more thing in his life, he was going to get to the bottom of this.

Chapter 41

Warm pizza aroma floated over Ethan as Skip walked back to the table to retrieve his iPhone. "Kid, I'm sorry about what happened; it was a long time ago. If you want to talk more later I'm at the office almost every day."

Ethan handed Skip his phone and nodded. His stomach was still ravenous, even after the pizza, but he was so upset now that he couldn't think about food. Skip shuffled towards the exit, then leaned against the door, pushing it open with his shoulder while cradling the pizzas in his hand. "I'm sorry I can't be more helpful, but right now I've got hungry people waiting for me."

Ethan followed him out the door and watched him get into his El Camino and drive away. The kid behind the counter was now locking the glass door and had just flipped the sign to "Closed."

Ethan felt aimless. He had spent eight years dreaming about coming home and now that he finally did, there was nothing here for him. Over the years, Ascot would frequently rant about how corporations were taking over the world, how the people were being manipulated and lied to, and that was why things often didn't add up.

One of Ascot's favorite rants was on the Kennedy assassination—how the people sitting on the grassy knoll who saw the real shots that killed the president had all mysteriously ended up dead.

Ethan, lost in his thoughts, started walking in no particular direction. Ascot's paranoid conspiracy views of the world now seemed to be making more sense. Maybe Ascot wasn't as crazy as Ethan had thought. Ascot had often said that it was easier to get away with a really big lie than a small one. Ascot was convinced that the moon landing was a hoax and that 911 had been an inside job. Ethan mused, "Maybe Ascot was right. Maybe I'm not willing to see how fucked up the world really is." Perhaps most people weren't willing to face the truth, so they lived in an idealized dream state, pretending that things were fair and honest when they really weren't.

It seemed possible that a company that was capable of building a secret space station and a secret air base could probably hide an accident. They would have no problem getting rid of anyone who might start asking questions and expose something that would make them look bad.

If this were the case, then his father's and Vanessa's deaths were no accidents. He knew history had many examples of this. It just seemed unlikely that a common kid from the San Fernando Valley, whose dad owned a gym, would be the target of a big corporation.

Even after the shootout at the pod in the desert, Ethan wasn't sure if it was Eden, Inc. that was behind everything, but the more he thought about it, the more it made sense. Now, in a bizarre way, it made him suddenly feel very significant. How many people have the kind of knowledge that warrants being put on a multi-national corporation's hit list?

Ethan clenched his jaw. The anger that enveloped his body made him feel powerful. He suddenly had a bigger bounce in his step. If Eden, Inc. killed Vince and Vanessa he was damn well going to do something about it. Fantasies of exposing Eden, Inc.'s lies and seeing the corporation fall to the ground like a giant redwood filled his mind, but then the idea of merely humiliating the company seemed trivial. If these assholes killed his only family and girlfriend then they probably did the same thing to all the other people who were working on the station as well. They deserved much worse than just going out of business. They needed to be terrorized—captured and slowly tortured.

Ethan's anger grew as he continued to walk aimlessly, fantasizing about all the ways he and his new strength could make those people pay for his losses. Ironically, the more he thought about it, the more the anger started to dissipate. It was hard to keep up the energy of a vendetta. Even with his new abilities, he wasn't sure if he could follow through with killing someone, particularly if it was premeditated. He knew he could defend himself if he was attacked, and if the assailant died, well then he had it coming.

He was bothered by the fact that there would always be a tinge of uncertainty. Suppose he was wrong? What if his dad really did die at the bench press, and Vanessa's death really was an accident. It seemed ridiculous and unlikely, but it wasn't impossible, inexplicable things happen all the time.

His head was reeling. He had no money, no ID, and all records of him said he was dead. Normally that would be daunting enough, but a deep gnawing hunger and a little indigestion had numbed his mind. After going so long without food, the slice of pizza had upset his stomach and what little fuel it offered had worn off almost immediately. He considered himself a fairly resourceful guy. He should be able to legitimately procure some real food.

He remembered talking with a group of guys at the gym about what they would do if they were suddenly homeless with no money. One of the guys was a musician. He told them, "I go to parties for a living. I know all the back entrances to all the hotels and nightclubs. I know all the Happy Hour spots and I know most all the caterers in town, so if I were homeless, as long as I had some respectable clothes, I could find a way to eat."

Ethan smiled at the memory. It was too late for happy hour, and he wasn't anywhere near a luxury hotel. Most of the San Fernando Valley shut down at night fairly early, and he was wearing a ridiculous red jumpsuit with blue boxing shoes. Even if someplace were open, no one was going to let him in dressed the way he was.

He walked through a quiet section of town that used to be small farms but had now been replaced with spacious residential ranch houses with long gravel driveways and no streetlights. "This street isn't going to get me anywhere," he thought. He turned a corner and far in the distance was a row of lights where businesses and restaurants still appeared to be open. He headed towards what seemed to be the hot spot of the Valley. With each step, his hunger grew and the option of possibly stealing something just this one time didn't seem so bad.

Chapter 42

Naked, strapped to a stainless steel table, probes and body scans of all kinds were measuring and cataloging every inch of Ascot's inner and outer body. A staff of doctors and scientists in lab coats filled the examination room. Several consoles with screens and computer terminals beeped and hummed, filling the room with static electrical energy, adding to the stifling chaos.

Unable to move, Ascot watched with trepidation. None of the doctors were explaining anything to him. They treated him like an inanimate object, a curious fossil that they had found and were carbon dating, trying to decipher.

Eventually a short, white-haired man, with a pencil mustache and a contrasting tan face, seemed to appear out of nowhere. He addressed Ascot directly. "Hi, I'm Dr. Conrad." His surprisingly husky voice and no-nonsense demeanor seemed familiar to Ascot, but he couldn't place him. "I'm going to be doing some tests on your spinal column. I'll need you to answer some questions as I go through the procedure."

Ascot nodded. The doctor attached a metal brace to Ascot's legs with a cable that ran up and connected to his spine. Then he held up a computer tablet. "Let me know when you feel a tingling sensation or a change in temperature."

Again Ascot nodded. Dr. Conrad pushed a few keys and a diagnostic program appeared on the screen and began running through its cycle. Within a minute, Ascot's body involuntarily trembled. "I feel something." His voice came out cracked and airy.

Dr. Conrad looked at the computer screen. "Excellent, that's a good sign." After about a half hour of testing, with Ascot speaking up every time he felt something, the doctor finally unstrapped Ascot, removed most of the tubes and wires, and then adjusted the braces on his legs. He positioned Ascot so his legs were dangling off the side of the table, then sat down and typed something on the computer keyboard. "I want you to try to move your legs."

Ascot looked humiliated, "Why? You know I can't!" His voice was very defensive. For eight years he had been suppressing his emotions and forcing himself not to deal with the reality of his injuries. Ethan had done his best to ignore it and treat him as if it were a temporary inconvenience. Now the reality was hitting him hard and he wasn't enjoying the process.

The doctor rubbed his thin mustache and gave Ascot a knowing grin. "Humor me!"

Ascot took a deep breath and tried, but nothing happened.

The doctor looked at him with another smile. "That was good." He typed a command on his keyboard. "Now, try that again." This time Ascot's leg convulsed wildly and both of them began to laugh. "I told you. Around here you must always expect the unexpected!"

Just then, Casper walked into the examination room, demanding the results of the medical team's findings. Ascot was once again ignored. What little tinge of light-heartedness that had existed was instantly sucked out the moment Casper set foot in the room.

Ascot's naked body was readjusted so he was lying on his back. He was covered with a sheet and strapped in again. He felt the Velcro straps press against his chest and stomach, making it uncomfortable and harder for him to breathe. All the men in lab coats left the examination room and assembled in an adjacent observation room separated by floor-to-ceiling glass. Ascot was suddenly alone and the energy of the room instantly calmed. He could see that all the lab coats were on one side of the room and the bald guy was on the other side, listening.

Casper had started the day extremely curious as to how in the hell these two guys, Ascot LaRouch and Ethan Stone, survived the Valhalla accident. He wanted to know everything he could about the effects eight years of space had on them. He was told that the one who had gotten away seemed to have extraordinary abilities. Casper wanted to know exactly what these "extraordinary abilities" were. He was disappointed to find out that the guy they had captured was a paraplegic. "How friggin' difficult is it to capture a cripple?" That didn't seem extraordinary at all. He wanted some answers and he wanted to be impressed.

The scientists examining Ascot were determining if his exposure to space life had changed him physically or biochemically. The questions were: Did space exposure give these men extra abilities? If so, could it be duplicated here on Earth? Did they accidentally discover something that could revolutionize humanity? If so, what were the possibilities of these findings?

The team of doctors and scientists lined up and gave Casper a quick layman's explanation of their findings. The first person to speak, starting the ad hoc presentation, was Dr. Chen, a stocky Asian man, with medium-length hair and owl-like glasses. He was a biologist whose specialty was the research of viruses, pathogens, and cellular mutations. He took two cautious steps forward, looking like a man who just volunteered for a suicide mission. "There aren't any bacterial or viral abnormalities, but there is a list of interesting and unique variations that have occurred due to his exposed time in space."

Casper nodded in anticipation. Chen adjusted his glasses and pushed a button on a computer terminal. A photo of a cell popped on the screen. "From what we can tell, the subject's cells have become dense—we believe due to increased gravity. Ironically, they went into an environment with no gravity, but the artificial gravity must have been increased, possibly as much as ten times Earth's gravity. As a result, the subject's skin is almost impossible to penetrate, making it practically tough as steel, but it is still skin; it's flexible and elastic, it's just not permeable.

Casper's eyes widened and he stood up and looked into the examination room at the guy strapped to the metal table. "Are you telling me this guy is bulletproof?"

Chen fidgeted nervously, thinking about the question. "Perhaps, that is a possibility." Casper sat down in a chair, a maniacal smile spreading across his face.

Chen stepped aside as if he had just passed the baton in a relay. Next up was Dr. Walton, a thin-lipped, emaciated man with salt-and-pepper hair who was clearly the tallest person in the room. His bony arms stuck out like thin sticks from his lab coat. Ironically, his specialty was kinesiology, skeletal structure, and muscle development. He spoke in a high monotone. "The subject's increased cell density has also caused increased muscle tension and tensile strength, off-the-chart capabilities. He could very well have the strongest upper body strength of any human being on Earth, yet his cells are still fluid and supple, allowing them to perform their functions. They seem to be behaving like a non-Newtonian fluid; the harder they are impacted, the stronger they become."

"Hmm." This time Casper didn't move; obviously thinking.

Dr. Walton waited for Casper who remained lost in thought. Unsure what to do, he looked at his colleges for instructions. They all meekly shrugged, so he hesitatingly moved on. "It also seems his body has created an unusually high level of ATP, the fuel that muscles cells use to contract, so he has an unusually high level of endurance."

Casper sat back in his chair, his fingertips lightly touching in front of him. "So, is this guy ready to work as the strongman in a freak show?"

Walton smiled, his thin lips making a tight slit across his face. "He certainly could qualify for that position were he to so choose."

Casper's fingers lightly bounced against each other in front of his chest. His face betrayed no emotion, only deep concentration. Dr. Walton nodded to Casper and the next specialist stepped forward.

Dr. Aaronoff was the complete opposite of Dr. Walton. A portly man who seemed as wide as he was tall, he had a broad, flat nose, a big mouth, and a ring of brown hair that started at his ears and partly circumnavigated his head, leaving a few hapless strands combed over the top. His area of expertise was the human central nervous system. He tried several times to clear his throat before he was able to speak. "The subject's nervous system has also evolved. The nerve fibers are transmitting at a rate five times faster than that of a normal human. We believe that this rapid increase of neuro-transmission supports our hypothesis that the subject was indeed subjected to an increased gravity environment. All falling objects or anything affected by gravity would move at a more rapid speed. It appears that the subject's brain and nervous system adapted to the increased speed, so objects falling at five to ten times the normal speed would now appear to him to be falling at our normal Earth speed. Which I'm sure you know is ten meters per-second squared."

Casper gave a grunt, signaling that he was listening and indicating that he expected the doctor to continue with better and more interesting information.

Aaronoff cleared his throat again. "With this increased cognitive function comes superior reflex speed, so his awareness and upper body motor skills are abnormally fast. From what we can tell, everything to him appears to be happening in slow motion. This indicates that the human nervous system is more adaptable than we ever thought possible. We have no idea what our human potential is, because the earth has limited our parameters. We believe—"

Casper cut him off. "Thank you." He tried to keep the impatience out of his voice, but the science was not as interesting as the subject. "I want to talk to him."

Casper stood up, and it was as if the Red Sea had just parted. The lab coats all scattered to their designated spots. The door was opened and straight in front of him, strapped to a steel table, was Ascot.

The space was dead quiet, the hum from the machinery gone. Casper stepped into the examination lab. All the doctors and scientists seemed to hold their breath as Casper came into their world, walking across the sterile white linoleum floor. The click of his twenty-five-hundred-dollar Italian shoes reverberated, but he hardly heard the sound, so intent was he on his prey.

Casper gazed down at Ascot, who appeared to be sleeping. "I want to talk with him alone." Without another word, the lab coats all scurried into the adjoining conference room and then continued out of sight. When Casper looked back down, Ascot was staring up at him, contempt and curiosity visible on his face. He spoke as gently as possible. "Hi, I'm Casper Degas."

Ascot nodded. "I've heard of you."

"It appears you have undergone a seriously stressful eight years."

"Yeah, you might say that."

"It seems you are better off because of it."

"You think not being able to walk, pushing myself around in an office chair for eight years while no one does a thing to try to help us or even see if we survived is being better off?"

Casper unfastened the restraints, and then helped Ascot sit up. "I owe you an apology. I truly am sorry about what happened to you and your friend, as well as the entire crew of the Valhalla resort. It was a tragic accident and we made the false assumption that no one could possibly have survived. Finding a thousand pieces of a space station scattered throughout space is virtually impossible. I just never thought I would be speaking to a survivor. I want to make it up to you."

"How are you going to do that?" The words spat from Ascot's mouth before he could stop himself.

Casper kept his tone quiet, yet charming. "Look, I know you're pissed off. Who wouldn't be? But you have to see things for what they are."

"How's that?"

"You are extremely lucky."

"I don't feel that lucky right now."

"I'm sure you don't. I've read your file, it says you're an idealist."

"Really. That's bad?"

"Bad's not the word, but it's not practical. Look, you're obviously an intelligent man or you wouldn't have survived the way you did, so I'm going to put things in perspective. I know you will understand and appreciate what I'm about to say."

Hands behind his back, Casper began pacing around the room. "There are two kinds of people, those who see the world and complain that it's not the way it ought to be, and then there are we who see things as they are without judgment. Sure things could be better, we should all get along, live in peace, clean up the environment, erase poverty and all that crap. But it's never happened, and it never will. That's the reality. Years ago we thought if we just got rid of the Soviet Union, we could stop the arms race and all our problems would go away."

Casper stopped and gave Ascot an ironic shrug. "So we got rid of the Soviet Union and nothing changed. Why? Because that's not the way the world works!" Casper's eyebrows lifted and he continued without drawing breath. "We will always find a new enemy and if none steps up to the plate, we will invent one. I choose to see things for what they are and profit from it. I didn't create this mess—I simply make it work for me."

Ascot gave him a wry smile. "So, you have no soul and you don't stand for anything."

"Quite the contrary, my angry friend. I stand for what is real and what is inevitable. We live in a complicated world where corporations call the shots. This trend is irreversible, so it boils down to picking a side and deciding: do you want to pick the winning or the losing team? I choose the winning team; that's why I'm the head of a large corporation with assets all over the globe and in space. That's why I have congressmen and senators kissing my ass—they work for the highest bidder and that's me. You and your idealistic friends can point your fingers at me and say, 'That's not fair!' And you know what? You're right! But that's the way it is!"

Ascot was amazed how crazy people could, in a strange, twisted way, make sense. His celebrity ex-wife, Queie, had that same ability. She was so passionate that she could convince thousands of people to rally around an idea even if it was completely absurd. Ascot sat and looked at Casper, a flood of thoughts racing through his brain. There was something both compelling and revolting about the man—clearly he was a highly intelligent sociopath, used to getting everything he wished for.

Ascot swallowed before speaking. "So what the hell do you want from me?"

Casper pulled up a chair from a nearby workstation and sat down next to Ascot. "You are a unique individual, a survivor of an accident that we made disappear. So your amazing survival and return is something we don't want to leak to the public. Our next generation of outer space resorts is getting ready to launch. We don't want rumors or bad PR. So I can either stop you by force, or I can have you on my team."

"If I'm so idealistic, what makes you think I'll join 'your team?'"

"I can offer you more than anything you could ever acquire on your own."

Despite himself, Ascot found Casper's confidence intoxicating. "Like what?"

"I can give you almost anything you could ever want—no limits, a new beginning with, money, prestige, power. I'm talking real power: the power to do anything you want, anywhere you want, at any time you want."

"What do I have to do?"

"First of all, I want to find your friend. He is also very valuable to me, I need you to help me find and recruit him."

Ascot closed his eyes, musing. "I know where he's headed and what makes him tick, but I can't speak for him or promise he's going to go along with your program."

"I think he will. I pulled his file, too. He is young and impressionable and you are his mentor. When you get right down to it, there isn't much to consider. He has no family, no place to live, no proof of identity, and no way to make a living. It's a brutal world out there, and there are enough other people to make his life a living hell. It won't take him long to swallow his pride."

"So, if this is so inevitable, and he's going to jump at the opportunity, what do you need a cripple like me for?" Ascot winced at his own harsh tone, the finality of his words. But Casper responded kindly, moving in for the kill.

"Speed. I don't want to waste time, I don't want him getting in the news and having people start asking questions. I think you can convince him to live by a newer set of principles. Besides, you're not going to stay crippled for long."

"What do you mean?" Ascot was suddenly skeptical.

Casper grinned and raised an eyebrow. "This is Eden, Inc. We have the most advanced medical technology on the planet. One of our divisions is dedicated to the advancement and improvement of human performance. That's also why we want you two around. You have achieved some staggering results, and we'd like to find a way to create those same results on Earth. So if you join our team, we'll have you up and walking within a week."

Ascot considered the possibility that Casper might not be all bad. It even seemed possible that, in a strange way, he could be rather generous.

"You want me and Ethan to be your lab rats?"

"Not lab rats, but rather prize specimens that warrant further study."

"How do you propose I will walk again?"

"I believe Dr. Conrad already got you started. Our weapons department has developed high-tech exoskeleton combat suits that give our soldiers massive strength and speed. We are using this technology to outfit paraplegics with exoskeleton leg braces. The difference is that the hydraulic joints are trigged from the nerve reflexes that flow down the spine, instead of by gross muscle movements."

Ascot sat wide-eyed, hanging on Casper's words.

"This technology is at the vanguard of science. I believe with the newer lightweight, hydraulic braces, we will have you walking and running better than before your accident. Typically the challenge is balance. It will take some practice, but we will get you running faster and longer, jumping higher and beyond what would normally be possible. We believe the speed and strength of your legs should match that of your upper body."

Ascot was now enthralled. "Really? – Wow!"

Casper stopped pacing. "This technology isn't flawless, but with it I can offer you new hope and opportunities that you would never have thought possible."

Ascot sat under the glaring lights that reflected off the polished white floor and let the smell of disinfectant and warm electronic components fill his senses. He looked around the room, considering his choices. He could join the corporate giant, live the rest of his life in luxury, and disregard the principles he'd lived by his entire life. Or, he could leave and have nothing: no place to live, no money, no means of transportation, not even a wheelchair, let alone a high-tech pair of legs that could outperform his real ones. Then again, after this conversation, he could end up dead. He seriously doubted that Casper would just let him walk away, so the more he thought about it, he really had no choice.

Ascot cleared his throat, choosing his words carefully. "There is a time when a person has to re-evaluate what's important. I'm too fucking old to keep fighting the system. I fought it, got beaten up and never made a dent. Bottom line, I want to walk again, I want to be able to do all the things I always wanted to do—go places and see things that I could never afford to do before. If you can deliver that to me, I'm on your team."

Casper loved converting people to his way of thinking; he nodded his bald head in approval and straightened his thousand-dollar silk tie. "Do you think you can convince Ethan to work with us once we find him?"

Ascot shrugged. "I will do my best."

Casper nodded again. "With the two of you on my team we will be unstoppable— we will have more power than you could ever imagine."

Ascot ran his hand over his head, and then rubbed his chin, calculating. "Ethan is young, idealistic and he still has his legs. If you want him onboard—"

Casper burst in. "I need to know what makes him tick so I can make the right offer."

"He's never had money," Ascot mused, "so he doesn't know the power of having lots of money. In fact, I'm not sure I really do, to be honest."

Casper was impressed at Ascot's insight. For a moment, he spoke from the heart. "You're right. You have no idea. Most people have no idea. They think if they win the lottery all their problems will go away. They think they would know what to do if they suddenly had real money, but they wouldn't. Money complicates things. It's like having a very powerful racecar—if you don't know how to drive it, you'll crash. That's why the lottery winners usually end up worse off than they were before. When you have real money like I have, you have serious responsibilities, and an obligation to shape the world."

Ascot was now very intrigued. He sat and thought about Ethan, trying to sum up key behavior points that he had noticed during their time together in space. "Ethan has a needy side—he likes attention. He had no mom growing up, so being popular with the ladies is a big goal for him. He wants to be influential. He was hoping that our return to Earth would make him famous so he could have a voice, talk on TV, have his opinions discussed and evaluated. You give him that and I think he will give you whatever you want!"

Casper walked up and put out his hand for Ascot to shake. "It is a pleasure to have you on board. I will have Dr. Conrad and his staff outfit you with your new legs ASAP. I predict within a week you will be running and jumping like Steve Austin." Ascot's face was blank. "You never saw the TV show, 'The Six Million Dollar Man?'"

"Nah, man, I grew up in the 'hood—we watched 'The Cosby Show' and thought it was all BS."

Casper nodded and headed out the door. Ascot watched as the well-dressed executive strutted across the lab, through the glass-enclosed conference room, and out of sight. A few seconds later, all the men in lab coats began to file in again. Ascot lay back, his head swimming. He was beginning to feel like he had just made a deal with the Devil.

Chapter 43

Flyers for the Raunchy Texan Cowboy Bar littered the gutter as Ethan jogged towards the San Fernando Valley nightlife. Ethan picked one up and brushed the dirt off. There was a photo of a cowgirl with big boobs, wearing tiny cut-off shorts, cowboy boots, a tight shirt with her mid drift showing, and a big cowboy hat. It was possibly the most erotic thing Ethan had seen in eight years. The flyer advertised "Meatball Mondays, all-night Happy Hour, bull riding, and bar games!" The address was just a few blocks away. His stomach growled in anticipation of free Happy Hour food.

Red neon outlined the large white letters of the sign that proudly jutted over the front of the Raunchy Texan. The building was painted barn red with a big white door. A burly bouncer covered in tattoos, his head shaved, stood at the door checking IDs. Ethan had no ID and this guy didn't look like the type to cut anyone some slack.

Ethan's hunger pangs grew; he wasn't going to give up right away. He walked towards the back of the building. The kitchen door was open and a busboy dressed in blue-grey coveralls stepped out of the back door carrying a trashcan. The restaurant's dumpster was overflowing. The busboy contemplated the situation, then plopped the can down next to the dumpster, turned around and walked back into the kitchen, all without noticing Ethan.

Ethan saw an opportunity and figured he had nothing to lose. He scanned the area to make sure no one was looking, and then leaped eight feet into the air and landed on top of the dumpster's plastic lid. The trash compacted instantly, making the lid level. Ethan hopped off the dumpster, grabbed the trashcan the busboy had just left, and emptied it into the newly reconfigured dumpster. Carrying the trashcan, he walked into the kitchen as if he had worked there for years. A skinny kid washing dishes looked at him inquisitively, then went right back to loading beer mugs onto a dish rack.

A few seconds later, Ethan was standing in a room full of noisy, drunk people. Across the room, in the shape of a covered wagon, was the Monday Night Meatball Buffet. The crowd seemed to be more interested in drinking, so the food was largely ignored. Ethan felt a surge of desire pulse through his body—he wanted to sprint across the room and start stuffing his face. As cool as possible, he casually strolled across the room, past a pool table, a mechanical bull, and then finally a row of high bar tables and stools. By the time he arrived, the smell of grease, salt, and sugar was so overwhelming it was erotic.

Ethan had spent his whole life living with a strict body builder who only ate low fat, high protein, and unprocessed food. For Ethan, looking at the trough of barbecued meatballs slathered in sauce, white bread, chicken wings, potato skins, and buttered popcorn, was like watching pornography. Ethan marveled at how guilty he felt. "Sorry, dad, but what choice do I have?" He grabbed a plate.

Ethan piled a small arsenal of meatballs, chicken wings, and potato skins onto his plate, and popped a meatball into his mouth. The second the sugary coating touched his tongue, his insulin levels spiked and sent a message to his brain demanding more sugar. Ethan tried not to act like a starving piranha, but his mind was a blank; he was on autopilot, eating like a zombie. There is nothing more satisfying than the densely-packed calories of warm, greasy foods. After three plates, Ethan slowed his eating and relaxed, his body floating on a surreal cloud. He was buzzed from all the carbs and fats. His stomach was in shock, trying to break down the poly-unsaturated, hydrogenated, nitrate-infused, preservative-ridden, mystery meat that he had just consumed. The experience left him warm and sleepy. It was the best he'd felt in years.

It's no wonder Americans were fat, Ethan thought. This type of food was like a drug, but even in his peaceful delirium he still felt a tinge of self-disappointment. He had always had the discipline to resist eating junk food. He decided to make this his one exception.

With his eyes at half-mast, Ethan made his way across the bar to a soft chair near the corner of the room overlooking the bullpen. The moment he sat down, he began to nod in and out of sleep. A minute later, there was some commotion as a group of Japanese tourists lined up to ride the mechanical bull. Everyone not riding either had a video camera or was snapping pictures on their cell phone. Almost instantly, a crowd gathered around the pen, blocking Ethan's view. Still dozing, he continued to sit and let his body absorb the calories, as the shouting, hooting, and clinking of beer bottles escalated. Finally, the enthusiasm around the bullpen brought Ethan out of his stupor. With renewed energy, he rose and walked over to take a look.

The rules were clearly spelled out on a big sign over the bull pen: each ride cost ten dollars, the rider could only hold on with one hand, if the rider touched the bull or the strap with the other hand he was disqualified. Stay on the saddle for 10 seconds and win $100, plus $20 for every second afterwards. There was an electronic sign displaying the name of the rider and a giant stopwatch on the wall. It started and stopped as each rider got on. Next to the stopwatch was a money clock, which also started at zero. For every second the rider stayed on, $10 would roll by.

Everyone watched the money clock because it was inherently more interesting to see the dollars roll up. Next to the dollar clock, was a gaudy light bulb-encrusted sign that said BONUS! This would light up if someone ever made it to ten seconds. At least once a week, the owner, supposedly a cowboy who had ridden real bulls in his youth, would ride the mechanical bull and hit the ten-second mark to show the crowd that it could be done. That was generally the only time the bonus light ever went on.

Ethan watched as a series of ambitious drunk people got on the bull and then got tossed off a few seconds later. There was kid in a booth operating the bull. He was good at keeping people on for about five seconds then dumping them; so far, the best ride of the night had been six seconds. Ethan walked around the room, looking at the mechanical bull from different angles while listening in on people's conversations. He heard a guy wearing jeans, boots and a cowboy hat say between guzzles of beer, "This is for pussies! This ain't like ridin' no real bull! There ain't no foam pillows at a rodeo."

His inebriated friend challenged, "Well, if it's so goddamn easy let's see you do it!" but nothing came of it and they started talking about something else.

After watching several people attempt the ride, Ethan knew he could do it with no problem. This was an opportunity to make some money, which he was desperate to do. The problem was he needed ten bucks first. Ethan thought about asking someone for money. He figured he could easily pay back double and still have plenty left over, but he looked around the room and didn't see anyone who looked approachable.

As Ethan glanced around, he noticed a wadded-up flyer inside a pile of popcorn. Something about it beckoned. Ethan causally walked toward it, knelt down, pretending to tie his shoe, and picked up the paper, then nonchalantly he walked to the quietest corner of the bar. When he uncrinkled the paper, the hottie cowgirl stared up at him, a fake-Texas angel offering him his future. Next to her inviting mouth and come-hither eyes, were three crumpled fives and two single dollar bills.

Ascot used to say things that Ethan thought were silly, like, "When you are clear in your purpose, the Universe will provide for you." Standing in a shitty San Fernando Valley cowboy bar that smelled of old beer and reheated meatballs, surrounded by screaming, drunk tourists, and wearing a ridiculous red jumpsuit, Ethan Stone had the most profound spiritual moment of his life. He promptly thanked the universe for looking out for him, and then walked over to the sign-up sheet to ride the mechanical bull.

A blonde girl who resembled the photo on the flyer stood behind a glass display counter that sold tacky belts, hats, plastic bulls, and other crap—marketing gimmicks for The Raunchy Texan. When Ethan approached, he could smell her floral shampoo. It reminded him of slow dancing in high school, that rush from getting close enough to girls to soak up their fragrant essence. Ethan put two of his five-dollar bills on the counter. "I want to ride the bull."

She smiled, nodded, and then handed Ethan a waiver. It was the usual legal stuff: if you fell off and broke something, the Raunchy Texan was in no way responsible. The rider assumes all liability, yadda-yadda. Ethan read through the paragraph that laid out the legal protocol, then looked up at the girl behind the counter. Locks of blond hair cascaded from underneath her ten-gallon hat. She just stood there, her breasts popping out of a red-and-white checkered shirt tied to resemble a bikini top. It was as if her job was to just stand there, look pretty, and not say anything that might spoil whatever fantasy was going on in the minds of the customers. It worked. Ethan smiled back, his groin charging with renewed vigor. Then he started filling out the sign-up sheet.

As he was about to put his name on the page, a thought struck him. He was on some corporate hit list, so he should use a fake name. Since he didn't have any ID, it didn't matter what name he put down. The girl wasn't checking. The first name that came to him was Vince. He would make up for eating all the junk food by winning the prize money in his dad's name.

Chapter 44

J.W. Owens had moved to LA to become an actor. His biggest obstacle was that he had such a heavy Texas drawl he was only good for cowboy films. When those rare auditions came, he usually got nervous, so he didn't book many parts. Other than a few scenes here and there as a member of a posse or an outlaw gang, his acting career never took off. To stay alive, he had opened the Raunchy Texan. Originally he wanted it to be a barbeque/strip club. He imagined naked girls chewing on big sloppy ribs and getting sauce all over their naked bodies. He figured guys would pay good money to lick it off.

As it turned out getting permits for such things was much more difficult and expensive than he had anticipated, so instead of naked girls and barbeque, he ended up with a mechanical bull and meatballs. He got a good deal on the bull. Since there weren't any real cowboys in LA, the cowboy-bar-craze had pretty much disappeared on the West Coast, but with some creative marketing and a cash incentive to ride the bull, J.W. was able to lure people in. Within a few years, he had built up a loyal following of regular customers and a reputation as a colorful tourist destination.

J.W had hired a nerdy, punk-rocker kid named Javier to be the mechanical bull operator. A joystick controlled the movements of the bull. Javier could make the ride easy or rough. The one rule J.W. had was, "Make sure the riders get knocked off before the ten seconds are up! I don't ever want to pay." That wasn't very difficult to do. A professional rodeo rider only had to stay on a real bull for eight seconds, and most of them didn't make it that long.

J.W. was in his office talking on the phone with his third ex-wife, a bartender with perfect breasts. The only redeeming qualities that J.W. could remember about her were that she made a good Bloody Mary, and she looked great in a tank top. That was about the depth of their relationship. She was crying and asking for an advance on her alimony check. Her 200 lb. Rottweiler needed hip replacement surgery. J.W. was working up the courage to tell her he had always hated that dog. In his opinion, the fact that it couldn't walk was an improvement, but before he could say anything he heard screaming and yelling coming from the bar downstairs.

He immediately knew something was wrong. There was the usual enthusiastic screaming, and then there was screaming like someone had just won the bull-riding prize. Unfortunately, Javier had a weakness for cute girls in short dresses. One time he had gotten so mesmerized by trying to look up a girl's dress he had lost track of time and she won the $100. J.W. made sure the little pencil dick paid the prize money out of his paycheck.

Then there was a time when the bull had malfunctioned. It bucked about as hard as one of those horses in front of the 99¢ store that three-year-olds ride. Fortunately, the rider was very drunk, so when the bouncer tackled the guy and knocked him off the bull, he had just assumed he had been thrown off. When one of his slightly-less-drunk friends tried to collect the prize money on his behalf, he was told in no uncertain terms to fuck off—the bull had malfunctioned. Just to be nice, J.W. gave them a pitcher of Papst Blue Ribbon, and by the end of the night the incident had been erased from their memories.

Without hesitation or explanation J.W. cut off the ex. "Something's up—I'll call you back!" and hung up. He hurried down the "not-to-code" plywood staircase he had built himself, doing his best not to stumble in his size 14 ½ boots.

When he opened the door, the energy in the room nearly knocked him over. In all the years he had owned the bar, he had never seen anything like this before. Everyone in the room was huddled around the bullpen, and the Bonus light was flashing. His jaw nearly hit the floor and his stomach clenched. When he got closer and could read the name of the rider displayed on the wall; he was confused. Vince Stone? "That's not a chick! What the fuck, Javier?"

The money clock was up to $600 and popping up another $20 every second. The bull had just been worked on and J.W. knew it was in perfect condition, so what the hell was Javier doing? J.W. was even more mystified to see the perplexed Javier absolutely terrified, and the mechanical bull going completely ape shit.

There was no way in hell any human being could ride that bull. It was at full throttle; spinning and bucking like a possessed demon. One second it would be completely vertical, with its horns straight up in the air, and a second later, it would flip forward and be completely vertical, ass to the ceiling, all while spinning around in circles and bucking, putting the rider completely sideways. J.W. watched in amazement and horror as the money clock cranked up to $900. And who was this character in a red janitor's jumpsuit? Clearly this guy was a human barnacle who wouldn't let go. To add insult to injury, the son-of-a-bitch was laughing.

J.W. had ridden professionally for a short time, and as far as he knew, there was no one on Earth that could ride a bull that long. By the time he pushed his way through the crowd to Javier's control panel, the money clock was up to a $1000. He threw the kill switch, and the money clock ground to a halt at $1060. A flea couldn't ride a bull this wild for 58 seconds. "That's over seven times longer than professionals ride!" he thought, running the math in his head. Something was seriously wrong and he was going to find out.

J.W. sized up the crowd. They were a rowdy bunch and all their shouting had filled the room with the smell of half-digested beer and barbecued meatballs. Even J.W., who regularly enjoyed the consumption of these two basic food groups, felt his stomach turn slightly as he breathed in the raunchy air, justifying the bar's name. He grabbed the microphone to announce the winner of the largest prize in the history of the Raunchy Texan Cowboy Bar. He was rapidly running out of ways he could get out of paying this guy, when an angel from heaven appeared in the form of an armed gangster.

Clearly the thug pushing and shoving his way through the crowd was a bad-ass. He was wielding a large gun, a pissed-off scowl, and was trailed by several other rough-looking guys, all of whom had their sights set on the man climbing off the bull. In the seven years that J.W. had been in business, he had never had any dealings with the underworld. His only bit of extortion came in the form of corrupt city officials who had squeezed money out of him for bogus licenses. If J.W. were lucky, this gangster and his team, whoever they were, would shoot this barnacle and his problem would be solved.

Suddenly a woman shouted from across the room, "Ethan! Look out!"

Ethan was shocked to hear his name, even as he looked up to see the name "Vince" in capital cowboy font letters on the wall, next to "$1060!" Who the hell had recognized him? Particularly since he was supposed to be dead and forgotten.

J.W. ducked behind the mechanical bull controls where Javier was already hiding, and looked at Javier with burning eyes. Javier shook his head frantically at his boss. "I did everything I could to throw him off—I swear I did, I promise!"

"Something's not right! If I find out you're in on this, I'm going to wear your balls as a necklace!" J.W. peeked from behind the controls to get a look at the crowd. A beer mug flew at his head, missing him by a few inches, then shattered against the wall behind him.

The crowd was booing, calling J.W. an asshole.

"What did I do?" he yelled into the air. He suddenly realized they assumed that this gangster was working for him, and this was how he treated the winners. Sure he didn't want to pay, but he hadn't gone so far as to hire a hit man.

Ethan saw the big man in a suit pushing his way though the crowd towards him. "That didn't take long!" He recognized the bruiser from the desert, and everything clicked into place: he really was on a corporate hit list, and they knew how to find him.

The crowd didn't appreciate being pushed by thugs in suits, so they started shoving back. Then someone threw a beer mug, hitting one of the thugs in the shoulder. The gangster responded by punching a random guy in the face, knocking him to the ground. Within seconds, the room was in pandemonium. Food and drinks were flying though the air, not aimed at anyone in particular. The anarchy continued to crescendo until a gun went off. A light fixture, made of beer mugs and bullhorns, exploded, spraying glass and chunks of horn all over the floor and pool table. Immediately, those less drunk ducked for cover, hoping not to get shot, while the more inebriated yelled profanities, throwing popcorn and meat balls at anything that moved.

J.W. stayed hidden behind the bull-riding console next to Javier, wondering how the hell things had gotten out of control so fast. J.W. wasn't very political, but he had street smarts. He knew that during the past several years, people all around were feeling squeezed. In fact, he felt it himself. Nowadays he seemed to be working harder and longer and getting less for it, while big corporations and the super-rich always seemed to be getting tax breaks and bailouts. He knew that if he felt frustrated by the system, then other people must be feeling the same way. J.W. figured that was why the Raunchy Texan was packed on Monday nights. People needed an escape, but he wasn't naïve. Under these conditions, when things are inherently unfair, people will eventually snap. All it takes is just a little push over the edge and the next thing you know, you have a riot.

J.W. considered the possibility that this dumb barnacle could be the catalyst that sparked a citywide riot, and a shiver ran down his spine. If something like that originated from his bar he would be responsible for the aftermath. J.W. was a Texan and a full-fledged conservative and he didn't like the idea of starting something that he wasn't 100% behind. He realized he had to deal with this somehow—find a way to release the tension and end the chaos.

The tossing of beer mugs had subsided. J.W. carefully stood up and watched as Vlad, a three hundred pound Russian bouncer, cornered the kid in the red jumpsuit. J.W. had hired Vlad because he was big, strong, and scary-looking. J.W. observed with anticipation, fully expecting Vlad to squash the little bug, summarily stopping this cluster-fuck.

His smile of triumph lasted less than a second. Suddenly the biggest, meanest, and ugliest bouncer J.W. had ever known had a look of bewilderment on his face, as he was being tossed twenty feet over the heads of the fake cowboys and cowgirls. Unaccustomed to being used as a human projectile, Vlad shouted something in Russian before slamming into one of the gun-wielding thugs. They collided into a huddle of drunk cowboys, like a bowling ball hitting pins, knocking bodies in all directions.

The two big men landed on top of the wagon-shaped Monday Night Meatball Buffet. The table's sneeze guard exploded, shattering safety glass across the room. Vlad and the thug were barely conscious, lying in a puddle of meatballs and BBQ sauce, which added a surreal grotesqueness to the goings-on.

J.W. wasn't sure what to do. People were trying to leave the building, but most of them were so drunk they were going the wrong way and bumping into each other like some old Keystone Cops movie. The room was in worse shape than he could have imagined. During the single minute he had hidden behind the mechanical bull console, an unbelievable amount of damage had occurred. Tables, chairs, and bar stools had been tossed around the room. Thousands of dollars of booze bottles were shattered and the smell of alcohol permeated the air.

J.W. made a dash across the room towards his office to call the police. Hopefully, everyone would be arrested. He'd file a report and a padded insurance claim, and it would all be paid for. He would make out fine. As he ran towards the door, he saw a red blur in his peripheral vision. A second later, he was standing face-to-face with the barnacle in the red jumpsuit. All around them people were still fighting, but he ignored them. He couldn't help staring at the guy who he had watched demonstrate phenomenal feats of strength and speed. He stood in awe, fully expecting to encounter a larger than life persona with the deep resonant voice of a god, or at least something that sounded like James Earl Jones.

"Hi," Ethan said awkwardly, with a voice of a kid who seemed very uncomfortable around new people. "Um, sorry about all this. I didn't do it. I mean, I didn't mean to do it, it just, I don't know, happened. Someone wants to kill me—or something…but I did win the money fair and square."

J.W. was stunned, and more than a little disappointed. If his bar was going to be destroyed, he wanted it to be by someone of epic proportions. J.W. was hardwired to not pay whenever possible, but surprised himself by saying, "No one has ever gone that long before. I'm not sure the bull was working correctly. I'm going to need to look into the situation before I pay out that much money." He had a hard time keeping a straight face. He knew that the bull was working perfectly well and that every word he just said was utter and complete crap. But he stood his ground.

Then Mitch the big, bald, bouncer with arms covered in ink, walked up and stood beside J.W., "Is there a problem here?" Mitch said in a menacing tone.

"No," said J.W. in a self-assured voice. "This is Vince." He pointed to the name still on the wall next to the sign that affirmed: $1060. "I was just telling him that before I can pay him, I'll need to make sure everything is legit, or it wouldn't be fair."

With the speed of a frog's tongue grabbing a fly, Ethan heaved Mitch twenty feet across the room, where he landed straddling the mechanical bull. J.W. grabbed his balls in sympathetic pain, then watched as the burly tattooed bouncer fell into the foam pit, writhing in agony.

Ethan grabbed J.W. by the throat and stared at him, not saying a word. J.W. saw a pair of crazy eyes. Even crazier than his Uncle Bill, a bona fide homicidal sociopath who had been sentenced to life in prison for having killed six women. Suddenly J.W. got a bizarre burst of respect for the kid.

"I want my money!" This time Ethan's words came out clear and direct. There was no mistaking his intention. He was a serious person who meant business.

"I don't know how much cash I have." J.W. reached into his pocket and pulled out a wad of bills, and started counting. "Here's $820. I can pay you the rest later." Ethan squeezed his throat harder and picked him up off the ground. J.W.'s voice went high, wheezy and faint.

"I promise I'll pay you the rest later!" Ethan grabbed the money out of his hand, shoved it into his pocket, and then tossed J.W. against the door to his office. The cheap, hollow door collapsed on impact, the hinges tearing from the wood. J.W. struggled to his feet, but his size 14 ½ boots slipped on the beer, BBQ sauce, and popcorn-coated cement floor. He fell back and slid down the broken door onto his butt.

Ethan looked around the room. All around people were still fighting, which was good because the henchmen in suits were disarmed, out-numbered, and being kept busy by what seemed to be a fairly well-organized group. He got what he came for: he had eaten and made some money, and now the goons who were after him were getting their butts kicked. All things considered, things were working out pretty well.

He was heading toward the door when he heard someone shout his name. Who the hell recognized him after all these years? He turned around and a young woman with shoulder-length red hair, wearing jeans and a T-shirt, ran up to him and pulled him along as she sprinted though the kitchen and out the back door.

As soon as they stepped outside into the alley a car pulled up silently, as if the engine were off. Ethan looked surprised, "It's electric," said the girl, stepping towards the car. Ethan stayed put as he watched her open the rear passenger door, not sure who to trust, where to go, or what to do next. He was trying to get a look at the driver when the woman climbed into the back seat and turned back towards him, beckoning. "Ethan—it's me, Vanessa!"

Ethan looked at her in disbelief. Her hair was much shorter and a completely different color. Her body had changed, too—she was less curvy and more athletic, and her cheeks, chin and eyes had angles to them that weren't there before. He blurted, "I read that you were dead!"

"You're supposed to be dead, too."

"Huh?"

"You need to come with us! I'll explain more when we get to the safety zone. This is much bigger and deeper than you know."

A voice erupted from the kitchen, "He went out the back!"

"Get in!" ordered an unknown voice from the driver's seat.

Ethan hesitated, confused from all the distractions around him. Suddenly a guy raced past, leaped over the hood of the electric car, grabbed the front door handle and hopped in. It was all very fluid, as if he had practice doing it.

"Forget him, let's go!" barked the man in the front passenger seat, slamming the door.

"Get in now!" yelled Vanessa.

Ethan stopped thinking and reacted. He jumped in as fast as he could. Before he could fully shut the door, the silent electric car was speeding away. Behind them, the men in suits rushed out of the kitchen into the empty alley.

Chapter 45

Sirens blared in the distance as they sped down the street. The car's electric motor was silent, but its wheels squealed as it raced around corners, sliding sideways and swerving to avoid potholes. Ethan grabbed hold of the seat in front of him to stop himself from being tossed around. Falling to Earth in an untested escape pod was less scary than sitting in the back seat of this car with a stranger driving like a B-movie stuntman.

After a couple of miles, the sirens faded into the distance and Ethan felt his body relax. He realized he had been holding his breath for most of their journey.

He sat back as best he could and looked at Vanessa. It wasn't just her physical exterior that had changed. Ethan sensed that she had a completely different presence.

Every day for the eight years while he was lost in space Ethan had fantasized about seeing her, then abandoned the idea when he read she was dead. Now he was sitting next to her, emotionally confused. Though he was extremely happy to see her, the feelings of love that were so strong between them all those years ago now seemed lost.

He couldn't blame her. He supposedly had died eight years ago and she had obviously moved on. He couldn't take that personally. Nonetheless, Ethan still felt incomplete. Should he pursue her and try to pick up where they left off, or assume that things could never be what they were? All this seemed very stressful—all he knew was he was relieved she was not dead.

As the car slowed to a more normal speed, Ethan let go of the seat in front of him and turned towards the girl who had just saved him from being captured.

"Vanessa, uh—I read that you died several years ago. It was in the Northridge Campus News."

Her tone was clipped and intolerant. She was no longer the sweet, innocent, Valley girl whose ambitions were to spend the summer at Club Med. "Vanessa did die. My name is Cameron."

"What?" Ethan looked at her again carefully, not sure what she meant.

She stared at him hard, trying to size him up, then fluid as a newscaster, switched subjects.

"I would go and see your dad almost every day after you left. We suspected something went wrong when we never heard from you. You quit calling, emailing, and texting. That was completely out of character. So Vince and I started getting suspicious. He made several inquiries to Eden, Inc.'s public relations department. They told him all information about your whereabouts was classified for security reasons. Vince didn't buy it and suggested that you had been kidnapped or killed, and that they were somehow responsible and were covering it up."

Ethan watched her lips as she spoke, her warm, clear eyes dredging up memories from a painful past.

"Ironically, I was taking a history class and we were studying the rise and fall of the Third Reich. I was reading about the tactics the Nazis used to transfer wealth and power from the middle class to big businesses and the super-wealthy. When people complained, Hitler would make them disappear. If their family and friends made inquiries or questioned their disappearance, they too would disappear."

"Okay..." Ethan was surprised; she was sounding a lot like Ascot.

"One day Vince didn't show up at the gym. And there was a for sale sign on the door. I called the house and he didn't answer. It made no sense. Vince had no life outside the gym."

Ethan nodded; that was true enough.

"I wondered what could have happened to him, so after a few days when he still didn't show up I went to the police to file a missing person's report, but because I wasn't a relative or a co-worker, they wouldn't take my statement. I suggested that maybe some thugs were trying to extort money from him. At the gym a week earlier, I had seen some strange guys in black suits talking to

Vince and he looked worried. It was obvious they weren't there to work out. When I mentioned it to the police they just laughed and told me I should mind my own business."

Her eyes started to water, but she still avoided eye contact, just staring into space. Ethan turned to look out the window as the car silently sped down the road.

"I knew something wasn't right. Talking to the police reminded me of the documentaries I watched about the Third Reich. I started to be very suspicious of everyone and everything."

She turned and looked Ethan in the eyes, her face full of sorrow and anger.

"The next day I went by your house and there was a Salvation Army truck and workers loading up and hauling away all your stuff. None of the guys spoke English very well, so when I asked what was going on, they just said: 'We take away! No more here!' Vince had no reason to leave. All his friends were in the Valley. He had roots here."

Ethan was emotionally overwhelmed, his mind was swimming with the pictures Vanessa painted for him. He nodded absentmindedly. Then he realized that he was staring at her breasts, imagining what they looked like under her pale green T-shirt.

"The more I thought about it, the more freaked out I got and the more parallels I saw to the Third Reich. It was the same old tactics: uncaring, corrupt cops, private, for-profit religious organizations out legally stealing people's stuff, and not a word of objection in the media. It seemed so obvious to me, but I was the only one who seemed aware of it. Any time I said anything, I was dismissed as a nutcase. Then after what happened next, I decided it was wise to disappear."

Ethan sat, not saying a word and not moving, eagerly awaiting what came next. He scanned the car. No one else in the car was paying much attention to her, they had obviously all heard the story many times before. She looked at Ethan hard, this time assessing whether or not to let him into her world, knowing if she told him what was next there was no going back. He would either think she was crazy or see things her way. Ethan nodded enthusiastically, wanting to know more.

"My roommate, Cameron, had just dropped out of college."
Ethan nodded, "Oh yeah, I remember her."

"She had gotten into a huge fight with her parents, who were divorced and very messed up, and she didn't want to have anything to do with them. She was out of control and quickly becoming a little barfly. She was only nineteen so she would often borrow my ID and go to bars and clubs. We looked similar enough that it worked. Ironically I had cut and colored my hair so Cameron's hair length and color matched my ID more accurately than my own."

Ethan nodded, again trying not to stare at her breasts.

"One night some cops came to the house at 2:00 AM, asking if Vanessa Montel lived here. I'm standing right there, but I didn't say anything, I just nodded. The cop asked me to confirm the identity of a body that was found in an alley. The cause of death was a hit-and-run. There were no witnesses, no motive, no leads, so they told me it was an accident. Poor Cameron was dead, but they thought it was me. That's the day I became Cameron."

The guy sitting in the front passenger seat unexpectedly turned around and jumped into the conversation. "Right after that is when we met your friend here!" He was a thin, muscular man with high cheekbones, a strong jaw, and short dreadlocks. He was so dark that he looked as if he was carved out of ebony. His voice was very low and he had a thick African accent. "We found out about her situation so we took her in our confidence. We helped her to clearly see what was really going on, although she was already starting to figure things out for herself. She's a very smart bird."

Ethan was slow to respond, the man's low voice and musical accent took a moment for Ethan to translate.

Vanessa—Cameron—laughed. "Thank you, M'buy" She pronounced it em-boo-yae, and Ethan thought, "Cool name."

Ethan wanted to know more about Vanessa—Cameron: "How were you able to change identities?"

Cameron smiled mischievously. "It pays to be paranoid. I never let on that it was my ID that they had. I explained to the police that her parents lived out of state. Apparently a death certificate is a state document so the police only have limited jurisdiction over the body. I told them I would contact the family and find out what they wanted to do with it. They were more than happy to give me that assignment. It was less work for them and they didn't really care one way or the other about what happened to her. After a few days, I picked up the police report and the death certificate, and had the body cremated. That took care of all the legal loose ends."

Ethan watched M'buy nod in agreement, then saw that Cameron had her eyes closed as she dredged up the past. "But what about your parents? Didn't anyone ask questions?" Ethan was very intrigued and mystified as to how she could have pulled something like this off.

Cameron smiled. "I had to make up a story so if anyone were to call my mom in South Carolina, which was very unlikely, she wouldn't freak out. I called her and told her that a girl in my college with the same name as me had died, and that there was some confusion. I suggested that if anyone were to contact her it would be easier to just go along with it and thank them for their condolences."

"Did anyone ever call your mom?" asked Ethan. Cameron shook her head. "What about your dad or any of the rest of your family?"

"They all live on the East Coast, so I'm out of sight and out of mind. They think I work in a lawyer's office and have absolutely no free time. Every now and then I talk to my mom, I tell her things are good and not to worry about me."

"So how did you manage all the legal stuff?" Ethan wanted to keep her talking. There was something about her mouth that captivated him.

"I'm dead, what's to look for? As Cameron I acted quickly. I transferred the title to my car to Cameron," and she pointed to herself. "I closed my bank accounts, and Cameron became the executor of my estate, so all inquires, notices and everything that pertained to the dead me came to me. No one else had any idea what was going on. I had all of Cameron's IDs and her computer. Patik, who you will meet later, helped me access all her passwords, so I had access to everything of hers. I got a new driver's license in her name, so before I knew it, I was Cameron."

"What about Cameron's friends? None of them noticed that she wasn't around?"

"I canceled her phone and told everyone who came by that she moved back home, and I had no idea where that was—Colorado, Nebraska or someplace like that. She didn't have many friends that actually cared about her. They were just party people who wanted to hang out and get high. So they all quickly moved on."

"What about Cameron's family?"

"She hadn't spoken to her family in years."

"No one got suspicious?"

"Why? They think she's alive and well and going to college. Every once in a while she'll get some emails, so I return them."

"They can't tell it's not her?"

"I say just enough to keep her parents satisfied. They wrote her off a long time ago. She was a trust fund kid, and her parents felt they had done their duty since she was financially provided for, forever."

"Wow, that sounds harsh."

"Harsh?" Cameron suddenly got much more animated, her hands making large gestures in the car's small interior. Ethan suddenly remembered that Vanessa had Italian genes. "Cameron is dead because someone wanted to kill me and they thought she was me. What choice did I have? So now I'm her, and I've been living under the radar. I'm using her monthly trust fund deposits towards a noble cause!"

Ethan smiled. "You certainly have changed. I remember your idea of a noble cause was going to Club Med."

She looked disgusted. "Having your eyes opened to the extreme corruption and injustice around us has a way of changing a person."

M'buy chimed in, his bass voice a contrapuntal contrast to her alto. "Tell him what got you involved in our movement."

Ethan sat up and turned slightly so he could see her better. Cameron nodded. "It's both sad and funny. Just after Cameron was killed, I read online that the last whale in the wild had died. It was a female. She died when a group of scientists tried to impregnate her with frozen whale semen. The stainless steel and rubber device that they used to insert the semen got lodged in the whale's uterus, creating severe urinary and fallopian tube blockage. This unique pain caused the whale to become disoriented, and in an attempt to get away from the inserting scientists, she swam into an iceberg, causing a large piece of the sharp ice to fall off and impale her."

Ethan arched his back in sympathetic pain. He was still trying to take in the information that the whales were gone.

She continued. "This seemed to be the ultimate case of do-gooders blundering away and just making things worse. I started looking into what was going on with our environment and was shocked that no real progress had been made over the years; in fact, things were systematically getting worse."

Ethan wasn't sure where this was going, so he just nodded. She started talking and moving more animatedly, working herself up into a bit of a frenzy. "What I learned was that for years, big business has been infiltrating our government buying congressmen, senators, and even the president. Every year more and more of the laws intended to protect" —she made air quotes— "'we the people,' from the predatory behavior of big business were gutted. So things that used to be considered illegal and despicable are now perfectly legal and commonplace. It's unbelievable!"

Her rant sounded remarkably like Ascot's when he would start bitching about how screwed up things were. As she talked, a warehouse of stored memories began opening. Ethan wasn't sure if anything Ascot said was credible or could be trusted. Now he was hearing these same things for the second time, from a new source— a source he knew and trusted. It gave them credibility. Suddenly it all became more real and relevant to him. Now he was beginning to believe it.

Even more animated than before, she went on. "It's all an extreme example of the fox guarding the henhouse, and the average person is so caught up in the trivial day-to-day bullshit that they fail to notice what's really happening around them, let alone do anything about it."

Ethan was completely speechless. Her commitment and passion was ramping up his sex drive, which after eight years of living in solitary confinement was extraordinarily high to begin with.

He tried to focus on what she was saying, but he kept staring at her breasts through the thin green T-shirt. He barely noticed that she was on a roll.

"Now a smaller group of people have more power than ever before, and these people's greed has no boundaries. They have no concern for our future whatsoever. Because of them we are rapidly heading to a point of no return. If pollution levels get any higher it will cause our planet's ecosystem to be so out of balance that it can never recover." Her passion was so extreme that she looked possessed. "It's imperative that these people be stopped!"

Chapter 46

Without missing a beat, M'buy jumped in the conversation, his low resonant voice breaking the spell that Cameron had cast over Ethan. Now that M'buy had commanded the floor, Ethan looked up and was fascinated by the man's dreads; he looked as if pipe cleaners were sprouting out of his head.

"She's right, man! We live in a world where everything is opposite. They pass laws that sound like they are protecting the environment: the Clear Skies Initiative, The Healthy Forest Act—yet they all dismantle previous environmental laws and make it easier for big business to pollute and pillage."

"It's all a smoke screen!" added Cameron

"They used the big lie theory," continued M'buy. "The bigger the lie, the easier it is to convince people that it's true." Ethan remembered Ascot saying the same thing. Cameron jumped in as if it were a tag-team wrestling match. "The media use emotional issues to manipulate the uninformed and get the masses fired up over inconsequential bullshit, like 'who's cheating on their spouse,' while the corporations screw us over every which way!"

"Yes!" It was M'buy's turn again. "Everything in the media is fear-driven. They create enemies out of everything. They make us question the people around us. They make us afraid of our streets, our schools, our businesses, everything. The more irrational our thinking, the more control they have over us."

Ethan was doing his best to follow as the two of them fired off rounds of information. He hadn't slept in forty-eight hours or so, and had recently consumed several plates of sugary, fatty meatballs, and the combination was starting to detract from his ability to concentrate.

He popped back into the conversation as Cameron was firing up again. "Daddy save us! That's their strategy! They create a boogieman, then say that only they can protect us from him. It's the oldest trick in the book."

"And it works every time," M'buy chimed in.

"That's right," said Cameron. "Their arrogance is so phenomenal that they expect us to believe the impossible just because they say it is so!"

Somewhere Ethan had skipped something. He wasn't exactly sure what they were talking about now. Supposedly the conversation was for his benefit, but they were so wrapped up in it that he was feeling more like an eavesdropper.

"That's why they create a war on everything." This time it was the driver adding his two cents to the conversation. Ethan was sitting directly behind him so all he could see was a patch of the man's brown hair between the headrest and the back of the seat.

"That's right!" nodded M'buy. "They create a task force. Then that becomes a war on whatever they can use as a distraction, as well as a vehicle to take away our civil liberties."

Cameron turned to Ethan and took over M'buy's line of thinking.

"There is now a war on—" she started counting them off on her fingers: "drugs, crime, terror, dead-beat dads, secular humanists, immigrants, unions, creative agitators (aka political satirists), documentary filmmakers, activists, pornography, and several forms of science."

"Basically, anyone who isn't in agreement with the status quo gets shut down and becomes a de facto enemy of the state," said M'buy, but before he could take a breath Cameron jumped back in.

"That's why there is now a curfew in most parts of the country, so people will stay isolated and ignorant, and not rock the boat."

Ethan shifted in his seat uncomfortably. "This all sounds so extreme. How did all this happen while I was gone?"

"Don't be so naïve!" thundered M'buy. Ethan unknowingly seemed to have hit a nerve. "America has had a policy of oppression since the days of slavery. Nowadays slaves aren't born to plantation owners, they don't work in the fields, and they aren't broken by angry overseers. Now they are created by zero tolerance laws that target minorities! Once someone is caught with a particular drug or doing a particular petty crime, they are labeled a criminal. Then once they're in the system, there is no way out! There are now minimum mandatory sentences for every drug and gang-related crime. These laws were all put there by corrupt politicians manipulating a scared, closed-minded public for the benefit of the private prison industry. Prisons are the fastest growing business sector in our country now."

Ethan was looking doubtful. "Why would a country want to imprison its own people? That doesn't make any sense, and why wouldn't the media expose it?"

Cameron laughed mirthlessly. "None of this is ever mentioned in the news because the media is owned by the same people who profit from the corrupt laws. They are the ones who lobby the politicians and get their bills passed. So they can get away with their corrupt behavior legally. They make sure that no information that is incriminating gets leaked. The job of the news outlets isn't to dispense information, but rather to regulate and black out information."

"Keep the public ignorant!" said M'buy.

The silent car cruised through an industrial part of the valley near the airport. Ethan tried to identify the area as the vehicle slipped off the road into a black tunnel leading to a subterranean parking structure.

Cameron touched Ethan's shoulder. "We are part of an underground revolution working for the greater good of humanity. Our purpose is to restore freedom and idealism in our country and to expose the injustice that is corroding our way of life."

M'buy faced Ethan. "The men who are after you are corporate hit men. The people they work for control everything around us with total immunity. They make the worst of the CIA look like Cub Scouts. No one dares to touch them. The fact that you got away tonight is a miracle. I'm sure that those thugs are really pissed off right now." He leaned over the seat and gave Ethan a high-five.

Ethan looked out of the window, surprised. They were driving through an empty parking garage, passing old piles of rebar and dusty bags of cement. The place looked like it was abandoned years ago in the middle of a renovation. He didn't know where they were taking him, but he wasn't expecting this sort of place.

At the end of the underground structure, Ethan assumed that the driver was going to park somewhere among the rubble, but instead, he maintained his speed, heading straight towards a cement block wall. Ethan tried to say something but nothing came out, so he braced himself for the impact. Suddenly the car lurched downward and they were in a pitch-black tunnel. M'buy watched Ethan expectantly, chuckling knowingly. "It's quite clever, isn't it?" Ethan exhaled with relief and nodded in agreement, then relaxed slightly and leaned back into his seat. A moment later the car was inside a dimly-lit, clean, metal garage full of electric cars. The car pulled into a spot that seemed to be reserved for them and parked.

Ethan climbed out of the car. He held the door open and watched as Cameron slid across the seat, following him. He marveled at how much she had changed. The girl he knew before he left would never be caught dead in a place like this. She hated anything dirty or unfinished. She was a girl who wanted to go party at some exotic locale and watch soap operas on TV. This was the last thing he would expect from her, but Ethan was impressed. Perhaps switching her identity from Vanessa to Cameron was more than symbolic or opportunistic. It allowed her to completely reevaluate who she was and to make decisions about her purpose in life. She had allowed herself the freedom to make new and bold choices, steering her life in a totally new direction.

Ethan was inspired; perhaps he should do the same. After all, who was he now, anyway? He didn't have a dad or a gym to help support. He didn't have a place to live, a job, or anywhere to be. Plus, he was physically transformed and could do amazing things, he reminded himself.

He admired Cameron as he followed her through the garage. She looked more statuesque than he remembered, too; now she walked with an air of authority. He was impressed with her group. They seemed to be fighting the good fight, at least in their minds. Clearly that was their intention. But Ethan could tell he didn't share their level of passion, so he wasn't sure he was going to fit into their club.

He didn't want to deal with trying to fix a screwed-up world. At least for the time being, he just wanted to have some fun using his new abilities. He thought he would go and make some money, get a nice car, a nice pad, and hang out with lots of hot chicks. He had never had the chance to really live. He had been stuck in outer space since he was barely more than a kid.

Ethan followed the group through a maze of car parts and electric motors. He realized that with every step he took he was getting in deeper and deeper. They had saved his ass, trusted him, and brought him to their secret hideout. Getting out of this gracefully was going to be tricky.

Chapter 47

Rows of desks with large 3D computer screens cast a multicolored glow throughout a large concrete and metal room. Ethan followed Cameron and M'buy through an arsenal of high-tech gadgets. Small dots of colored LED lights flashed on and off, indicating that the devices were on and doing their job. On one side of the room, a half-dozen electric cars sat in various stages of construction. Cameron noticed Ethan's curiosity. "We have to convert gas guzzlers into electric cars in secret. It's crazy! The oil companies passed laws that prohibit zero emission vehicles. So by law we are required to pollute."

Ethan looked flabbergasted. "Why would any lawmakers pass that?"

Cameron snorted. "Because that's who pays the bills." Ethan was getting very frustrated with the idiocy of the world.

M'buy seemed to sympathize with Ethan's confusion. "They managed to get an electric hydrogen fuel cell car to blow up and the media immediately declared that all electric and hydrogen powered vehicles were dangerous."

Cameron finished his thought. "They had weeks of footage of the Hindenburg blowing up, with supposed experts saying, 'This could be your car.'"

M'buy chuckled, his low rumble echoing off the concrete and metal walls. "Yes, trying to save the world has made us all wanted men!" Cameron glared at him. "And women," he corrected.

The person in charge of all computer operations was Patik, a medium-framed Indian man in his early thirties who was neither ugly or hansom. He had no features that were particularly interesting, and he sported a nondescript haircut that only added to his plainness. His entire wardrobe consisted of all-white linen clothing. Whenever he was asked why he always wore the same outfits, his response was, "This way everything I have matches and I don't have to concern myself with fashion. Therefore I can use my brain for more important things."

Patik got up from his computer station and walked towards the new arrivals. Cameron was in the lead, quick to quell any suspicions anyone would have about Ethan. "Patik, I would like you to meet an old friend of mine, Ethan Stone."

"Has he been vetted?" asked Patik suspiciously, before reaching out to shake hands.

"I can vouch for him, I've known him and his dad for over eight years."

M'buy added, "Casper's goon squad was after him—he's definitely not playing for their team."

As he shook Patik's hand, Ethan felt proud and important, not for doing anything spectacular, but for just being. It was the first time he felt like he was being introduced as an equal to someone. It occurred to Ethan that he left Earth as a kid and never had an opportunity to be an adult, since Ascot was older and had taken on the role of being his coach and mentor. Ethan never felt like they were equals. Now he was in a secret underground hideout being introduced to the leader of a radical anti-government organization. It made him feel special, like an adult who had some influence on the world.

Ethan smiled, possibly for the first time since he had landed back on Earth. He stood up straighter and looked Patik in the eyes.

"We have been following the activities of Eden, Inc. and Casper Degas for a long time. Years ago we hacked into their server and learned about the Valhalla project, its destruction and its cover up. Cameron suspected that you might have been on the station and that was why you had disappeared. We had practically forgotten about it until the other day when we intercepted an encoded transmission stating that a space pod had been found in the desert with two survivors, Ascot LaRouch and Ethan Stone. Apparently there was a skirmish and one survivor escaped who exhibited extraordinary abilities. I suppose that was you?"

"Yeah," said Ethan.

"I take it they weren't particularly happy to see you?"

"Apparently not."

"Well, if you were to pop in from outer space you could blow the cover off Eden, Inc. and send their stock prices down the loo." Ethan rolled his eyes and shrugged. Patik continued. "Cameron predicted that you would head back home, so we sent teams to keep an eye out hoping to find you before Casper's henchmen did."

"So all this wasn't as serendipitous as I had thought."

"I will confess I had some reservations, but if Cameron can vouch for you, then you must be okay. Welcome to R.A.D." He slapped Ethan on the shoulder.

Ethan cocked his head, a little confused. Patik picked up on his body language and filled him in. "R.A.D. stands for Restoring American Democracy. We have rebel cells all around the world. Our mission is to take back the power that has been systematically stripped away from us by large transnational corporations, and to stop them from polluting our planet."

Ethan saw the dedication in his eyes. He looked around and understood that everyone in the room shared that commitment. There was no doubt in anyone else present that their cause was worthy of risking their lives. It occurred to him that perhaps this was the bravest group of people he had ever met.

Ethan and Patik stood, not saying a word, sizing each other up.

Finally Ethan broke the ice, pointing to the electronics all around the room. "So, what is all this stuff?" Patik walked toward a rack of gear with small flashing LED lights. As he explained, he pointed to each item. "Here we have police scanners, global weather monitors, pollution monitors, carbon emission monitors. All these devices have been hot-rodded and can out-perform any off-the-shelf, state-of-the-art gear out there. With our equipment we are able to tap into massive amounts of data, analyze that data, then determine where to concentrate our efforts to be most effective."

"Effective in doing what?" Ethan wanted to know.

Patik nodded. "As I said before, we have clear goals and they are massive, so the trick is to find ways to influence things without exposing ourselves."

Cameron joined the conversation. "Patik is a computer genius and can hack into any system, bust through firewalls, break encryptions, and override all kinds of security software." Patik gave a modest shrug. "He's the reason we get our political leverage and stay invisible."

"What does leverage mean, exactly?" asked Ethan.

Cameron took a deep breath, giving her time to organize her thoughts. She needed to decide where to start, so that it would make sense to someone who was getting all this information for the first time. "We've gotten to the point where our politicians don't represent the will of the people at all. These guys buy their way into the "Washington Club." Periodically they will spew out a few sound bites, so it appears as if they care about something. In reality, they completely ignore the desires of their constituents. Instead, they do the bidding of their corporate sponsors."

"Don't people notice that these guys aren't looking out for them or doing their job?"

"Sometimes," answered Patik. "But not usually. Only when people get emotionally riled up about an issue do they pay attention and notice that their representative is on the wrong side, and that's when we have some leverage. We can expose them and show people who they really are. Sometimes that's enough to win an election, but the truth is, the candidates who have the most cash usually win elections. Since we don't have that kind of cash, we need to use leverage."

Cameron took over again. "Essentially what Patik does is find out where a politician or an organization is vulnerable by accessing their files. Files that would destroy them if they were released publicly."

"That sounds like blackmail," said Ethan.

"Yeah!" chimed Patik and Cameron in unison. They smiled at each other, enjoying the synchronicity.

"Look," Patik suddenly got very serious. "Blackmail is for personal gain, and that's not why we do what we do. These politicians are stealing from us. They are using their elected offices for their own personal gain at our expense."

Cameron jumped in. "And at the expense of the health of the planet."

Patik continued, "We tried to lobby Congress. We went out and got signatures for a particular piece of legislation, then went about trying to make change through the conventional channels. But it didn't work. The system is simply too corrupt, so now we make corporate bank accounts disappear, or put politicians' dirty secrets on all prominent websites and on the TV so their careers are ruined. That's how we can start to move things back into a more positive direction."

"A direction that helps people and the planet, not just us!" added Cameron.

M'buy emerged out of the shadows of the computer gear. "What we are doing is unraveling the trend towards American Fascism that's been a long time in the making."

"Fascism?" interrupted Ethan. Perhaps these people really were nuts after all. "Didn't we get rid of Fascism when we got rid of Hitler?"

"Not even a little bit. "You're thinking Fascism is a dictatorship; it's not, sure we got rid of the Nazis, but Fascism is when government is run by big business and the people are serfs working for the desires of business interests."

"Otherwise known as supply-side economics," interjected Cameron.

Ethan looked confused again. M'buy responded to his body language. "We believe business should serve the needs of the people by making goods and providing services that we all need. But when a business gets big, they start to control the economy and everything gets turned upside down. Now the need is for the people to serve the business by buying unnecessary stuff. If people don't buy enough useless things then the government has to step in and bail the business out because, 'it's too big to fail.'"

Ethan nodded, a little uncertain.

"You may not see a big difference, but it's huge," said M'buy. "I assume you eat breakfast."

"Sure," said Ethan.

"The purpose for you to eat breakfast is to nourish your body."

Ethan nodded. "Sure..."

"Let's say the government was owned and operated by Denny's, and they passed a law that said, 'You must go to Denny's every morning and eat a stack of pancakes and three strips of bacon.' If you don't the police will come and arrest you and put you in jail. Because it is more important to the system that Denny's stays in business than it is for you to have any choices as to what and where you eat."

"Okay," said Ethan skeptically. "But who would want to live like that?"

"It depends where you're sitting. Are you eating the pancakes or serving them? Big business, banks, the military, the police—they all love Fascism. It gives them ultimate power. They decide what they want to make, what services they will provide, and what information they are willing to release; we the people have to go along with the program or face the consequences."

Cameron jumped back in as Ethan tried to digest what M'buy had said. "Did you know that in 1933, right before Franklin Roosevelt was about to take office, there was an attempted coup d'état organized by the big business leaders of the day: JP Morgan, Dupont, and Prescott Bush. They all liked Hitler and thought a similar government in the USA would be preferable to the one Roosevelt was proposing. Fortunately they picked the wrong man for the job. They asked four-star General Smedly Bulter to assemble one hundred thousand World War I vets to storm the White House so he would become the de facto dictator of America. Afterwards he was supposed to let the business tycoons run the country, but he ratted them out and the plot never got off the ground. Roosevelt tried to cover it up, not wanting to go into office with the stigma that he didn't have the support of the business community. The point of all this is, these people never went away. They have been systematically unraveling our country, our laws, and our constitution to serve their agenda. Now these people own the media and have entrenched themselves in positions of power."

Ethan nodded as M'buy spoke. His serious voice resonated throughout the room. "Have you ever wondered why over the years the peacemakers are always the ones who get assassinated? Gandhi,

Martin Luther King, the Kennedys, Malcolm X, all fought to unite and empower their people. To give them hope for a better future. That is always a threat. So they were killed. But the warmongers always serve the interests of big business and they are always protected!"

"I thought America was the freest country in the world," said Ethan.

Cameron laughed. "We are so brainwashed and uniformed — our lifestyle and our personal freedoms rank at number 97 out of 180 countries! Also, we have the worst social infrastructure of any industrialized nation in the world. The propaganda in our media is strong and our collective ego keeps us in denial so we don't see things as they really are."

Patik stepped forward out of the shadows, looking like a sage in his all-white outfit.

"If you can't see things for what they really are, then you are stuck and you can't move forward. Our job is to understand what really works, then do what we can to improve the situation." He raised his hand, counting off on his fingers as he spoke. "Our objectives are as follows: to restore the freedoms and collective values of America, to change the laws back to what they used to be so they look after the interests of the people and not the corporations, to remove Fascism in America and make it a democratic Republic again, and to change the environmental laws, punish polluters and implement clean alternative forms of energy and a more sustainable way of living."

M'buy's voice erupted again, shaking the room. "It's ridiculous that we have to do the things we do in secret. But that's how out of balance things have gotten. Besides covertly converting cars to non-polluting electric or hydrogen vehicles, we also build and convert houses to be self-sufficient. They can be completely off the grid by making solar, wind, and geothermal electricity. We capture rainwater and make water from condensation machines. Most water can be filtered and recycled. We use all kinds of renewable technology that the government will not allow. Not because it's not safe or efficient, but because it's not profitable to the right people."

Cameron jumped into the conversation, arms passionately waving. "Meanwhile greenhouse gasses are escalating, water pollution is increasing, and every day our people are getting sicker and sicker. Yet these corporations are relentless and fight every attempt at making a cleaner environment for everyone. I mean, how screwed up is that?"

"The world is certainly not logical or fair," thought Ethan. "But can these few guys fix anything?"

Patik held up a finger. "As you can see, we are fighting on several fronts at the moment. For starters, we are working on ways to dislodge the stranglehold that corporations have on government. Senator Amanda Goldman is the only senator who has the courage to draft a bill that ends corporate lobbying and limits campaign spending. She needs lots of support and she's not getting it, so we are using her bill to do some serious house cleaning."

"Exactly!" said Cameron, "Patik has hacked into half the Congress and Senate's computers and dug up all kinds of dirty little secrets that they would prefer to remain secret."

Patik resumed. "We are using the information we have collected to create a scenario where these politicians must support her legislation or be exposed. Our organization is involved in many acts of corporate sabotage."

"Sabotage?" Ethan asked doubtfully.

"It sounds worse than it is," boomed M'buy. "Corporations have no mercy or conscience. By law they have to first and foremost do whatever will make their shareholders the most money. So in many cases this gives them license to behave like sociopaths."

Ethan shook his head, confused. "I don't understand!"

Cameron jumped in before M'buy could respond. "Corporations, by law, have all the rights and privileges as a living, breathing human being, but they're not. They are immortal business entities with a narrow agenda to do one thing, amass as much wealth as possible. As an entity, a corporation doesn't care and legally can't care how it achieves its goal. So if, for example, a logging corporation decides it needs to cut down an entire forest, then sell the land to a strip mining company and destroy the habitat for hundreds of species of animals, because that's going to give them a boost in their quarterly profits, then they will do it! It's crazy!"

M'buy's low sing-song voice was purposely more calm, trying to bring the mood of the room down to a more rational level. "We have, in extreme cases, engaged in acts of destruction of corporate property. We don't think of it as terrorism. We don't kill people. We have done things like blowing up a dozen logging trucks before a company goes to cut down old growth forests, or we blow up pipelines and oil drilling equipment before they move into Yosemite to drill for oil, or we cover an underground nuclear warhead launch-site with twenty tons of concrete. All these stunts are nothing more than a big, expensive nuisance to a big corporation. Our strategy is to be relentless and make it too expensive for them to operate destructively, so eventually they will stop, since all they care about is making money."

"Also," said Patik, now holding two fingers up. When we do this it often brings about public awareness to the situation. The reason these corporations are able to get away with all this destruction is because no one knows it's happening. When we expose it, we start a debate. We put the corporations on the defensive so that they have to spend all kinds of money on lawyers and PR. That digs into their bottom line. If we are consistent and persistent, it will be too costly to operate destructively, and they will change their ways."

Ethan looked around the room; a dozen battle-ready faces stared intently back. He thought, "I just got indoctrinated into an organization that I'm not sure I really want to be in."

Not wanting to look nervous, he faked a smile.

Chapter 48

Light flashed and there was a loud boom. The smile on Ethan's face was replaced with a sudden dread. Disoriented, he stood motionless, as clouds of dust and debris blew through the room. Ethan watched as coordinated shadows entered through a massive hole blown in the side of the hideout's wall. Cameron, M'buy, and Patik were nowhere to be seen. Their training had taught them to always expect the unexpected, and to do whatever was necessary to stay alive, so they had already taken cover.

As Ethan's head cleared, the shadows moving about the room began to resemble specific shapes, men dressed head-to-toe in black Kevlar, running in formation with precise movements. He realized that the underground hideout was being invaded by some kind of SWAT team.

A couple of kids who had been doing computer work across the room sat stunned behind their desks, disoriented from the explosion's shock wave, and blinded from the flash. Their heads were bobbing as their hands groped around their desks.

Ethan watched as gunmen slowly emerged from the shadows with drawn weapons. The kids were easy targets. Ethan took in a deep breath, tasting the hot dust and gunpowder, then yelled, "Get down!" His voice, dry from the dust, came out thin and scratchy. Deaf from the concussion, the kids behind the desk didn't react to his cry.

A second later, there was a burst of machine gun fire. The fight-or-flight survival reflex deeply lodged in Ethan's brain instructed him to fall down onto the ground and hide. He watched the kids sitting behind the desks convulse as their bodies were riddled with bullets. Blood splattered across the desks and onto the computer screen. Their limp carcasses slid off their chairs, leaving a snail trail of blood.

Ethan crawled on his stomach away from the gunmen who were filing into the room through the hole they had just created.

Suddenly there was a series of small pops. In front of him, Ethan saw several small silver canisters oozing out a noxious gas. Immediately his lungs burned as the smoke rose, filling the room with a stinky haze. The rebels hiding in the room began to cough, giving away their locations to the gunmen.

Ethan continued to crawl on his stomach, staying below the rising smoke. He held his breath, picked up a smoking cylinder and tossed it towards the hole in the wall. Still not completely acclimated to Earth's gravity, he missed the hole and hit the wall. There was a series of plinks as the canister bounced on the ground, followed by a burst of machine gun fire in his general direction.

Ethan slid across the floor towards the corner of the room, tossing all the smoking canisters he came across back toward the gunmen. The smoke was very disorienting and he almost stood up, to walk towards the hole in the wall to catch his breath, when he realized what he was doing and fell back down onto his stomach under the cover of the rising smoke.

Finally he hid behind the chassis of an old car that was being converted. Hiding in the corner, he watched as the camouflaged men, not a millimeter of skin exposed, methodically fanned out across the room. Their faceless suits made them look like aliens exploring a smoking, newly- discovered planet.

He watched and saw that although they were well-armed, their Kevlar combat suits with all their gear made them slow and clumsy. His strength and speed would be a tremendous advantage in an up-close, hand-to-hand fight. The only way out of this was to go on the offensive and take them on one at a time.

Patik, M'buy and Cameron were hiding in a secret compartment the size of a handicapped person's public bathroom stall. Their hideouts were equipped with secret exits and compartments. Getting raided by various government agencies or by private hit squads was not a new thing. This had been happening to R.A.D. since the beginning. Homeland Security had raided their last hideout and they had narrowly escaped. Now, if their security were ever breached, all three would immediately jump to action and take cover in the closest hiding spot.

The room was practically airtight and from the outside the door blended seamlessly into the metal wall making it practially invisible. The only light in the room came from Patik's Smart-phone, which was being used as a flashlight. Both M'buy and Patik glared at Cameron.

Cameron moved her lips in an exaggerated fashion to make her silent words understood: "It's not my fault!" She pointed to the main room, "Ethan's not one of them!"

Patik responded with a look that said: "You better be right!" then calmly started fiddling with his smart phone. Both M'buy and Cameron relaxed slightly. Patik's manner had a soothing effect, allowing them to focus on the business at hand. How long could they stay in this hiding spot, and could they sneak out unnoticed and get to their vehicles quickly enough to get away?

Patik automatically began to back up all the data using his smart-phone. The data was too large to store on the little device so he used it as a remote to access the main computer to upload all the important files to a remote server.

The noxious tear gas was slowly starting to drift into their hiding spot. Apparently the room wasn't one hundred percent airtight. Patik worked as quickly as he could. He assumed the goons would probably either take or destroy all their equipment. So he doubted he had much time to preserve all their vital information.

Patik typed in the final command, uploading the last of the data. Then he accessed the cameras on each of the networked computer monitors. The three of them crowded around the little display screen and watched as dark figures passed through the room looking for people to shoot. Cameron was the first to point out the blood trail on the chairs.

They held their collective breath, watching as the small army that was looking for them passed just behind the false wall then spread out across the room. Then there was a large explosion. The hidden door buckled, letting in a thick cloud of gas and smoke. The three of them slid to the ground and covered their heads. They squatted in cannonball position, still watching the activity in the adjacent room from the little phone's screen.

The sound of gunfire echoed throughout the room. Bullets ricocheted off the buckled metal door. Sparks filled the screen as all their equipment was being riddled with bullets. A second later the acrid smell of burnt electronics blew into their hiding spot. They watched a small grenade bounce in front of the camera; simultaneously there was a flash on the screen and another explosion in the room that sent more smoke and debris onto their heads. Immediately the phone's screen went blank.

Every raid had some collateral damage but the Kevlar raiders were intent on destroying everything. Cameron, Patik and M'buy knew if they stayed put, any second they would be discovered. They needed to sneak out now while the goons were distracted destroying their gear. There was a secret exit not far from their hiding spot, but the armed assassins were just a few feet away. In the glow of the smart-phone, Cameron, Patik and M'buy gave one another a knowing nod; it was a risk they had to take.

M'buy went first, with Patik and Cameron close behind. Holding their breath, they crawled on hands and knees under the cover of smoke. Cameron was having a harder time seeing and breathing. When she crawled out from behind the broken door she couldn't see either M'buy or Patik and wasn't exactly sure which direction she should go. The smoke and noise had her terribly disoriented. She followed the wall, hoping she was going the right way, more afraid of screwing up their mission than of dying. She was already in some trouble since she was the one who had brought Ethan here.

Cameron, with her head low and T-shirt pulled up over her face to filter the dust and smoke, quietly and cautiously crept on her hands and knees along the wall of the room. She groped her way around until she arrived at a stack of car tires. A burst of anger shot through her. She had screwed up big time, somehow she had gone the wrong way. Now she was in the garage area where they did the conversions; the opposite side from the secret exit. She needed to get her bearings. The smoke was thick on the floor. If she could only see over it, she would know which way to go. She got off her knees and squatted onto her feet. Slowly and quietly she slid up the side of the wall. When she was almost standing straight up she saw a gunman turn toward her.

Immediately she fell to the ground and began crawling as fast as possible under the smoke cloud and away from the gunman. A spray of machine gun fire blasted the wall where she had been standing. Small chunks of concrete exploded off the wall and covered the floor with jagged grey chunks.

Ethan, hiding in the corner, saw Cameron's head pop up out of the smoke for a split second, followed by the deluge of gunfire. He watched the gunman cautiously take two steps out of the shadows towards Cameron.

As Ethan watched the gunman, anger seethed through him. All the primordial male hormones and instincts that draw a man into battle, so as to protect his loved ones from harm, surged though him. He lost all fear and rational thought. He was focused on making sure nothing happened to Cameron.

Ethan was about thirty feet away from the gunman. With a leap that even surprised Ethan, he sprang out of his hiding spot across the room and tackled the gunman. The momentum and Ethan's weight was enough to crush the guy, who could now barely move. Ethan grabbed the man's helmet and bashed it on the ground like a monkey trying to open a coconut, until he heard the Kevlar crack open. The man's rifle was lying beside him. Ethan grabbed it and slammed the butt into the soldier's face mask. The plastic shattered and blood oozed out. A second later, three more gunmen were shooting at him only a few feet away.

Ethan picked up the bloody body and tossed it like a sack of flour at two of the charging gunmen. Instinctively the men shot at the incoming object. When they realized what it was, they stopped firing and froze. The flying gunman came crashing down on the two baffled soldiers, knocking them to the ground. Ethan leaped and grabbed the remaining soldier and tossed him across the room against the concrete wall.

The man hit the wall with his shoulder and fell to the ground. He managed to hold onto his weapon and started shooting the moment he hit the floor. Ethan dove for cover and the soldier got back on his feet. Feeling triumphant, the gunman pointed his rifle towards the ceiling. Ethan, seeing nothing but pure anger and hatred, charged the man at full speed.

The plan, if there was one, was to smack the guy against the concrete wall. At the last second, the soldier leaped out of the way, like a matador, and missed getting squished by mere inches. Ethan's heavy and dense body hit the wall with the force of a wrecking ball, bursting through it as if it were made of Styrofoam. Grey concrete dust and blocks flew in all directions. There was a big, irregular shaped hole with bent rebar poking out, which now resembled a giant Venus flytrap. The hole created a change in pressure, and the smoke that had been lingering inside the room was quickly sucked out into open air. It became instantly easier for everyone inside to breathe, but harder to hide.

Ethan sprang to his feet. Through a swirl of concrete dust and debris, he saw the gunman step through the broken wall, this time with his weapon at the ready. With lightning speed, Ethan leaped towards the mercenary, grabbed the machinegun and tried to pull it away but it was tightly strapped to the gunman's body. All Ethan could do was jerk the Kevlar warrior around, lifting him off the ground and then shaking him from side to side. It looked like an awkward interpretation of a Brazilian Capoeira dance.

This continued for a few seconds and its lack of effectiveness really pissed Ethan off. With a loud grunt he twisted his wrist and bent the machine gun's barrel upward by twenty degrees, and then pushed the mercenary to the ground. The surprised gunman bounced on his ass and instinctively did what his years of training had taught him. He looked up, pointed his weapon and pulled the trigger.

Ethan watched as the gunman's hand, arm, shoulder and black Kevlar suit exploded, as the machine gun tried to shoot fifty rounds a second though a twisted barrel. It looked as if someone had forgotten to put the lid on a blender full of Bloody Mary mix before pushing "frappe."

Chapter 49

Franco Arana and Steve Hughes, known to their squad as, "The Pitbull" and "Maverick," were the two gunmen assigned to guard the vehicles in the alley behind the building. They were to wait as the team breached the hideout and do what they called a de-infestation. These were usually quick in-and-out jobs. The targets, unarmed computer geeks hacking their way into systems.

Maverick was sitting on the hood of the Hummer and had just taken his Kevlar helmet off because it was hot and itchy. He thought it was ridiculous to be "armored up" in a non-combat situation. Especially when the engagement was inside a concrete bunker with only one entrance and exit. If the enemy were somehow to make it past the team, which was extremely unlikely, he and The Pitbull had the exit covered and could neutralize the enemy before they took one step out of the combat zone.

Maverick was complaining to The Pitbull, "We always get the crap assignments! I mean, what's the point of all those years of training if we never get to do anything? Come on! We should be in there doing the fun stuff." He drew his rifle and pretended to shoot at a bunch of moving targets.

The Pitbull stood at attention. His back was up against the concrete wall. His helmet and combat gear were on, his rifle at-the-ready. He was taking his assignment very seriously. He believed that all aspects of the operation were vital, and that guarding the vehicles was as important as any other part of the operation. He got very tired of listening to Maverick bitch and moan. But he knew it was pointless to say anything. They would just end up arguing and neither of them would change their minds. He clenched his jaw to avoid saying anything, and just kept his eyes on the exit. It was obvious to him that Maverick wasn't disciplined and could easily disrupt the chain of command in a combat situation. That's why he always got guard duty.

Maverick spat on the ground, then wiped his mouth with the back of his hand. "I can shoot better than half the team. Certainly a hell of a lot better than Bowen or Spitz, and they always got in on the frontline. If I was in there now, I would be charging and chasing down those SOBs, no mercy, no hesitation, that's how you get it done!" He hopped off the hood, stomping his feet on the ground when he landed. "Man, if I was in there, we would be done by now!"

At that exact moment, the wall behind The Pitbull, who was standing at perfect attention, burst open as if a cannonball had hit it, discharging a shrapnel spray of concrete blocks and chunks. Maverick stood staring like a deer into headlights. He was confused. There wasn't an explosion; there was no heat, no smell of gunpowder or C4.

Maverick ducked behind the Hummer as big chunks of rubble crashed into it, breaking the windshield and headlights. Rocks bounced off the hood and front end, leaving big dents and scratches. The Pitbull's body was catapulted across the alley into the adjacent building. His body lay upside down and lifeless in a pile of rubble. His neck, arms and legs were all twisted in an unnatural way, like a rag doll that had gotten tossed in a trash bin.

Maverick watched in amazement as a man in a red jumpsuit popped up out of the rubble, tossing large concrete blocks as if they were papier-mâché. Next he watched Bowen step out of the hole. Then the guy in the red jumpsuit sprang like a tarantula, tossed Bowen around and pushed him to the ground. Maverick snickered. Bowen was over-rated and this was proof. A second later, Bowen's weapon blew up in his hand, blowing off his arm and splattering blood all over the hole.

Maverick felt his insides squeeze in excitement and his breathing get heavy. Finally some action! He would show the team leader what he was made of, and that he should be on the front line. Maverick crouched beside the Hummer's front passenger door. He listened as the man dusted himself off and began walking towards the vehicle. Maverick could hear the man's movements much better without his helmet on; he felt like a real stalker. He grabbed his machine gun, wet his lips, and thought to himself: "This is it. I'm going to show the team that I'm not to be overlooked." In a fluid and practiced move, Maverick jumped to his feet, stood in a solid stance, and pointed the machine gun into the dusty man's face. "Freeze, motherfucker!"

Ethan didn't flinch or even break his stride. He swatted Maverick as if a large insect had just flown in his face. The gun flew out of the stunned mercenary's hand and over the roof of the Hummer, followed by his own upside-down body. The airborne commando desperately tried to grab a hold of something, but there was nothing to grab, only his fingernails were able to scrape along the top of Hummer's metal roof. Finally Maverick came down headfirst, hit the edge of roof, bounced off, and before he could gain control, fell into a tight space between the driver's side door and the large side view mirror.

The mirror was very strong and for a long few seconds Maverick's body was suspended upside down in a metal headlock as if it were some medieval torture device. His shoulder was caught under the mirror and his ears were stuck tight against the bracket. He couldn't lift his arms up to grab anything to try to stop himself from falling over backwards. He felt his neck wrench and bend to its absolute limit. Instinctively, he closed his eyes and tightened his neck muscles then tumbled over as if doing a summersault. Finally his head popped out and he hit the ground hard, landing flat on his back.

He opened his eyes. He was looking straight up at the side view mirror, his vision blurry from the trauma. It appeared that something was stuck on the bracket. He tried to focus and see what it was, but it was hard for him to concentrate because both sides of his head burned. Just as he realized what he was seeing, both of his ears fell off the car and bounced off his face. They landed next to him in the dusty alley near a growing pool of blood oozing from his head. Once he had put together what had happened, the pungent smell of his own blood made him queasy. The last thing he thought before passing out was, "I guess I should have kept my helmet on."

Chapter 50

Amped up and pissed off, the four remaining Kevlar-clad mercenaries rushed out of the smoking hole, ready to take revenge on the guy who'd just taken out five of their fellow gunmen barehanded. The second the gunmen were out of the hole, they started wildly firing at anything that moved. Ethan ducked behind the armored Hummer as the bullets ricocheted off the vehicle, making a sound like spit on a hot griddle. Seeking better cover, Ethan ran to the rear of the Hummer. The gunmen slowed down their fire, conflicted; it didn't seem right to shoot up one's own vehicle. One of the soldiers got the bright idea of shooting under the car at Ethan's feet.

Ethan hopped around to avoid the cascade of badly-aimed bullets; it looked like a slapstick sketch from an old silent movie. Then Ethan had his own bright idea. Crouching like a linebacker, he leaned into the Hummer and started pushing. The big car's parking brake was engaged but Ethan continued to push, as the four gunmen cautiously approached the Hummer it began o skid down the alley, quickly picking up speed. The soldiers retreated. In less than a few seconds the big vehicle slammed into the side of the building, pinning two of the soldiers against the wall. The other two managed to jump out of the way and began shooting at Ethan through the Hummer's windows.

Crouched behind the armored vehicle, Ethan ducked the gunfire and shattering safety glass. When he looked back, he was surprised to see that the R.A. D. team had cautiously started crawling out of their hideout, armed only with bats and rocks. This seemed extremely risky. Suddenly a stream of debris began flying from the hideout's hole, over the Hummer, hitting the two remaining gunmen with surprising accuracy.

Ethan watched the teamwork and resolve of the rebels as they systematically exited the building. Here in the open space the two forces didn't seem so mismatched. The remaining gunmen took cover around the corner of the building, calling for back up. The R.A.D. team's main objective was to distract the soldiers so they could get to their electric cars and get away.

Once the bulk of the rebels had snuck out of the hideout, the flying debris was replaced by rifle fire as the remaining rebels made their getaway. Ethan stayed undercover, watching the R.A.D. team go through their maneuvers. They were keeping the mercenaries at bay behind the building, shooting at the gunmen whenever they tried to leave their cover. Cameron, M'buy, and Patik were finishing rounding up all the rebels and making sure everyone got to their vehicles safely.

Just as the last team was about to leave, two large armored Hummers came racing down the alley and an entirely new squad of mercenaries arrived.

Ethan watched Cameron push a skinny computer geek with bad acne into a getaway car. As the car sped away, she ran for cover dodging a spray of bullets. A blind rage filled Ethan. He leaped from his hiding spot and pounced on the hood of the arriving Hummer, crushing the front end like an aluminum can. Warm green antifreeze squirted in every direction. The passenger door opened, but before the first gunman could get out, Ethan stepped up onto the roof, grabbed the soldier by the back of his helmet, and like a paperboy tossing the Sunday edition, heaved the startled soldier head-first towards the Hummer trailing closely behind. The Kevlar covered mercenary flew like a human cannon ball, crashing through the windshield, pinning the driver and front seat passenger in a tangle of bodies and safety glass like a gruesome game of Twister.

Ethan saw everything as if in slow motion, actually seeing the bullets travel through the air towards him. Feeling more confident he leaped off the roof. Wanting to make himself as hard a target as he possibly could, he bounced around the ground as if he were on a trampoline. Suddenly bullets were flying in all directions as the confused gunmen wildly tried to shoot the wildly zigzagging target.

A soldier was stepping out of the rear passenger door, and was preparing to shoot, when in one fluid motion, like a gymnast doing a floor routine, Ethan leaped and slammed into the door crushing the gunman's legs. Using his momentum, Ethan bounced off the door, cartwheeled over the Hummer's roof, and pounced on the mercenary who was climbing out the opposite side. Ethan landed with both feet on the Kevlar helmet. There was a sound of a muted crack, and the soldier's body instantly began convulsing. Ethan grabbed the flailing storm trooper by the pants and jacket, picked him up, held him like a shield, then charged the second Hummer.

This new batch of mercenaries weren't as sympathetic towards their fellow soldiers. The first one stepped out of the rear driver side door and immediately started shooting, not seeming to care one bit that he was riddling his fellow fighter with bullets. Ethan tossed the limp bloody body over the roof at a mercenary who was climbing out of the rear passenger door. The body hit the gunman with astounding force pinning him to the ground like a scene from a morbid wrestling match.

Now Ethan was back, face-to-face with the first shooter. He swatted the rifle's barrel to the side, then kneed the startled warrior in groin, squashing his protective Kevlar cup like it was paper. The warrior buckled, and fell to his knees in agony. Caught up in the heat of the action, Ethan stepped on the mercenary's rifle, crushing the gunman's trigger finger while pinning him to the ground. With one arm Ethan grabbed the man's belt, jerked him into the air, and tossed him twenty feet into the wall of the adjacent building. Every inch of the warrior was still covered in protective armor except for his finger, which was exposed and bloody. Ethan looked under his foot and found the torn piece of the black glove laying beneath the rifle's trigger.

In the front seat of the Hummer the men were trying to dislodge themselves from under the hurled soldier and crumbling safety glass. The gunman on the side of the vehicle had unpinned himself from the grisly wrestling pose and was now crouching beside a lifeless bloody body, waiting to get a good shot at the freak in the red jumpsuit. Ethan was getting tired of the battle. He wanted to get back and help Cameron, so they could all get the hell out of here before another group of soldiers showed up.

Ethan squatted, grabbed the bottom of the heavy armored Hummer's side panel, and with a massive heave, tipped it up on to its side. The mercenaries in the front seat fell on top of each other, upside-down and tangled up, making their exit attempt all the more difficult. The squatting gunman, hiding on the side, had tried to jump out of the way, but got his leg caught under the vehicle, and was now pinned like an animal in a trap.

Ethan moved towards the hole where Cameron and the remaining R.A.D. team members were hiding, waiting for their electric car. Suddenly there was a big outburst of gunfire, as if everyone was cued to simultaneously start shooting. Bullets were flying, ricocheting off the walls of both buildings. Ethan felt a hot sting as the bullets and debris hit him. His jumpsuit was torn up, but there was no blood. He took cover behind the first Hummer that he had slammed into the wall; the soldiers were still pinned and were yelling obscenities at him.

Ethan sneered at their insults bewildered why they would want to piss someone off who could easily crush them like a bug. To shut them up, Ethan bumped his hips against the side of the Hummer. The car lurched a few inches and the two pinned soldiers screamed in agony. "Dipshits!" Ethan thought.

There was more gunfire and Ethan took cover behind the Hummer. He examined his skin underneath his torn jumpsuit. Nowhere was the skin broken. He was covered in welts that burned, but the injuries were more annoying than lethal. He was amazed. Apparently his adaptation from space had made him bulletproof. Ethan smiled with a new level of confidence.

An electric car silently arrived in the alley. Ducking gunfire, M'buy, Patik and Cameron ran from their hiding spot towards the car. Ethan watched as the wounded soldiers slowly got back on their feet and rearmed themselves. Ethan just needed to disable them a short while longer so Cameron could get away.

From behind the cover of the Hummer, Ethan grabbed several chunks of concrete and started tossing them at the soldiers, drawing their fire away from Cameron and the rebels and towards himself.

A second later, Ethan heard a loud, high whine, then a whoosh. Cameron started screaming. Ethan turned around towards the noise and didn't see anything. M'buy and Patik were standing halfway between their hiding spot and the escape car. They were staring dumfounded up into the air. There was suddenly a strong chemical odor, it reminded Ethan of the smell of jet fuel at the airport. Ethan looked up and saw what he was dealing with. "Oh my God," he wondered, "will this never end?"

Chapter 51

Flying up to the top of a twelve-story building, Myron Tucker, aka "The Fly," released the screaming woman he had just snatched from the ground and deposited her onto the roof. He had examined the roof earlier to make sure there was no way off, not even a drainpipe to crawl down.

Casper had given him an assignment: to find Ethan Stone and bring him back alive. Casper mentioned that Ascot, his fellow castaway, had shown remarkable strength, cognitive function, and speed. But the accident had left him paralyzed, so Ethan might be a bit more of a handful. From the looks of it, he most certainly was. The guy had just taken out an entire battalion without a single weapon. Impressive, but The Fly had some tricks up his sleeve; he was confident that he would capture and deliver this freak to Casper.

Before swooping down from the roof The Fly watched the R.A.D. team and the guy in the red suit fight the infantry. He had noticed right away that Ethan had a thing for the girl. The first step was to get some leverage. Grab the girl and hold her hostage. He had found an indirect attack to be very effective. Now that Mr. Stone's object of affection had been taken away, and was in the hands of a uniquely well-equipped, ruthless killer, perhaps they could have a constructive conversation.

****

The Fly was a practical man who approached his missions logically. Emotions, he thought, get the better of people every time. He learned this as a kid. His father was the only African-American test pilot at Edwards Air Force Base, and always felt like he had to prove himself. There was no overt racism; in fact, the military was pretty good at treating all people equally badly, and they usually promoted a person based on merit. But Myron's dad, Lloyd Tucker, was a very passionate man who would give two hundred percent to be the best. Myron always thought this was because, underneath it all, he felt like he wasn't good enough and needed to prove his value.

His need to prove something became his undoing. Lloyd was testing an experimental high-altitude space plane that could go past the stratosphere. It was a very risky test and Lloyd wanted to show that he wasn't afraid to take on the assignment, particularly when the other test pilots thought the plane wasn't ready. The story that was repeated to Myron was that his father had flown so high that he had left Earth's gravity. He had actually circled the earth, but when he tried to reenter the atmosphere, the plane didn't have enough heat shields. The aircraft got so hot that it turned into a blob of molten metal and fell into the ocean somewhere.

Like his dad, Myron was obsessed with flying and thrill-seeking. When he was ten years old, Myron had learned to skydive on the Air Force base, and at twelve, to mountain climb. At fourteen, he would hang out with the engineers who built the experimental aircraft. He was a smart kid and they enjoyed teaching him aeronautics and aerodynamics. He became a gifted student. When looking at schematics, he would often find ways to improve the design of the aircrafts they were working on.

After his dad died, he, his mother, and his sister were forced to move off the base. They moved back to Cleveland, where his mother was from. Almost immediately, she got remarried to a large, white plumber named Toby, who was an abusive alcoholic. One night, Toby drunkenly tried to molest Myron's sister, Tyra. Myron zapped Toby with a live electrical wire he had fashioned from an extension cord. While the big man was recovering from the shock, Myron beat the crap out of him with a baseball bat. Toby just barely survived.

Ironically, the injuries made Toby a much nicer guy. He had severe and permanent brain damage that made him slow, thoughtful, and unable to work. As a result, he collected SSI and Workman's Comp, increasing his income and eliminating the family's financial stress. The pain medication made Toby very mellow and unable to drink any alcohol. As a therapeutic measure, Toby started painting, mostly watercolors of buildings. He began to see the world with an eye of an artist and the wonder of a child. His relationship with Tyra and her mother had become like a kind, older brother. His sexual desires became nonexistent and the thought of him perpetrating any kind of sexual abuse seemed laughable.

Unfortunately, the Cleveland district attorney wanted to score points by being "tough on crime" by throwing the book at Myron. The attorney had campaigned on cleaning up all gang-related violence. Myron's case had absolutely nothing whatsoever to do with gangs. But somehow a black kid beating up a white guy got labeled as a gang-related incident. So Myron disappeared. He left Cleveland and never looked back, changing his name and his identity. He decided if he was going to be hunted down as a criminal, he might as well be one. So he developed his natural skills and found ways to both make a lot of money and live invisibly.

Myron was a small-framed man. He stood five feet, eight inches tall and weighed one hundred and thirty pounds. He was very strong for his size, and could easily do fifty pull-ups and over two hundred push-ups. Physically he was perfectly equipped for climbing up walls, breaking into skyscrapers, base jumping and flying around on a jet pack.

No building was impermeable to him. He could climb straight up a glass wall one hundred stories with suction cup shoes and gloves, in just a little over the time it would take to go up in an elevator. He had developed a very compact jet pack that could sustain forty minutes of airtime and travel up to Mach speed, earning him his professional nickname: The Fly.

****

At the bottom of the twelve-story building, Ethan looked up, amazed, as he watched a flying man drop Cameron onto the roof. Where the hell did this guy come from? An amplified voice, thin and tinny, as if it were being spoken through a bullhorn, blasted down from the roof of the building.

"Mr. Stone, we need to talk!" His voice was smug and confident and it really pissed Ethan off. "I believe I have something you want." Cameron's face was pushed to the side of the building, looking over the ledge. It seemed as though she was about to say something before she was yanked back by her hair and tossed out of sight. All gunfire had ceased and all eyes turned upwards. Several soldiers were now on their feet, walking or limping towards Ethan, weapons at ready. Patik and M'buy stood next to the electric car, hands in the air, their faces worried. They didn't think the soldiers were planning to take prisoners.

The tinny voice continued: "My men will refrain from shooting you and your friends, even though I know they would like to." There was a collective moan of disappointment from behind the masks of the soldiers. "We need to be civilized and come to an agreement."

Ethan was trying to quickly assess a strategy to get out of this mess, but at the moment it seemed that the guy on the roof and his cronies had the upper hand. Ethan looked for an angle.

"Mr. Stone, my employer would like to meet you." The tinny voice droned. "He has an affinity for people with unique abilities. You and I have something in common: we are both one-of-a-kind. A one-of-a-kind object has value, lots of value. You have more than you know."

Ethan yelled up to buy himself some time. "Thank you, but I'm not ready to sell out yet!"

"Suit yourself!" The Fly made a quick gesture with his right hand and the mercenaries all sprang to attention.
Ethan wasn't surprised. In every movie and TV show he could think of, the bad guys never fulfilled their end of the bargain. Why should this be any different? M'buy and Patik took cover behind the electric car. It was an old lime green and fuchsia D9 Citroën from the 60s, all tricked out with pink, purple and green neon lights around its edges. As Ethan reached down to grab an armful of concrete chunks, he thought. "Of all the cars, there couldn't be a more ridiculous getaway car in the entire world. That thing wouldn't blend in anywhere."

Once again bullets started flying. In less than two seconds the rainbow glow from the neon lights on the escape car was transformed into glass confetti. Ethan leaped from behind the Hummer and tossed the concrete chunks with deadly accuracy at the three gunmen who went down like targets at a shooting gallery. Two remained. One ran and took cover behind the corner of the building and the other was on the opposite side of the Hummer.

Ethan crept towards the gunman, as expected, the soldier countered his move maintaining his distance. Once they were crouched on opposite sides of the vehicle, between the front and rear doors, Ethan repeated his earlier strategy, only this time much faster. He reached down and flipped the Hummer on to its side, crushing the unsuspecting mercenary.

Looking down from his perch on top of the roof, The Fly had had enough. He was getting impatient. This bumbling bullshit needed to end now! He needed to take his leverage with him, perhaps knock her unconscious in front of Ethan. That usually got some cooperation. Cameron was on the opposite side of the roof, trying to find a way down, but the only way down was to jump, and at twelve stories, she knew that wouldn't end well.

The Fly fired up his jet pack. It made a high-pitched whine as he hovered three feet above the roof. Cameron turned with panic in her eyes. The Fly grinned back. They were standing off on opposite sides of the roof, the bull facing the Matador. "Let's kick the tires and light the fires!" shouted the tinny, bullhorn voice over the whine of the engine. At jet speed, The Fly shot across the roof and grabbed Cameron by her waist. His gloves were electrified, so the second he touched her she was hit with a disabling electric shock that made her body go rigid and her jaw clench shut. A second later, they were two hundred feet in the air, circling back toward the alley.

The Fly hovered above Ethan, holding Cameron with one arm, arriving just as Ethan flipped the car onto the soldier. The Fly looked at the commotion and thought, "enough is enough!"

Strapped to the side of each forearm were two gun barrels, he pushed a button to load riot control bullets. Typically one hit was enough to disable the average person and leave a big bruise or welt. The Fly swept down and showered bullets on top of Ethan's head. Startled, Ethan responded as if he was being attacked by a swarm of bees, but he wasn't hurt, if anything, it just seemed to just piss him off.

The Fly landed ten feet from Ethan, just opposite the shot-up Citroën, holding a stunned and rigid Cameron.

"What did you do to her?" demanded Ethan, as he massaged his stinging head and upper torso.

"She's fine, she's tough. In a minute she will be as good as new."

A shot came from behind the building and hit Ethan in the back.

"Oww!" Ethan arched his back, rubbing the spot with the back of his hand. The jumpsuit was torn but there was no blood. The Fly noted that the bullet didn't even break the skin.

"Stand down, soldier, I got it!" said the tinny voice. The Fly let go of Cameron, who stood as if at attention, her body shaking slightly.

On impulse, Ethan lunged at The Fly, tackling him to the ground. The Fly was covered from head-to-toe with armor, weapons, and gadgets. His suit was an exoskeleton robotic suit made from a very strong titanium alloy, which made him extremely well-protected, strong and very fast. He was also a highly-trained assassin who was used to killing or paralyzing people quickly with little effort. Ethan was fast and strong, and his years with the Ultimate Sparring Partner had shaped him into a formable adversary.

Cameron, just barely able to walk, started taking tiny steps towards the car. M'buy and Patik jumped out from behind the car and scrambled to open the rear doors, disregarding the shots being fired from behind the building. When M'buy pulled a rifle from the back seat and shot back, the gunman retreated. Both M'buy and Patik went to help Cameron as she inched towards the car.

The two were locked in Struggle, each throwing fast combinations, blocking, ducking, and weaving. Ethan was doing everything he could to Keep the Fly engaged and to pull the attention away from Cameron.

M'buy and Patik grabbed Cameron and dragged her to the car. As they were bending her rigid body into the back seat, a gunman from behind the building started shooting again. M'buy was quickly climbing into the car, when a bullet grazed his ass and he let out a loud, low-pitched scream. He fell on top of Cameron, and before the door was even closed the driver stomped on the accelerator and electric car sped off.

The Fly literally had tricks up his sleeve. His forearm gun-barrels could shoot out a half-dozen different projectiles, and of course he could fly. But real hand-to-hand combat was out of character, since he normally didn't need to exert this much energy. It reminded him of the old days before he had developed his gadgets and weapons. Back then, he had to rely on his fighting skills.

The Fly grinned. He was actually enjoying himself. Finally he had a worthy opponent. With a smile, he blocked another one of Ethan's jabs, and then ducked a strong right hook. If the punch had connected the fight would have been over.

The Fly didn't like close calls. It wasn't logical to take unnecessary risks with an unpredictable adversary. He decided right then it was time to end this. Ethan lunged towards him and The Fly leaped back, blasted his jet pack and flew straight up. Ethan stumbled from missing his target, caught his footing, leaped forty feet into the air, and grabbed The Fly's legs with the grip of a bear trap. The jetpack lost much of its upward thrust and went into sporadic zigzags. Ethan twisted his body shifting his enormous weight and The Fly fought to maintain control and avoid hitting the buildings.

The Fly's assignment was to deliver Ethan to Casper alive. He was about to ignore that order and shoot Ethan at point-blank range, but then thought better of it. Instead, he blasted Ethan with several dozen sticky bright green goo balls.

Ethan's face, hair, and shoulders were covered. One goo-ball hit his eye and glued it shut. While continuing to hold on Ethan tried to remove the sticky object, first by rubbing his face against The Fly's leg, then by digging it out with a finger. The more he messed with the goo, the more it spread and stuck to him. Ethan thought, "What's the point of this shit?"

Just then, he felt an excruciating pain, the sticky goo was an electric conductor that The Fly could remotely activate. Ethan lost his grip and fell four stories, crushing the front end of a Hummer like an aluminum can.

The Fly regained control of his flight, then landed with expert precision next to Ethan's body that was engulfed in the metal. The Fly surveyed the wreckage. Two Hummers were on their sides, one shot up and smashed against a wall, the other crushed. The Fly was both impressed and annoyed. As Ethan started to climb out of the wreckage, The Fly walked over towards him. "You may be strong, but your body is not immune to electrocution." He grinned. "You, my friend, are no match for me."

With that Ethan lunged for The Fly's throat, but was hit by a blast of chloroform gas from the Fly's gloved hand. Ethan's eyes crossed, and became instantly droopy. His left knee buckled and he lost his balance. Then he fell to his side, bounced off the crushed Hummer, and onto the dusty cement alley. Ethan tried to get up and crawl, but passed out before he was able to move a single inch forward.

Chapter 52

Beads of condensation dripped down two half-full champagne glasses onto a linen tablecloth in a lavish penthouse apartment. Cameron appeared, wearing a vintage bright orange terry cloth jumper that looked like something a Bond girl would wear, and picked up one of the champagne glasses. Her hair was unusually long and flowing, and the skimpy one-piece showed lots of cleavage. Ethan sat on a fuzzy, zebra-striped La-Z-Boy with the seat fully reclined. His legs were stretched across the footrest, as he watched her walk towards him.

Every inch the temptress, she slinked across the room her feet barely touching the ground, hovering like an apparition in front of Ethan. A sensual melody wafted from a soprano saxophone and softly filled the room, enveloping them in a sonic pillow. Cameron, with the practiced moves of a professional courtesan, began to remove her jumper. Moisture glistened on her breasts as she began to slide out of the top.

Ethan was getting very aroused. He hadn't touched a woman since the day he had left over eight years ago. Now, finally he was going to release the pent-up sexual energy that had been building up. He stared at her in awe. She looked like a goddess. Just as she slipped one arm out of its sleeve, exposing a large, soft, perfectly-shaped breast, a foul odor filled the room.

Ethan looked around as the walls changed from a rich sunset orange to a muddy brown. A large rhinoceros beetle flew into his cheek, and he winced from the sharp sting. When Ethan looked back, Cameron was gone. Now the room was filled with boxes of cleaning supplies. In the middle was a wheeled bucket with a mop sticking out of it. In front of him were two stinky, filthy restrooms he was responsible for cleaning. He got up and walked toward them, pushing the mop and bucket. With each step, the smell got worse and worse. Out of nowhere, another beetle flew into his opposite cheek, and again he felt the lingering sting. Then everything around him started to melt: the walls, floor, bucket, and mop all began to swirl like he was inside a giant toilet.

Ethan realized he was sitting in a chair. His arms were handcuffed behind him and his legs were shackled to the seat. A creepy-looking man was staring at Ethan, occasionally scratching his big nose and pockmarked face, with razor stubble poking out between the scars. His thinning, greasy hair was combed over starting at his left ear. He leaned in and slapped Ethan's face one more time to make sure he was fully awake, his breath reeked of cigarettes, coffee and spicy food. Ethan's mouth soured and puckered. He jerked back to get as far away as he could from the horrific smell and the man's hideous face.

"Goddammit!" shouted Ethan. Every time he was about to have a good erotic dream something interrupted it. Ethan looked around, evaluating his situation. He was in a sterile room, unable to move. The most sadistic-looking person he had ever seen in his life was staring at him maniacally.

He tried to break free, struggling, but couldn't break the chains. Out of nowhere an electrical current zapped him, neutralizing the nerves in his spine so he couldn't move his body from the neck down. Ethan's entire body became tingly, then went numb.

He was just getting used to the idea that he was invincible and could do anything. Now he was completely helpless. He was angry for having been captured. He should have let the guy in the jet pack fly away. Perhaps then he could have run away and he wouldn't have gotten caught. Just then a light went on and he saw that he was sitting in the middle of a strange medical office crammed with a plethora of computers and sophisticated medical diagnostic equipment.

The door opened and a fit, bald man wearing a dark expensive suit walked into the room. The creepy man with the ridiculous comb-over took one last murderous look at Ethan, like a fat man looking at the last donut in a box, and then walked out.

Casper Degas pulled up a chair and sat opposite Ethan.

"I heard you gave my men a run for their money."

"They started it." Ethan had a hard time getting the words out as the electrical current continued to flow through his body, immobilizing him.

"I don't take it personally, it's just business, and when you are in my business sometimes things get rather nasty." Casper motioned with his hand.

Two doctors in white lab coats, one tall and one short, walked into the room and stood next to Casper. They looked curiously at Ethan. Casper introduced himself and the two doctors. Then Ascot walked into the room wearing a very fashionable sweat suit, the kind celebrity trainers wore when they brought their rich clients to the gym. Casper stood up from his chair. Ascot stood smiling beside Casper. Ethan's eyes widened, revealing as much surprise as possible under the influence of the electric numbing device.

Casper grinned. "As I was telling your friend," Casper said patting Ascot on the shoulder, "I'm very sorry about what happened to the Valhalla Resort. I'm both impressed and amazed that you two survived. I know you are upset that no rescue attempt was made. But you have to understand you guys weren't in Mexico or Iran or someplace that I could just send a rescue team. By the time we figured out what had happened, Valhalla was in pieces, and you two were floating through the deepest depths of outer space. There was no way to get to you, no matter how badly we wanted to."

Ethan stared at Ascot. Ascot lifted up his pant leg to reveal a thin, elegant metal brace that ran down his legs. It was so small that Ethan could barely see it under his clothes. "Pretty cool, isn't it?" asked Ascot rhetorically. "I have full use of my legs again, thanks to these guys here." He pointed to the two doctors, who smiled as if on cue.

Casper stepped forward. "We have all kinds of technology that can make your life better.... or worse." With that, he touched a button on his wristwatch and the electric current that was immobilizing Ethan's body shut off.

Instantly he was able to move freely. Casper sat back down in the chair in front of Ethan. He lost his formal air and spoke as if he and Ethan were old buddies.

"You do realize that, since you are already considered dead, the simple thing for us to do would be to just go ahead and kill you, to avoid having to explain why you are still alive. Which, I'm sure you understand, would be a bit awkward from our perspective."

Ethan wiggled in his chair, his arms and legs still bound. "You make it sound as if it was somehow my fault."

"Sure, like I said, it's just business, and we have to do whatever is best for our bottom line. But I think you are much more valuable alive than dead."

"That's good to hear. Why?" Ethan was surprised at the almost-cocky sound of his own voice.

Casper held up a folder. "I've been reading your medical file."

The short doctor stepped forward. "We took the liberty of doing a battery of tests on you while you were unconscious."

Casper interrupted, "We did what should have been a week's worth of tests on you in two days." He pointed at Ascot, "We know all about the molecular and cellular transformation that went on while you two were in space."

The short doctor held up a sheet of paper. "We have charted in detail Ascot's exact levels of increased bone density, cellular density, muscle tension, strength, speed, and cognitive ability. From what we can tell from your tests, you seem to have even higher levels, which is quite amazing."

Casper nodded in agreement. "You have become an extraordinary human being. I dare say if you wanted to, you could become the world's best boxer, weight lifter, football player, you name it. I'd say just about any sport that requires speed and strength."

"Do you want to be my agent and take twenty percent?" The room burst out laughing. Ethan sat stone-faced.

Casper cocked an eyebrow at the insolent young man. "Because you are scientifically unique, we are willing to make a substantial investment in your future. We would like to see you working for us here at Eden, Inc."

Ethan looked dumbfounded. "You just sent a hit squad out to kill me. Now you're offering me a job? I don't get it!"

Ascot took a few steps closer to Ethan. His gait was a little bit awkward but if you didn't know him you wouldn't notice. "Do you remember the expression, 'Business and politics make strange bedfellows?'"

Ethan nodded.

"This is an example of that sort of strange relationship. You have something they want and I think they can give you something you want. So everything that has happened in the past is irrelevant."

Ethan nodded suspiciously. "Okay, what is it you want me to do for you?"

Casper patted Ascot on the shoulder, then took the floor. "Eden, Inc. owns literally hundreds of different companies that do thousands of different things. Your muscle and your abilities will be very useful to us."

"Okay," said Ethan suspiciously, not sure what he was getting himself into.

"You have to realize," said Casper, "you will be part of the inner coalition, you can be sitting at the top with us as we oversee everything that goes on."

Ethan turned to look at Ascot in surprise. This was exactly what Ascot would endlessly rant and rave about, only from the opposite position. Now suddenly he had switched sides... just like that. Ascot was about to say something but Casper lifted his hand, cutting him off. Ascot took a few steps back. Casper crossed his legs, sat back in his chair looking more relaxed, then snickered. "There are some things you have to understand. People need to be led. It's true everywhere. Even the 'so-called' leaders need to be led. We do what is necessary for society to function. We are the strong who have been ruling the world for thousands of years. It requires conviction. It's not at all emotional. We use emotions as a tool to distract and manipulate the masses so they will do whatever we need them to do: fight our wars, buy our products, clean up our messes, and so on. That's how the world works, and it's how it's always worked. Leo Strauss advocated that we should use religion to manipulate the masses. Some call us ruthless." Casper shrugged. "Like that's a bad thing. They simply don't understand. We aren't dealing with the little stuff here. We have to be ruthless because the consequences are too great."

Ethan, who was starting to tune into Casper's hypnotic voice, began to nod his head in agreement.

Casper continued. "Because you are unique you have been given a very rare opportunity to be invited into our inner circle. In fact, most people don't even know we exist. Some people have heard about the Freemasons, the Bilderberg Group, the Illuminati, and other such groups, but their existence is always downplayed. When people try to bring public attention to them, we always make sure they get labeled as some kind of kooky conspiracy theorists." Casper gave Ethan a knowing wink. "Now is the time to jump onboard, because you only get one chance."

Ethan didn't say anything. He just sat staring at Casper and Ascot. His conflicted look prompted Casper to continue.

"We are on the brink of a one-world corporate government and there is nothing anyone can do about it. This has been in the works for a long time, hundreds of years. The corporate and banking community both have a clear vision of how they want the world to operate. After seventy years of think tanks, we have slowly and steadily shaped and manipulated the laws and governments of the world to achieve our vision. It's the natural order of things. Mankind has tried to create equality but the truth of the matter is, all men are not created equal. Look at you!" Casper patted Ethan on the back. "You are unmatched, therefore it's only right that you take your place among the elite and embrace the fact that the dreams of the ruling class are about to come to fruition."

"Hmm," Ethan grunted.

Casper stood up, excited. "They say God rewards those who are strong; perhaps that's why we are rich and powerful. To rule over the masses! The Romans understood this concept well, and they ruled most of the earth for almost a thousand years. Now is our time, I have decided to believe that God is favoring me. He has made me rich and he has given me power, and it's my obligation to use it for the benefit of the people I choose. That is why you have come here. God sends me extraordinary people to help me build my empire and reap the rewards of being on top."

Ethan lifted his handcuffed arms as high as he could behind his back and shook them at Casper in frustration. If he was "on top," why was he still handcuffed to a chair? Growing up, Ethan had seen lots of people with extremely large egos. It went with the territory of bodybuilding. It took a certain kind of person to stare at themselves for hours flexing in a mirror, but never did those iron-pumping fools ever suggest that God was on their side. Casper's ego was in a league of its own.

Ethan knew he wasn't a particularly good debater; all things considered, the mood was reasonably peaceful. If he could just keep his mouth shut and let things play out, things would stay civil, but the hypocrisy was nagging at him. Listening to this madman's rationalizations and self-aggrandizement was just too much. He had to say something. Knowing that he was dealing with a person who could snap at any instant, Ethan tried his best to keep his tone calm.

"How can you believe in God when you lie, cheat, and kill people?"

Chapter 53

Everyone in the room stopped breathing for a moment and immediately looked at Casper, who seemed to regard the question seriously. He looked around the room, sizing up his team. "I would like to speak to Ethan alone for a moment." Without saying a word, Ascot and the doctors filed out of the room.

Casper closed the door behind them, then redirected his attention to Ethan. "I don't usually tell anyone this, but I'm sure you have heard the expression: 'God helps those who helps themselves.'"

Ethan nodded.

"The secret is this: God is non-judgmental, so I do what I need to do to win. God rewards conviction and commitment. God is not moral. Morality changes with the times, while convictions and commitment are a constant. God is infinite and can only deal with constancy. Inconsistent rules are man-made constraints. God doesn't reward someone for following the rules. Murdering, cheating, stealing—God doesn't distinguish between these sorts of petty, right-from-wrong stuff. No, God rewards fortitude. Whether or not it's self-serving or altruistic is irrelevant, so the question I have for you is, now that you are back, how do you want to live?"

Ethan just stared, not sure what to say. He didn't have a plan. Yesterday he was just trying to find his Dad and girlfriend and now everything had been turned upside down.

"It's really not that hard a question," said Casper as he walked back towards the door. "How do you want to live? Do you want to be wealthy or poor, famous or obscure? Do you want to have an effect on the world and leave a legacy, or do you want to be an insignificant drone in a giant colony of ants?"

Ethan continued to stare, confused. Everything seemed so extreme and unreal. Casper opened the door and the team reentered the room. Casper stood next to Ethan, waiting for the last person to close the door.

"Look" said Casper, "life is surprisingly simple. There are things that give pleasure and things that create pain. I'm in the position to give you whatever you want that will give you pleasure. Ascot now sees the big picture; he realizes we are living in a dog-eat-dog world and the top dog has the good life while the rest struggle. He wanted to walk again, I gave him his legs back. I can give you hot chicks, fast cars, money, vacations to exotic places, whatever you want. If you join me and get on the winning side, I promise you will have a great life."

Ethan smiled; he had to admit that the thought of driving a Viper or Lamborghini with Cameron in skimpy clothes sitting in the passenger seat was very appealing.

Casper interrupted his fantasy. "I have more power than you can imagine. I can buy anything. I have control over legislation, I tell the Congress what laws to pass. Nowadays laws are written by those who put the politicians in office." He pointed to himself. "Not by our politicians—they are just puppets. I am the puppet master, so I use the system to get what I want; more money, more power, more leverage. Poor people see the law as a form of oppression, the middle class sees it as protection, but for me it's a tool to get what I want, pure and simple."

Ethan was thinking about what it would be like to have whatever he wanted. Would he go crazy like Casper? He wondered if Casper's wealth made him crazy or did his craziness make him wealthy? "Do you ever have enough?" asked Ethan.

Casper thought for a moment. "It's not about acquisition. It's about doing something amazing. The more you want to do, the more you need to have to do it. Every day the bar gets raised. So the question I have for you is, what do you want? Seriously, ask yourself that question and be fearless. If you could have anything, what would it be?"

Ethan was shocked to find that he didn't know. Whatever dreams and desires he once had were abandoned long ago. Now he was literally being offered anything he wanted and he was completely overwhelmed. Besides surviving, he hadn't really achieved anything in life. He was going to be the first person in his family ever to graduate from college, but that only lasted two semesters. Now the world was opening up to him. He could make a quantum leap into any arena. At this moment, anything was possible; he just had to point the way. This was everyone's dream come true, and his mind was a blank.

Casper laughed. He could tell that Ethan was melting down. He spoke very seductively. "I can make you world-famous in two weeks. Like I said before, you can be the best at a lot of things, and for the rest of your life you will have money, girls, and the adoration of the masses. You'll be given a free ride everywhere you go. Everything you ever wanted is available to you."

Casper's eyebrows rose in excitement. "You have no idea what money and fame can do for you. Believe me— it's fun!" He paused to let the words sink in. Ethan sat blankly. "Only, you can't tell anyone how you got this." Casper pointed at Ethan's body. "Your incredible strength and speed is a result of Eden, Inc.'s proprietary muscle-building supplements and training formula." Casper laughed, "Hell, we pay that numb-nuts baseball player Tyrone Jackson a million dollars a year to endorse our products. You can easily be worth ten times that."

Ascot delicately stepped in. "Ethan, I'm sure you're confused. I remember all the stuff I advocated all those years while we were training. I was being idealistic and unrealistic. I was viewing the world as 'us and them,' black and white with no shades of grey. When I got back to Earth, and was crippled, I saw clearly how temporary and short our life really is."

He turned and paced, thinking what to say next. "I could continue to try to swim upstream and fight a losing battle because— " he made quotation marks in the air— "it's the right thing to do. But some things are simply inevitable and fighting them is ultimately a waste of energy. You might delay something for a short time and feel victorious, but it's an illusion. So for the last few decades that I have left in life, I'm done fighting losing battles. I don't want to be in fight mode all the time. I just want to relax, maybe find a nice girl, settle down and enjoy my life."

Ethan stared at Ascot in disbelief. This was one hundred and eighty degrees opposite from everything he had ever stood for. He remembered his dad had a theory. It wasn't typical of Vince to have theories, so this stuck out for Ethan. He called it the love-hate teeter-totter. Simply put: the level of love and passion people have for something or someone is equal to the level of hatred they will have when they fall out of love with that same something or someone. Love and hate takes the same amount of energy, so it's like a teeter-totter that requires equal weight to go up or down.

Vince got the idea when he learned, to his amazement, that early in his career Ronald Reagan was a New Deal Democrat who had fought hard for the unions and the rights of the working class. Later he switched sides and became a right wing zealot who did more to bust unions and divide the middle class than anyone in American history. This, along with the love and hatred Vince had felt for Ethan's mom, Delilah, were the inspiration for Vince's theory.

Now Ethan looked at Ascot, thinking that last week he was very passionate about the environment, peace, freedom, democracy, and the rights for all mankind. Ethan cringed at the idea that if Ascot had flipped sides, what kind of person had he become?

Ethan licked his lips and asked if he could have a drink of water. The doctors looked at each other, then at Casper. Casper nodded and the tall doctor left. Casper pushed a button on his watch and suddenly Ethan's handcuffs broke free.

He looked at Ethan. "I can trust that you will behave yourself and I won't have to turn the magnetic cuffs back on?" Ethan nodded, and brought his hands in front of his body. On his wrists were electro magnetic bands that looked like thick metal watchbands. When an electric current ran through them, they became magnetic and would stick together, turning them into handcuffs. The tall doctor came back with a plastic water bottle and handed it to Ethan.

Ascot continued. "Since we have been gone, a lot has changed in the world. The population has grown; there is more famine, disease, pollution, and chaos. Clearly people are not capable of adequately governing themselves. World population is too big now to let people do whatever they want. The days of freedom are over. People can't handle it, they abuse it and ironically they don't appreciate it anyway. Someone needs to tighten the reins if we are going to survive."

Ethan drank down his water and looked around, not sure where to put the empty bottle, then set it on the ground next to his shackled ankle. Ascot was pacing back and forth in front of Ethan, collecting his thoughts for the next round. "History is just the perspective of the winner. Had Germany won World War II, today the Nazi perspective would be deemed, just, right, and even moral."

Casper tapped Ascot on the shoulder and took over the conversation. "You have to understand that most people don't ever see the truth. You remember the line from that old movie, 'You can't handle the truth.'" Ethan was surprised. Casper did a surprisingly good impression of Jack Nicholson. "It's true, people don't want to know what's really going on, and they don't need to know. They don't care about war or peace. Most people don't even know it's happening, and those who do sign up to fight, know what they were getting themselves into. No, most people want to be distracted. They just want to do their jobs, watch the game on TV, and go to the movies on the weekends. They are happy being told what to do and how to think. For them, that's a productive, peaceful life, so we are the ones who are giving them exactly what they want. What's wrong with that?"

Ethan thought about his options. He had no family, no place to live, no money, no job, and no transportation. If he joined Eden, Inc. he could have anything he wanted. He looked over at Ascot, who seemed to have teeter-tottered over to the other side.

Ethan was intrigued with what Casper and Ascot were saying. It seemed to make sense. What's wrong with wanting a lifestyle filled with champagne wishes and caviar dreams?

But there was something nagging at him. He thought of Vanessa, now Cameron, and how caught up into R.A.D. she was. He admired her commitment. There was something very noble about dedicating one's life to others and to the idea of making the world a better place.

But how much power and influence did R.A.D. really have? They were a bunch of computer hackers and second-rate saboteurs. Surely he could have a bigger impact on the world and do good things if he were in a position of power like Casper, and he could do it while living the good life. Ethan felt the teeter-totter start to drop.

He was thinking what the future could hold for him: smoking hot cars, faster girls, and exotic vacations. The chance to live the American dream.

Chapter 54

Two taps on Casper's wristwatch and the magnetic shackles that pinned Ethan's ankles to the chair suddenly released, as Casper sought to establish a new level of understanding with his quarry. Ethan stood up and stretched his legs, Casper turned to Ascot. "Would you excuse us?" Ascot looked over at Ethan, concerned, then shrugged and walked out. Ethan waved at his departing back. He was still intrigued by Casper's offer, imagining what it would be like to have his own private helicopter... Or better yet, a blimp. With a big blimp he could float silently over the city and have wild parties filled with beautiful women.

Just as his vivid imagination was conjuring all the freedom and opportunities that lay before him, Ethan's body suddenly went ridged. It felt like an invisible bus had hit him. The next thing he knew he was crumpled to the floor like a tossed wet towel, unable to move any part of his body. Casper stood over him, stone faced, speaking firmly like a strict parent. "Ethan? I know you can hear me. You are probably wondering what's going on. Well I just electrocuted you from the inside out. Nano-bots have been inserted into your spine." Casper held up and tapped his wristwatch. "With this, along with some proprietary satellite technology, I can, from any location on Earth, control all your body functions and nullify your super strength and speed in the blink of an eye. As you can see, I can make you as helpless as a snail inching across a freeway."

Ethan lay crumpled on the sterile floor. The two doctors just stood next to the medical equipment, watching and observing neutrally. Casper tapped his wristwatch again. Suddenly, Ethan went from being quadriplegic to paraplegic.

Casper chuckled. "I have total control over your nervous system." Casper tapped his watch again and Ethan's body went into convulsions. "This is just to show off the nano-bots' capability and versatility." Ethan's body suddenly froze. He lay on his back perfectly straight, his arms at his sides. Involuntarily, his arms shot up above his head, then back down, his legs spread-eagled, then closed.

Playing with Ethan like a child would play with a video game, Casper maniacally tapped on his wrist keypad, changing the speed that Ethan moved, making him repeatedly hit himself to see how loud a noise it would make. As the game went on, Casper's laugh got more and more sinister.

Ethan's whole body stung, his hands and face were red from having slapped himself. Now his upper body was working again, but his legs still tingled and he couldn't move them at all. He stretched his arms and wiggled his fingers.

Casper walked over to Ethan and stood looking at him like a cat toying with a mouse. "So, if we do business together and you are on the payroll, you need to know one very important rule." His jaw clenched and he suddenly resembled the mannequin from the Ultimate Sparring Partner. "Any malicious act against me or Eden, Inc. and I'll shut you down for good. Understood?"

Ethan nodded. He lifted himself up onto his elbows and then up to a sitting position. The idea of having tiny robots in his spine that could turn him into a marionette at any time made his stomach turn. He expected some level of quid pro quo but this was way beyond his imagination. Ethan's good mood and fantasies were knocked right out him and he was engulfed in a feeling of dread.

Casper nodded to the two doctors. They both moved mechanically over to the medical equipment and began to turn it on. Casper tapped his watch and the tingling in Ethan's legs immediately subsided, enabling him to move freely with no side effects. Casper gestured to Ethan to get off the floor. "Something else you should know."

"Great," Ethan thought, "What now?"

"Your entire body is covered in nano-bots. You can't feel them, see them, smell them, or taste them. They are completely undetectable. They monitor all your body functions and then send us updated information every few minutes on how and what you are doing."

"Like what?" wondered Ethan.

"Like your exact location."

"You mean I'm lo-jacked?"

"Yes, and we monitor your heart rate, your pulse, your uh—" Casper looked over at the short doctor to help him out.

The doctor picked up the sentence. "—digestion, insulin levels, blood pressure, brainwave activity."

"Why?" interrupted Ethan.

"I want to make sure my investments are safe." said Casper. "Also they serve a utilitarian function."

"What's that?"

"The nano-bots can become an extra eye and ear." Casper got very excited when talking about the technology. "They can see infrared and X-rays, then send us that data, so everything you see, everything you hear, as well as the things you can't, all get automatically recorded." Casper pointed to a hard drive.

The short doctor chimed back in. "Also, the nano-bots can combine and assemble themselves into literally thousands of different functions. If, for example, you were to get into an accident and become unconscious and your carotid artery were severed, the monitoring computer would detect the problem and instruct the nano-bots to assemble themselves into a sub-dermal clamp and close up the wound to stop the bleeding. Then the bots would stimulate your nervous system and revive you. It's very useful technology."

Casper looked proudly at Ethan. "Like I said, I want to make sure my investments are safe. Once you and I agree to get started, I believe we are going to transform everything around us." He patted Ethan on the back. Ethan felt strangely honored and simultaneously creeped out.

Casper stood near the door looking down at Ethan. "Another perk for being an Eden, Inc. team member is you get your own apartment."

Ethan stared up at Casper, his face questioning.

Casper smiled enthusiastically. "Come, I'll show you."

Chapter 55

Walking out of the medical examination/interrogation room was a huge relief. Casper, Ascot and The Crusher surrounded Ethan in the hallway. Ethan was still in his battered jumpsuit and everyone else was nicely dressed. He felt like a prisoner being escorted to his cell. The hallway to the elevator was dead quiet and smelled like floor wax. Their footsteps echoed through the corridors. Ethan became aware of the shuffling sound that his jumpsuit made from the cloth rubbing when he walked.

The elevator door opened just as the men approached it, as if anticipating their arrival. Casper slid a card through a reader that accessed the VIP section of the building. A second later, the door closed and they were rushing to the top of the building. The elevator moved so fast that Ethan could feel the G-force. Less than a minute later, the door opened and Ethan's ears popped.

They stepped out onto the roof. The air was cool. There was a refreshing breeze and Ethan could smell the salt from the ocean, only a few miles away. At first glance it looked like a ground floor apartment complex. There were lots of trees, walkways and a large pool in the center. Surrounding the pool were two and three story apartment units with large windows looking out over the city.

It was serene, the grounds so lush that Ethan forgot he was on a roof. He could smell the trees and the flowering bushes that lined the pathways. While below him was the hustle and bustle of the city.

Ethan walked beside Ascot. "It's awesome that you can walk so well and so quickly." It was the first time Ethan had a chance to talk with Ascot since he first saw him. Each of Ascot's steps looked effortless; he was walking as if he had never been paralyzed.

It was awkward having Casper and The Crusher next to them. Both Ethan and Ascot could both feel the tension. Ascot looked over his shoulder at the two listening men, then turned back to Ethan. He made a subtle face acknowledging their lack of privacy.

"It's amazing, we are very lucky. Without Eden, Inc. we would be fish out of water. We have no IDs or jobs, we'd be homeless and penniless, and I would spend the rest of this life being crippled. I say we hit the jackpot." Ethan nodded, wondering if the words coming out were for his or Casper's benefit.

"We are living in a Brave New World and we are blessed to be sitting at the top." As Ascot continued, Ethan studied his body language; he seemed to be happy with his new situation. The old idealist seemed to have vanished in a puff of high society smoke. Ethan was usually the one to play it safe and Ascot was the rebel, but it seemed as if their roles had reversed.

Ethan wanted to tell Ascot about his encounter with Vanessa and how she switched identities and became Cameron, and that he was concerned for her safety and well-being, but there was no way to talk about it with Casper there. Ascot had actually met Vanessa once just before they had left, and Ethan had talked about how he felt about her quite a bit.

Ethan assumed that Casper was going to ask him to betray Cameron and her R.A.D. team members. If so, was all this really worth it? Previously Ascot had been good with these sorts of questions, but now Ethan had some doubts since he seemed to have switched sides. Ethan had spent almost a third of his life with Ascot and still felt like he could trust him. He wanted to find a way to talk with him in private, but even if they were able to be alone, Ethan's nano-bots meant there was no way to be sure that someone wouldn't be listening. From now on, nothing that he said or did was ever going to be one hundred percent private.

The group arrived at a large stainless steel door framed by two jacaranda trees. Casper pointed to a little touch pad on the side of the door. "Touch the keypad with your right index finger." Ethan did as instructed. There was a soft click and the large steel door automatically opened.

The entryway had a two-story ceiling and a black marble floor with matching columns. The living room sported plush white carpet and a black marble fireplace that matched the entrance. Ethan looked out of the floor-to-ceiling windows over Westwood Village. There were streams of cute UCLA girls darting in and out of shops, like ants scouting for food to take back to their colony. Casper, The Crusher, and Ascot stood in the entryway and watched Ethan explore.

Everything was very elegant and cushy. The style reminded Ethan of Valhalla. "Probably the same interior designer," Ethan mused. Although very impressed, Ethan felt uncertain about calling this place home. It would be like living as a fish in a bowl inside Casper's office. Everything he did from now on would be monitored. He looked around the elegant living room, with its white couch, glass coffee table, and built-in entertainment center. He wondered if all the rooms had hidden cameras and if the place was bugged? "One doesn't get to be in Casper's position without being a little bit paranoid," Ethan mused. He had no doubt that Casper always had his ass covered.

Ethan scanned the room and considered his situation. "I suppose this is what it's like once you get to the top," he thought. "The President and his family don't have any personal freedom really. They have the Secret Service monitoring their every move. I suppose that's the price you have to pay to live like this." What made him uneasy was he was being showered with all these gifts and threatened in the same breath, and he was still unsure what purpose he would serve. Being a unique human specimen and having some special skills, what did that really mean?

He thought for a moment as he looked around the kitchen, dining room and bedrooms. Ascot took Casper's offer. Apparently he was willing to live in the fishbowl and be Casper's tool, to be used when needed.

"What do you think?" asked Casper.

"It's so opulent, I'm speechless," responded Ethan.

"There is twenty-four-hour room service." Casper handed Ethan a menu. "And a maid comes in twice a day." He gave Ethan a knowing look. "She'll do anything you want her to do.... anything!"

"Ah," said Ethan, not sure if he had caught the correct innuendo.

Casper walked toward the kitchen and pulled out one of the four chrome and black leather barstools that stood next to the counter. He gestured for Ethan to sit, pulled out another stool for himself, then produced a folder. "Check this out and tell me what you think." The folder held pictures of more than a dozen cars. All were expensive and exotic: Mercedes, BMWs, Ferraris, Corvettes. "Pick one."

He gestured to The Crusher to bring him his briefcase.

Surprised, Ethan looked over at Ascot for advice. Ascot said nothing and shrugged his shoulders.

"Pick one?" said Ethan.

"It will be your company car. It's important that you have a stylish ride."

"A stylish ride, huh? Why is that important?"

"Because you are important and you need to be seen as important. We have to change your middle-class mindset! Image is reality! And reality is relative."

Ethan looked confused, not sure what he meant.

Casper hopped off the barstool. "Show some enthusiasm! Get excited! Have some fun! It's just stuff and it's all temporary! So enjoy it!"

Ethan wasn't sure why, but the nervous sinking feeling that was lodged in his gut seemed to lift out of him and evaporate into the ether. A smile spontaneously appeared on his face and he just felt happy. Ethan looked over the sheet of cars with a new, cavalier feeling. His mind was chanting: "Go for it, it's just stuff! Go for it, it's just stuff!" As he struggled to decide which hot, exotic car to pick, it occurred to him that the last car he personally drove was his Dad's beat-up 1965 Ranchero. That car, although potentially cool, was no status symbol.

He wanted a car that was cool and impressive and said to the world: I'm important, I'm rich and I deserve only the best. He scanned the pictures one more time. "I'll take the convertible Maserati coupe."

"The red one or the black one?" asked Casper, matter-of-factly, as if Ethan had just ordered coffee and he was clarifying, "regular or decaf?"

"The red one!"

Casper pulled a small device from his briefcase and handed it to Ethan, who looked at it blankly. "The key," Casper looked at it solemnly. "This is what keys to hot, exotic cars look like." Casper reached into his briefcase and sat back down on the barstool. Then like a card sharp he dealt Ethan a new driver's license, passport, social security, and ATM card. Then he topped off the pile with an American Express Platinum Card.

"We have sort of given you a new identity."

"What do you mean sort of?"

"All your numbers are different: social security, driver's license, passport, and so on, but your name is the same. So according to the system you are a different person."

"They won't notice that I died and then came back to life?"

"Not at all," Casper waved his hand dismissively. "You are a completely different Ethan Stone. We even padded your records. The new Ethan Stone has a credit score of 850, is a college graduate, has served in the military, gets vet benefits, and will receive a government pension when he turns fifty-five. He also has a history or charitable contributions to the March Of Dimes."

Casper gave Ethan a thumbs-up. "You, my friend, are squeaky clean. Not so much as an unpaid parking ticket on your record. There is absolutely no reason for anyone to suspect anything."

"I was under the impression that with all the new security measures, that they would catch anything fraudulent like this."

Casper chuckled. "No way. The irony is, the more people they catalogue, the bigger the system grows and the more difficult it is to manage, therefore the less efficient it becomes."

Ethan looked through the pile of cards, then put them down on the counter.

Casper hopped off the stool. "All we care about is that you are a legal citizen in good standing." He pointed to the IDs and credit cards. "This all states that you are!"

The Crusher walked into the kitchen and opened the refrigerator. Ethan got a quick glimpse inside and noticed that it was full of food. A hairy, muscular arm handed Casper, then Ethan, each a bottle of beer. It was a brand he had never heard of, written in a language he couldn't read. Casper took a long draught and Ethan followed. It was the first time he ever drank beer socially as an adult. As a kid he got drunk a few times at high school parties, but Vince was a hardcore teetotaler and had gotten really mad. His main objection to Ethan drinking wasn't that he was under age, it was that alcohol contained hundreds of empty calories.

It felt good to sit back in a super-luxury apartment, look down upon the city with one of the most powerful men on Earth, kick back, drink what he assumed was a damned good bottle of beer, and bond.

There was a ding in the kitchen. The big man pulled a white china plate covered with little pizza hors d'oeuvres out of the microwave, then put them on the counter. Ethan looked at this guy, who he knew for a fact to be a killer, serving him. He grabbed a mini-pizza and thought, "I could get used to this lifestyle." He imagined being among the high-powered jetsetters, having the finances to travel first class or in a private jet. Staying at five-star resorts, eating the best food at fine restaurants. It was a big leap from cleaning the locker rooms at Blood-Sweat-N-Tears Gym. It would be hard to go back.

Casper finished chewing and wiped his mouth on a silk handkerchief that seemed to magically appear. Then he pointed to the ATM and credit cards. "For the time being, I can offer you a corporate account with an unlimited line of credit. It's available to you so you can purchase whatever is essential, or in the case of an emergency. I don't think you are the type of person who would abuse these privileges." Casper looked over to Ascot, who nodded in agreement. "Anyway, I doubt you will need it. I think you will find that most everything you need is provided for you. He handed Ethan a map of the Eden, Inc. headquarters, which resembled the Valhalla Resort. There were restaurants, shops, nightclubs, spas, a gym, a swimming pool and a Jacuzzi. In what looked like a second shopping mall, there was a pool hall, video arcade, bank, post office, and movie theater: Casper was right; there was practically no reason to ever leave the building.

Ethan took another swig of beer. He was feeling pretty good, but did he really need Casper? He thought about what he could do with all his new powers. He could probably be the world champion at something, make lots of money and create an awesome lifestyle for himself. But, he didn't need to build that lifestyle; he was living it. All the goodies he ever dreamed of were at his fingertips. Everyone around him was treating him with the utmost respect, and wasn't that what was most important: commanding people's respect? When he thought about it, except for the nano-bots, what was there to complain about?

Casper opened a large-floor-to ceiling sliding glass door and stepped out on to the balcony. The faint sound of traffic blew in with the cool, salty air. Ethan followed him. Standing against the balcony rail, Ethan felt like a king looking down upon his subjects. Casper's eyes bored into Ethan. "Are you ready to take on your first assignment?"

Ethan took another sip of beer, contemplating. "This is it. I could toss him off balcony and walk away. I doubt he would be able to tap his watch and zap me. Or?" He nodded. "You've made me an offer I can't refuse. I'll take it."

"Before you take anything, and before we let you in, I need to know that you are serious. This first assignment is a crucial test." Casper had that same maniacal look in his eyes as he'd had when he was electrocuting him with the nano-bots. "All secret organizations, from street gangs to Skull & Bones, triads to the mafia—even the Harvard Law Review and the Carlyle Group—they all have tests. Any organization with as much power as Eden, Inc. has to have a serious test to prove the commitment of anyone who wants to join. I have to know without a doubt that you are loyal. That your strength, speed, and fearlessness are going to be used for me, and not against me."

Ethan nodded, and took another sip of beer. There wasn't much left. He considered: Should he guzzle down the last bit before Casper told him what the assignment was, or wait until he knew and then polish it off?

Casper continued. "You shouldn't be surprised that once you step into this realm there is no going back. The reason secret societies can do covert stuff for thousands of years and not be exposed is because they all have tests... Serious tests."

Ethan looked puzzled. "Like what?"

"Things that no one could ever confess to, or expose like: the Kennedy Assassination, 911, or the Oklahoma City Bombing."

"But we know who did those things."

Casper smiled with a knowing look. "Really? Are you sure?"

Ethan Shrugged.

"Lets just say, those are what initiations into a super secrete society looks like."

"Really?"

Casper grinned. "And you can bet that the people involved went on to became very high ranking public officials."

Ethan looked inquisitively: "Presidents? Vice presidents?"

Casper smiled. "Perhaps. Very few people get that high up in the world without some blood on their hands."

"Really?" asked Ethan naively, hoping that what Casper had just said was an inflammatory joke.

"Are you kidding?" said Casper. "The United States government is full of ruthless people who came to power from underhand tactics. It's the reality of the world. If you want to be in the big leagues then you have to step up. If you don't, someone else will, and then they will be running the show, so the choice is, either them or us. Let's face facts; we can't change the system, so the smart thing is to use it to our advantage!"

Casper headed back into the apartment. Ethan took the last sip of his beer, then followed him inside and closed the big sliding glass door. The Crusher and Ascot were sitting in the living room, eating the pizza hors d'oeuvres, not saying a word to each other.

Ethan continued to follow Casper who went to his briefcase, pulled out an envelope, and then moved to the dining room. He flipped on the light switch and the crystal chandelier made the glass table top with its black marble base sparkle. Casper pulled out a carved ebony chair with a plump white leather seat and gestured to Ethan to pull up a chair beside him. He obviously had something important to show him.

Chapter 56

Photos slid out of Casper's envelope and across the glass table. Ethan picked up the stack. He shuffled through images of ransacked and destroyed chemical labs, of monkeys, rabbits, and dogs running loose through the streets. The last two were of a shipping truck toppled over and burning.

"This is what your R.A.D. friends did to one of my companies! Their delusional views of reality have cost me millions of dollars." Casper was clearly upset.

"Hmm," said Ethan, trying to see things from both sides.

"These people are crazy. They see testing chemicals on animals as cruel, eating animals as cruel. They don't realize that these animals wouldn't exist without us breeding them for these purposes. What's more important, saving some lab rats and monkeys or doing research that will help us develop products that will benefit the world and all of mankind?"

Ethan nodded, he had a point.

"These radicals are hindering the growth of science. We need to experiment and see how things work biochemically. You can't do that on a human being. We have a symbiotic relationship with these animals. Their usefulness to us helps their species survive. These rebels, who think they're on the side of the angels, need to realize that these creatures are thriving more now because we need them and they need us."

Casper pulled out more photos, briefly captioning each one as he slid it across the table.

"Here's an oil pipeline, a refinery, a fleet of logging trucks, two fishing boats, a chicken ranch, for God's sake! People have to eat! Here's another research lab, a nuclear power plant site. All of these were targets by these R.A.D. idiots." Casper was very animated, barely staying in his seat.

"As you can tell, I have a problem. These people are costing me hundreds of millions and it's slowing down my progress on other fronts. One of the reasons I haven't been able to get Asgard Resort, aka the Valhalla Two, finished is because I constantly have to deal with this shit. I want it resolved!"

Ethan's stomach knotted up and a sour taste came to his mouth. He knew where this was going and he could feel himself sweat. He nodded and said nothing.

"Tomorrow you are to go out with some of my elite squad. There is The Crusher," he said, pointing to the living room. "The Fly, whom you met, The Valkyrie, and the Blood Hound. I want the R.A.D team that you helped escape captured. I want to use them as leverage. I want to find out where the other cells are, how they communicate, who's in charge and where they plan to strike next. I want to crush them once and for all, so others don't just take over and fill their shoes."

Ethan nodded blindly.

"This is your test! You do well and you get all this." He spread his arms wide over his head and gestured to everything around him. "I want to see how well you work individually and with a team. As soon as you have them all captured I want all their equipment taken. Anything with information on it, I will have my tech guys analyze. I will be monitoring you at all times to make sure nothing goes wrong. You got it?"

Ethan swallowed. He regretted not saving the last swig of the beer for now. His mouth was very dry and his throat was scratchy. He fidgeted in his chair, then with a voice that betrayed his feelings, muttered, "Got it."

Casper got up and walked to the door. The Crusher and Ascot met him in the entryway. The Crusher opened the door. Casper turned and looked at Ethan. "Eat some good food, relax, get some rest, get laid, and I will see you tomorrow." The three men nodded goodbye, then stepped through the threshold. A second later the big steel door silently shut itself.

Ethan stood staring at the door, feeling like he had swallowed a brick. He walked around his apartment and looked at all the stuff. There were three bedrooms. Each looked like a master suite, with lots of mirrors, walk-in closets and private bathrooms with large Jacuzzi tubs. He was confused. He had everything a person could ever want and yet he felt more alone now than he did when he was stuck floating in outer space thousands, even millions, of miles away.

He wandered into the family room and stared at the entertainment center's giant blank HD-3D-TV screen. There was nothing he wanted to watch. There was nothing he felt like doing. There was no one he could call. To have all this he would have to betray Cameron and her comrades who passionately fought for the rights, freedoms, and safety of the common man. He would have to show his loyalty to a rich and powerful psychopath.

If it were an abstract choice, it would be easy. No one wants to be beholden to a psycho, but here he was, sitting in a multimillion-dollar apartment, overlooking one of the premium parts of Los Angeles, holding the keys to a half-million dollar car and a limitless credit card in his pocket. It wasn't an abstract question; it was real.

Ethan realized that in his entire life he never had to make a seriously tough decision. The hardest decision he ever made was to leave his dad and work at Valhalla, and that didn't turn out so well.
He had to choose the life he wanted to live. How important was money compared to having a clear conscience? How important were the people in our lives?

Ethan's head was jammed and he didn't want to deal with anything. His whole body was upset. He imagined that, at that moment, some doctor or scientist was probably sitting in a lab thirty floors below, analyzing his stomach acid and stress levels. Ethan went up to the top floor to the largest master bedroom. He lay down on a fuzzy white comforter on top of a king-sized bed. He took some deep breaths, trying to calm his racing mind. Not sure what to make of it all, he decided, "This will make more sense tomorrow. I'll deal with it then."

Chapter 57

Five AM. Ethan woke up lying on his stomach on top of the bed. He was still in his jumpsuit and feeling grimy, although technically he wasn't dirty; they had cleaned him up at the lab. The electric curtains were open and the endless lights of the Los Angeles skyline dotted the horizon. He was starving; since he had landed back on Earth he hadn't had a proper meal—just some hors d'oeuvres and happy hour junk food. That's probably why the beer knocked him out.

He walked downstairs to the kitchen. There was a wall of mahogany cabinets. Ethan remembered the general area where he had seen The Crusher opening a fridge, but there was no fridge. He stood, confused for a moment, since it was early and he wasn't fully awake. Then he realized that the double-size refrigerator and freezer were seamlessly blended in with the mahogany cabinets, the appliance doors artfully disguised to match. Very clever, he thought. Another rich folks' amenity that he wasn't used to.

The fridge was packed with all kinds of stuff: sausages, eggs, milk, soy milk, ground beef and turkey. There was an array of cheeses from around the world and every condiment he could imagine. There were also things he had never seen, like tiny pickled ears of corn.

He opened a cupboard next to the fridge and stared at rows of brightly colored boxes: crackers, snacks, cookies, instant mashed potatoes. He thought of how horrified Vince would be at all this processed food, but Ethan didn't want to have to cook anything. He found a package of a dozen individual-sized breakfast cereal boxes, wrapped and stuck together with cellophane.

He grabbed the cereal, the container of milk, and then went looking for a bowl. The set of dishes in the cabinet were nice, but the bowls were small. For Ethan's current needs they seemed pointless. He continued looking through the cabinets and found a large salad bowl and a large table spoon. With the bowl and spoon in one hand, the milk in the other, and the boxes of cereal under his arm, he shuffled out of the kitchen and into the living room, plopping himself in a reclining massage chair. Parked next to the chair was a small table—its purpose seemed to be to hold the remote controls for the entertainment center and to put one's beverage on.

Ethan tore open the cellophane and a rainbow of boxes spilled onto his lap. Without bothering to look, he began to tearing them open and dumping them into the bowl. Once the bowl was three-quarters full, he drenched it with milk. Then he picked up the remote, turned on the TV, leaned back, and began to shovel the concoction into his mouth.

The first thing to appear on the TV was an old episode of *I Love Lucy*. "My God," he thought, "this show is still on the air?" Ethan watched in amazement. He would bet that since the moment he was born, not a single day had gone by that *I Love Lucy* wasn't broadcast somewhere in the world. The fact that a TV show could endure so long seemed unreal. He wasn't particularly a Lucy fan, but he didn't care. He just wanted to watch something for the novelty of seeing a large HD-3D-TV.

Lucy and Ethel, in hunting outfits, were trying to prove to their husbands that they could shoot a duck. Ethan finished a spoonful of cereal and reached for the remote; then, in front of Ricky, Lucy pointed and shot her gun into the air. This signaled Ethel, who was hiding in a tree, to toss a dead duck out of the branches, the carcass landing at Ricky's feet. The charade was exposed when Ricky picked up the bird and revealed that its feathers were already plucked, and its head, feet, and guts had already been removed. Ethan was amused enough by this to not change the channel. Instead he put the remote back on the table and dumped the few remaining boxes of cereal into the salad bowel, doused it with milk, and started another round of shoveling.

Curious as to what the buttons on the chair did, he pushed one. Instantly the chair started vibrating and squeezing in and out. Firm rollers went up and down his spine, back and forth across the small of his back, and around his shoulder blades. It felt awesome. He leaned back and tried to continue eating his cereal, but the vibrations made the milk dribble out of the spoon and onto his chest, so he held the bowl to his lips and just pushed the food into his mouth. A few minutes later the cereal was gone. He tossed the bowl onto the carpet next to the dozen mini-cereal boxes that littered the floor like multi-colored confetti.

Lucy and Ethel were apologizing to Ricky and Fred for wanting to be more than just housewives and for daring to venture into the realm of hunting, where clearly only men belonged. Ethan thought, "If that same TV show were written today, the writers would be ridiculed as sexist pigs." Perhaps it was good that this show was still on the air. It was a way of monitoring our progress as a culture. A commercial popped on. There was a pleasant-looking man in a suit standing on a busy New York street corner, but the moment he opened his mouth everyone around him started to choke, then melt like the characters at the end of *Raiders Of The Lost Ark*. Apparently his breath was incredibly bad. Before the cure to lethal halitosis was revealed, Ethan grabbed the remote and hit the mute button, then closed his eyes and let the vibrating chair do its thing. Now that he was full of food and relaxed, within seconds he nodded off.

A loud, clangy version of Beethoven's "Ode To Joy" rudely awakened Ethan. Apparently someone had rung the doorbell. Now the sun was out and Westwood village, UCLA, and the Santa Monica Mountains had replaced the evening lights that had dotted the horizon. Ethan pushed several buttons before he found the one that turned off the humming chair. The doorbell rang again.

"I'm coming!" he yelled, climbing out of the chair and heading towards the door.

Ethan opened the door and looked up at The Crusher, who practically filled the large doorway. The big man was dressed in a nice suit, already sporting two-day-old stubble.

"Get ready, we got to go!"

"Now?"

"We've been trying to call you for over an hour, but you didn't answer the phone."

"Can I at least take a shower and change my clothes?"

"No time. You're dressed fine. They're waiting for us downstairs. I'll fill you in as we go."

Chapter 58

Walking quickly to the elevator, they took it down to the parking garage, where two black Hummers were waiting for them. The Crusher opened the rear door of the first Hummer and gestured for him to get in. Ethan climbed in and the big man closed the door behind him, then walked out of sight.

Sitting next to Ethan was a stocky man in military fatigues holding a GPS device the size of an iPhone. As soon as Ethan sat down the device beeped. He turned towards Ethan, his bulldog face was framed by a crew cut that prickled out from under his camouflage cap. A hand with stubby fingers shot out. "Mr. Stone. I'm Captain Travers."

Ethan shook Travers' hand, then reached over to fasten his seatbelt. The Captain's voice was short and clipped, with a hint of a Midwest twang. "Our intel located the R.A.D. hideout late last night. Your mission is to infiltrate the R.A.D team, gain their acceptance, then, take out the leader. Then signal us and we will come in and clean up the mess."

He held up the GPS. "We have the nano-bot data here. We have a GPS reading on you, accurate up to three centimeters. We will be monitoring all your body functions, and can receive audio. The visual capabilities are limited today due to software updates. We should have that fixed very soon, so we will have you fully covered."

Ethan understood that from Travers' perspective, being able to track his every move was a good thing, but for Ethan the thought of being under someone's watchful eye twenty-four/seven made him very uneasy.

The Hummer pulled out from the underground parking garage. It was still fairly early and the streets were just beginning to fill with people going to work and opening their businesses.

Ethan thought about the mission before him. Casper has said the reason for this mission was that the "R.A.D. idiots" were a threat to him, and this assignment would show his loyalty to Eden, Inc., but something didn't seem right. In the scheme of things, how could this little band of rebels be a serious threat to a big multi-national corporation? Eden, Inc. had its own army. Why did they need him to take care of this problem? It seemed that Casper was asking this of Ethan solely to prove his power over him. He wanted to see him betray his friends. It seemed like a sick fetish. Ethan sat still, his mind flashing through his options as they drove across town. Ethan was intrigued by the possibility of the new life that lay before him. He had dreamed of being rich and he always wanted to have nice stuff, but now he had to decide what price he was willing to pay.

The Hummers pulled up to a neighborhood of abandoned buildings and stopped in the shadow of a row of overgrown palm trees. Travers pointed to a building a block away. "That's the place." Behind an imposing twelve-foot fence with razor wire sparkling on top stood a boarded-up, three-story, Asian-style, jade green and blood red building. There was a large broken neon sign that looked like it had once illuminated several large Chinese characters.

Ethan grabbed the door handle and was about to open the door, when he turned to Travers inquisitively. "What is this place?"

"Used to be a Korean nightclub," said Travers matter-of-factly.

An Asian soldier sitting in the front seat turned to face Ethan. "It was called 'Tae Pyung Yang,' Korean for 'Pacific Ocean.'"

Ethan nodded, and then addressed Travers, who was a little put out by the interruption. "What happened to it?"

"Apparently, the upstairs doubled as a brothel. A rival gang who wanted to corner the market on Asian prostitution sprang a surprise hit on the building, killing over forty people. The news media created a sensational story. They said the attack was an act of terrorism by a well-organized, deadly Asian gang. Every night for months, the TV news showed explicit pictures of the carnage and did bios of all the victims. All the bad publicity killed the commerce in the neighborhood, and eventually the businesses in the area shut down. That was over four years ago."

"How do you know they are in there and not some of these other abandoned buildings?"

Travers looked at Ethan like a parent who just told his kid to go to bed for the third time. His voice suddenly became edgy. "I trust our intel-ops. One of Casper's Elite Team specialists tracked them from the previous battle. Also, we got a reading that the electricity and the water have been illegally turned on. So we know there are people living in there."

Ethan nodded, then opened the Hummer door. There was a stillness that came from the absence of life—no dogs, cats, birds, or squirrels—just an eerie quiet and the smell of dry dust in the breeze. It had all the attributes of a ghost town in the middle of the city.

There was a soft thunk as the door shut. Then the car backed away, out of sight from the abandoned nightclub. Ethan walked towards his destination, hiding as best he could in the shadows cast by the abandoned buildings.

Positioning himself behind an old dumpster in the alley; Ethan scanned the target. Though the chain link and razor wire fence he saw an underground parking garage similar to the one at R.A.D.'s previous hideout. A large rusty chain was pulled across the driveway, blocking the garage's entrance. Clearly no cars had come in or out in years, but something instinctively told him it was probably a way in. Ethan figured the R.A.D. team had probably turned the old nightclub into a fortress. No doubt they would have someone guarding the premises at all times. He figured that if he could get past the guards and talk to Cameron, M'buy or Patik first, he would have a better chance of avoiding any conflict. He was afraid of running into some trigger-happy guard who didn't know who he was.

The building next to the hideout was a square, flat-roofed, concrete block industrial structure that stood a story taller than all the other buildings in the neighborhood. Each floor had a row of boarded-up windows with commercial grade security bars covering them.

Without over-thinking his options, Ethan crept out from behind the dumpster and leaped up to the top of the second-story window. Like a cat, he grabbed the top row of the horizontal steel bars, used his momentum to propel himself up onto his feet, and immediately pushed off, leaping up a story to the next barred window. His weight and momentum stressed the bolts that held the bar in place, and a small plume of concrete dust puffed from the wall as chunks of stucco crumbled to the ground.

His final leap sent him soaring upward, perpendicular to the flat, rocky roof. He grabbed the old rusty rain gutter, twisted his body, shifted his weight, and flipped himself over. He tumbled inward toward the center of the building. A second later Ethan was on his feet, standing on the highest perch, surveying all that was below him.

Just like the old Korean nightclub, many of the neighboring buildings were fenced off, and all were boarded up. All the trees and bushes in the area had been dead for years. The only sign of recent activity was the fast food wrappers, beer cans and other trash scattered throughout the streets.

Ethan noticed a building kitty-corner to the nightclub, which also had an underground parking structure. Because the two buildings faced opposite directions, their backs were separated by an alley, making them appear to be much further apart than they were. From Ethan's vantage point he could see their actual proximity. The interesting part was that the underground parking lot for the other building wasn't chained shut, like it had been used more recently. Ethan's instincts told him that the R.A.D. team was parking in the adjoining underground lot then tunneling into the nightclub parking structure. "Very clever," he thought.

This was good. Casper's soldiers probably didn't know about the entrance. He could go in and warn Cameron and her team that they were about to be raided and they could escape. Then he could tell Travers that the place was empty. Just then, two new black Hummers with heavy artillery pulled up and blocked the secret entrance. "So much for that idea," thought Ethan. Now he wasn't sure what to do. Was he going in to warn them or to destroy them? He had to get off the roof and get inside before the soldiers did.

Ethan ducked out of sight so the soldiers in the Humvee wouldn't see him. He figured he could probably jump off the roof and be okay, but it was farther than he was willing to risk. After a quick survey of the rest of the roof's rim, Ethan saw that there wasn't anything to hold onto. He considered going down the way he came up, leaping from one barred window to the next. Then he noticed that the security bars had been pulled from their sockets and were just dangling in place.

His imagination conjured images of jumping and grabbing the bar, only to feel it tear away. With the bar in his hand, he imagined falling helplessly backwards seven stories, banging and bouncing against the bars and windows, snagging and tearing his clothes. Then he would land with a heavy thud, while the other bars, landing beside him, bounced and clanged on the ally's pavement making a deafening racket. Then to add insult to injury, concrete dust and chunks of stucco would fall on top of his immobile, injured body. "There must be a better way down," he thought, shaking the images out of his mind.

Ethan climbed over and straddled the corner of the building like a koala bear hugging a tree. He dug the sides of his blue boxing shoes into the mortar gaps between the concrete blocks. He squeezed, holding on for dear life, and the concrete gave way. It felt like sandstone on his hands and feet.

He methodically climbed slowly down, leaving a trail of holes on both sides of the building's corner. When he was halfway down, he leaped. He felt like he was floating to the ground and when he hit the asphalt, it gave as if it were a rubber mat. He considered that he could have probably jumped from the top and been fine, but he was still getting used to his abilities and wasn't sure what he was his limits were.

He jogged over to the chain-link fence surrounding the nightclub. Then, with a elegant leap, he cleared the razor wire by three feet and landed on his feet with the grace of a ballet dancer. Once he was on the property, he inconspicuously jogged to the back side of the four-story building. All the windows and doors were boarded up, except for a lone door hovering two stories above the dilapidated remains of an old fashioned fire escape.

Ethan needed to find a way inside, but then what? "No matter how you slice it," he thought, "there is no good scenario."

Chapter 59

Ethan climbed what was left of the tattered staircase and easily leaped up and over the missing sections of steps. Once at the top, he jumped up two stories towards the door. While airborne, he grabbed the handle and pulled. The door didn't budge and the handle broke off in his hand. Thinking fast, he kicked the door, which burst off its hinges and flew into the room. As Ethan began to fall he leaned forward, grabbed the door jamb with the fingers, and pulled himself into the room. He landed on top of the broken door and slid into a dark hallway like a surfer. The door rammed into a pile of debris and came to an abrupt halt. He tumbled off onto a musty-smelling carpet and banged into a wall. "So much for a subtle entrance." he thought. Ethan rolled onto his back and looked up. Dust sparkled in the sunlight that streamed in from the empty doorway. Ethan got up, looked down the hallway and saw a faint light at the end of the hall.

He was about to shout Vanessa's name when he caught himself, and instead yelled "Cameron!" His voice echoed through the dark, empty building. He headed toward the light at the end of the hall, which was a stairway leading down. He called Cameron's name again. The room was still and quiet, his voice and footsteps being the only disturbances. He cautiously walked down the stairs, each step making a little creak. The old nightclub stank of stale beer and cigarettes. Ethan was beginning to think that perhaps the intel guys had gotten the place wrong and this wasn't inhabited after all.

Just as Ethan's foot stepped on the landing, he felt the barrel of a machine gun press against his temple.

"What do you want?" whispered a low-pitched voice with a hint of an African accent.

Ethan instinctively froze. Out of the shadows emerged a dozen other R.A.D. team members, each pointing some kind of firearm at him. Ethan really didn't know what to say. He didn't want to turn the rebels over to Casper's gang of mercenaries, but he had to go through the motions if he was going to live in his penthouse and drive around town in a convertible Maserati.

Ethan stood there, his hands in the air, contemplating who he should be loyal to. There was a palpable tension in the room. The R.A.D team was getting impatient with him, standing there with a dumb look on his face, they interpreted his soul-searching as obstinacy. Finally a skinny, curly-haired kid broke the silence by cocking his high-powered sniper rifle and aiming it at Ethan's forehead. M'buy held up his hand. "What do you want?" he repeated, a bit more ice in his voice.

Ethan's head was swimming, when Vince's voice came back to him. "When in doubt, tell the truth. It's the easiest thing to remember, and people can tell when you are being honest."

Ethan looked up at M'buy, whose face showed that he was a man who didn't play games. He took a deep breath. " I don't know."

Several gun-toting R.A.D. members took a step forward and raised their weapons. M'buy gestured for them to back off. Keeping the barrel to his head, M'buy stepped closer, his voice softer. "Who sent you?"

Ethan shook his head, gesturing for something to write with. He moved his lips, exaggerating. "I'm bugged!"

M'buy pressed the machine gun barrel against his temple and had Ethan step forward into the light. Then he gestured with his head, asking Ethan to repeat what he had said. Ethan pointed at himself, then made little spidery motions with his hands, mouthing over and over, "I'm bugged!" M'buy's eyes widened as he realized what Ethan was saying. He gestured for him to walk and the rebels started marching towards a room on the opposite side of the building.

Ethan was led into a large white-and-gold-tiled room, decorated with black and red Oriental-style furniture and a mirrored ceiling. It had been the part of the brothel where girls would shower the men, massage them on a rubber mat, cover their bodies with a slippery seaweed gel, and then flop around on top of them naked. It was very popular, and several rooms were outfitted to accommodate this.

Now the R.A.D. team was using the room to block all radio waves, cell phone transmissions, and infrared signals. The thick, tiled walls were covered in layers of foil that blocked all signals from entering or leaving. On top of that, there were several different types of electronic signal jamming devices.

Silently, M'buy led Ethan into the room, followed by a dozen R.A.D. members with guns pointing at his back. The moment they entered the room, the door was closed and a large foil barrier was pushed over, covering the door. The combination of all the high-powered electronic circuitry and the water from the showers gave the room a strong ozone smell. It had a sanitized sting to it that Ethan found very pleasant.

Once the room was secure, M'buy pulled the machine gun barrel away from Ethan's temple. Ethan exhaled in relief. He turned to see that behind him was Patik and Cameron, flanked by a small army of rebels, all still pointing guns at him. Patik and Cameron gave him hard stares, then Patik stepped into the uncomfortable silence. "Why are you here? They obviously sent you."

Ethan didn't say anything, ashamed. His eyes scanned the room, looking to see if it was safe to talk. Patik picked up on his fear. "This room is clear. No signals can get in or out."

Ethan put his arms up over his head like any stick-up victim and walked a few steps toward a crud-covered mirror. The R.A.D. team nervously trained their guns on him, ready to shoot at the slightest false move. Ethan slowly and carefully wrote, "Nano-bots," in the crud.

Patik and M'buy glanced at each other. M'buy looked at Ethan suspiciously, but there was enough firepower to take care of him, even with his extraordinary strength and speed. M'buy nodded. "Nano-bots, that's a bit trickier, but they can't get out of this room either." He turned to Patik for assurance.

"They can't get past the electronic signal blocking perimeter," Patik agreed.

Ethan put his arms down now that some tension had subsided. "I'm covered in nano-bots inside and out. They can hear everything I say and see what I see. They can make me do things remotely that I can't control."

M'buy pointed to the dozen guns pointed at Ethan. "I think we will be all right."

"Who sent you?"

"Casper Degas himself."

"What were you supposed to do?"

"Break in and capture some of you. Then send in the team that's waiting outside."

"Is that what you are planning to do?"

Ethan stared down at his feet. "No, I didn't know what I was going to do. I didn't have much choice. I had to go along with the program or they would just fry me and send a squad in after you guys."

Cameron spoke with an icy tone. "Did they re-educate you?"

Ethan raised his eyebrows.

Patik interjected. "What did they tell you about us?"

"Oh. He showed me lots of photos of labs, buildings and bulldozers being blown up, and said you were responsible for it all. As a result of your radical, anti-establishment viewpoints, people have gotten hurt and killed."

"That's bullshit!" Cameron erupted. "We have never killed anyone! And the only time we have destroyed property was to prevent something bad from happening." Everyone in the room nodded in agreement. "So like, we did blow up some logging trucks because the logging company was planning on cutting down a hundred acres of protected forest. Technically what they were about to do was completely illegal, but the company was so big that they owned all the politicians and police force, so there was no one to enforce the laws. They were planning on cutting down an entire forest, paying some puny penalties and still making tons of money, then leaving town. By destroying all those logging trucks, we got the insurance companies involved and it became a nationwide story. It put the spotlight on the company and exposed their corrupt logging practices. After the dust settled, they were charged with over two thousand counts of illegal logging. That was one of Casper's many companies and those types of things are exactly why he hates us!"

"I'm sure Casper is very persuasive" added Patik.

Ethan nodded.

"And no doubt he offered you a lot of carrot to go with your stick."

Ethan nodded again.

"The problem is he is a complete sociopath. When you sell your soul, at the end of the day what do you have? A bunch of stuff, and it can all be taken away from you. But when you live with integrity and you stand for something, nothing that really matters can be taken from you."

Ethan looked around the room, suddenly feeling very immature. It was like he was a kid who just did something really selfish and was being reprimanded by his parents. No one spoke as the mood in the room got very reflective.

Cameron broke the silence. "Do you know the story of Christ being crucified on the cross?"

Ethan was startled by the seeming randomness of her question. "Yeah, sure, He died for our sins and that's why there is Easter."

Cameron looked at Ethan seriously. "No that's not it at all, that's what most preachers will say and it's nonsense. "The real meaning of Christ on the cross is simple and profound. It states that when you stand for something, live by a set of principles and values that puts the good of the many above the good of the few, and above your own comfort. When your commitment to the greater good is unshakable no matter how much pressure or pain is put upon you, that's when your life has real meaning and purpose. Christ got the living shit kicked out of him. He was tortured and crucified, but he never wavered from his commitment to his people, and never sold out to the Romans. He understood that we are all human and we will all die. What really matters is, what did you do when you were alive?" Cameron stared hard at Ethan, letting the words soak in.

M'buy's low voice broke the silence. "All men die, but not all men live!"

Ethan looked down at his bright blue shoes and tried to remember what movie he had heard that line in.

Cameron nodded. "When you stand for what's right and do great things, you will be immortalized. Martin Luther King understood this, Steven Biko understood this, and Mahatma Gan¹hi understood this; that's why their spirits are immortal."

Ethan scratched his head. "I never did understand what, 'he died for your sins' meant."

"Preachers, politicians, Federal Reserve chairmen, they use confusion to keep people in line," said M'buy. "It's an old trick. People assume that if someone credible speaks with authority but doesn't make any sense, then they must know something that you don't, so therefore they must be smarter than you."

Cameron chimed in. "That's why preachers are always mixing up Bible quotes that make no sense, then adding some random interpretation. Its all elementary mind control techniques."

Patik cleared his throat. "Did you know that if you give a fish a lobotomy, all the other fish will follow it?"

"Really?" Ethan was puzzled. "Why is that?"

Patik didn't expect to elaborate, but took a moment to think it over. "Hmm, perhaps when an individual is significantly different, they are interesting and therefore seen as special, so perhaps they have some kind of profound insight. Since leadership and survival go hand in hand, people and fish will follow an individual who is outgoing and charismatic even if they are completely crazy, particularly if they perceive that that individual has the answers to life's compelling questions."

Ethan shrugged. "How deep are the thoughts of a fish?"

"I don't know, but I don't think we humans are as smart as we think we are, so they are probably not as different as we may imagine."

Ethan grinned. "Then are you saying that our leaders are really just crazy people?"

Patik laughed. "Maybe not all of them, but there are plenty of preachers, politicians, talk show hosts, and corporate executives who are absolutely nuts. Particularly your friend Casper Degas."

All the eyes in the room focused on Ethan. After a few tense moments, Cameron broke the ice.

"What do you want to do?"

Chapter 60

A dozen faces waited for Ethan to speak. He imagined what his new life working for Casper could be like: flying all over the world in the corporate jets, meeting important heads of state, taking hot models and famous actresses to all the happening Hollywood parties in his new convertible Maserati and then afterwards up to his Westwood penthouse. Looking into the eyes of the rebels suddenly made everything Casper had offered him superficial and shallow. But, Ethan wondered if he could live with that nagging feeling of, "what if?" Both Vince and Ascot had said the only things in life they had ever regretted were the things they didn't do. Perhaps that's why Ascot took Casper's offer.

Ethan looked around the room. These supposed rebels were all clear about who they were and their purpose in life.

M'buy's mellifluous voice broke the silence in the room. "Look... We are a nation of laws made of the people, by the people, for the people. Whoever's in power gets to make the laws, and there are two kinds of laws. Laws that protect the people from assholes and ones that protect assholes from the people." Ethan looked around the room; heads nodded in agreement like they were in church. "We are working to undo the laws that protect the assholes from the people, restoring the balance of power. You could help us."

Ethan nodded, too; Ascot would rant about this sort of thing during boxing practice. The idea of actually helping Casper and Co. make the world a more unjust place seemed absolutely ludicrous. A switch flipped in Ethan's head and everything became clearer. "I don't want to have anything to do with Casper Degas, I want to rid myself of these nano-bots and help you do what's right."

M'buy and Patik looked at each other, then Patik gave M'buy a nod. M'buy faced Ethan. "The only way we can rid your body of the nano-bots is to short-circuit them."

"Okay," said Ethan, cautiously, not liking the sound of that at all. Across the room was an old-fashioned, claw foot bathtub where the girls would bathe the men before performing their slippery Asian massage. Cameron started filling the tub with water.

M'buy looked at Ethan intensely. "If you want to rid yourself of these nano-bots, then you will have to trust us. We've done this before, but it's not pleasant. You will have to do exactly as we say."

"Okay," Ethan said again. All eyes in the room analyzed his every move.

"First thing," M'buy continued, "you need to take off your clothes and get into that tub of water." He pointed to the tub as he and Patik dashed out of the room.

Ethan hesitated, feeling uncomfortable getting undressed in front of the rest of the R.A.D. team. Cameron noticed his shyness and smirked. "This is no time to be modest. Get your clothes off and get into this damned tub!"

Just like old times when she was Vanessa and his girlfriend, Ethan jumped to attention and did what she said. The water was freezing cold. He squatted slowly, putting his body in the water. "Does it have to be this cold?"

"Yes," came a chorus of voices. Apparently everyone in the room knew the routine.

Ethan continued to slowly submerge his body. It was so cold that he had difficultly breathing. His body immediately was covered in goose bumps and he started to shiver.

M'buy came back into the room and walked to the tub, carrying a pair of electric heart paddles that he seemed to have pulled from nowhere. Behind him stood Patik, holding a pair of jumper cables and pulling a cart with a large battery pack.

Ethan's eyes bugged out. "What's that for?"

"Just relax," said M'buy in a soothing voice. "Patik is going to administer the voltage that will short-circuit the Nano-bots. Once they are shut down and disarmed, we have to hurry. We don't have much time before they reboot. While they are out of commission, we need to flush them out of your body.

M'buy pointed to a bald, tattooed, ominous-looking character they called TNT. He was standing behind Patik, holding a rubber hose and an electro-magnet. His voice had an uncanny resemblance to Rocky Balboa. "You will be ahh, unconscious for a few minutes, while I flush the disarmed bots from your body, then draw them out with the magnet."

"I'll be unconscious? Can't I do this awake?"

"That's not possible," said M'buy. Ethan's eyes asked why.

Cameron knelt next to the tub, her face inches from his. "Technically you will be dead for a few minutes while they blast water through your lungs and sinuses. Then they will magnetize your body to flush and pull the bots out."

All eyes glared at her.

"What?" she protested, standing up to face the team. "I'm telling him the truth! He deserves to know what's going on!"

Ethan looked at M'buy, hoping to hear that what she just said wasn't true. He just nodded. Ethan felt like jumping out of the tub.

"She's right!" said Patik. He looked at Ethan with honest concern. "Are you ready for this? We believe it's your only chance."

Ethan nodded and Patik submerged the two ends of the jumper cables into the cold water. Then he reached behind and flipped a switch on the battery pack. Instantly there was a loud crackling sound. The crowd watched in fascination as Ethan convulsed and flopped around in the tub, splashing the cold water over the porcelain rim. The intense electricity in the water began filling the room with the stinging smell of ozone. TNT commented, "It's not every day you get to see a guy get electrocuted."

Patik was staring intensely at his watch. The timing was critical. One second too long and they could kill Ethan. A second too short and the nano-bots would not be short-circuited and the moment they stepped out of the radio-free room, everything they had discussed and had done would be transmitted to Casper and his goons.

Patik held up three fingers to indicate seconds. TNT stood ready with his hose and magnets. Just then Ethan convulsed, snapping his legs hard against the tub. His extra-dense body weight and incredible strength broke the tub in half with a loud crack. Electrified water poured out onto the floor.

Patik reached to shut off the battery pack just as his torso was drenched in electrified water. His body convulsed as he fell unconscious on top of the console. Miraculously, his flopping hit the switch with his chest, shutting the unit down. TNT saw the light on the side of the battery pack go off and Instinctively reached over, grabbed Patik by his collar, and pulled him off the console before he could accidentally switch it back on.

Amid the confusion, M'buy looked at the tattooed man. "You got ninety seconds to do your thing."

Chapter 61

Captain Travers looked at his watch. It had been over twenty minutes since he heard from Ethan. His orders clearly stated that this assignment was a test for Ethan to prove himself, so Travers was to give Ethan some space. Normally, he wouldn't leave his men out of his sight or out or communication for more than a few minutes, so he was feeling a little edgy. His instincts were starting to warn him that something might be wrong, but he didn't want to panic. It was important that Ethan do this job on his own. If Travers were to jump in too soon and screw up the mission, then he would have to deal with the wrath of Casper Degas, so Captain Travers was doing his best to suppress his growing concerns.

The handheld nano-bot tracking unit made no sense to him, as Travers was functionally illiterate when it came to electronics. He particularly didn't like things that didn't have buttons or had one button that did different things depending on which window was displayed. He stared at the blank device and gave up. Then he looked out of the Hummer window through a pair of binoculars. He could see the building and nothing seemed to be happening. He would give Ethan ten more minutes before he and his team would spring into action and smash into the building. If he barged in too early, then he would deal with it. Better to be too early and safe than to have something bad happen to Ethan on his first assignment. There could always be other assignments for him to prove himself.

Travers held the nano-bot tracking unit so no one else could see its display. He didn't want anyone to see that he didn't know how to use it. He particularly didn't want Chow Mein, the know-it-all Asian guy, to see him struggle with it. Chow Mein was smart and good with doo-dads. Travers didn't want a lecture from him.

Chow Mein's real name was Tony Ozeki. He was Japanese, not Chinese, he grew up in the San Fernando Valley, and didn't speak a word of his ancestor's language. He just happened to know his way around Korea Town and the name of the nightclub because he once dated a Korean girl for about a year, and they hung out there a lot. It turned out that she was on a mission to marry an American so she could get her green card. Before Tony, she had dated a white guy, but when she brought him home her parents flipped out, crying that she had brought disgrace to the family. She couldn't handle the pressure or the rejection so she dumped the guy and found Tony. At least he was Asian, and being Japanese wasn't nearly as bad as being Caucasian, so, as far as the family was concerned, he would do. But Tony figured out what was really going on and dumped her. Last he heard, she had moved back to Korea.

Tony got the nickname Chow Mein when Vern Porter, a big corn-fed redneck recruit almost twice Tony's size, picked a fight. Vern had called him a "little-Chow-Mein-eating-bitch." Tony decided the best way to deal with the situation was to nip it in the bud. Without hesitation, Tony beat the living crap of Vern, and in the process, broke Vern's jaw. Ironically, Vern's mouth had to be wired shut, so all he could eat were noodles and a few other soft foods. While Vern was recovering, Tony made a point of delivering Chow Mein to him daily, with a little note saying: "Who's the Chow-Mein-eating-bitch now?"

Travers was so engrossed in the Nano-bot unit that he didn't notice when three more Hummers pulled up behind him. A loud banging on the passenger side rear window interrupted his concentration. Travers was so startled that he dropped the nano-bot unit, which fell onto the floor next to his feet. Travers hesitated, perplexed whether to first pick up the unit off the floor, or deal with the man in a strange uniform staring at him outside his door. The man looked pissed off. Travers thought it was best to see what the guy wanted and deal with that first.

Travers looked at the man curiously. He had all kinds of high-tech electronic devices on him. An electronic earpiece, some kind of electronic goggles, and a suit that changed color like a chameleon, depending on what he stood next to. Travers knew about Casper's team of assassins. Each had a unique skill. This guy, he rightly guessed, was The Bloodhound. Apprehensively, Travers rolled down the window, hoping he was wrong and that this wasn't another one of Casper's Elite team. If it were, he would most likely pull rank and take over the mission.

"What can I do for you?" asked Travers, staring into the strange man's goggles and noticing that the color of his suit blended into the grey-black pavement.

The man leaned toward Travers and barked loudly in his Hillbilly accent: "You can get your ass out of this damn vehicle and salute your commanding officer, you stupid numb nut!" The man's breath smelled like a rotten dog turd and Travers held back his gag reflex, got out of the Hummer, stood at attention, and saluted the strange man. The Bloodhound stepped in between Travers and the Hummer; immediately his suit blended into the black paint job. This time his bark was softer and more menacing. "Why has your recon man been off line for over eleven minutes?"

"Shit!" Travers thought, "No wonder the stupid nano-bots weren't responding. I've been trying to operate a broken GPS."

"Listen here, you worthless pile of pig shit!" The Bloodhound continued, barely pausing for breath.

Travers thought, "Each time I'm forced to deal with these 'elite team guys', one's worse than the other!" Travers clenched his jaw and stood tall; ready to take the abuse this asshole was about to dish out. Travers had no idea that the goggles that The Bloodhound wore were three- dimensional computer screens tied into an online computer. As The Bloodhound looked at a person, a camera in the goggles took the image and matched it with a worldwide database using state-of-the-art facial recognition software. Within a second, the person's name and stats appeared on the three-dimensional screen in front of his eyes for him to read.

"Has it occurred to you, Captain Travers, that Mr. Stone might be playing you for a fool and be in the middle of a double-cross?"

Travers was confused. It hadn't occurred to him that there might be a double cross going on. If there were, it was not his problem. That wasn't covered by his orders. Travers just stood there not moving, not changing his expression, and waiting for the abuse to continue.

"May I remind you!" barked The Bloodhound, his breath melting Travers' sinuses, "this is a military operation, and when there is a SNAFU we expect our commanding officers to take immediate action and deal with the situation professionally?!"

The Bloodhound spat on the ground, stared through his goggles and waited to see if Travers was going to respond. Travers continued to stand and show absolutely no emotion. He didn't change his expression and didn't say a word. "All right, let's get this goddamn show on the road!" The Bloodhound looked over at the Korean nightclub down the block. "Get back in your damn vehicle. We are going to shock and awe those commie mo-fos and blast their asses to oblivion! Do you understand me, soldier?"

There was an awkward silence. Travers had clenched his jaw so tight to avoid barfing that now he couldn't unlock it. Finally, with a shallow breath, he coughed out, "Yes, sir!" Then he turned and climbed back into the Hummer.

Chow Mein and the other soldiers looked at Travers expectantly. "Gentlemen, there has been a change of command and a change in orders. We are going in."

Five Humvees pulled up along the chain link fence that surrounded the abandoned nightclub. The Bloodhound stepped out of the lead vehicle. Travers and his men sat in their car, waiting for instructions. They watched The Bloodhound walk up to the metal chain link fence and reach out with a gloved right hand. The instant his fingers made contact with the chain, a shower of sparks erupted. Travers and his men sat dumbfounded as The Bloodhound cut through the metal as quickly as if it were tissue paper. The men marveled as the fancy suit changed colors, the bottom of the pants blending into the grey-black asphalt near the ground, the jacket with the silver grey diagonal pattern of the fence. Suddenly it began to mimic the shower of white and orange sparks. It was like the 4th of July.

After a few seconds, The Bloodhound had cut a door-sized hole in the fence. There was a metallic thwack as the chain link hit the ground. He motioned everyone to get out of the vehicles and follow him through the newly-cut opening. The men jogged in single file through the opening, weapons in hand, cluelessly stomping on the broken fence and making a huge racket. They stopped and lined up six feet from the boarded-up door. Travers thought, "So much for a surprise attack. With all this noise, a fucking deaf person would know we had arrived." Travers had orders to not blow their cover, let Ethan infiltrate the rebel hideout, then wait for him to disarm the enemy. This was the antithesis what they were now doing.

The Bloodhound motioned a group of men to go around back then pointed at another group to go to the side of the building. On his wrist was a tracking unit similar to the one that Travers couldn't figure out how to use. A faint signal of all of Ethan's vital signs was being registered, despite the fact that he was supposedly in a room that blocked all signals. The Bloodhound suddenly looked very upset. He sneered over at Travers. According to the vital sign readings, Ethan had been dead for over two minutes. "No more time to waste," shouted The Bloodhound to all the men lined up at attention, "Time to bombard this shithole and clean up the mess."

The Bloodhound lifted a gloved hand. A spray of gelatinous pellets shotgunned out, peppering the wood and metal sheets that covered the doorway. He stepped back from the building and stood in line with the other soldiers. There was a soft sizzling sound as the gelatinous pellets began to dissolve the wood and metal. In less than a minute, the blockade to the nightclub door was gone, and the men followed The Bloodhound into the building.

Chapter 62

People assumed that TNT got his name because he was good with explosives. His real name was Timothy Nathaniel Troy, but that was no name for a six-foot-six-inch 280 lb. guy who looked like a Hells Angel on steroids. Timothy liked the power he got from looking scary; he simply needed a name that was complementary to his image. TNT was a logical choice, making it inevitable that he would eventually go into the business of explosives.

He first worked as a bouncer, which led to a job as a security guard, then bodyguard, so blowing things up seemed like a natural progression. His demolition mentor, Dano, was the best in the business. One day Dano was showing TNT how to rig a car bomb. Somewhere in the process Dano managed to blow himself up. TNT literally saw pieces of Dano shoot off in every direction. Dano's head flew thirty feet straight up into the air and then landed at TNT's feet like a soccer ball. TNT was covered in blood and guts and couldn't hear anything for a week. Needless to say, the experience gave him second thoughts about going into the demolition business. Years later TNT still had a faint ringing in his ears. It was a constant reminder not to act impulsively whenever the temptation to try explosives again arose. Nonetheless he still kept the nickname. Now when people met him, they made the false assumption that he could, and would, blow things up if he wanted to. That made Timothy Nathaniel Troy a badass dude without his having to risk death on a daily basis. That part he liked.

Ethan lay on his back, naked on top of the remaining shards of the broken bathtub. He looked like a giant oyster whose shell had been cracked with a hammer.

TNT pushed a piece of the tub out of the way and stuffed the beige rubber tube up Ethan's nose. The tube was attached to a bucket. TNT didn't tell anyone, but the apparatus he was using was originally made for administering home colonics. He once sold them as part of a network marketing company and ended up with a garage full of buckets and rubber tubes.

He held the bucket at his chest level, regulating the water pressure, carefully watching it pour into one nostril and seep out the other.

M'buy stared at his watch. "You have fifty two seconds left!" said the African urgently. TNT nodded. A few seconds later, the last of the water emptied out of the bucket. Quickly the tattooed giant pulled the tube out of Ethan's nose. Cameron held Ethan's head back so his jaw would hang open and TNT stuffed the tube down this throat. Another full bucket of water went pouring into Ethan's lungs. After a few seconds, the bucket was empty and his lungs were full.

M'buy had the heart paddles in each hand. "We have twenty seconds before I have to zap him!" His voice was edgy, the tension in the room rising fast. The idea was to pick Ethan up and lift his legs above his head so all the water would pour out of his lungs. TNT would run the magnet across his body at full power, grabbing all the remaining bots that didn't get washed out. Then M'buy would hit him with the paddles and bring him back to life before there was any brain damage.

One oversight that became quickly apparent was that Ethan weighed four or five times more than anyone else his size, and he wasn't particularly small to begin with. TNT, who prided himself on being strong, couldn't even budge Ethan. Without anyone needing to say a word, all the rebels spontaneously ran over and grabbed Ethan's legs and arms, doing their best to hoist him awkwardly into the air. A few seconds too long and Ethan might not recover. The unspoken thought got everyone focused.

Ethan was heavy and slippery and there weren't many places to grab hold of on a naked body. The wet floor and shards of broken bathtub made it difficult to get a firm stance. After a few seconds of yanking, tugging and slipping, someone got the bright idea to get on their hands and knees and become a bridge that the team could rest Ethan's naked butt on. Two guys got on all fours and the remainder of the group heaved Ethan's body up onto their backs. This made it easier to keep Ethan's legs elevated and his torso upside down. The team all watched the water spill out of Ethan's lungs, while TNT quickly passed the strong electro-magnets over his body, and M'buy counted down the final seconds. "Five, Four Three...." Suddenly the door into the room burst open and an explosion interrupted the countdown.

M'buy fell on top of Ethan, the defibrillator paddles pressing against Ethan's lifeless chest. Surprised and disoriented, M'buy quickly pushed himself up and untangled himself from the pile of people scattering like cockroaches. The R.A.D Team instinctively took cover as they tried to figure out what the hell was going on. Without thinking, his head ringing from the explosion, M'buy zapped Ethan with the paddles at full voltage. Ethan violently convulsed, flopping around like a fish on land, water still seeping out of his lungs.

Cameron and M'buy were suddenly alone. It was as if everyone else had instantly evaporated into the flying dust that filled the room. Cameron tilted Ethan's head backwards, pinched his nose, put her lips on his, and then strongly blasted three quick breaths into his lungs. M'buy immediately followed, pumping Ethan's chest. Nothing happened. Cameron repeated the breaths and, after a last tense moment, Ethan began to cough water out of his mouth and nose.

M'buy sat back to give Ethan a chance to recover. Suddenly bullets started flying in all directions as men in Kevlar raided the room. Ethan managed to roll onto his side and continued to cough violently. Cameron, forced to abandon further CPR, took the moment to make her escape.

M'buy looked at Ethan, trying to assess whether or not the kid would recover. The next thing he knew he was face down on the floor, his shoulder burning. He was bleeding badly from the gunshot and he knew he'd better get the hell out of the open before he got hit again. He crawled over Ethan's writhing body and scurried across the floor to a temporary hiding spot behind a couch. A trail of blood followed in his wake.

Bullets were flying in both directions. The rebels were used to their enemies' Blitzkrieg tactics and consequently were never far away from their arsenal of weapons. Ethan was lying naked and coughing in the middle of a full-blown firefight.

The Bloodhound put his electronic goggles on infrared so he could see the heat signatures of everyone in the room. Then, like an air traffic controller, he spoke to his men in their earpieces, telling them where and when to shoot. Within a few minutes, all the rebels were either dead or had escaped. There was still a little sporadic gunfire coming from a distant source, but the room had been cleared.

The Bloodhound stood over Ethan, who was trying to get on his hands and knees, breathing hard and sporadically coughing up the last bit of water from his lungs. The Bloodhound ordered two of his men to lift Ethan and take him down to the vehicles, while Travers and the all the other men pursued the remaining R.A.D. members.

The Bloodhound normally didn't do any heavy lifting. That wasn't his gig. He was a recon man. He found people who didn't want to be found and things that no one else could find, so as far as he was concerned, his job today was done. The moment Ethan had gone offline, the team at Casper's headquarters had known something was wrong. They called him in to get Ethan back, and he had fixed it. What had been chaos was now orderly. With his assignment complete, he was feeling pretty good about himself. This job was a cakewalk, he thought.

He watched as the two soldiers struggled to pick up Ethan, who wasn't cooperating at all. They were both baffled by his enormous weight. A guy his size should be easy to lift, but when a heavy, slippery, naked person doesn't want to be picked up, it's not easy.

Ethan's mind was still a little fuzzy and he was just getting oriented. It's not every day a person gets electrocuted, drowned, and then revived, only to find himself in the middle of a gun battle. Ethan's first clear thought was, "This will be a day to remember." As soon as his vision cleared, Ethan immediately recognized the black uniforms from the last battle. "Déjà vu," he thought. "Only this time I'm naked." The two soldiers couldn't get a strong grip on Ethan to pull him along. Ethan just relaxed and did nothing, trying to sort out what he should do. He didn't want to go back to Casper. He would have to explain how he ended up in a radio-free room, naked in a bathtub, and having all the nano-bots taken out of his body. Not a pleasant conversation.

Finally The Bloodhound, who was leaving the room, saw the two men struggle to lift Ethan. He was about to call in for more help, but decided he should just do it himself, an out-of-character act of exertion.

Ethan was now lying on his back with three men hovering over him. He hadn't said a word and as far as the men were concerned, Ethan was so out of it he was unable to speak. The two men agreed to grab Ethan's arms just under his shoulders and lift him so he would be sitting upright. Then The Bloodhound would grab the naked waist and the three of them would lift him onto his feet and drag him to the car.

The moment the two men squatted down, Ethan, with cheetah-like speed, grabbed the defibrillator paddles and sandwiched the two men's heads together. There was a dull clunk as their Kevlar helmets bashed into one another, instantly followed by a loud electric blast. The two men collapsed on both sides of Ethan and convulsed. Surprised, The Bloodhound leaped back but just a micro-second too slow. Ethan spun around and slammed one paddle into his face and the other into his crotch, blasting sixty thousand volts into two very sensitive areas. The Bloodhound flew backwards, landed on his back — just missing a big shard of the bathtub — and began to convulse.

Ethan stood up and watched the three men flop around on the floor like some kind of weird modern or punk rock choreography. He was freezing cold and still wet, so his first order of business was to dry off and put on some clothes. Suddenly, he heard the rhythmic blast of machine gun fire. Apparently the fight wasn't over; they had just taken it to another part of the building, and now they were on their way back.

Ethan hopped over the myriad debris and went looking for a towel. He had spent his life working in gyms and spas, and this was sort of a spa. It was the place where the VIP patrons would have their "long time" soapy massage and sex sessions with all the newly-imported girls from Asia, so there must be a towel somewhere.

The gunfire was getting closer and he could hear muffled voices yelling in the distance. He frantically opened an Asian-styled cupboard. He found boxes of condoms and several pairs of tiny flip-flops. He was close, so he opened the next cupboard. Covered in dust and rat shit he found a stack of what looked like towels. Fortunately they were individually wrapped in plastic. Amazed at his luck, he carefully pulled two out from the middle of the stack, trying not to disturb the filth on top.

He tore open the bags and discovered that the towels were actually bright neon yellow and pink satin robes with an Oriental print. He donned one — the robe barely covered his genitals and had just slightly more ability to absorb water than Saran Wrap. Ethan was hoping to change his clothes, but this outfit was even more ridiculous than his red jumpsuit. At least with his jumpsuit, his private parts weren't dangling out. He urgently began rubbing his head with the second robe, attempting to dry his hair, but stopped when he realized it wasn't working.

The gunfire was occurring in bursts. The yelling was becoming more audible, but it was still far enough away that he couldn't understand what was being said. The three men had stopped flopping and were now breathing hard, trying to get to their feet. Ethan ran over and kicked each one of them in the nuts. One by one they fell down and resumed writhing on the floor.

Ethan found his jumpsuit covered in splinters and dust. He picked it up and shook off all the debris. Half of the right leg was wet and there was a bullet hole in the left sleeve. Ethan thought, "There have to be some clothes stashed around here!" Then a spray of bullets riddled the wall and floor next to him. With cat-like reactions he jumped out of the way, leaped fifteen feet across the room and hid behind the cupboard. Without hesitation, he put the raggedy jumpsuit back on. Then he saw his bright blue boxing shoes, just a few inches from The Bloodhound's head.

Ethan waited. After a moment of silence, when the coast seemed clear, he took a chance, darting out from behind the cupboard and reached for his shoes. As he was about to snatch the second one, Ethan felt a searing pain. The Bloodhound had grabbed

Ethan's ankle and the electric blowtorch glove was burning into his skin.

Ethan kicked the hand free, and then smacked The Bloodhound in the face with his boxing shoe. The Bloodhound rolled out of the way and onto his side. It was now Ethan's turn to be surprised. As The Bloodhound jumped onto his feet, goop shot out from his wrist. Ethan dodged the slime, leaped towards The Bloodhound, and slammed his knee into the man's face, crushing his electric goggles. The Bloodhound was dazed, but not down for the count. Ethan grabbed his opponent by the collar and belt, hoisting the fighter over his head. The Bloodhound's camouflage suit changed colors blending into the peppered remains of the gold and white tiled room. With the man wriggling over his head, Ethan carried him to the opposite side of the room then slammed him against a boarded-up window.

Ethan saw the event as if it were happening in slow motion. He watched The Bloodhound's body hit the board and the suit instantly mimic the color and pattern of the strained and bending plywood. Ethan was preparing for The Bloodhound to bounce off, but just before the sheet was ready to snap back, the nails that held the plywood in place gave way. Instantly there was a bright light as the sun poured into the room and The Bloodhound's body fell three stories to the parking lot below.

Ethan covered his eyes from the sudden glare, leaped back into the shadows, and put on his shoes. He could hear Cameron's voice yelling, followed by more gunfire.

Chapter 63

Falling backwards, lying against a big sheet of plywood, The Bloodhound found himself in a tricky predicament. He was no stranger to dumb luck. He had a long history of evading death in the most inexplicable ways, like a cat who had renewed his nine lives contract many times over. Born Bobby-Joe Elrod Dooley, he grew up in South Carolina. His first bit of dumb luck started when he was just a baby sleeping in his crib. His alcoholic father had raped then beaten Bobby-Joe's mother until she was unconscious, and then fell asleep while smoking in bed. When the house caught fire, Bobby-Joe's crib happened to be next to the hot water heater. The tank erupted in such a way that it caused a steady spray of water to create a wall between the fire and the crib. By the time the fire department arrived, the house and everything in it was leveled and burnt to a crisp, with the exception of one soggy wall, a prolifically spraying hot water heater, and a perfectly preserved baby's crib. Bobby-Joe never even woke up.

The fireman who found the sleeping baby just happened to be a born-again Evangelical Christian, and was convinced that God had spared this child for some divine purpose. The local Christian paper declared that this child must be the Second Coming of Jesus because there was just no other explanation for the miracle. Several parishioners tried to adopt him. After all, who wouldn't want to be the one to raise the Second Coming of Jesus? But the courts stepped in and the child went to his only living relative, his Uncle Elwin.

Compared to his alcoholic and abusive brother, who had died with no less than two hundred thirty-one unpaid parking tickets, Elwin was a decent guy. He only had a dozen unpaid parking tickets and a ticket for an illegal U-turn. Elwin would only agree to raise his brother's child as his own if the judge would forgive all his traffic violations. The judge, not wanting the case to linger and have the child go into the nightmare of the child services system, agreed. Strings were pulled and Bobby-Joe moved in with Elwin, who quickly realized that babies were a pain in the ass and required an enormous amount of work. This inspired Elwin to marry his girlfriend, Brandy Mae McLeod, so she could take care of the boy and feed him at 3:00 AM. It turned out that she loved being a mother so much that she and Elwin ended up having four kids of their own.

The financial pressure of raising a family got Elwin to take his life more seriously. He soon became the general manager of the trucking company he worked for. He started making a solid middle class living and he responsibly paid all his bills, even the few parking tickets that he occasionally got. Consequently, Little Bobby-Joe Dooley grew up in a reasonably normal household.

However, every so often while he was growing up, an overzealous born-again wanted to see the "miracle child" and would ask to be healed or blessed by him. Bobby-Joe was so put off by their religious fervor that he didn't want to be seen in public. To get away from people, he started spending his time tracking and hunting in the woods. He got very good at reading the land and he soon knew the local woods better than anyone.

When he was a teenager, the local sheriff asked Bobby-Joe if he could find a body that a murderer had confessed to hiding. They knew it was out there, but the FBI couldn't find it after looking for a week. In less than six hours Bobby-Joe found the corpse. That's when he got the nickname The Bloodhound. He continued to hone his tracking skills and was often hired by hunters to track wild boar and deer.

He got into paintball and air-soft war play and competed in championship tournaments. He thought that going into the military would be cool. After all, he was the paintball champion, but before he was able to sell his soul to the Army, he came to the awareness of Casper Degas. Casper showed him the money and lifestyle he could have if he worked for the corporate world, as a corporate assassin. Casper explained, "There are no more nations left to fight. All the fighting now occurs among corporations. That's where the real action is." Immediately after meeting Casper, Bobby-Joe Elrod Dooley, AKA The Bloodhound, signed up and starting working for Eden, Inc. He never looked back.

Since that time, The Bloodhound had been in a variety of death-defying situations. He had been shot at by a helicopter gunship. Hundreds of fifty caliber rounds strafed the ground inches from his feet, and somehow all of them missed him. Once, he was running through a large empty parking lot and an SUV came out of nowhere with the clear intention of running him over. Unarmed, the only thing he could do was run. The SUV came at him at nearly one hundred miles an hour and there was nowhere to hide. Inexplicably, the SUV ran over the only beer bottle in the entire ocean-sized parking lot. It hit the front tire in just the perfect way and at just the perfect time as to cause the tire blow out while the homicidal driver was turning. The SUV, being top heavy, flipped onto its side and tumbled across the parking lot. The driver was a fat man and seat belts made him uncomfortable, so he hadn't bothered to wear his. Consequently, his body was catapulted through the windshield after the third tumble. The Bloodhound stood and watched as the fat man's heart, liver, lungs, and wallet, shot out from underneath the SUV and skidded across the parking lot pavement. The wallet, filled with hundred dollar bills that the fat assassin had just received as payment for agreeing to kill The Bloodhound, came to rest in front of Bobby-Joe's feet. The SUV continued to tumble over the dead assassin's body. The Bloodhound walked away, upset that the bounty on him was only a meager twelve grand.

This morning, in true Bloodhound dumb luck-style, the tree in the middle of the parking lot of Tae Pyung Yang was the only tree on the property and one of only a few trees in the neighborhood. It wasn't practical to have it, because it took away a potential parking spot. But the nightclub's Korean owner said it was good feng shui to have a tree there, and that Chinese Maples brought good luck, so it stayed.

Now The Bloodhound rode the sheet of three-quarter-inch plywood through a series of branches; miraculously not a single one had even scratched him. A second later, the plywood came to a gradual stop, then got lodged between the two main branches that split from the trunk. The Bloodhound found himself sitting on a plywood ledge, about seven feet from the ground, looking down at the only patch of dirt in probably five square miles. With the nonchalance of a man getting off his daily bus ride, The Bloodhound hopped off his perch and returned to the fight. Now he was pissed. He would get even with that little shit-head, Ethan Stone.

Chapter 64

Inside Tae Pyung Yang nightclub, M'buy crouched behind an empty Jacuzzi filled with chunks of drywall, old beer cans and layers of dust. His shoulder was numb. He had lost a lot of blood and was dizzy; white spots floated and danced in front of him everywhere he looked. With TNT's help, he had managed to get himself to a more secure room in the building: a spa area with a dressing room attached. It had a strong metal door that locked from the inside.

TNT and the rest of the R.A.D. team had left the room. M'buy pressed a wadded-up T-shirt against his wound trying to stop the bleeding. In the distance, he could hear gunfire and shouting. Frustrated that he couldn't help, he concentrated on making the pain go away, so he could regain his strength and help fight Casper's mercenary goons.

M'buy closed his eyes and took several deep breaths. Suddenly there was a hissing sound. Then the strong smell of sulfur and melting metal came charging through the room. The acrid smell got so thick that M'buy started to cough. Then, as if his cough were a cue, there was a pop and the door blew apart, showering debris into the room. Standing in the doorway, the light silhouetting him from behind, stood The Bloodhound. He wasn't particularly large: five-foot-nine-and-a-half barefoot and one-hundred-seventy-eight-pounds naked. But with his high-tech suit and boots on, he looked much more imposing. All the gear that he wore—body armor, weapons, and computer interfaces—made him look like a half-man, half-cyborg killer freak. On top of that, he was extremely pissed off and was looking to hurt someone.

The Bloodhound assumed that Ethan would be hiding behind the locked metal door, and was surprised to find instead the tall black dude he had shot earlier. It was obvious that the wounded man had no weapon in his hand and only one of his arms was working, so The Bloodhound casually walked into the room. "You still alive?"

M'buy looked up at him with absolute contempt. There was nothing to say, so he just sneered. When the cocky cyborg looked away for a second, M'buy lunged for a gun he had hidden under his leg. Immediately there was a loud pop, and before M'buy's hand even touched the gun, his left knee exploded, shooting excruciating pain up and down his leg, knocking him onto his back.

"That was a dipshit move!" said The Bloodhound, as he stood above the African's shattered leg. He was having fun. He got great pleasure out of kicking his opponents when they were down. It was one of the fringe benefits of being a psychopathic assassin. His job satisfaction came when he got to torment and torture his victims. He nonchalantly walked up to M'buy and kicked him in the ribs, knocking the wind out of him. Then he reached down and grabbed his gun. It was a .38 special six shooter revolver.

He held the gun in his hand, feeling the weight and admiring its balance. He had a spontaneous idea. He opened the chamber and emptied all but one of the bullets out of the gun, then closed it back up. Raising the gun above his head, he spun the cylinder like he was playing Wheel of Fortune. Then he pressed the gun into M'buy's head, the barrel getting lost in his dreadlocks, and pulled the trigger. There was an audible click. The Bloodhound burst out laughing. "You are a lucky bastard!"

He grabbed the gun, overwhelmed by a sudden urge to point it at himself. Some bizarre compulsion to play Russian roulette had always occupied some dark corner in the back of his brain. With a nervous snicker, he kicked M'buy so that the African was lying on his back looking up at him. M'Buy concentrated on taking shallow breaths, trying to quell the pain.

The Bloodhound took a deep breath, looked down into the confused eyes of M'buy, then stepped on his neck so as to hold his head in place and lock on his gaze. He put the gun to his own temple and pulled the trigger. There was another loud click. The Bloodhound roared with laughter. He felt more alive and lighter than ever. He jumped back off the black man's neck and did a quick little hillbilly jig. "Ah Lordy Lordy, this is fun!" he shouted, like a man overtaken by the Spirit at a Pentecostal revival.

Then as quickly as his euphoria had erupted, his mood flipped. He looked down menacingly into M'buy's eyes and smiled psychotically. "Now it's your turn!" Just then, there was a burst of machine gun fire and the sound of men running towards the room. The Bloodhound realized he was getting sidetracked. The euphoria of playing Russian roulette had kept him from doing his job. He needed to either kill this guy or take him prisoner. Just then a R.A.D. member ran into the room. He saw The Bloodhound standing over his comrade and reached for his weapon. The Bloodhound instinctively aimed the gun that he had in his hand, regardless of available ammo, and pulled the trigger. The one bullet hit the rebel square in the forehead. His neck snapped back and his head hit the ground hard, making a noise like a cantaloupe being cracked open.

M'buy, realizing that his attacker had no more bullets, feebly attempted to lunge, grab his attacker's leg and tackle him, but The Bloodhound's unique chameleon suit was made out of a Mylar fabric that utilized a matrix of reflective surfaces and was extremely slick. It was like trying to grab a Slip-and-Slide. The Bloodhound easily sidestepped and got out of the injured man's pathetic grasp.

The Bloodhound pointed to the dead man's body blocking the entrance into the room. "That was your bullet!" he snarled, as if M'buy had just cheated him in a poker game. He pointed a gloved fist at him. "You should be dead!"

More voices came from the hallway. The Bloodhound stuffed the .38 into his waist, grabbed M'buy by his dreadlocks and dragged him into the adjacent room. Confused, M'buy tried to shout out to his friends for help, but the pain was too great.

The Bloodhound kicked him in the kidneys, snarling, "I'm not done with you yet!" As he dragged M'buy through the door at the back of the room, Cameron appeared in the opposite doorway, wearing a gas mask like it was a hat. She crouched next to the body lying on the floor. Patik and TNT stood, guns in hand, on opposite sides of the door and covered her. She checked his pulse, confirming that their comrade was dead.

Patik and TNT tried to shoot The Bloodhound as he quickly slipped into the adjacent room, being careful not to hit M'buy, but the chameleon suit confused them. As soon as The Bloodhound crossed the threshold into the opposite room, TNT charged in commando-style, his semi-automatic rifle pointed in front of him.

The room was dark. TNT loomed near the doorway and slowly surveyed the room, looking through the night-vision scope mounted on his Armalite AR-10. In the middle of the room, he spotted M'buy, lying on the floor helplessly with large bloodstains on his pants and shirt. Cautiously he continued his survey, staying as covered behind the doorway as best he could.

Out of nowhere, a gloved hand grabbed his rifle, which suddenly it became electrified. TNT's body convulsed, squeezing off a burst of semi-automatic fire into the room. The next thing he knew, he was lying on the floor looking up at The Bloodhound, who was pointing a gloved hand at him. Then a fluffy grey foam shot out of his glove. The second it hit his body, it expanded like shaving cream. Within a few seconds, TNT's entire body was covered in grey bubbly foam. Instantly the room filled with a harsh petrochemical smell. Satisfied by what he had done, The Bloodhound casually disappeared into the shadows of the dark room.

TNT's body was still reeling from the shock. He could barely move and now he was covered in this awful foam. He had no idea what the point of it was, other than to make him sick from the smell. He tried to wipe if off his face and onto the floor but the stuff was super-sticky. He managed to spread enough away from his eyes so he could open them. He tried rolling on the ground, trying to get this stinky stuff off, but that didn't help. Then he felt the foam quickly begin to grow hotter. A second later he was getting so hot that it felt like his body was going to burn up. He heard some snickering from inside the dark room and realized he was being played. Not wanting to be an amusement for someone's sick fetish, he quickly got on his feet and stumbled back into the spa room, out of sight from The Bloodhound's perverse view.

TNT tried to tear off his clothes, but they were stuck to his body as if they had dissolved from the foam. The fabric just peeled off in soggy little strips. Patik and Cameron moved towards him, trying to help. "NO!" shouted TNT. "Stay away!" He looked very perplexed. "I don't know what this stuff is but I don't want it to get on either of you!" Confused and helpless, Cameron and Patik watched as TNT ran around like a crazy person.

Cameron looked at Patik. "I'll go find a towel, maybe that will help."

Patik nodded, "I'll stay and cover him."

The foam was starting to seriously burn and TNT was getting desperate. He stumbled toward an old Jacuzzi that hadn't seen water in years, trying to think of some way to get the stuff to stop burning. This was the old spa room, after all, there had to be some water somewhere that he could wash himself off with. Behind a dusty old Japanese screen was a water closet that had a sink and a toilet. He pushed the screen out of the way and opened the door to the tiny room.

There was an old chipped coffee cup sitting on the sink. He grabbed it and turned on the water but the pipe had burst long ago. He looked in the toilet. At the very bottom was an inch of water. He tried to scoop some up, but the cup was too big to get to the bottom of the bowl and he couldn't reach it. Each passing second the burning and itching increased; he had to do something quickly. In a last ditch effort, he opened the back of the toilet's tank. To his amazement, the tank was half full of water. He dunked and scooped out a full cup of water. He stood up as tall as he could. As he was about to pour the soothing water over his head, he saw Cameron run into the room with a towel in her hand. As he turned his wrist and dumped the cup of water onto his head, a voice from the opposite room shouted: "Yee-hah!" The Bloodhound appeared in the doorway, watching them with great amusement.

Instantly there was a loud WHOMPFF, as TNT's body was covered in a bright blue flame. Cameron screamed. Patik turned to shoot The Bloodhound, but he was out of sight. Only his maniacal laugh reverberated among the crackle of the flames. They both watched helplessly as TNT's body melted and burned in a white-hot phosphorescent heat. Within seconds, the big tattooed man was a pile of ash. The Japanese screen he had been standing next to caught on fire and the room quickly began to fill up with black smoke.

Anticipating that the commando goons would use tear gas, Cameron, Patik, and TNT had grabbed their gas masks and had come to the spa room looking for M'buy to give him his. Cameron and Patik simultaneously pulled down their masks from the top of their heads and watched as their friend, who had been committed to equality and justice, burned completely. Cameron's heart sank. She often wondered if the fight was worth it. No time in human history had there ever been true justice. Were they fighting for a pipe dream that would never be a reality? Perhaps human beings were incapable of equality. Perhaps humans liked hierarchy and exploiting one another. Perhaps some people even liked being exploited. Maybe that was the natural order of things, and what they were fighting for was going against the grain. It seemed that no matter what happened in history, there were always forces that suppressed, exploited, and destroyed. Perhaps that was just what humans had to live with. Maybe all this fighting and dying for a noble cause was just a big waste of time. She watched as TNT's ashes began to scatter about the room, lost in despair.

Then another feeling washed over her. No! There had to be balance! She and her comrades were the ones who brought balance to the world. They were the light in the darkness. Watching the last of TNT's body turn to ash, Cameron restored her commitment to their cause. She wasn't going to let her friend who, time and time again, had acted bravely, die in vain. Cameron let out a roar of frustration and anger. She was determined to save M'buy from an equally horrific fate.

Chapter 65

Freezing cold and still a bit fuzzy-headed, Ethan took some deep breaths to try to regain his focus. It was a technique that Ascot had taught him to use in between boxing rounds. After three deep breaths, he doubled over in pain, then hacked out the last ounce of water from his lungs onto his shoes. He stood up, propping himself against the cupboard. He felt his body quickly recover as oxygen filled his lungs.

A few seconds later he felt much better and started to warm up. He had no idea which way to go or what lay beyond the room he was leaving. Taking the path to his right, Ethan walked as quietly as he could, then came to a stairway. Suddenly, above him, he heard Cameron scream. Without caution, he bound up the stairs to rescue her.

The moment Ethan was on the top floor, he saw two gunmen in fatigues duck behind a shower and take cover in response to Cameron's scream. Ethan wasn't sure, but it looked like they might have been the guys in the Hummer with him earlier that morning. Their strategy appeared to be to lie and wait, then ambush her as she stepped from the adjacent room.

Ethan felt no fear; his longing for Cameron and his inability to get anywhere with her now made him particularly aggressive. These two unsuspecting henchmen were about to receive the brunt of his anger and frustration. If it turned out that they were the same guys from the Hummer, then they were just mercenaries; they had no moral or ideological compass. That mentality infuriated Ethan, who watched like a predatory cat from the cover of the stairway as the soldiers burrowed into their hiding spots, clueless of his presence. Once in position the gunmen seemed to relax slightly, focusing their attention on the voices coming from the adjacent room.

With all his years of Ultimate Sparring Partner training, Ethan's fighting mind sprang into action. He surveyed the area, memorizing where on the floor plan the soldiers were hiding.

Stealthily, he descended the stairs and compared the upstairs floor plan with the floor plan directly below it. From what he could tell they were almost identical. Ethan moved to where the soldiers were hiding one floor above him. He squatted, and with the fierce determination of an Apache warrior, jumped and crashed up through the ceiling.

Captain Travers and Chow Mein were about three feet apart, crouched behind a shower stall, looking through their scopes. They could see the flickering shadows of two R.A.D figures walking out of the room towards their dead comrade's body. Both mercenaries were in sync and ready. Travers had his finger on the trigger and was anticipating bagging two more R.A.D. rebels. He wanted to create a stack of dead bodies on top of the one that was already lying there.

Suddenly the floor beneath him exploded. A hand with an iron grip grabbed the back of his neck. The next thing he realized, he had dropped his weapon and was airborne. Out of the corner of his left eye he saw the very puzzled and surprised face of Chow Mein. He too was weaponless and was being grabbed by his neck and catapulted towards the ceiling. Then, in a blink of an eye, Travers felt his face slam into Chow Mein's. The blow hurt but it didn't knock him out. He could taste Chow Mein's saliva on his lips. Then he felt his nose swell up and blood filled his mouth.

Travers realized he was falling. The iron grip on his neck tightened and his body wasn't just free-falling; he was being pushed downward.

For Ethan, everything felt like it was happening in slow motion. With a scumbag mercenary in each hand, Ethan did a jack-knife, like he had learned during his summers at the Northridge Public Pool, kicking his feet above his head and pushing off the ceiling. Now Ethan was diving straight down towards the hole in the floor. He blocked his fall through the broken floorboards with the faces of the two soldiers. For Ethan, plowing through the layers of building material felt like tearing through tissue paper. Ethan landed on top of the two soldiers on the floor below and then did a dive roll like he had learned to do in fifth grade tumbling class. The next thing he knew he was back on his feet. Travers and Chow Mein both lay on the floor immobile, their faces now a crushed, bloody mess. The only sign of life they exhibited were tiny bubbles of air in the blood seeping from their noses and mouths.

Ethan's successful surprise attack had excited and stimulated him. Now he was ready for more. Without hesitation, Ethan jumped up to the next story through the hole he had just created, determined to help Cameron.

The Bloodhound had watched with great amusement the dumb, tattooed idiot pour water on his head, giving the phosphorous foam the needed hydrogen to combust. Once the white-hot flame ignited, there was no stopping it. He had seen enough. He slammed and bolted the door that connected the two rooms. The room had no windows or lights that worked. The Bloodhound touched something on his sleeve. Then his suit began to glow, filling the room with a soft light. He pulled out the .38 special that he had stuffed in his pants and looked down at M'buy, still lying helpless on the floor. Then he pulled a single bullet out of his pocket. "We are doing this again!" He opened the chamber, dumped out the used round, put a new bullet in, and spun the cylinder. "You first!" And The Bloodhound pressed the gun's barrel onto M'buy's forehead right between the eyes. M'buy glared at him. If he was going to die, so be it, but he wasn't going to cower or beg.

Then to M'buy's surprise, The Bloodhound pulled the gun away. "This isn't right. I want to see you pull the trigger."

"Fuck you!" rumbled M'Buy's wheezy voice.

"I know that deciding how to die is a difficult decision." He grabbed M'buy's dreadlocks, dragged him a few feet and propped him up so he was sitting up against an old metal locker. After he was properly repositioned, The Bloodhound found a plastic crate and moved it so he was facing M'buy. He sat and stared at the ravaged blood-covered man.

"I'll make you a deal."

M'buy just glared.

"Here it is. You are most likely going to die. I can shoot you, or I have a dozen other tricks up my sleeve that I can kill you with, or you can play a little game with me."

M'buy almost said, "Kill me and get it over with," but instead, just continued to glare.

"Here's the game, and as far as I can tell, it's your last chance to stay alive. I spin the chamber and you get four shots to your temple, that's a percentage of... uhh—" He paused, trying to figure out the math.

After about thirty seconds, M'buy muttered, "It's a one in three chance of survival."

"Okay, mister math whiz, one in three! That sounds like pretty fucking good odds, because if you don't do it, there is a one hundred percent chance I will shoot you right between your fucking eyes." The Bloodhound waved the gun in front of M'buy's face and then spun the cylinder. "So, you feelin' lucky?"

M'buy nodded and lifted his right hand. The Bloodhound was about to hand him the gun, then stopped. "By the way, my suit's magnetized and completely bulletproof, so don't bother trying to shoot me. If you do, all bets are off, and I'll torture you, then kill you!"

The Bloodhound scooted back so he could see a bit better and avoid getting any blood splatter on his suit. "Ok, you ready? Let's play." He leaned over and handed M'buy the gun.

Ethan cautiously walked toward the smoke that was coming from the doorway where the dead body lay. He could hear muffled voices from inside. He peeked inside the adjoining room and saw Cameron and Patik standing next to a bonfire wearing gas masks. Once Ethan, had determined that the coast was clear he eagerly went into greet them.

Without saying hello or suggesting that she was even glad to see him alive, Cameron pointed to the closed door that led to the opposite room. "Ethan, M'buy is in there with some psychotic-sick-fuck. We are out of ammo and we are trying to figure out how to stop him before he kills M'buy like he did TNT." She pointed to a small pile of white ash that was the only thing left of their comrade-in-arms.

A short stack of cardboard boxes and what was left of a Japanese screen were smoldering in the corner next to him. The tiled spa floor and walls were like a brick oven. The fire had been contained and was extinguishing itself.

Ethan was getting the picture that he was just muscle to them, a body without a soul to do their bidding. Perhaps that's what happened in all war? People got reduced to their ability to perform some useful task. Despite this emotional letdown, Ethan was still pumped up and in the mood to kick some ass. He marched toward the door "Well, we're not going to get anywhere by just standing here!"

Cameron stopped him. "If you just barge in then he will definitely kill him." The smoke in the room was almost gone.

Patik took off his gas mask and looked Ethan in the eyes. "It's The Bloodhound and he is equipped with all kinds of gadgets that even you are no match for." Ethan was reminded of the pain he still felt in his ankle from the blowtorch glove. Nonetheless, they both looked at him with the expectation that he was going to go in and rescue M'buy, regardless of the risk.

Ethan thought for a second, then walked over and picked up the dead body that was lying in the doorway. Cameron looked puzzled, "What are you going to do with him?" she asked. Ethan held up the body, "I'm going to toss him through the door as a distraction. Then bust through the wall on the opposite side of the room and get M'buy. Cameron looked horrified at the idea of using one of their dead team members as a battering ram.

Patik read her expression perfectly and put his hand on her shoulder. "Hey, he died proudly fighting, and he can only die once, so now he can continue to help us in our battle."

Cameron nodded and Ethan, body in hand, marched toward the door.

Inside the room, The Bloodhound sat on the plastic crate about four feet away from M'buy, watching the bloody man intensely. There was a faint click and The Bloodhound burst out laughing, then stomped his feet on the ground in excitement. "That's three! One more and you're a free man." M'buy was covered in sweat. His dark skin had turned to ashy grey from all the blood loss. He put the gun to his temple for the fourth time. Even if he did survive this last round of Russian roulette, the other two bullet wounds would probably do him in anyway.

The Bloodhound stared at him, licking his lips like a hungry dog. M'buy was about to pull the trigger for the last time when the door busted open. Light broke in, stinging his eyes, which had adjusted to the light of the psychotic man's glowing suit. Propped up, gun to his temple, M'buy watched in surprise as wood splinters exploded from the door jam, followed by an airborne R.A.D team member who landed with a harsh thud in the middle of the room. Furious over the interruption, The Bloodhound jumped to his feet, and began shooting the man on the floor, his back towards M'buy.

M'buy took this opportunity to see if The Bloodhound really was bulletproof. He yanked the gun from his temple, aimed it at the middle of his glowing back where he knew he would absolutely not miss, and pulled the trigger. The single bullet in the chamber went off and The Bloodhound was knocked to the ground.

"Bulletproof, my ass!" M'buy mumbled, thinking he had gotten the last word. He leaned back, smiled, and relaxed slightly.

Almost as quickly as he'd fallen to the ground, The Bloodhound rose and turned to M'buy. "Oh, no you didn't!" The cyborg freak shouted, looking extremely pissed off. "Oh, no you didn't!" he repeated. There was no blood on him and he wasn't hurt. The glowing suit, surrounded by a super dense magnetic field, had protected The Bloodhound. The bullet had knocked him to the floor, then ricocheted off into the ceiling. It hurt all right, like getting punched in the back, but it wasn't the least bit fatal. Now The Bloodhound had a gun in his hand and a scowl on his face. "Oh, no you didn't! That was your bullet! That's twice you've cheated me."

The Bloodhound angrily walked towards M'buy. When suddenly the wall next to them exploded. Drywall and chunks of 2X4 flew through the air. Undaunted, The Bloodhound grabbed M'buy by his hair, dragged him a few feet towards the opposite side of the room, and put his knee on the injured man's neck. Instantly The Bloodhound's suit changed colors, blending into the dark grey of the dying African's skin and The Bloodhound forced a gun into M'buy's mouth. Ethan stood in the hole in the wall, but stopped when he saw the situation.

"Listen, dickhead!" roared The Bloodhound. "You move and your friend here is history!" Ethan didn't budge an inch. The

Bloodhound spit in Ethan's direction. "Now you and your friends can go play with yourselves. Mr. Rastafari and I have some unfinished business to attend to."

Ethan stood tall, and with as much authority as he could muster, barked, "Let him go and I won't hurt you!"

Dumbfounded, The Bloodhound looked at him incredulously. "Let him go? You hurt me? Who the hell do you think you are?" Without warning there was a flash and a spray of pellets like buckshot hurled towards Ethan. Even with his heightened senses, Ethan could barely see them coming. At the last second, Ethan dove out of the way, through the hole in the wall and back into the spa room. The pellets splattered against the wall and the floor around him. Ethan watched in awe as the pellets dissolved, burning holes through the wall and the tile floor. He noticed that one lone pellet had grazed the bottom of his left shoe, and now the heel was melting.

The Bloodhound turned back to M'buy. He wanted to finish the game of Russian roulette, but there wasn't any more time. He needed to get back to his troops and finish this assignment. Ethan was strong and fast, but he was no soldier. The Bloodhound was confident that his training and experience was more than enough to handle him and the situation. Besides, he had to get even with Ethan for throwing him out of the window. "Let's see if Space Boy is as lucky as I am!" he thought.

M'buy still had the gun in his mouth and was looking up at The Bloodhound with absolute indifference, showing no respect for the fact that The Bloodhound controlled his fate. This infuriated The Bloodhound, who got off on terrorizing his victims. Violently, he pulled the gun out of M'buy's mouth and pressed it hard between his eyes. M'buy closed his eyes and took as deep a breath as he could. M'buy's calmness sparked a new and deeper level of anger inside The Bloodhound. He pressed the gun harder into M'Buy's forehead, breaking the skin. A single bead of blood pooled around the gun barrel, slid past the black man's closed eyes, and down the bridge of his nose.

"Look at me, you asshole!" The Bloodhound shouted. M'buy kept his eyes closed. "Look at me!" He dug his knee deep into the big man's chest, knocking the wind out of him. "Look at me!" he shouted louder, but the large, dark eyes stayed closed. In a state of absolute rage, The Bloodhound pulled the trigger.

About a minute before the shot, an officer on The Bloodhound's team had discovered the rebels ammunition stockpile of C4 explosives, bullets and grenades. Excited, he called all of his tactical teammates to take a look at his impressive discovery. If properly positioned, there were enough explosives to obliterate an entire city block. They needed approval to confiscate it, but for some reason The Bloodhound had turned his headset mic and receiver off. The men were all gathered around stockpile, deciding how they should proceed now that the chain of command was once again in question.

In less than half a second, the bullet flew through the front of M'buy's skull, passed though his brain, out the back of his skull, through the carpet, though the floor boards, though a large bundle of electrical wires that sent power to the entire building, and into the secrete metal ammunition depot.

The ambient electrical current, along with the heat and force of the bullet, traveling through the wire, was just the right combination of events to set off a charge. The dumb luck of The Bloodhound had just run out. Within a few milliseconds a fireball blew the roof, along with one side of the building wide open. Arms, legs, and disembodied pieces of The Bloodhound and all his men flew a hundred feet into the air, and then began to rain down like giant meaty puffs of popped corn. In less than a minute, the parking lot looked like a slaughterhouse floor.

Ethan was wondering what to do about his shoe when he noticed that Cameron and Patik were gone. He had just gotten up onto his feet and was thinking of another approach to rescue M'buy when he heard the almost-simultaneous gunshot and loud explosion. A second later, a giant fireball erupted from the room as if a dragon had just come out of hibernation. Surprised, Ethan leaped in the opposite direction towards the door that led to the hallway. Ethan was fast, but the fireball caught up with him and like a wave crashing over him, engulfed his body and knocked him to the floor. The flame was short but very hot. He could feel and smell that his hair had caught on fire. His instincts were to rub his head and roll on the ground; luckily the fire went out right away.

Ethan turned and looked at the damage. Most of the explosion had blown away from him. The roof that was on the opposite side of the building was completely gone. The side he was on was shaken but structurally fine. Ethan's ears were ringing, his head was fuzzy and his entire body ached. His jumpsuit was made from some kind of synthetic fabric that had shrunk and stuck to him like wax. "This can't be good," Ethan surmised "Skin needs to breathe, after all." He tried to peel the melted fabric off his arm, but it just crumbled and broke apart like an uncooperative hard-boiled eggshell, while yanking out the hairs on his arm.

To Ethan's surprise, he discovered his skin wasn't really burnt. Apparently his extra-dense molecular structure also made him somewhat impervious to fire. He should be covered in blisters and third-degree burns, but instead was walking away with nothing more than a mild sunburn. The melted fabric felt like he was wearing a wetsuit. He liked the tightness and pressure against his body. It made him feel like a warrior.

The spa room had a dressing area with a mirror on the wall, which had miraculously managed to stay in one piece. Ethan looked at himself, still a little fuzzy-headed, and laughed. Now he really was wearing a silly superhero outfit, a complete ensemble consisting of a bright red skintight suit, with a melted Eden, Inc. logo on his chest that looked like something Salvador Dali had doodled, and bright blue shoes. To complete the new look was an uneven mop of burnt hair about two inches shorter than it had previously been, with all the ends singed and curly. "Whatever," Ethan thought, turning away from the mirror. He had more important things to deal with than his image.

He heard fighting going on down the hall, and jumped into action.

Chapter 66

Furious fighting was in full force between Cameron and a masked ninja in the nightclub's top floor ballroom. The stealth assassin in black had burst out of the shadows and caught Cameron and Patik off-guard, but to the surprise of the ninja, Cameron fought back like a trained professional. Patik had tried to jump in and help her, but got instantly clobbered. He was now lying on the floor, delirious, blood oozing out of his mouth.

The fight raged for several minutes, utilizing every square inch of the large ballroom like an elaborately choreographed Hollywood movie scene. A relentless stream of kicks, blocks and punches erupted from both fighters. The two were remarkably well-matched in ability and size. Neither seemed to be able to land a strong solid punch. The ninja was more aggressive, and if Cameron were to let her guard down for a fraction of a second, the assassin could deliver a deathblow. Cameron had amazing stamina and used that to her advantage. She figured if she could wear the fighter out, she had a chance of surviving and maybe even landing a lethal blow herself.

Ethan walked in and saw Cameron block a roundhouse kick to her left temple by her masked opponent. Cameron countered the move with a kick to the groin that her attacker blocked.

Ethan ran towards the fight just as the ninja was being backed up against the wall. Suddenly, like an old Gene Kelly dance routine, the assassin faced the wall, ran up it, and did a back flip over Cameron, landing a solid kick to the back of her head on the way down. She fell to the ground like a sack of potatoes. The ninja landed firmly on the ground and was about to deliver the coup de grace when Ethan leaped across the room and collided with the masked assassin. The two bodies went tumbling across the room.

Ethan began untangling his body from the stunned ninja. The melted suit, still warm and smoldering from the fire, was now starting to itch. This was becoming a serious distraction and he couldn't decide if he should first finish the fight or scratch his back. Unexpectedly, the ninja stood up, and like a magician, produced a handful of razor-sharp throwing stars. Like tiny bolts of lightning, a deluge of stars began flying toward Ethan. Scratching his back would have to wait.

Ethan leaped towards the fleeing ninja, the stars missing Ethan's body by just a few inches. He grabbed the assassin by the back of the neck then slammed the masked assassin face first into the floor. The ninja lay motionless on the ground. Ethan took this brief respite to scratch. The suit was tough and bumpy; this was what he imagined rhino hide would feel like. The more he scratched, the more the itch spread. The next thing he realized, he was lying on his back, wiggling around the splintered floor, trying to get that impossible-to-reach spot.

Cameron and Patik were both dazed and bleeding slightly. They both got back up on their feet wondering what the hell Ethan was doing. They stumbled over to their writhing comrade and watched him scoot across the floor in apparent ecstasy. Finally, when his itch was quelled, Ethan sat up, looked at the bewildered Cameron and Patik, and said, "I can't tell you how much better that feels."

Cameron and Patik nodded, staring at the unfinished business in front of them. Ethan reached over and tore off the ninja's mask. Long locks of blond hair cascaded from beneath the mask. Ethan pushed the body onto its back, revealing the face of the unconscious Valkyrie. The three were taken aback.

"Bitch!" Cameron screamed, kicking the woman on the side of her hip as hard as she could, then stormed out of the room. The Valkyrie moaned and rolled onto her side, her eyelids fluttering. Ethan and Patik watched in curious fascination, like a mother hen seeing her eggs hatch for the first time, as the blonde ninja started to show signs of waking.

Two minutes later, Cameron stormed back in, dragging a hose similar to the one that TNT had used to flush out Ethan's nano-bots. Ethan and Patik were still, crouching next to the assassin, waiting for her to become conscious. Without warning Cameron blasted a hard stream of cold water into the prostrate Valkyrie's face, splashing water on Ethan and Patik. Startled, the two men instinctively jumped back.

Cameron was brutal, spraying a hard, wide stream of water onto the assassin's face for what seemed like much longer than necessary. Patik ran out of the room while Ethan stayed, watching The Valkyrie get soaked.

Finally the assassin began coughing and blowing water out of her nose. Cameron finally stopped spraying when Patik came in, carrying the jumper cables he had used to wipe out Ethan's nano-bots. He scowled and then touched the two ends together, creating a shower of sparks. Ethan easily held the assassin down as she looked up at the R.A.D team glaring at her. Unused to being in a compromised position she was flabbergasted.

Cameron snarled, "What is Casper up to? And what does he want with Ethan?"

The assassin glared up at her captors and said nothing. The team stared down at the blonde ninja and waited. Eventually they began to lose patience. Sensing that the focus had been broken, The Valkyrie seized the opportunity, and kicked Patik while reaching for a gun hidden in the side of her boot. The second the gun was in her hand she fired.

Ethan saw her move as if it were in slow motion. He grabbed and twisted her wrist. The bullet that would have hit Patik went straight into the floor instead. Ethan was now holding her gun, Cameron was kicking her in the ribs, and Patik was stumbling back towards her with the two hot battery leads in his hands. The Valkyrie attempted once more to break free, but this time Cameron's knee dropped onto her chest, knocking the wind out of her. Ethan saw a fan of blond hair create a halo around the assassin's head as she lay on her back. To help contain things, Ethan stood on her hair, pinning her to the ground, his blue boxing shoes pressing against her ears.

Patik yelled, "Cameron, get off her!" It sounded like he was objecting to the World Wrestling Federation tactics she was using, but then she realized that Patik was pressing the leads of the jumper cables against their prisoner's thighs just below her crotch. There was a loud crackle, then for several seconds she convulsed, flopping like a fish.

Cameron shot her with the hose again, making sure to get water up her nose. "Let's try this again!" Cameron barked. "What is Casper up to? And what does he want with Ethan?"

The Valkyrie was panting with her head pinned to the ground; her ribs hurt, her legs were numb, and her heart was racing from the combination of electricity and adrenaline. "There's nothing I know that you guys don't already know."

Cameron looked at her, "I don't agree!" She gestured to Patik to electrocute The Valkyrie again.

Panic came over The Valkyrie's face. "Look, Casper and his cronies are simply power mad. No matter how much they have it's never enough, so for years they have been tweaking the system to favor them. Most of the people don't have a clue about what's going on and that's the way they like it. You guys pay attention and object to their having obtained this level of unprecedented power, so they want to shut you up before people take notice."

Cameron scowled, "We know that!" She pointed to Patik and he zapped her right on her knees caps.

Beneath his feet Ethan felt The Valkyrie's hair tear away from her scalp as she convulsed. Cameron shot her in the face with water again. "See this routine we have? How many more times do you want to go through this?"

The Valkyrie blew water out of her nose. It dribbled down her checks and onto Ethan's slightly melted boxing shoes. "Okay, okay, I get it!" The Valkyrie took a deep breath. This time she actually seemed sincere. "For years, Casper has been gaming the system so he can control space as if it were real estate. He sees it as the new frontier. He has everything in place. The Valhalla II Off-world Living Resort is almost complete." She tilted her head back to look at Ethan. "And it's three times bigger than the one you were on. Casper is selling the idea to the super-rich that they can live in paradise above the crime and pollution, like the Greek Gods on Mount Olympus. But they're not buying it like he thought they would. Now Casper is sitting on a mountain of debt, and a possible hostile corporate takeover of his company."

An electrical crackle of two jumper cables touching interrupted her. She looked up at Patik fearfully. "Why aren't they buying?" he asked.

She clenched her jaw, contemplating whether or not to say anything. Patik zapped the cables together again, and as if on cue she started talking.

"All the environmental awareness, pollution laws, nuclear nonproliferation, and policies that help reduce poverty..."

"You mean all the stuff we've been fighting for all these years?" snapped Cameron.

"Yeah. Well it's slowly and quietly been working. So things like crime, pollution, unemployment, aren't as bad as the media reports, and not nearly as bad as Casper had thought and had hoped they would be. So he needs to create a new incentive for them to leave." Cameron and Patik looked at each other, seriously concerned. "Casper planned to use Ethan and his friend to help sell the idea of living in the resort to his clients," The Valkyrie gazed up at Ethan, "since they are the only two people who have ever lived on an Eden, Inc. space station."

"Well plans change," said Ethan. "Besides Ascot and I know the real dangers involved, and how friggin' boring it really is up there. I doubt we would be good for sales."

"That's why Casper wants to make sure you two are close by and on his side."

"So what's Casper's 'incentive' that will sell billions of dollars worth of bullshit real estate in space?" asked Patik.

"I don't know!"

"Bullshit!" Cameron blasted water into The Valkyrie's face until she started coughing. Ethan almost told her to take it easy, but realized it was best to stay out of her way.

The Valkyrie turned her head and coughed water out of her lungs. "Look, there's nothing you can do about it, anyway. This is too big for anyone to change."

"We will be the judge of that!" Cameron interjected, venom in her voice. "What is Casper planning?"

"He's going to detonate a dozen loose nukes, scattering them over each continent."

"That's crazy!" said Patik. "He will be irradiating millions of people, and possibly destroying what's left of the ozone layer!"

"Maybe," said The Valkyrie. "But these are old Soviet bombs. Most likely they aren't operating at full capacity."

"Nonetheless, there will be lots of radioactive fallout and skin cancer rates will rise and—"

"That's exactly the point," interrupted The Valkyrie. "So the people who can afford to leave will suddenly want to."

Ethan looked astonished. "You have to be kidding. You are telling us that Casper is willing to destroy the world just so he can make more money. He already has tons of money. How much does he need?"

The Valkyrie rolled her eyes up at Ethan. "You don't get it. It's not about money. It's about power and control. Guys like Casper want to play God and we are their toys. They control corporations and governments so they can play their global chess game with each other. They see people like a farmer sees a crop of corn. If they need to burn or spray or plow some to win the game, they'll do it."

There was awkward silence as Ethan, Cameron and Patik stared down at their wet prisoner, waiting for more information. When none came Patik tapped the jumper cables together, making a loud crack and a shower of sparks.

Like Pavlov's dog, The Valkyrie continued, "They want the population to be just smart enough to build their things, buy their products, do their work, and be good, law-abiding citizens. Then be distracted by safe, stupid, trivial and superficial events. They have been systematically dumbing down the population all over the world. They are afraid of people who are smart enough to notice that everything we do just feeds the machinery of repression. It's a war that's been going on since before the Roman Empire."

Patik and Cameron both nodded their heads in agreement. Ethan cleared his throat inadvertently, getting everyone's attention. "Why do you work for these assholes?"

The Valkyrie laughed. "For the same reason you did! Or did you already forget?" Ethan looked down at his melted blue shoes, ashamed.

The Valkyrie continued. "Look, they will do whatever it takes to get their way, and they always get their way! You guys can have your high ideals and hide underground and be hunted like rabbits. Personally I would rather live out in the open and to be the hunter."

An explosion interrupted her rant. The sound was deafening and very disorienting. Ethan watched the ceiling peel away. Dust and debris floated down like snow, filling the room. There was a barrage of gunshots and the floor exploded around Ethan's feet. Cameron and Patik immediately ducked for cover, ignoring their prisoner. Instinctively Ethan jumped out of the way, while trying to see where the gunshots were coming from.

The room was so cloudy with dust and smoke that Ethan could hardly see anything. The gunman—or more likely gunmen—could be hiding anywhere. Ethan stumbled backward until he literally banged into a portable bar that was parked in the corner of the nightclub's dance floor. He climbed behind it as exploding bullets continued to randomly tear up the floor. A faint, high-pitched whine reverberated though the room. Frustrated, Ethan wanted to jump out and fight, but he couldn't see anything and had no idea how lethal the bullets were. He had been shot already and the bullets hadn't broken his skin, but these bullets were exploding when they hit the floor and he wasn't ready to take that chance. Ethan wished he had a weapon so he could fire back, hold off the attackers and help Cameron and Patik escape, but when he looked for his two teammates he couldn't see where they had gone. Ethan realized once again that they could get along fine without him.

The mysterious whine was getting louder and louder. Ethan peeked over the top of the bar trying to see the source of the sound, but the hardwood dance floor and mirrored walls were very reflective, enabling the sound to bounce around and making it impossible to detect its location. The Valkyrie was on her feet, crouched on the spot where she had just been pinned. She started navigating her way through the exploding gunfire and out of the room.

Movement, from where the explosion had blown a hole in the ceiling, caught Ethan's attention. He looked up to see if there were any mirrors on the ceiling; when he realized there weren't, he did a double take. The Fly was walking upside down on the ceiling, shooting down at the floor. It was so surreal that he thought he must have been imagining it.

The dust was clearing and the visibility was improving. Some of the other R.A.D. team members had heard the explosion and come to investigate. Now they were hiding in the corners shooting up at The Fly, who was dodging bullets and making his way towards The Valkyrie.

Ethan pushed the bar towards The Valkyrie, using the thick wood and metal as a shield, while peeking over the top and keeping The Fly in his vision. When The Fly got close to The Valkyrie, she made a dash towards him through the massive gunfire, but, just as The Fly swooped down from the ceiling with his jet pack to grab her, Ethan leaped up from behind the bar and hit The Fly like a human swatter, tackling him in midair. The two crashed through the tattered ceiling, then began tumbling down the pitched tile roof. As the two slid towards the edge, The Fly managed to wiggle out of Ethan's grip, blasted his jet pack, and was instantly airborne, flying above the building.

Ethan tried to grab the tiles and do whatever he could do stop himself from sliding towards the parking lot, four stories below. He managed to dig his hands through the tiles and successfully slow himself down. Just as he was coming to a complete stop, less than a foot from the edge, the Fly passed overhead and a grenade fell from above and landed on Ethan's lap.

Without thinking, Ethan tossed it like it was a hot potato and it lobbed over the edge of the roof without much force. The grenade went off, blowing a hole in the side of the building, weakening the awning where Ethan was precariously perched.

The next thing he realized he was falling four stories onto the concrete parking lot below. He saw that about ten feet to his left was a tree and surrounding the tree was soft dirt. At the last possible second, Ethan pushed off the building towards the tree. He was on a trajectory towards the dirt, but didn't quite make it. He landed right smack on the concrete less than three feet from the tree, then somersaulted onto the dirt.

Ethan came to an abrupt halt with his feet straight up in the air, straddling the tree trunk. Now he was really pissed off. That was twice the Fly had gotten the better of him. He had to get back and help Cameron and Patik.

Chapter 67

Hiding in the shadows, dodging gunfire with her backup gone. The Valkyrie was doing her best to stay alive. The very annoying Ethan Stone had decommissioned the Fly. Since she wasn't sure what had happened to the two of them, she had to assume she was on her own. She was running out of time and needed an escape plan.

The Valkyrie quietly crept and hid behind the same bar Ethan had used. She wasn't as strong as Ethan, so pushing the heavy object across the floor proved to be very difficult, but she managed to slowly make her way towards the side of the building that was blown wide open.

She was suddenly disoriented by a blinding flash and two muscular men in bloody Kevlar vests and helmets appeared out of nowhere and pounced on The Valkyrie. It happened so fast that her cobra reflexes were caught off-guard. The next thing she knew, she was lying face down on the ground with her hands tied behind her back.

"Good job, men!" Cameron reappeared, followed by Patik and two other R.A.D team members also wearing newly-acquired Kevlar body armor, with bits of flesh and skin still clinging to it from the massacred Bloodhound's team. Cameron pointed to The Valkyrie, who was now lying on her back.

"Let's get out of here before more troops come!" The two armored men lifted her onto her feet.

A high-pitched whine suddenly poured in, echoing through the room. Tear gas grenades began to rain from the exposed sky like a candy from a piñata, exploding all around the room. Instantly there was a chorus of coughing. The Valkyrie seized the moment. In one fluid move, she wiggled away from her captures then hopped through her arms, as if they were a jump rope. With the speed of a rattlesnake, she smacked the unsuspecting guard in the jaw, knocking him to the ground, then bolted towards the hole in the wall.

Just then, the Fly swooped in through the hole in the ballroom ceiling. A barrage of exploding bullets rained down like a hailstorm. Cameron, Patik and the remaining rebels were forced to duck for cover.

Being a six-foot-four-inch, two-hundred-forty-pound ex-marine, fighting was something that Dale Buck enjoyed and was very good at, so the fact that he just got knocked down by a girl whose hands were tied didn't sit well with him. Dale had been recruited to fight for R.A.D after his wife had fallen and broken her arm when the stairs in their apartment collapsed. Their twelve-year-old daughter had been sick, so his wife, Susan had come home early and brought her office work home with her. The insurance company refused to pay for the broken arm because they claimed it was a work-related injury, which they didn't cover. There were several attempts to get medical help, a dozen lawyers got involved, and it got dragged through the legal and medical insurance bureaucracy for months.

Meanwhile, Susan was stuck with a broken arm that was never properly set, and was using a makeshift sling. She had just finished dinner and was helping their eight-year-old son with his math homework, when she suddenly went into a seizure and died. Apparently, a blood clot from her untreated arm had lodged in her brain. Dale was so upset with the system he vowed to change it. When he learned how institutionalized the problems were and how thoroughly big pharma had corrupted the laws, he concluded that the only way to make any improvements and change the system was to literally fight back with weapons. Leaving his beloved children with Susan's parents, Dale had been embedded with the R.A.D. team for over a year.

Dale chased the Blonde ninja towards the broken wall, determined to get his prisoner back. He was so focused that he failed to notice The Fly in the air behind him. Dale never felt the exploding bullet hit the back of his neck, between the Kevlar vest and helmet. It happened so fast that there was absolutely no pain. The explosion was contained inside the helmet, allowing the bullet fragments to bounce around like pieces of ice inside a blender. Dale's well-developed trapezius muscles kept his head from falling completely off. Even after his head had turned into soggy meatloaf, Dale's big body had so much momentum that he continued to stay on his feet and move forward.

Four stories down, Ethan lay on his back, looking up at the sky. His feet stung from the impact. His head ached from tumbling on concrete, and his body itched from the partially melted plastic suit. He replayed the fight he had just had with the Fly in his mind, trying to figure out how he could be wiser the next time he did battle with a villain who was so well-equipped with gadgets of destruction.

At a burst of gunfire overhead, Ethan looked up and saw The Valkyrie leap off the top floor like a skydiver, her legs spread-eagled, her hands overhead tied together. Right behind her was a big guy in a Kevlar suit who fell off the ledge straight, down like a walrus sliding off an iceberg. A wave of tear gas frothed over the ledge behind the bodies. Ethan watched in fascination, anticipating where the two bodies would land, then out of the smoke at supersonic speed, the Fly swooped down towards the falling Valkyrie. Just as she was passing the second story, he grabbed her in mid-air, and the two flew over the parking lot past the row of meat-covered Hummers.

The two assassins landed on the sidewalk a block away, where The Valkyrie had her motorcycle waiting. The escape move was so spectacular that Ethan paid no attention to the big man that used to be Dale as he hit the pavement. Ethan rose to his feet in the parking lot, brushing the rubble and debris off of his skintight suit.

Across the street, The Fly cut the wire that tied The Valkyrie's hands together. She rubbed her wrists, stretched her arms, and then abruptly climbed onto her bike. Ethan watched her speed away, her long blond locks blowing in the breeze. The Fly turned to Ethan, then flipped him the middle finger. "I'm not done with you, asshole, I'm declaring war!" Satisfied that he had said what he needed to say, the Fly shot straight into the air and within a few seconds was out of sight.

Ethan wasn't sure what he meant by "declaring war." Wasn't that what was going on already? He heard one of the Hummers start up, then peel out of the parking lot. Chunky, bloody goop slid off the hood and roof and onto the pavement. Apparently some of Casper's soldiers had survived after all.

Ethan raced back into the building through the melted front door. Everything was in shambles. All the walls and floors were destroyed from gunfire and grenades. When he got to the third floor, Cameron and Patik were staggering down the stairs, followed by two big Kevlar-covered rebels carrying a dead team member. The quartet was scratched up but none of them were seriously injured. They put the body with the other dead team members.

Ethan looked surprised. "Where are all the dead mercenaries?"

"Casper's men stuffed the bodies in the back of a Hummer and left," said a muffled voice from behind a Kevlar battle helmet.

Cameron interjected. "They never leave any trace of who they are or where they've been."

Patik looked out the window that Ethan had tossed The Bloodhound through. "Except this time they didn't have time to clean up the mess they left in the parking lot."

"Oh, they'll be back!" said Cameron, "and we need to get our stuff out of here before they return with reinforcements."

Cameron looked at Ethan coldly. "What are you going to do?" Ethan was surprised by the question.

"I figured I would stay with you guys." Cameron and Patik looked at each other for approval. Ethan seemed baffled. Didn't he just prove himself by helping them battle Casper's goons? Ethan clenched his jaw and put some edge in his voice. "I just seriously burned a bridge. I think I've shown my intentions to help you fight your cause."

Cameron shook her head. "Do you really want to help us and be part of this, or did you just realize you had made a deal with the devil and that you needed our help to get you your freedom back?"

Ethan stood his ground and looked deep into Cameron's eyes, speaking deliberately. "If living the high life was what I wanted, I could have busted through that door and wiped you all out. Then had the back-up team come in and finish the job. Then I could have gone to my new luxury apartment overlooking Westwood Village, and dined on gourmet food served to me by a beautiful, naked housekeeper. I could have taken my convertible Maserati for a spin and spent a stack of cash at the most exclusive nightclub in Beverly Hills." He paused and looked at Patik, then back at Cameron. "But I didn't do that! I chose to stay and fight for what will make our community, our country, and our planet a better place for everyone."

Patik and Cameron exchanged glances, their eyes betraying nothing. "Look!" said Ethan. "I know my awareness of the issues aren't up to your level. I was off-planet for eight years!" Cameron shrugged.

"Also, I will admit Casper is very persuasive and I was confused. He duped me when he explained how the world is run"

Cameron's cocked her head. "How things are run isn't necessarily how they should be run."

Ethan took an exasperated breath and looked Cameron in the eyes. "I realize that. That's why I'm here and ready to join your team. I've walked away from everything that was offered to me. The only thing I have left is my strength, and you guys."

Patik looked out of the window and pointed at a fleet of combat helicopters coming towards them in the distance. "I think we have sorted things out well enough for now. We have about a minute to gather our things and get out of here!"

Chapter 68

Standing proudly, ten stories high, on the Tarmac of Eden, Inc.'s secret desert air base, the shuttle reflected the early morning glow of the rising sun on its gold heat shields. The dozen Soviet-made nuclear warheads were being slowly loaded into the cargo bay. Casper, The Crusher, The Valkyrie and the Fly all stood in Casper's office and watched the procedures through the oversized tinted windows.

The grand plan was in full swing. In two hours, the shuttle would launch, then as the shuttle silently circled Earth at supersonic speed, the bombs would be released and detonated in the air. Radioactive fallout would rain down. In most cases it wouldn't be powerful enough to kill people right away, but it would scare the hell out of everyone. Almost immediately, discomfort, crime and violence would escalate dramatically, followed rapidly by famine and disease.

Casper sat back in his chair and imagined the phone calls from all the people who had previously placed an order but then changed their minds. They would get a rude awakening when they found that the price had just quadrupled. He predicted that in a week all the spots on Asgard would be sold out, and Eden, Inc. stock would be worth ten times what it was worth now. Any thought of a corporate hostile takeover would be eliminated. Casper knew that he and his team were on top of their game.

He would deal with the turncoat Ethan and the prior day's botch-up in Korea town later. Casper had been optimistic about Ethan's allegiance. He thought Ethan understood that working for Eden, Inc. would put him on the winning team and provide him an opportunity that rarely ever comes once in a lifetime. He was still angry about it. He had ordered his team to let Ethan prove himself, and he did. He proved himself to be a selfish traitor. If it weren't for that psychotic hillbilly, his men would have prevailed, wiped out the rebels, and Ethan would be in his custody.

Despite their failure, R.A.D was almost completely eliminated, and Casper smiled thinking about that. Although Ethan and some of their key players had escaped, they weren't any threat to him. He was the winner!

Ascot walked effortlessly on his new exoskeleton legs as if nothing had ever happened to him, sipping on a Mocha Frappuccino. He took a look at the shuttle as the penultimate bomb was carefully being loaded. Ascot looked at Casper: "Do you expect Ethan and his R.A.D. friends to show up?"

The Crusher turned and answered before Casper could get a word out. "And do what?"

"I don't know exactly, but they do seem to be rather resourceful," Ascot replied nonchalantly.

"They got lucky," protested The Valkyrie. "That won't happen again."

The Fly nodded, "If there is a next time, we're not holding back and we will take care of them once and for all."

Casper looked up at Ascot. "We are sitting in a secret base in the middle of nowhere. It's so remote that even the government doesn't know about it, and we're surrounded by the most sophisticated security system on Earth." Casper got out of his chair, walked over to the window, and pointed down at the row of hangars. "If any aircraft comes within a hundred miles in any direction, our fighter jets will shoot them down, so Ethan may be strong and his buddies may be resourceful, but they are no match for us."

There was a soft knock on the door and Hayley Halgreen, one of Casper's secretaries, walked in wearing a short skirt, high heels, and a tight top that showed off her ample cleavage. She was carrying a large tray of exotic cut fruit and fancy pastries. She placed the tray on the table in the middle of the room then stood next to it, smiling. "Thank you, Miss Halgreen," said Casper, pointing to the food. "Everyone please help yourselves, this will be a launch to remember." Ascot and the trio of assassins grabbed something to eat, as they sat back to watch the shuttle, prepare to take off.

* * * *

Security officer Thomas Payne relaxed in his air-conditioned office surfing the Internet, while sipping his green tea with soymilk. A blip on the radar screen interrupted him. When he turned to take a look, it vanished. He checked to see if any of the noise detectors had picked anything up. Nothing. It was his job to be suspicious, so he diligently checked it out. So far, during the two years he had worked at Eden, Inc.'s secret desert air base, nothing had ever happened.

Thomas started working for Eden, Inc. after spending six years as an electronics and radar specialist in the air force, stationed in Iraq, where actual fighting took place. He had assumed that civilian life would be more profitable, and more fun, so a high-tech security job monitoring the perimeter of Eden, Inc.'s secret desert base seemed like a perfect fit. He had no idea that it was going to turn out to be the most boring assignment ever.

In the beginning, there had been an incident on the Northeast corner of the barren desert. A strong wind had kicked up a wave of sand so dense that it triggered the radar. Thomas sent a fighter jet out to deal with it. When it turned out to be nothing, he found himself sitting for the first and only time in Casper Degas' office, being told harshly, "Screw-ups like that won't be tolerated ever again." Since then, he was much more careful about sounding the alarm.

As a kid, Thomas Payne got teased about his name, starting in the fifth grade when his class learned about the American Revolution. Consequently he ended up getting into more than his share of fights. His hypersensitivity to his name and his willingness to engage in hand-to-hand combat eventually led him to join the Army. There, he learned about military strategy and specialized in security.

Thomas figured that if anyone were to try to attack the base, it would be at the main gate, which was guarded by four armed guards and out of his jurisdiction. The other logical choice would be to try to fly in under the radar, but that would be nearly impossible. They had state-of-the art radar, which was by all accounts impermeable, but if someone were to somehow trick the radar with some kind of stealth technology, the perimeter was equipped with noise detectors that could hear any sound coming from the sky or ground. There was also satellite imagery that monitored the area around the base as well. Thomas was confident in their redundant security system.

The most unlikely scenario would be a ground assault from the Northeast. In that scenario a vehicle would have to travel undetected for over three hundred miles over open desert with no roads, contend with seventy miles an hour winds and sand storms that could destroy a vehicle's paint, windshield, and engine. To be stranded out there with no shelter, the sand could blast the skin off a person's body in a matter of minutes. Was it worth the risk?

The radar had indicated something twenty miles off the Northeast side of the base. Then it vanished. No sound was detected other than the howling of the desert wind. The satellite showed that there were no planes anywhere in the sky. The ground visual showed a big cloud of dust from the wind blowing up the sand. Finally he looked on the infrared monitor system. There was nothing. He surveyed all the other security monitors. When everything seemed fine, he looked at the time on the top right of his computer screen. He made an entry in his security log that at 10:32 AM there had been another anomaly caused by the desert sand, then he went back to surfing the Internet.

He had twenty-eight minutes until Dewey got back from making his security rounds. Thomas looked over his shoulder just to make sure that no one else was in the room. He clicked on Flexi-dynamos.com. It was a porn site full of female gymnasts who seamlessly blended all kinds of near-impossible acts of contortion with hardcore perversion. It was one of Thomas Payne's few guilty pleasures. A window popped on the screen stating that anyone entering the site had to be eighteen years old. "Like that's going to stop any kid," he thought. Then a window popped up, showing: "Today's featured video." It was titled "Olga." It showed a supposed eighteen-year-old Russian girl lying naked on her stomach as if she were doing a push-up, with her back arched so far backwards that her feet were on the ground and her heels were next to her ears. Excited, he clicked on the video, then as if on cue there was a loud explosion that shook his seat.

The monitors and alarms went crazy. Lights flashed and sirens screamed. Thomas looked up at the security monitors and saw that the perimeter fence at the Northeast side of the compound had been breached. He switched cameras so he could get a visual. Out of the desert sand, crashing through the fence, came a completely silent combat tank with armored stealth plating. He stared transfixed at the unique vehicle. "How the hell did anyone pull that off?" he heard himself say out loud. There was another loud explosion and he felt the room shake. Flustered, he immediately dispatched the security force.

Ethan, Cameron, and Patik sat in the back of a custom-made tank that their fellow R.A.D. Member and engineering genius, Simon Morgan, had built. Simon had built a six-hundred horsepower engine that used Nicola Tesla's magnetic coil technology to build a near-perpetual motion engine. It was a work of genius and it was simple. The bottom line was that his engine was the size of a thirty-five pound barbell weight, could power a car, and easily drive from LA to Chicago without ever having to stop. It used no gas and didn't produce an ounce of pollution. His first prototype car held six passengers, had a large trunk and used solar panels to charge its battery. It had looked like a Corvette SUV and could go from zero to sixty in 1.6 seconds.

Simon figured that he was going to change the world. No longer would big oil companies and automakers drive American policy. He had proven that an eco-friendly, efficient means of affordable transportation could now be made available to the world. Like any proud inventor, he applied for a patent and made a video showing off his creation. Excited and naïve, he went out to seek funding, showing his car to investors and automakers. To his surprise he landed an appointment with lobbyists from the big three American automakers. He did his practiced presentation and he thought it had gone well. His audience seemed to be very intrigued by what he had created and wanted to know more. They even set up an appointment with some elected officials and upper management from the big three automakers for the following week.

The next morning, Simon was in the attic looking through some old boxes, when he heard a loud scream, he looked out of a small porthole and watched in horror as his eleven-year-old daughter ran across the backyard. Then got shot in the back of the head. A second later, her body was being dragged back into the house by a man dressed in black wearing a black ski mask. A team of masked assassins had broke into his house and gunned down his entire family, killing even their pet dachshund and their three hamsters. Simon, discombobulated, pulled out his cell phone and dialed 911. When the operator answered, he couldn't talk coherently, but he managed to get out the word "murder." Apparently that got the cops out quickly. Almost immediately there were sirens in the distance. By the time he was off the phone, his house was ablaze. Forced to leave early, the masked assassins torched the house hoping that Simon would be trapped inside.

Simon managed to break, and then squeeze through, the small window, slicing up his arms and legs, before jumping two-and-a-half stories to the ground, breaking his ankle. What could have enriched the world, instead destroyed his life. Simon saw first-hand the depth of corruption that permeated the auto business.

With a draconian sense of retribution, an appetite for revenge, and the hot headedness that redheads and Scorpios are known for, he wasn't about to let these thugs get away with this.

As fate would have it, he soon found himself in the company of M'buy and his very determined R.A.D. team. M'buy believed in Simon and wanted to help get his invention out into the world. They explained to Simon that the business status quo would never allow something that could put them out of business to come onto the market, no matter how good it might be for the world. M'buy showed Simon examples that suggested that those who had tried to mess with big corporate gangsters had ended up dead. Simon was extremely lucky.

Simon agreed to join in their cause and use his genius to build whatever they needed to help them in their fight. In return, R.A.D. would help him find the guys who killed his family. That had been over three years ago. Since then, several of the gunmen had been found, questioned, and then handed over to Simon. What he did with them no one dared to ask, but there were rumors that Simon was a scholar of medieval torture techniques. That, combined with his electronics genius, made for something potentially very twisted and lethal.

Through these interrogations, it was discovered that Casper Degas had stolen Simon's nascent patent and was using Simon's engine for his own purposes. Needless to say, Simon was very upset, and he had thought long and hard about what he would do if he ever did meet Casper Degas.

Simon's ten-passenger stealth tank, from a distance, looked like a large, flat, desert rock. It had grenade and missile launching systems that magnetically shot large caliber exploding shells without creating any sort of heat signature, making it invisible to infrared monitoring. It had an ultrasound blaster beam and a laser beam. The magnetic engine also created no heat and no sound. Its unique stealth shape and armor-plated material deflected radar, making the vehicle essentially invisible to every sort of electronic surveillance device.

The tank had plowed through the perimeter fence as if it were a combine moving though a cornfield. With a single blast from the ultrasound cannon Simon disintegrated the block wall. Concrete blocks and dust erupted, creating a Sahara sandstorm. The tank barely slowed as it trudged over the rocky remains and headed towards the center of the compound.

Chapter 69

Hit by surprise, Casper's army was at first startled and disorganized, but they were well-trained and welcomed the excitement. Within seconds of hearing an explosion and sirens going off, a dozen men with high-caliber machine guns were on the scene and riddling the tank with bullets. When it was obvious that they were just bouncing off the armor, backup was called in and a half-dozen men with bazookas showed up. They triangulated the metal beast, then to create the maximum impact, they all fired simultaneously. There was a loud boom and a massive shock wave that shook all the windows and reverberated throughout the compound. Despite the vehicle's enormous weight, it flew six feet into the air, flipped over, bounced, then skidded on its side across the Tarmac. Its treads blew off and the barrel of the missile launcher snapped off like a branch.

The armored mechanical beast slid out of control towards a very large airplane hangar. The guards frantically shot at the tank's undercarriage, hoping to hit its fuel tank and make the thing explode. Instead bullets bounced off the undercarriage. The massive stealth tank's momentum crashed through the metal and concrete wall like it was made of Styrofoam, then sliced through a fully fueled F16 fighter jet like a steak knife though a banana, pouring hundreds of gallons of jet fuel onto the floor.

Ethan, Cameron, Patik, and Simon, along with six other men, sat inside the tank. They were tired from the long journey across the desert, but once they busted through the fence and the bullets started flying, everyone's adrenaline was pumping.

Cameron had insisted that they all keep themselves harnessed in until they came to a complete stop and then go about their planned exit procedure. When they found themselves upside down, and sliding out of control, everyone was happy they had done as she had requested.

The tank continued to slide, then grounded to a stop in the middle of the hangar. Cameron gave everyone a smile as she unfastened her seat harness. "I guess this is it!" she said. "Start our exit process." Everyone on board was a bit dizzy, their ears were ringing from the blast, nonetheless they all nodded, eager to get out and fight.

Casper's private army, excited, all rushed towards the hangar, knowing that there was no way for the intruders to get out except through the hole they had just created. This was going to be a turkey shoot.

Leading the charge, with an M16 in one hand, driving a topless Jeep with the other, was Sergeant Rodolfo Zepeda. For three years, guarding this place that no one even knew about had been excruciatingly boring. Finally, his ten years of military training was going to be utilized, and if he were lucky, he might even get to shoot someone.

All of the other private military contractors who worked at Eden, Inc. had fought wars for various corporations around the world, and they were thinking the same thing. Like Rodolfo, they wanted to show off their combat skills to their fellow soldiers. They weren't about to miss this opportunity, so all the guards had gladly left their posts and gone rushing off towards the action.

They all took positions outside the hangar and methodically started moving in. Rodolfo stationed himself behind his Jeep and watched. The soldiers were all well-trained and moved as if they could read minds. Rodolfo put the M16 to his shoulder, looked through the scope, and licked his lips with anticipation. He was both shocked and excited by these ballsy rebels. Perhaps they had something more up their sleeve. He moved in closer and smelled the harsh flammable chemical smell of the jet fuel. A moment later, it began to spill from the hangar.

Climbing out of the destroyed tank, the R.A.D. team looked like Neanderthals carving the carcass of an over-cooked mastodon. Before leaving his creation, Simon checked the weapon systems; they were all inoperable. When he designed it, he hadn't planned on a half-dozen simultaneous bazooka blasts. Nonetheless, he was still proud of his machine. Everyone inside had survived and the bundle of C4, which was packed in what he considered the trunk of his invention, had been protected and hadn't gone off.

A deluge of gunfire came from the hangar's opening. Ethan, Cameron, and the rest of the R.A.D. team ducked for cover and retreated towards the back of the building. Casper's army was moving in with practiced SWAT team tactics.

Cameron, who had assumed leadership after M'buy was killed, analyzed their predicament. Even with the extra men, they were way outnumbered. She felt the onset of panic but knew she had to stay focused on the purpose of their mission: do whatever was necessary to stop the shuttle launch and prevent the nukes from being detonated. Now with their tank out of commission and Casper's army backing them into a corner, it was going to be harder to get the job done.

The R.A.D. team took cover and focused on preventing any more of Casper's men from entering the hangar. Lugar, a big German guy who had joined the team after he was kicked out of the Marines for having a short fuse, was standing in the open and had already shot two of Casper's guards as they had tried to enter the building. Just as he was about to score his third kill, he got shot in the stomach and leg, by a sniper hiding in the opposite side of the building. Lugar doubled over, fell down, and crawled behind a forklift for cover, where no one could help him.

Ethan's main concern was making sure that Cameron was safe. A tear gas grenade flew into the hangar, landing a few yards from where Ethan, Cameron, and Patik were hiding. Ethan, abandoned is cover, immediately bullets started flying at his feet, he ran towards the grenade, scooped it up just as it was about to go off. He held his breath and tossed it out of the hangar door. The grenade popped in midair as he ran back to his hiding spot. "Let's get out of here before they decide to use real grenades," said Ethan.

"Are you kidding? And damage all these planes?" said Cameron. "Casper likes his toys way too much to blow them up just to get us."

"Huh? I hope you're right," said Ethan.

Cameron motioned for Ethan to move to the back of the building. "Let's do this!"

Cameron, Patik and Simon followed Ethan, while Lugar and the rest of the team slowly and carefully lured the mercenaries deeper into the building.

Ethan and the team faced a solid brick wall in a storage room, out of view of the entrance, on the exact opposite side of the building. The three of them looked at Ethan expectantly. "You ready?" asked Cameron. Ethan nodded, mustered his brute strength, then used his shoulder to ram a hole through the concrete block wall.

"Let's go!" shouted Cameron, guiding everyone through the hole. Cameron waited as her team, having drawn the guards into the hanger, ran past her.

Two of her men weren't moving. "Retreat!" she yelled as loudly as she could. When they didn't respond, she could do nothing but assume they had been killed. Lugar, who was seriously injured, reluctantly left his hiding spot and limped as best he could towards Cameron. As soon as he was out in the open, he was instantly hit with a dozen bullets. The big man hit the ground and slid on his own blood. He looked back at Cameron with a resolute grin, just before his life-force vanished.

Cameron said a quick thanks to Lugar for giving his life to the cause, leveled the flare gun she had been holding, shot two flares into the large puddle of jet fuel, and then ran like hell out the hole in the back wall.

Rodolfo Zepeda watched in fascination as every guard that worked on base, regardless of where they were stationed, came pouring out from their posts to join in the fight. He had grown up in South Pasadena, a small town, where he had noticed that any time there was a crime every cop in town would show up at the scene. Rodolfo always thought that seemed a bit absurd. "Was it really necessary to deploy twelve cop cars to catch a junkie who had just tried to rob a liquor store?" Also, every time he saw the cops go through their routine he thought, "Who's minding the store? Wouldn't now be the best time to rob a bank?" Watching the guards enter the hangar he suddenly understood: everyone wants a piece of the action. Recognizing this pattern of human nature, Rodolfo figured perhaps he should be the one who didn't go in. He should be the one who kept an eye on things and made sure nothing else happened while all this was going on.

He listened to all the guards shouting. They were finally seeing some combat. Curious to see what was going on up close, Rodolfo drove the Jeep up to the opening of the hangar. He got out and watched as the R.A.D. team ran towards the back of the building into a storage room. Clearly they were trapped and it would all be over in a few minutes. A second later, he saw two flares shoot out into the middle of the room, then a gigantic ball of flame blew the hangar apart.

The last thing Rodolfo knew he was flying backwards over his Jeep, his skin peeling off him like barbecued pork. He was conscious just long enough to think, "Shit! I knew I should have stayed in the Jeep!" The moment he hit the ground he was dead, a few seconds later his body was covered with two feet of burning rubble.

Cameron, Ethan, Patik, Simon and the three remaining team members ran like the wind, mere inches from where the hangar debris began slamming to the ground. They turned and watched as the last standing hangar wall collapsed, falling onto the burning remains of a pair of charred fighter jets. Like cave men hundreds of thousands of years earlier, they stared transfixed by the roaring fire, awed by its destructive power. As the smoke cleared, standing proudly in the middle of the fire and rubble like a phoenix, was Simon's tank. The blast had knocked it upright again.

They had just successfully wiped out Casper's army. It wasn't how they'd planned it, but they did it nonetheless. A wave of confidence washed over the team. They could do this. Now they needed to stop the shuttle. Cameron started towards the large main building where they assumed the shuttle's launch controls were. Patik, Simon, and three soldiers followed. Ethan didn't move, continuing to look at the burning ruin. Cameron stopped and watched him for a moment.

"Ethan, we need you. We need to complete our mission!"

"I know! But I have an idea."

Cameron looked peeved; this was no time to break ranks.

Ethan started back towards the destroyed hangar.

"What are you doing?" she called after him.

"Go without me. I think I see an opportunity to shut this thing down!"

"Let him do his thing!" said Patik, raising his gun. "We have enough firepower to get the job done."

Ethan ran back toward the remains of the hangar, and the rest of the team ran toward the main building.

Ethan had tried to take off the melted jumpsuit the night before, but it was stuck on and he didn't have enough time to deal with it. Now that he was running back into a fire he thought that perhaps it was a good twist of fate that he'd kept the suit on. Maybe it was less likely to catch on fire again since it had already been burned up and had lost most of its flammability.

In the middle of the chaos and rubble, Ethan arrived at Simon's tank. The treads had been blown off but the wheels still turned. Other than the damage from the bazookas, the tank was still fairly intact. Ethan looked up and saw the shuttle, about two football fields away. It was standing at a forty-five degree angle launch position with its back half inside the giant magnetic rail-gun.

Realizing he didn't have much time, Ethan started pushing the tank towards the shuttle, knocking charred debris out of the way. One of its wheels was bent; it scraped along the ground, creating sparks and pulling the vehicle towards the right. Ethan just pushed harder and the heavy tank quickly picked up speed. Like a charging rhino, it barreled down the Tarmac towards the shuttle.

Chapter 70

Looking down onto the Tarmac from the floor-to-ceiling office windows, Casper, The Valkyrie, The Fly, The Crusher, and Ascot watched as all hell broke loose below them. The Fly was ready to suit up and join the fight, but Casper thought it would be better to let security handle it. When the hangar exploded, they watched in horror as charred and dismembered body parts flew out of the wreckage. Anger seethed in Casper as he watched the final wall fall and the hangar burn.

The cherry on the cake was when that bastard, Ethan Stone, ran out from behind the adjacent building, towards the burning rubble. That was the final straw. Casper looked like his head was going to explode. He turned to his team of assassins and snarled, "Go kill him!" It was the call to action they had been waiting for.

Most of the building was filled with office workers who weren't privy to the impact that Casper's operations had on society and the world. They had no particular military or combat training. They shared no political or social ideology. They just worked at an office, in the middle of nowhere, running the day-to-day operations of a private corporate air base.

When the explosion happened, most reacted by trying to either hide or get the hell out of there. A herd of people got to their cars, creating a traffic jam in the parking lot. The long driveway to the main entrance was quickly clogged up with cars. People with SUVs and Jeeps pulled off the paved road and drove towards the exit on the scraggly desert terrain.

Those too scared to leave their offices hid under desks, in closets, in pantries and bathroom stalls, hoping that whoever was attacking the base had no interest in them.

The Fly walked into his office on the ground floor, located exactly four stories below Casper's office. He walked past his wall of experimental aviation photos, past a secretary's desk that never once had a secretary in it, then into a conference room. The room looked nice but it never once got used for its intended purpose. Without breaking stride, he went straight to the back of the room to a nondescript locked metal door. When he got within three feet it automatically opened. Here was the research lab where he made jet packs and designed weapons, the tools of his trade. It was also where he spent most of his time.

He put on his combat flight suit and jet pack as quickly as he could. He had no plan as to how he was going to deal with Ethan. He needed to approach the situation calmly and rationally. If he had too strong of an emotional reaction, he ran the risk of making a bad decision. He wasn't going to do that again. Out of sheer luck Ethan had evaded him the last time they fought. This time he was not going to hold back. He wasn't going to capture him and bring him in alive so the scientists could do their experiments and learn more about his unique abilities, or so Casper could recruit him and add him to the team. This time he was going to kill that son-of-a bitch once and for all.

He was about to walk out of the door when a thought occurred to him. He had been experimenting with a new shoulder-mounted laser that was linked to the sightline of his helmet, so that he could shoot wherever he looked. Now, seemed like a good time to try it out. If it could cut through two-inch solid steel in a second, it would have no problem cutting through Ethan Stone. He strapped the laser weapon onto his shoulder and walked out of the door.

* * * *

When Simon realized what Ethan was about to do, he thought he could help, so he and one of the team stayed back while Cameron, Patik and the two remaining members made their way to the main building. Cameron's plan was to get into the building, find the control room, have Patik hack into the computer system, and shut down the launch. After that, they would hack into Casper's system and grab as much data as possible.

Cameron, Patik and the two rebels carefully approached the building in a practiced military fashion. When they entered the building, they were surprised to find the lobby and the offices all empty. With their weapons drawn, they cautiously explored the room.

* * * *

Near the shuttle's magnetic launching system was a small nuclear reactor that generated millions of watts of electricity to create the huge magnetic push it took to hurl the enormous machine into high altitude. Onboard the shuttle was a pressurized solid oxygen fuel reservoir that would kick in once the ship reached its stratospheric altitude, shooting it out of the earth's gravitational pull and into orbit.

Ethan figured he could use the armored beast he was pushing to ram the shuttle and crush it. It would be risky with all the loose nukes onboard and the reactor so close by. Ethan imagined the worst: the nuclear bomb going off and the reactor cracking. The thought of being vaporized and having Eden, Inc.'s secret desert airbase becoming a big radioactive hole in the ground made him think twice. Still, as horrific as that scenario was, it was better than what Casper had in mind.

Ethan continued to push the tank until it slammed into the giant rail-gun apparatus supporting the shuttle, wedging the heavy metal beast under the shuttle's solid oxygen fuel container. Ethan had pushed hard, but the impact didn't make a dent.

With brute force he pried open the tank's trunk. Even after all the explosions and fires, there were still intact stacks of C4 plastic explosives inside. Just as Ethan was about to grab an explosive, there was a deluge of gunfire. Several bullets hit him and they stung as if he had fallen on a hornet's nest, but they didn't break his skin. Ethan abandoned his plan and ducked for cover behind the shuttle's magnetic launch pad. Frantically he looked for the origin of the shots, but he couldn't see anything. Bullets blasted all around him, keeping him stuck behind pillars of metal and concrete. Ethan's current strategy was to lie in wait until an opportunity came for him to go out and grab some of the C4 sticks.

Across the Tarmac Simon and his teammate arrived at the blown-up hangar and began to head towards the shuttle. Simon had watched Ethan push the stealth tank into the shuttle, then try to grab the explosives from inside the tank. He wondered if Ethan knew that the explosives had to be detonated remotely. Simon felt his front right pocket where he had the detonator. It was the size and shape of a fancy car key, and only he knew the code.

Simon was thinking about how he could help Ethan disable the shuttle, when a muffled groan came from the rebel standing next to him. When Simon turned to look, a lighting-fast foot kicked him in the face, breaking his nose. His eyes swelled shut and his ears began ringing; he could barely see or hear anything. In a feeble attempt to ward off his attacker, Simon blindly began punching and kicking the air around him.

He felt a fist slam into his neck and for a moment, he went into a coughing spasm and couldn't breathe. Then at lightning speed his right arm was wrenched behind his back, pushing him up onto his toes. A hand grabbed his hair and violently yanked his head back until it felt like his neck was going to snap. Pinned with his back arched, unable to move, he detected a familiar fragrance, a floral shampoo. It was something that his wife wore and the scent immediately made him ache for the life that had been taken from him. A soft voice whispered in his ear, "Do exactly as I say or I will break your fucking neck."

Chapter 71

The familiar, high-pitched whine of the jet pack got louder as The Fly flew towards Ethan. Now he knew where the endless stream of bullets had been coming from. Ethan could sense that The Fly was out for revenge. Ethan would have to come up with a new approach if he was going to survive this battle. He needed better cover and the closest possibility was the launching tower, a gigantic mechanical scaffold unit that was used to load everything into the shuttle. When it was time to take off, it lifted the shuttle and slid it into the magnetic rail gun launcher. At this moment, it offered the only place for Ethan to take cover from The Fly's relentless shooting.

Ethan waited as The Fly buzzed past him overhead, firing a stream of bullets down at him. When The Fly swooped past, Ethan made his move. He leaped out of his hiding spot, dashing towards the launch tower, and leaped up to the second-story scaffold. From there he climbed until he was almost halfway up the ten-story structure, taking cover behind a large metal beam.

The Fly made a sharp U-turn above the Tarmac, and then headed back towards Ethan. Even with Ethan's ability to perceive things in slow motion, The Fly was still fast and hard to follow. Watching from behind a metal beam, Ethan braced himself for another assault, but this time The Fly wasn't being as aggressive; it appeared that he was being careful not to create any collateral damage to the launch tower. The Fly flew past the tower much more slowly, and carefully fired only three rounds, each hitting a metal beam. "Apparently there were serious consequences to shooting at this thing," thought Ethan. This insight gave him an idea. "If you want to catch a fly, you need to think like a spider."

The launch tower had several moving parts: large gears, hydraulic hoses, fuel hoses, liquid oxygen hoses, airtight hallways, and sterile air ducts where germ-free materials were loaded

The Fly was now doing circles around the tower, bobbing, weaving, and zigzagging in the air, trying to lure Ethan out of his hiding place so he could get a clear shot at him. Ethan could see that The Fly was getting frustrated because he no longer had the upper hand. Ethan could hear him swearing even over the sound of his whining jet pack. The Fly was losing his cool and his anger was starting to show.

Ascot constantly told Ethan, "In the boxing ring, always keep your cool! When a fighter gets emotional, he sets himself up to make a mistake. Whenever you see your opponent get mad, seize the opportunity, coax him, do whatever you can to get him really mad. Inevitably he will open himself up and give you the opportunity to take the winning shot."

The Fly flew by, took another shot at Ethan and missed. When The Fly had his back to him, Ethan jumped out from behind his hiding spot, ran across the scaffold, and leaped down to the scaffolding one story below. The Fly quickly changed course and came up behind him, firing his shoulder laser. The beam missed Ethan's foot by less than an inch, just as he took cover among the hydraulic pumps and gears that moved the giant arms.

Each gear was at least twenty inches across and weighed at least a hundred pounds. This gave him another idea. He tore out three large gears, exposing an electrical conduit. He followed it and saw that it ran into a sub-panel on the opposite wall. Next to the panel was a fire extinguisher. This gave Ethan an even better idea. He grabbed the fire extinguisher and put it next to the gears.

The Fly was buzzing around in a very unpredictable manner, making him a difficult target. Ethan baited him by popping his head out of his hiding spot. The Fly blasted three shots. Ethan ducked and a large plume of white smoke fanned out. The Fly flew in closer to inspect the mysterious smoke. There was no sign of Ethan lodged inside the mechanical workings of the tower's arm. Confused, The Fly slowed down to inspect the situation, hovering in the air when out of nowhere, a greasy metal sprocket came flying towards him like a Frisbee. Instinctively, he blasted his jet pack to get out of the way, but when he shot straight up into the air he flew directly into the path of another, even larger sprocket, coming from a different direction.

The large gear from the tower's winch system hit The Fly hard, its sprockets crushing, digging, and lodging into his jet pack, making his weight imbalanced. The high-pitched whine of the engine started to descend. He tumbled five stories head-over-heels.

The Fly hit the ground face first, knocking the bug-eyed faceplate off his helmet and the heavy sprocket off his back. He lay motionless on the Tarmac less than fifty feet from the shuttle. A second later, the fuel line on the jet pack ignited and he went shooting across the Tarmac like a funny car off the starting line. His body slid and tumbled, his face scraping the ground. Twenty yards and few long seconds later, The Fly was lying on his back in the middle of the black asphalt runway. His bloody face dripped and blood pooled around his head. His eyelids had been nearly scraped off, and he was staring up at the desert sun.

Ethan stood at the open end of the fourth story scaffold and looked down at The Fly, imagining how that must feel. "If he's not dead, he probably wishes he were," Ethan thought. Then to his astonishment, The Fly's right arm moved, then his head, and then he got back onto his feet. He stood there, his flight suit full of holes, his jet pack blown apart, and his face a bloody mess. Ethan was so impressed he felt like congratulating the guy. "Damn!" he thought. "Anyone who could survive that deserved to fight another day."

The two stared at each other for a long moment. Ethan was in such utter disbelief that he failed to realize that The Fly was still a lethal adversary. Neither man moved until finally The Fly, staring at Ethan's chest, gave him the middle finger, and then blasted his shoulder laser.

The newly created shoulder-mounted laser had turned out to be fairly ineffective weapon during this battle. It really just weighed him down, making it harder to maneuver. Now, finally, he would get a chance to use it.

Ironically, during his crash landing, the laser got bent off its axis and was no longer lined up with the guidance of his helmet. When The Fly looked at his target and fired, he was confident that he was going to get to kill this pain-in-the-ass once and for all. The tracking was still working only it was now pointed sideways, so instead of hitting Ethan, the laser beam went straight into The Fly's neck. The Fly convulsed uncontrollably, violently shaking his head, and the more he moved, the more he sliced though his own neck and spinal column. Finally he fell to the ground. His trachea and the skin under his chin were the only things left that kept his head from rolling down the Tarmac.

Immediately after being flipped off, Ethan watched The Fly spaz out and then fall to the ground. Puzzled, He wasn't exactly sure what had just happened, but it looked grim. This time he didn't think that The Fly would get up again.

Unsure of what to do next, Ethan figured he should reassemble the team and go help Cameron, Patik and Simon. With a few leaps, he was off the launch tower and running full speed past the shuttle, past the blown-up hangar, and towards the main building. As he was about to enter the main building, Ethan saw Casper running out of the opposite side of the building, wearing a high-tech robotic exoskeleton combat suit. The suit, which Casper was immensely proud of, made him a hundred times stronger and ten times faster than a normal person. Ethan stopped in his tracks and watched as Casper sprang towards the shuttle at an alarming speed.

Ethan was hoping that he could have a bit of a break for just a moment, but he knew he had to stop Casper from doing whatever he was up to. With a new determination to complete their mission and spare the world from Casper's plot, Ethan ran after him with everything he had.

Chapter 72

Hiding under her desk, Molly Asbjornson noticed that she had just broken the nail on her right middle finger. She had just got her nails done the day before. On Friday she would be going to her fiancée's brother's wedding, now she was wondering when she would have the time to get her nail fixed between now and then? It was almost a two hour drive to get to the air base from Thousand Palms, a suburb of Palm Springs where she lived. She would never have taken the data entry job, but it paid well. She hadn't finished college and didn't know what else she could do. She was pretty enough to be popular in school, get dates and have romantic relationships, but she didn't feel she was pretty enough to really capitalize on her looks, so she was stuck here, as an office worker engaged to a man who managed a Palm Springs Sizzler.

Entering the room, Cameron reached down and grabbed Molly by her shoulder-length brown hair, pulled her onto her feet, then put a gun in her face. Molly wasn't sure what to do with her hands. She instinctively started to put them over her head, and then thought maybe she shouldn't, so she put them down by her side, but maybe that was wrong, so she started to put them up again. Then she stopped, thinking maybe she shouldn't.

"Put your hands up, damn it!" ordered Cameron, steely-voiced. "All the rest of you stay on the ground! Do exactly as I say and no one will get hurt!"

The manager who had hired Molly had made her sign a statement: she was never allowed to discuss her job or any of the activities that went on at Eden, Inc. with anyone, but now how was she going to be able to explain to her friends and fiancée how she broke her nail, without giving away the fact that armed gunmen had raided her office and taken her hostage?

Cameron put the gun between Molly's shoulder blades and pushed her away from the desk, then past the cubicles that covered the main office floor. In the center of the room was a miniature model of the Desert Base, the shuttle, and Asgard.

"Where is the main computer terminal that launches the shuttle?" Patik demanded, coming up next to Cameron. Molly wasn't sure what he meant, so she led him out of the room and up the stairs to the large lab where the tech guys worked.

Patik expected to find something that resembled NASA's command and control center, like he'd seen on TV and in the movies, even though he knew that wasn't realistic. After all, that space race technology was ancient. The early Apollo 11 mission, for example, used a computer that was the size of a building, had the memory capacity of one megabyte, and required a dozen men to operate.

The phone in Patik's pocket had five-hundred gigs of memory and over a thousand apps, so a simple laptop could have more than enough power to enable a single person to launch a shuttle from almost any location.

Looking for a specific computer in a building that had computers everywhere was a little bit like searching for the proverbial needle in a haystack, but Patik intuitively knew he would recognize the launch site computer the moment he saw it. This room was not the place.

* * * *

Ethan had watched Casper leap out of the far side of the main building and clear a flight of stairs. He bounced over a cactus garden and was now on the Tarmac sliding across the ground like a speed skater. Eden, Inc. did all kinds of experimental research and built a wide variety of weapons and combat devices. Multi-national corporations who had their own mercenary armies were their top clients. Sometimes they sold to wealthy countries to arm their elite forces.

Ironically, the US Government, who funded the research, usually didn't have the funds to buy the products they had paid to create. Thanks to a few changes in a free trade law that Casper was able to manipulate, Eden, Inc. weapons products could simply be sold to the highest bidder. It was not unusual for Casper's high-tech weapons to end up in the hands of the very people that US soldiers were fighting. He loved capitalism.

Casper's exoskeleton suit was a masterpiece of kinesiology. The suit modeled every muscle in the body perfectly. Inside the suit, Casper's body was encapsulated in a cushioning gel that responded to the body's electrical impulses. Tiny muscle movements triggered the magnetic and hydraulic mechanisms that moved the titanium plastic alloy suit. The movements felt completely natural. Anything a person could do with the suit off, they could do with the suit on. The only difference was that with the suit on they could do it much faster, at a hundred times their normal strength. The suit's boots were equipped with rollerblade-type wheels that Casper could skate on, as well as shock-absorbing springs that enabled him to leap up twenty feet then land on the ground easily.

Even though Ethan had just finished battling The Fly and was exhausted, he pursued Casper towards the shuttle with dogged fierceness. As fast as Ethan was, Casper was faster. Within a few seconds, Casper was pulling the tank out from underneath the shuttle's fuel reservoir. Obviously, Cameron and Patik hadn't been able to hack into the computer, so the only thing keeping the shuttle from launching was the fact that there was an obstacle in the way. Ethan realized he needed to put the tank back quickly or the shuttle would be launched.

Casper had to be careful how he moved the tank lodged under the shuttle. If he wasn't careful, he could damage the shuttle and possibly even tear a hole in the fuel silo. Just as the burnt metal tank carcass slid freely from beneath the shuttle, Ethan ran up from behind and jumped on Casper's back.

Casper, who was a black belt in various martial arts, instinctively kneeled and tossed Ethan over his shoulder and onto the ground. Casper leaped up to stomp on Ethan's chest, but Ethan saw it coming, and rolled out from under the intended blow just as Casper's boot made a pothole in the Tarmac.

Ethan jumped onto his feet, and looked Casper squarely in the eyes. It seemed like a lifetime ago when they shook hands in the condo at the Eden, Inc. headquarters. Ethan had done some serious soul-searching and was finally clear on what kind of person he wanted to be, consequently he was now seeing Casper in a completely new light. It was not favorable.

The two men stared at each other. Each waited for the other to make the first move. Casper's sweaty bald head and small dark eyes reminded Ethan of a reptile. He was embarrassed to think that he had actually agreed to work for this bastard.

Ethan thought about all the techniques Ascot had taught him to regain his strength and focus when he was tired and beaten up. Ethan took four quick short breaths in his nose and felt oxygen permeate his cells. All the little bangs and dings he had gotten from The Fly were blocked out of his mind. He was now focused on Casper. This was it.

With venom in his eyes Casper planted his robotic boots and jump-kicked like a striking cobra. Ethan knocked his foot out of the way but received a phenomenally fast combination of punches and kicks. He kept his guard up and blocked Casper's attack, but he was clearly on defense and couldn't get a punch in. Casper leaped up and did a roundhouse kick, at lightning speed, that clipped Ethan in the shoulder, knocking him to the ground. Even with his ability to see things in slow motion, he could barely keep up with Casper's inhuman speed.

Ethan was trained to fight boxers. He wasn't prepared to fight airborne kicks and spins. He got up onto his feet before Casper could kick him while he was down. Casper came at him with a series of punches. While Ethan was struggling to block them, he unexpectedly felt Casper's titanium plastic alloy knee clobber him in the stomach. Ethan doubled over, leaving himself open for Casper to land a right cross square in the jaw. It was the first time since he was back on Earth that Ethan felt weak and beaten up.

* * * *

Cameron pushed the gun into Molly's back, trying to encourage her to walk faster, but her high heels and tight skirt forced her to take short, clumsy steps. One rebel stayed back to cover them while the rest of the team got a tour of the building as if a real estate agent were conducting an open house. It quickly became obvious that she was leading them around on a floor that she had never been on herself and that she didn't know anything useful. Finally Cameron got fed up and told the remaining team member to, "Take this dingbat downstairs and put her back with the others," while she and Patik continued to search. They had to be close, they were running out of places to look.

On the top floor, at the end of the corridor, they saw a large half-open door. They could hear people inside talking. Immediately Patik knew that was Casper's office and the controls had to be in there. He pulled out his weapon and the two quietly walked towards the door.

Inside, Simon sat on a desk with his hands tied behind his back. His eyes were swollen and dried blood was crusted around his nose and mouth. The detonator for the plastic explosives that had been in his pocket was now sitting on the shuttle's control panel, a few feet away just inches away from The Valkyrie.

The Valkyrie and Ascot stood and stared out the large window with their backs to the door. They were watching Casper and Ethan fight on the Tarmac like two gladiators. Ascot reached down and felt the exoskeleton braces on his legs, it was his way of constantly reminding himself that without Casper Degas and Eden, Inc. he would be a cripple with no place to live, no money, and no future. He watched the fight with a trained eye, and saw Ethan use combinations that he had taught him. He couldn't help but root for Ethan, even though he knew that he was no match for Casper in his robotic suit. Casper had told Ascot earlier that he still wanted Ethan on his team. Ascot felt that given a little more time Ethan would come around and see his situation in life more pragmatically. Then Ethan would realize what an incredible opportunity Casper was offering him.

* * * *

They found it. In the middle of Casper's office was the shuttle's virtual cockpit. There was a joystick, a panel of switches, and a large visual display—it looked a like a high-tech video game.

The shuttle could be flown: by a pilot onboard, remotely from the office, or completely by computer. Today's flight was going to be a computer-controlled mission.

Patik looked at Cameron and said nothing, but his eyes conveyed his desperation to stop the shuttle. As one, they prepared to attack, their intention to take out Ascot and The Valkyrie. Suddenly from behind there was a loud crash, followed by a gunshot.

Cameron and Patik turned to see their team member, down the hall, in the fierce grip of The Crusher. The armed rebel was returning from having just taken their useless tour guide back to the ground floor. The Crusher, who had been hiding in the shadows snuck up on him, grabbed him from behind, and slammed his head into the corridor wall. The rebel got off a shot, but didn't hit anything. The Crusher snatched the gun from the rebel's hand then head-butted him square in the nose. The rebel's limp body slid to the ground. The Crusher looked like Big Foot in a suit. He turned and stared at Cameron and Patik with fury in his eyes and blood on his tie. Then suddenly something at the end of the hallway distracted the behemoth. He turned, coming up the stairs was their last R.A.D. teammate.

Chapter 73

Face down on the Tarmac, Ethan felt the hot asphalt sting his cheek while the desert sun beat down on the back of his neck. Blows that would have been lethal to any other person were brutally administered to his face and body, courtesy of Casper, who was now fast, strong and impervious to pain. Despite Ethan's extraordinary abilities, he was still flesh and bones and that made it hard to compete with super-high-tech titanium-plastic alloy.

Woozy and barely able to move, he watched as Casper successfully dragged the tank further away from beneath the shuttle. There was no damage to the undercarriage. Now there was nothing to stop the shuttle from being launched.

Casper started back towards Ethan. Despite the fact that his face and bald head were covered in sweat, he looked very satisfied. Ethan knew this came down to life and death. Not just for him but for millions of people. He was their only defense. He had to do something.

Casper started to run, then took a big leap towards Ethan with the clear intention of squashing his head. Every primordial survival instinct in the limbic portion of Ethan's brain fired the needed synapses. As if guided by another power, Ethan found himself on his feet, running as fast as he could towards the tank. Ethan could see Casper's shadow closing in behind him. A small rocket shot out of Casper's arm. Instinctively Ethan dove to the ground, somersaulted behind the tank, closed his eyes, and covered his ears. The rocket hit the corner of the massive beast, crumpling its armor, and popping open the hood to expose the stacks of C4.

Ethan opened his eyes just in time to see Casper jump through the flames of the burning wreckage. Ethan got on his feet, faked left, then leaped to the right, successfully putting the smoldering tank between himself and Casper. If Casper moved so did Ethan, constantly maintaining a buffer of distance between them. As the game continued, Casper got frustrated. Ethan, backed by his boxing training, wasn't easily fooled. The two men edged around the tank.

Ethan found himself in front of the stack of C4. It was now his turn to go on the offensive. Doing the best sleight of hand he could muster, Ethan once again faked right, then lunged left, grabbing two packs of the C4 without breaking stride.

Both men seemed to have the same idea. Like a choreographed trampoline act, they simultaneously jumped over the tank towards each other. Ethan twisted his body and landed a knee into Casper's stomach. As Casper's body flipped over in mid-air, Ethan slapped the C4 onto Casper's back, right between his shoulder blades. Casper hit the ground with his heels, slid, then landed on his butt. Ethan landed on his feet. Finally grabbing the advantage, he flipped the tank onto its side and pushed it over onto Casper as he struggled to get up.

Casper had given The Valkyrie and Ascot instructions on how to launch the shuttle once he had pulled the tank out of the way. They were in his office waiting for him to give them the signal. Lying on the ground with a tank on his back, Casper took the opportunity to catch his breath and contact his office. He activated the speaker phone on his desk. He was immediately connected and he could hear the hum of the office. Then he heard Ascot and The Valkyrie talking.

"Launch the shuttle!" shouted Casper.

"I'm on it!" said Ascot. A second later, Casper could hear the tapping of a keyboard.

"Good," he grunted, as he crawled out from under the tank. "Asgard is a masterpiece of engineering and technology. It will revolutionize dozens of industries." Casper had crawled out from under the tank and was now sitting on the ground, prying his foot out from under the remains of the metal beast. "But people are thick-headed, that's why we need to give them an incentive. After we drop these bombs, I promise you all my contacts will be calling and.—"

A loud gunshot interrupted Casper's rambling. "What was that?" There was no response in his earpiece. "Can you hear me? Launch the shuttle now!" he shouted. Casper pried his foot out from under the rubble then looked up at his office window. The tinted window was intact. He got up as fast as he could, and saw Ethan running towards the shuttle. "There is no way I'm letting you mess this up!" shouted Casper, speed-skating across the Tarmac towards Ethan.

* * * *

In Casper's office, when The Valkyrie saw Cameron, blood-lust overtook her. She desperately wanted revenge from their last encounter. Ignoring her training, which would have had her strategically assess the situation and determine the best chance of winning, she simply charged Cameron like a Pit bull. Cameron tried to pull the gun she had strapped to her hip, but The Valkyrie knocked it out of her hand.

The Crusher saw that the two nerdy-looking rebels were going to be easily handled, so he ran down the hall, chasing the armed rebel in the combat suit.

Ascot was standing in front of the launch terminal keyboard when Patik ran towards him, pointing a gun.

"Stop!" shouted Patik. His voice was just loud enough to pierce through the sound of the two women fighting. Ascot watched Patik run into the room and decided that the little Indian dude in the white linen suit didn't seem particularly threatening, so he returned his focus to the screen, bit his lip, and then with a sudden burst of urgency, he typed in the last bit of the launch code sequence. Once everything was complete, Ascot pressed enter and a window popped on the screen, indicating that the countdown sequence had begun.

When Patik got within ten feet of Ascot, the once renowned boxing coach spun around and leaped toward the surprised Patik, grabbing the gun and wrenching it out of his hand. The sudden move caused Patik to lose his balance. Ascot grabbed the small-framed man by the collar and belt, then tossed him like a bale of hay over the table, right across the few pieces of fruit that still lay on the silver tray. Patik was a techie, a computer hacker—not a trained combat guy. This stuff was clearly out of his element. He slammed into the wall so hard he actually made an impression deep enough to suspend his body for a few seconds, before tumbling off onto the floor. When he hit the ground, every nerve in his body screamed in agony. He lay face down on the floor. The last thing he remembered before passing out was the smell of the very expensive, commercial carpet.

Ascot went over to help The Valkyrie. "I got this!" she screamed, while landing a right roundhouse kick to Cameron's left shoulder, spinning and knocking her off-balance. "This bitch is mine!" The Valkyrie grabbed Cameron by the hair, then slammed her face into the floor to a ceiling window. Cameron fell backwards onto the carpet as the large window vibrated. The Valkyrie, assuming Cameron was unconscious, casually leaned over to grab her throat, when Cameron fired an unexpected kick to the side of The Valkyrie's head.

Ascot reached for Cameron. "I got it!" shouted The Valkyrie, shaking Ascot off. Cameron seized the opportunity and landed a strong left jab and a right cross, knocking The Valkyrie to the ground. With a look of absolute fury in her eyes, Cameron leaped into the air, ready to land a lethal blow by stomping on The Valkyrie's neck, but Ascot grabbed Cameron's leg in mid-air and spun her around like a cowboy with a lasso. He tossed her across the room. She flew over the food table and into the same wall that Patik had just slammed against. There was a loud thunk and the two bodies lay on top of each other, neither moving a muscle.

The Valkyrie was caught between anger and gratitude for Ascot's help as he assisted her onto her feet. They looked at the computer. Large numbers slowly counting down the shuttle's launch filled the screen. 9-8-7...

Ascot and the Valkryie looked out of the window and watched Ethan stick a white brick onto the shuttle's solid oxygen fuel silo and then run towards the building. Casper was about fifty feet behind, gaining on him quickly. "Casper, the shuttle!" shouted The Valkyrie, hoping the speakerphone was still on. There was no response. Casper slid past the shuttle, continuing to chase Ethan. Ascot looked over at the countdown on the computer monitor: 5-4...

Simon sat motionless, his hands tied behind his back and his feet shackled. He knew now that no matter what happened, what was left of his team would all be dead anyway. Somewhere in his core came the realization that there was one thing left he could do. While The Valkyrie and Ascot were distracted, Simon hopped over to the console, grabbed the detonator, then slid back onto the desk. Without being able to see what he was doing, he concentrated as hard as he ever had in his life.

The detonator had three buttons, one that scrolled the numbers up, one that locked them into place, and the one that finally detonated the C4 plastic explosives. Simon carefully felt the small device like a blind person would. He felt every curve, making sure he knew exactly which button he was pushing. He blocked out all the chaos in the room. Then he methodically pushed the first button. He had to make sure not to lose count before locking the number in place and moving on. This was their last hope.

The Valkyrie and Ascot stared out of the window in anticipation of the shuttle's launch, when something occurred to Ascot. He looked over at the launch pad console. "Where is the detonator?" They immediately looked over at Simon, fiddling with something behind his back. The Valkyrie grabbed her gun, and without a second of hesitation, shot Simon in the head. With the remorse of a hungry spider, she watched the red-headed man fall sideways, roll off the table and bounce on the floor. He rolled onto his side, revealing a grotesque, quirky, blood-soaked grin.

* * * *

Ethan was running as fast as he could across the Tarmac towards the main building. Casper was gaining quickly. Within fifty feet of the door, Ethan felt Casper's strong hand grab his shoulder. Ethan spun around, taking Casper with him, then dropped to his knees. With all his forward inertia, Casper tumbled over Ethan and somersaulted back towards the shuttle. Then unexpectedly, the light on the C4 brick, stuck behind Casper's shoulder blades, turned from red to green. Ethan's stomach clenched, he knew he had less than five seconds to evacuate. He needed to get as far away from Casper as possible, but Casper wasn't going to just stay put and allow him run away. A few feet away Ethan saw a large desert rock, part of the cactus garden landscaping. He picked it up, and then tossed it on top of Casper just as he was getting up. The big rock was heavy and successfully knocked him back down allowing Ethan more time to run like a thoroughbred from a starting gate.

Ascot looked over at the countdown on the computer monitor: 2-1. He watched as the shuttle silently shot out of its magnetic thruster and into the air. At this point, they no longer had control; everything was automated. A second later, a sonic boom shook the windows.

Satisfied that they had gotten the job done, despite all the interruptions, Ascot and the Valkrie breathed a sigh of relief. It was now too late now for the R.A.D. team to thwart their plans.

Ascot awkwardly tried to embrace The Valkyrie, but when he stepped toward her she sidestepped, turned and put up her right palm for a high five. Feeling a little dissed, he settled for what he could get, and smacked her palm, then turned to watch the shuttle soar into the sky and begin its journey.

There was a moan from across the room. Unsure as from where it had come, The Valkyrie curiously walked over to Simon's body, got down on all fours, and pulled the detonator from his hand. She stood up, then froze for a moment.

"What's up?" asked Ascot, seeing the concern on her face.

She merely held up the detonator. The little red light had turned green. A half-second later, the C4 exploded on the shuttle, igniting the solid oxygen fuel tank onboard. The sky erupted in a blinding white flash, followed by a deafening explosion. All the tinted safety glass that lined the side of the building imploded, scattering shards like buckshot.

The concussion tossed The Valkyrie on top of Ascot. He fell back, knocking over the thick wooden table, serendipitously creating a barrier that protected Cameron and Patik from the flying debris. Another fluke: had The Valkyrie not heard the mysterious moan and moved to investigate, she and Ascot would have been positioned so that he would have landed on top of her. His steel-hard skin would have easily protected them from the jagged jigsaw of glass and metal that was now deeply lodged in her back and legs. Now she lay on top of Ascot, barely able to move, breathing shallowly, her entire body a bloody mess.

The tank disintegrated from the trunk full of C4, its armor blowing into a million pieces and flying into the air in all directions. Fiery tank and shuttle debris rained down from the sky, pelting the entire airbase, putting potholes and burn marks on the few things that weren't already destroyed. A row of helicopters, small planes, and cars, all parked on the Tarmac, did cartwheels down the runway. Crunching, scraping and exploding as the fuel inside them ignited, they caused a chain reaction of devastation.

The giant electrical cables that connected the small nuclear reactor to the magnetic launcher tore off like laundry on the line during a hurricane. Hundreds of thousand of volts of electricity arced as the two ends danced on the Tarmac, creating a massive moving Tesla coil. Static electricity filled the air with charged particles, electrifying the tiny amount of moisture in the desert air.

Within a half-mile radius all the insects, reptiles, and small rodents who were innocently going about their day suddenly experienced a strange new reality, as their small bodies were zapped as if hit by a bolt of invisible lightening.

The nuclear reactor stood intact, its dome stoic like a rock on the shore, as waves of fiery wreckage washed over it. It was a feat of engineering genius that it didn't break open and spew out radiation, which would have made the area completely uninhabitable for hundreds of miles and hundreds of years.

The dozen Soviet-made nuclear bombs shot out of the shuttle explosion in every possible direction, each bomb tumbling through the air like a bad kick-off at an amateur football game. Each was outfitted with a sophisticated detonator that required it be properly armed before it could explode. Not until a few seconds before deployment over it respective target would each warhead be armed. Their unimaginably powerful depleted uranium casings hit the ground several miles apart, and their weight caused them to bury themselves deep into the desert sand.

The explosion had tossed Ethan into and through the double-hinged glass doors of the office building. Glass and debris covered his body. He crawled onto his feet, stood up, looked out onto the Tarmac, and witnessed the massive destruction.

Ethan brushed the glass, dust, and debris off his tingling body, then out of his hair, now sticking straight out from the static electricity in the air. Ethan rubbed dust out of his eyes. His vision was blurry and his ears were ringing, but they had just achieved a one-in a-million victory! This blow was a game changer and he had a burst of renewed inspiration. They had accomplished their mission. Now they just had to get out alive.

Casper lay motionless across the room. He had just stood up when the C4, stuck to the back of his suit, exploded. The blast tossed him twenty-five feet into the air, tumbling into the window of the main building. He lay in the rubble, dazed. As he became more cognizant, he was pleased to discover that his suit, although extremely damaged and now non-responsive, had managed to stay in one piece. The shock-absorbing gel inside had protected him from the blast and from all the material that now covered him.

Ethan stretched his neck and arms. Then for good measure, he grabbed the large marble desk that had been knocked over by the explosion, and tossed it across the room as if it were some hybrid Olympian gladiator sport. The large slab flew over a sea of broken glass and office refuse, then landed right on top of Casper, making a loud solid thunk.

Satisfied that Casper wasn't going anywhere, Ethan set off, determined to find Cameron, Patik and Simon.

Chapter 74

Urgently Ethan raced through the rubble. The mangled mess and mayhem reminded him of the blown-out buildings in old WWII movies after the German blitzkrieg. Doors were blown off their hinges, the walls were torn apart, exposing the air-conditioning tubing, plumbing pipes, and electrical wiring. Ethan arrived at the stairway and didn't break his strid, leaping six steps at a time, straight up to the top floor. Instinctively he knew that if Cameron or any of the team were still alive, that's where they would be.

Propped up against the railing at the top of the stairs, as some kind of macabre warning sign, was a dead R.A.D. soldier. His gun was diagonal against his chest, and his head was perfectly balanced so he looked straight ahead. When Ethan got closer, he saw that the man's eyes were open and he looked as if he were still alive. Ethan waved his hand in front of the man's face, half-expecting to see him blink. Nothing. Then he slightly nudged the body and it easily tipped over. The gun slid out of the dead man's arms, bounced and tumbled down the carpeted stairs, then came to rest on the middle landing.

The top floor received the most damage. A thick cloud of dust hovered in the air and could be seen in the streaks of sunlight that poured through the holes in the walls. Sensing he was on the right track, Ethan cautiously walked towards the large office with the oversized double doors.

Halfway down the hall, lying among the burnt debris was the remains of the last R.A.D. soldier. His neck had snapped so that his head was perpendicular to his body. Chunks of glass and metal were embedded into his face so that the burnt flesh blended seamlessly into the piles of wreckage. Amongst the surreal collage of glass, metal, skin, and bones, was a perfectly intact left ear. Its irrefutable humanness sent a shiver up Ethan's spine.

Inside Casper's office, Cameron lay on top of Patik. Her head hurt. She heard blurry voices in the distance, like the murmur of a crowd filtering into an empty gymnasium. Then she started to become aware and remember where she was, and how she had gotten there. Finally she opened her eyes. She saw that she had drooled down the back of Patik's neck. She rolled off her comrade, sat up and rubbed her eyes, expecting to clear them, then realized that she was looking through a heavy layer of dust.

She heard a groan and instantly recognized the voice of The Valkyrie. Without making a sound, Cameron peeked over the heavy wood table. She was awed by the devastation. The floor-to-ceiling windows were gone. Small chunks of glass and metal covered the carpeted floor and had perforated the walls. She quickly felt her legs and stomach—no injuries, no blood. She checked the rest of her body. After her quick examination, she was pleased and amazed to find nothing wrong. The heavy table had blocked all the flying glass and detritus.

Sitting in a chair across the room was The Valkyrie and that douche-bag who had grabbed her and tossed her into the wall. He was bent over the bitch with his hand on her shoulder. It looked like he was softly whispering something into her ear. He stood up, surveying the room, and walked toward the back of the room to a wall of cabinets.

Patik groaned, sat up and watched Cameron peek over the table. He quickly remembered where he was and that he wasn't cut out for this sort of work. From now on, Patik vowed silently, computer hacking was all he was going to do. No more of this out-in-the-field combat shit. Cameron looked at Patik. He too was miraculously unscathed by the explosion. She put her fingers to her lips.

Now The Valkyrie was alone and an inner fury erupted inside Cameron. She pulled a small automatic handgun that was strapped under her pants on the inside of her left thigh. She looked over at Patik, then at Ascot, who was rummaging through the cabinets. Then she tossed Patik the gun. "Cover me!" she whispered. "I have a score to settle!"

The blonde assassin was sitting up with her head back and her eyes closed. Quietly Cameron stood up and noticed Simon lying on the ground. It was clear that he had been shot in the head. A burst of rage surged through Cameron. She jumped over the table and ran toward the wounded assassin. The noise from the crunching glass and metal alerted The Valkyrie to Cameron's approach.

Just as Cameron reached her, The Valkyrie opened her eyes and despite her injuries and extreme pain, she rose to her feet and threw a left jab at Cameron, surprising her surprise attacker. Cameron dodged the blow, so instead of getting a fist squarely in the jaw, she got clipped on the shoulder. Cameron fell backwards, tripping over a piece of an office chair, then landing less than two feet from a large window frame.

The Valkyrie reached down and grabbed a sharp metal shard about the size of a large butcher's knife. Desperate and determined, the warrior goddess screamed like a banshee and lunged. Cameron rolled onto her back just in time to block the crazed, shard-wielding warrior from leaping down on her. Cameron thrust her knees up, catching The Valkyrie in the stomach, grabbed the assassin's shoulders, and flipped her head over heals. As Valkyrie somersaulted she stabbed Cameron, with the shard, just below her left clavicle.

The Valkyrie landed on her back, halfway out of the open window, with her legs suspended in midair and nothing to grab onto. Cameron rolled onto her feet and watched as The Valkyrie, arms and legs flailing, began to slowly slide out of the open window. Cameron reached down and grabbed the crazed assassin by her long blond hair. Cameron's shoulder was bleeding and the pain was intense, but she stopped the assassin from plunging ten stories onto the pavement. Cameron wanted to kick The Valkyrie's ass but was suddenly conflicted. She had never actually killed anyone before and wasn't sure if she could do it. Then without rhyme or reason crazed assassin tried to stab Cameron again with the shard, and inadvertently sliced through half of her own hair. The remaining hair tore like a newspaper and she slid out the window. Cameron fell back into the room, holding a handful of blond hair.

Patik fired three rounds at Ascot, who Ignored the bee sting of the bullets, and grabbed Cameron as she fell back, wrenching her arm and pinning it behind her. Then he grabbed her hair, pulling her head back. He turned to look at Patik who wasn't sure what to do. He thought shooting Ascot might slow him down; even if he was like Ethan and bullets didn't penetrate his skin. Now Ascot held Cameron as a shield. Patik wasn't a very good shot. He wasn't about to try to shoot him again and risk hitting Cameron.

Ascot stood in the middle of the room, unsure of who he should deal with first: The geek who just shot him three times, or the spitfire who just tossed The Valkyrie out the window.

The situation seemed ridiculous to Ascot. This wasn't his fight. He just wanted to live a good life and finally settle down, fall in love and have a family. Casper created an opportunity for him to have money, power, and influence. He could do good things with that. He was once a community organizer, a political activist, and a TV fitness celebrity. Didn't these R.A.D. rebels realize that he had done good work and had helped people? Now everything was falling apart.

Ethan suddenly appeared at the doorway and saw Patik pointing a gun at Ascot, who had Cameron pinned in his arms. He realized immediately that this wasn't going to be a simple rescue. Ascot had working legs that were no doubt as strong as his own. Everything Ethan had learned about fighting he learned from Ascot, so if Ascot wanted to hurt him, he probably could. Ethan assessed that Ascot wasn't a bad guy, even now. That's why he was reluctant to cause Cameron or Patik harm.

There was no doubt that Casper had offered Ascot the life he had always dreamed of. Ironically, Ascot was the one who had taught him that when you hang out with crazy people, their craziness rubs off onto you. Their insane ideas start to make sense. He had said that's what happened to him with his ex-wife. It wasn't until her craziness started to really become destructive that he realized what was going on.

Ethan walked over to Patik: "I'll deal with this, you go!"

Patik nodded, knowing he wouldn't be very effective here. As a hacker, he had a greater purpose, and there was still a lot more work to do. This was his window of opportunity to get inside the computers of Eden, Inc. Patik trotted out of the room. He figured that Ethan knew Ascot better than anyone, and he knew Ethan cared for Cameron, so as difficult as it was, he had to trust Cameron's fate to Ethan.

Ethan's ears were still ringing, his vision was blurry and every part of his body hurt. He stood ten feet away, facing Ascot and Cameron. Ascot looked fit and unscathed. Ethan knew, particularly in the condition he was in, that he would get his ass kicked if he tried to fight Ascot, so a better strategy would be to appeal to his former mentor's higher nature. Ethan looked at Ascot: "Hi!" said Ethan awkwardly.

Ascot looked dumfounded. "Hi."

"How you doing?"

Ascot lifted Cameron into the air and pulled her head back until she gave a whimper of pain. "I'm great. I'm about to snap your girlfriend in half."

Ethan nodded. "So I see. Do you have to do that?" He paused, never breaking eye contact. "She just wants a better world."

Ascot loosened his grip. Cameron stood frozen, taking short shallow breaths. She was afraid to move and not at all sure where this conversation was going.

"Is championing humanity really a threat to you?" asked Ethan. "What happened to the progressive guy who taught me about corruption? How throughout history, equality and justice were always blocked by the greedy and powerful?"

Ascot just looked at him.

Ethan continued. "How the ignorant masses are manipulated by religion and TV, and don't know what's really going on?"

"Ha!" interrupted Ascot. "You know it's easy to be idealistic when you don't have anything, and the system isn't working for you, it's all an abstraction. But when you have something invested, the status quo doesn't look so bad."

Ethan nodded. "No doubt that's true. But what if the status quo is destructive! Which means if you support it, you are a destroyer of good things."

Ascot grabbed Cameron and pushed her towards the middle of the room, closer to Ethan. "I spent almost eight years in that floating sardine can, unable to walk. I don't want to struggle for the rest of my life. I did that already. I have an opportunity to be among the people who really run the world. I can have and do anything I want. I earned that!"

Ethan nodded: "That could be true, but power is like junk food. The more you eat, the hungrier you get, and the more you crave. And when all the money and power doesn't satisfy you, you start craving weirder and weirder shit."

Ascot snorted: "Look, you still have your legs! I don't! What am I going to do?"

Ethan shrugged. "I know it makes sense to you to be in Casper's corner. He has all the comforts a person could have, but you're the one who taught me in the boxing ring that the moments in life, the ones that have the deepest meaning, are when we overcome our biggest obstacles and when we do it on our own." Ascot listened, staring at the floor. "You have so much to offer the world that is positive. I believe you and I have survived because we have a greater purpose than to just be comfortable. You taught me that!"

Ascot lifted his head. "I thought the world worked that way but it doesn't. The rich get richer, the poor get poorer and the powerful get what they want. I was always on the losing side of things. I'm tired of losing!"

Ethan cocked his head and looked at Ascot, a little bewildered, like a dog staring as his master eating a sandwich. "If the powerful always win, then India would still be British, Germany would still be Fascist, and the US would have won in Vietnam. You know as well as anyone that real power comes from knowing that what you are doing is right. Doing what's right is a tangible, measurable thing. It can be tested and verified."

Ascot recalled when he had said this very thing to Ethan years ago, while explaining the South African apartheid system.

"What do you want your legacy to be?" asked Ethan, remembering how earlier that very question made him stop and think. Ascot felt sullen and confused. Ethan continued. "Do you go down Casper's path and stand for repression and self-serving greed, or do you want to stand for something better?"

Ascot gave Ethan the look of the teacher acknowledging that the student had surpassed him.

Ethan saw that he was making some headway. "You taught me that when a person stands for something bigger than himself, he transcends himself. His life represents an idea, and ideas are immortal, but that idea can be anything: good, kind, optimistic, loving, or it can be bad, cruel, and greedy. Do you really want to discard everything you've stood for most of your life? Could you really live with yourself?"

Ascot took a deep breath, then slowly began to release his grip on Cameron.

Chapter 75

Shocked, Cameron shuffled cautiously away from Ascot. Once she had taken a few steps beyond his reach, she bolted across the room and into Ethan's arms. They hugged. It was the first time since Ethan had been back that he felt the old, deep level of connection. Until now, there was always a cautious barrier between them. Now something had melted inside her and she was his. He felt her warm body press against his. He kissed her cheek and tasted the salty tears that ran down her face. She squeezed him as hard as she could.

Ethan looked over at Ascot, who had just turned his back to them and was now shuffling across the room, his eyes down at his feet. Time stopped for Ethan. For the first time in his life, he was one with someone. Ethan finally felt that his journey had come full circle, leading him to a positive purpose. Now he was complete. He ran his hands down Cameron's tousled reddish hair, feeling its silky softness. All thoughts of danger and emergency were gone. He was only aware of the ecstasy that he felt embracing her. He thought about what an amazing person she was. What an incredible journey they had gone through together, and how proud he was to be with her.

He kissed her cheek again. Then she turned her head and kissed his lips. A surge of passion flicked on as quickly as light filling up a room. Their tongues connected and his desire jumped off the charts. Since the day he left, Ethan had fantasized about kissing her, hugging her, and being with her. It was what motivated him to survive all those years alone. Now, finally, he was where he wanted to be.

A loud BANG snapped Ethan from his thoughts. Cameron's body jerked, then instantly went limp. Blood splattered across Ethan's left arm, putting bright shiny red dots on his burnt red jumpsuit. His arms and legs looked like a Jackson Pollock painting. Cameron died instantly, her lips still warm on his.

Casper stood in the doorway with a high-tech gun in his hand and a maniacal look on his face. He was wearing the muscle-contracting insulation of his exoskeleton suit. It looked like a wet suit covered in small fiber-optic wires. The wires sent an extra electrical current from his brain, stimulating his muscles, making them respond faster and stronger. Casper had similar strength and speed as he had before, but now without the heavy, clumsy armor.

Ethan held Cameron. Her warm blood dribbled out of her head onto his arm. A new level of hatred swelled through Ethan. He had never wanted to hurt someone so badly before in his life.

"Hey space boy, sorry to interrupt your fun, but I'm a little pissed off. When I get pissed off, things get a little unpredictable."

Ethan held Cameron's lifeless body close to his. Tears started running down his cheeks.

"Oh, boo-hoo, I see I made you upset," snarled Casper. "I told you that you could have all the pussy you wanted, but you had to go and fuck it all up." Casper pulled the trigger of his big gun and a machine gun burst of rounds flew into what was left of the ceiling. Debris and chunks of ceiling tile fell to the ground, exposing the pipes and wires hidden up there. Ethan and Ascot both jumped from the noise.

Casper smiled, as his shark-like eyes bore into Ethan. "I believe in the three-strikes-you're-out rule. I've given you at least three opportunities to do the right thing and be a team player. Every time you have failed and betrayed me. And I'm the one guy who could have given you anything you wanted!" He bounced his index finger off his forehead. "Not too smart!"

Casper looked over at Ascot and pointed to the ground where The Valkyrie had dropped her gun after shooting Simon. "Pick that gun up off the floor and kill this prick!"

Ascot looked resigned, then he spoke in a calm, measured tone. "I can't do that, and even if I did shoot him, it wouldn't hurt him."

Casper was furious. "You still on board or not?" Casper's face and bald head was beginning to turn fire-engine-red and his eyes squinted into tiny slits. "Did these R.A.D. idiots fill your head with their idealistic nonsense?"

"No, I just came to my senses." Said Ascot, as he thought about how he could be diplomatic. He considered that if he presented some universal principles of right and wrong, simple fairness, and appealed to Casper's ego, then perhaps he could talk some sense into the man. "You have the technology to do some real good in the world. The Valhalla II project."

"Call it Asgard!" growled Casper, interrupting.

Ascot nodded. "Asgard could be the best thing ever built to study our solar system, global weather patterns, the effects of man-made pollution on the environment. You hold the technology to reverse the damage we've done to the planet for the last four hundred years. Eden, Inc. could change the world, as we know it, for the better, and make tons of money in the process."

Casper spit on the ground. "Do I look like a fucking tree-hugger to you?"

Ascot stood up straight, puffed out his chest and spoke in his authoritarian coaching voice. "Think about what you are doing and ask yourself if there isn't another way you could get what you want?"

Casper pointed his big high-tech gun at Ascot. "I got news for you, tough guy. You may be strong and your skin may be hard, but you're not indestructible."

Ascot saw the tunnel-vision focus on Casper's Pitbull face and knew he wasn't getting through. With all his might, he lunged towards Casper. At that exact moment, Casper shot Ascot with sixty rounds of high velocity, gas propelled, fifty-caliber armor- piercing bullets.

"That's right, tough guy!" Casper shouted. "Go ahead, try to bully me!"

Ascot's steel-hard skin and heavy body withstood the first ten rounds, but then the force of the high velocity bullets stopped his forward momentum, and then began to penetrate his skin, tearing through his molecularly dense organs. His exoskeleton legs held him upright as the lethal bullets pushed his body backwards towards the open window. As suddenly as they had started, the bullets stopped. Ascot stood two feet from the window ledge, his blue and white sweat suit torn to pieces. Ascot looked sadly at Ethan. "I'm sorry, man," he whispered, drawing a last, raggedy breath.

Ethan looked at the man who has been a friend and mentor to him. "Ascot?"

Ascot's eyes closed for the last time, his chest exhaling weakly as the life drained from his body. The exoskeleton legs kept him on his feet, but Ascot was gone.

"Feel that?" shouted Casper as he waved the gun in the air, staring at the remains of Ascot. "That's real power!" Then Casper fired another burst of gunfire into Ascot's chest, knocking him off balance. His stiff legs tipped like a tree and he hit the carpet then bounced out of the floor-to-ceiling window.

Ethan stood frozen, still holding Cameron, not wanting to put her down. The blast of the gun snapped him out of his malaise and another burst of fury swelled though him. He carefully put Cameron's body on the ground, then lunged at Casper. The revelation that Casper's gun was no ordinary gun and was more than capable of blasting a hole through his steel hard skin should have made him think twice, but he had never been so angry in his life, so before he could think about this situation rationally, he was already airborne.

Casper turned and pulled the trigger at point-blank range. Ethan, still seeing everything in slow motion, clenched his jaw in anticipation of getting shot, but the gun didn't go off. Realizing that he had used all his bullets on Ascot, Casper moved with superhuman speed. His electrically stimulated muscle-suit made him amazingly powerful. He caught Ethan in mid-air, then using a jujitsu move, tossed the surprised Ethan over his shoulder. Ethan landed flat on his back, looking up to see Casper ready to stomp on his neck. Ethan rolled out of the way a fraction of a second before Casper's shoe hit the ground, making the floor shake. Hundreds of little puzzle pieces of safety glass popped into the air, creating a tiny fireworks display as the sunlight reflected off their jagged, uneven surfaces.

Ethan got on his hands and knees, positioning himself to leap into battle, when Casper's other foot punted him on the side like a football kick-off. Ethan felt the air blast out of his lungs as a sharp pain jolted from his kidneys and stomach. He tumbled across the floor. His suit and sweaty hair picked up pieces of glass like a lint roller. When he came to a stop, Casper tried to kick him in the groin, but Ethan blocked the kick, leaving his upper body unguarded. Casper swung around and kicked Ethan squarely in the jaw with his heel. The blow was perfectly executed and would have shattered any normal person's jaw, but for Ethan it was just demoralizing.

Once again he was feeling mortal. One of the things Ascot taught him when boxing was to always feel invincible. When you know you are losing, change your strategy but never lose your faith. As soon as you feel the other guy is better, you've lost your edge.

Ethan remembered the famous Muhammad Ali/George Foreman fight in Zaire. Foreman was bigger, stronger and twice as brutal as Ali. Foreman should have knocked out Ali in the first round, but Ali was a winner, and winners never allow themselves the luxury of feeling futile. Knowing that Foreman was bigger and stronger, Ali had to be smarter and think outside the box. He had to do something no boxer had ever done before. He did, and he won. Recalling this strategy, Ethan renewed his determination to win.

Casper grabbed Ethan by the hair, dragged him across the glass-littered floor, and then slammed his head into the heavy wood table that lay on its side. There was a loud clunk then, like a cue ball hitting an eight ball, the table scooted across the floor towards Cameron's body.

Ethan was exhausted. He hadn't eaten in hours, his mouth was dry, and he was dehydrated. He got back up onto his hands and knees, but before he could get up onto his feet. Casper landed another kick to Ethan's chest. Casper snickered as he watched Ethan cough and fall over onto his side.

As much as he tried to feel like a winner, it wasn't working. Everyone he had ever cared about was dead: Cameron, the only woman he had ever loved, his dad, Ascot, and the R.A.D. team. All their idealism and desire to change the world for the better had turned out to be a waste of time. The status quo marches on, leaving a wake of devastation.

Casper danced around the room like a fighter before the first round. His rage was palpable. He grabbed chairs and refuse tossing them aside, making a space to fight in the middle of the ravaged room. "Get up!" Casper shouted.

Ethan looked up at the dancing fool with blood lust in his eyes. The dust in the room had settled and Ethan was aware of the intense damage the blast had caused. The room looked like a construction site, the walls blown open, exposing the ventilation, water and gas pipes; air conditioning tubes and electrical wires dangled from the walls and ceiling.

"Get up and fight me like a man!" Casper demanded. Then he picked up a random filing cabinet and tossed it out the window. Ethan climbed onto his feet and stared at Casper, looking deeply into his eyes, the lifeless eyes of a reptile.

The two men circled the room, occasionally kicking debris out of the fighting area but never taking their eyes off each other. Finally Casper leaped into the air with a drop kick. Ethan blocked it, but Casper spun around and landed an elbow to Ethan's temple. Ethan was slightly stunned and staggered backwards. Casper charged, went for a field goal kick to the nuts. Ethan blocked it with his left hand and threw a right hook. Casper ducked the punch and landed a hard right to Ethan's solar plexus.

Ethan fired a left jab that clipped Casper in the jaw. This gave Ethan enough time to get back into his boxing stance and face his opponent. Ethan lunged forward and blasted Casper with a series of punching combinations. Now Casper was on the defensive. He was blocking punches and being pushed into the corner of the room. Ethan landed a solid right hook to the ribs, then a left jab to the side of his head, knocking Casper to the ground.

As he fell, Casper looked up at Ethan like an innocent, wounded animal. For a split second Ethan felt some compassion for this monster of a man and let down his guard, but the very second Casper hit the ground he sprang back like a cobra. He landed a perfectly executed right hook in the jaw, followed by a left hook on the other side of Ethan's jaw, then a kick to his stomach. Ethan fell flat on his back.

Casper bent over, resting his hand on his knees to catch his breath. "That's right space boy. Did you really think for a second that you were going to beat me?" His voice sputtered, breathing hard, then he paced, staring at Ethan's motionless body. "I don't lose!" he coughed out. "You understand? I don't lose!"

Ethan opened his eyes just a tiny crack and watched Casper as he paced and ranted. Then he realized that was subconsciously counting:

"One-one-thousand, two-one-thousand, three-one-thousand..."

This was what he did when he fought the Ultimate Sparring Partner. It was the one trick that even fooled the computer. Ethan looked up to where Casper had blown a hole into the ceiling. He saw a strategy. Ethan concentrated. Not moving, he focused all his energy on invigorating his muscles.

"...Four-one-thousand..."

Ethan hadn't given in to the dark side like Casper had. He wasn't cynical.

"...Five-one-thousand, six-one-thousand..."

He didn't exploit people. He stood for what was right and what was good about human beings.

"...Seven-one-thousand, eight-one-thousand..."

Now it was time to put this all to rest.

"...Nine-on- thousand..."

Casper had just turned his back to Ethan for a second. Ethan sprang to his feet and jumped up into the rafters of the decimated ceiling, grabbing the thick electrical conduit that brought power into the building. The cable pulled free and pieces of drywall burst from what was left of the ceiling and wall. Ethan pounced down on top of Casper like a spider grabbing its prey, then at a blinding speed twisted the heavy metal cable around Casper's body.

Surprised, Casper was immobilized in a cocoon of insulated electrical current. Ethan dug his fingers in, peeling off the metal conduit casing and exposing the heavy gauge Romex wires. With his fingernails, he scratched off a piece of the black plastic coating, exposing the thick copper wire. Casper struggled to free himself but could barely move. Ethan tore another hole in the conduit on Casper's opposite side, then peeled off the white plastic coating until the copper was free. The two exposed wires stood poised a half-inch from each of Casper's shoulders.

"Take this shit off me and fight me like a man!" snorted Casper, foaming at the mouth. He spat at Ethan, who easily dodged the loogie.

Ethan felt a burning hatred for this man consuming him. He wanted to tear Casper's head off, but for some inexplicable reason he just stood there. Some moral dilemma occupied the back of his mind. If Casper were to be electrocuted, Ethan would feel much better about it if Casper were the one who threw the switch.

At that very moment, Casper tried to kick Ethan, but the heavy wire and metal casing that pinned his arms to his sides made him lose his balance. He fell onto his left side, suddenly pressing the white wire against his shoulder.

Ethan stood and watched as Casper wrestled, trying to get out from the coils.

"I'm not sure that's a good idea!" warned Ethan.

"Screw you!"

Ethan brushed off the broken glass on his suit, then watched as Casper wiggled and writhed on the ground.

Then, as predictable as a sunrise, Casper rolled onto his right side and the black wire pressed against his shoulder.

Chapter 76

Sparks flew, lights dimmed, and a loud crackling noise filled the room, as 220 volts of electricity surged through Casper's suit and body. Ethan stepped back and watched Casper drool and flop around like he was having a grand mal seizure. He wasn't sympathetic. After all, Casper was a cold-blooded, sociopathic killer who had just perforated Ascot and put a bullet through Cameron's head, but Ethan wondered: was it bad karma to kill a killer or was it good karma? Was it murder? Or was he doing a public service?

The rage inside him subsided. He didn't like the idea of being responsible for frying Casper, but at this point there was nothing Ethan could do without getting electrocuted as well.

A strong odor of burnt flesh assaulted Ethan's nose, then he felt his feet tingle from the electrical current going through the floor. He had to get out of the room before things got worse. He was strong and molecularly dense, but he wasn't immune to high-voltage electrical current.

He ran over and grabbed Cameron's body and put her over his shoulder like a fireman, then stepped past Casper, feeling completely indifferent as the bald man in the rubber robotic suit continued to flop on the floor like a strip of bacon frying in a pan. Ethan carried Cameron's body out of the door and went to look for Patik.

Ethan stumbled around the top floor, looking in every empty office, trying to find the computer hacker. There was a lot of dust in the air from all the explosions and he had difficulty breathing and seeing through the haze. Now that the fight was over, Ethan's adrenaline rush was gone and his body was overwhelmed with exhaustion. He was ready to collapse.

At that same moment, Patik had found Casper's private computer terminal in a small windowless room just off Casper's big office, and was frantically typing. He was on a treasure hunt, as revved up as a prospector following a vein of gold. He had downloaded all kinds of private documents, including Simon's stolen patent for his magnetic engine and Casper's financial files. Patik felt empowered—this was what he was good at. It was a day of reckoning that was long overdue.

"Merry Christmas!" Patik said under his breath to himself, as he pushed the send key. In the blink of an eye, he had just redistributed Casper's wealth, anonymously transferring billions of Casper's personal and company funds into the accounts of various non-profit, environmental, and progressive political organizations.

Ethan had searched the entire top floor and was about to go downstairs when a flicker of light caught his eye. There was an unusual break in the pattern of the wall. Ethan quietly walked through the rubble and peeked through a door that was ajar. There sat Patik, looking as happy as a pig eating a truffle. Ethan watched as he hit the send key again, instantly sending Simon's zero-emission magnetic engine blueprints to every college, university, trade school and engineering firm on the planet.

Ethan stepped into the room with Cameron in his arms. Patik turned to face the pair, very excited and proud of his victory. "I know Simon was hoping that his invention would make him rich, but so long as one plays the game of commerce, the big fish will always have the upper hand and most likely win. However, take away the profit motive and we can change the world, right, Cameron!" As soon as he said that, he realized that Cameron's temples were a bloody mess. Patik's face fell.

Ethan had nothing to say. Patik stared at Cameron, a tear rolling down the bridge of his angular nose. After a few moments of silence, Patik wiped his eyes. "She was a strong, dedicated fighter who stood for what was right and lived with integrity!" Ethan nodded, holding back his own tears, took her body off his shoulder and sat her in a plush office chair adjacent to the one Patik was sitting in. The two men were silent for a moment.

Finally Ethan broke the silence. "Are you done?"

Patik shook off his feelings of sadness and turned back to the terminal. "I've just scratched the surface. There is a lot more here."

"Then get to it!" barked Ethan. "Make sure she died for a good reason!"

Ethan pulled up a third chair and sat down. Immediately, he felt his body melt into the soft cushion. He leaned back and the tension began to vaporize from his body. He closed his eyes and was instantly asleep.

A loud explosion shook Ethan awake. He had no idea if he had been out for an hour or just a few seconds. Leaning back in his chair, he watched the roof peel open like a sardine can. The bright desert sun poured in, soaking him and Patik with its blinding heat. A second later, the distinctive sound of a helicopter circling the building reverberated through the little room. Covering his eyes to soften the glare, Ethan searched the horizon for the source of the sound. Then out of the glaring sun came a fully armed, desert combat, helicopter gunship, prototype.

When it got closer, he saw to his surprise that sitting in the cockpit were Casper and The Crusher. Casper's electrified rubber suit had insulated him from the building's electrical current. The convulsions Ethan had witnessed were the result of his suit short-circuiting making his muscles involuntarily contract. Once he was able to wiggle free from one of the hotwires that was pressing against his shoulder, the current stopped and he was able to escape and quickly recover. Now he was determined to finish this fight as unfairly and as quickly as possible, using all of his last remaining resources.

Below him, Ethan's reflexes kicked into high gear. Instantly he was out of the chair and onto his feet. He didn't even allow himself the time to be baffled by Casper's escape. At this point nothing surprised him,

"Patik! We've got to go, now!" Ethan looked over and saw Patik racing through a stack of windows on the computer screen, sucking the last bit of data out of the terminal.

A burst of gunfire shot out of the helicopter. Ethan panicked and without thinking, grabbed Patik by the shoulder and lifted him out of the chair, then carried him under his arm like a surfboard. The tiny hard drive that Patik used to dump the data onto dragged behind them. Ethan ran out of the room and down the stairs. Patik tried to reel in the hard drive, praying that the cable that connected it would hold. When the hard drive hit the second step it popped up and bounced into Patik's hands.

A second later, a missile flew through the hole in the roof, hitting the floor ten yards from the stairway. The entire top floor erupted in a shower of flames and burning office furniture. A fireball consumed the stairwell, following Ethan like a snake chasing a rabbit down its hole. Ethan leaped as far as he could.

The moment Ethan landed on the floor below, he heard a loud "Woompf." The room burst into flames like the inside of a gas barbeque; the wallpaper began peeling, then igniting like thousands of matchbooks. The ceiling caved in and the stairwell collapsed from the shockwave. Within seconds, the room was engulfed in fire.

Ethan ran towards the emergency fire escape. He burst open the door, literally knocking it off its hinges and slamming it to the ground, making a loud bang that echoed through the concrete stairwell. He leaped down the concrete and steel stairs five at a time. Patik, petrified, stayed as rigid as he could under Ethan's arm. He was feeling utterly helpless and dared not move, afraid that he might wet himself in his fear.

Within seconds, Ethan arrived on the ground floor and kicked open the door. They were outside the back of the building, facing the parking lot. The top of the building was completely engulfed in flames. Thick black smoke rose into the sky.

Suddenly there were several more explosions. The burning building began to implode and started crashing to the ground like a controlled demolition. Ethan sprinted from the building as fast as he could, while burning refuse popped out the top of the building like a giant popcorn machine. Suddenly Casper's helicopter appeared out of the smoke and started shooting at them.

With Patik still under his arm, Ethan ran towards the concrete wall that surrounded the airbase. The helicopter's gunfire sprayed the ground behind them. Ethan leaped over the wall like a kangaroo. The wall turned into rubble as it shattered and crumbled from the bullets. Ethan grabbed a large chunk of concrete that had broken off, and, with all his strength, tossed it at the circling helicopter. It hit the tail rotor, spinning the helicopter around at the exact time that Casper pushed the button to fire another missile. The missile shot out while in mid-turn and went out into the empty desert. The helicopter seemed to regain control and took off in the opposite direction.

The chance of the missile hitting anything in the empty desert, where virtually nothing lives, was extremely unlikely. So it was more than unexpected when the high-yielding, conventional missile, scored a direct hit on one of the Soviet-made nuclear bombs, lodged deep in the desert sand. The explosion instantly melted the nuclear devices detonator, triggering it to explode.

The ground flashed and then erupted, blowing white-hot sand straight up into the air. The helicopter was blown upward by the shockwave, tripling its altitude in seconds and pushing it away from the building and parking lot. The helicopter tumbled rotor-over-tail and after a few seconds started spinning around like a Frisbee.

Ethan put Patik on the ground. Together, they ran towards the parking lot. He reflected that it took all their teamwork to bring down Casper, but now they no longer had a team; just Patik and himself. Was it worth it?

The mushroom cloud was sprouting in the desert and they needed to leave fast. The parking lot was about an eighth full. Most of the cars were regular pedestrian cars, nothing fancy and nothing to get excited about. Ethan and Patik walked past a few and looked inside. All of them were locked.

Ethan looked at Patik: " Do you know how to hotwire a car?"

"No!" Patik scoffed.

"They do it in movies all the time; how hard can it be?"

"New cars have all kinds of safety features that make it almost impossible to hotwire!"

As Patik finished his sentence, he walked over to the VIP section of the parking lot, which was indoors to protect the expensive cars from the sun, wind, and sand. In the corner was a valet key box. Patik raced over to it and opened it. He grabbed the expensive-looking key hanging on peg number seven. Parked in slot number seven was a bright red Dodge Viper. Patik grinned; he'd always wanted the opportunity to drive the "ultimate muscle car." He looked around the lot. There was a BMW, a Mercedes, and a Bentley. They needed something that would get them quickly away from the rapidly approaching fallout and to safety. There was no rule that said they couldn't do it in style.

Patik clicked the key and the car chirped, indicating that its two doors were unlocked. "I'm driving!" said Patik, as they both ran to the car and climbed in. The 750-horsepower, supercharged V-10 engine roared to life, giving Patik a rush of energy. He backed up out of the space, then carefully eased his way past the row of VIP cars. The second they were outside and had a clear stretch of road, Patik slammed the pedal down and the tires screeched, burning rubber. The car fishtailed, then shot down the long private driveway like it was a drag strip. The G-force slammed Patik and Ethan against their seats. Ethan turned to look behind them. The mushroom cloud was now at its full height and had created a monster sand storm that was rapidly approaching them.

"Step on it!" cried Ethan.

Patik was already going as fast as he could, driving at the edge of his ability. Every ounce of concentration he had was focused on reading the road and maintaining control of the powerful car. He was about to say, "You must be joking!" when he looked into the rearview and saw the massive grey storm that looked like a freak tornado. The fallout was rapidly expanding and getting closer every second. Patik clenched his jaw and floored the pedal as hard as he could.

* * * *

Charlie, the guard, was an Eden, Inc. fixture. Scheduled to retire every year for the last twelve years, he didn't know what he would do if he didn't have a job to go to every day. His wife had died, his kids all lived thousands of miles away and he didn't have any hobbies. Casper liked Charlie and kept him employed because he was extremely reliable, was never late, never complained, and did everything by the book. Charlie loved having a routine, loved knowing and following the rules, and liked the quiet isolation of his job. He spent his days happily sitting in his guardhouse doing crossword puzzles, making sure that only authorized personnel ever passed through his gate. That was his job and he did it well.

Earlier that day, when the perimeter was breached, all the younger guards, who had an insatiable appetite for violence, had abandoned their posts. They went to see if they could go shoot something. Charlie was flabbergasted by this generation's lack of discipline. He would never abandon his post.

When he heard the explosions and saw that the main building was on fire, he knew that wasn't his concern. He was assigned to guard the front entrance. He watched the cars zoom out of the parking lot like rats deserting a sinking ship, but he never questioned the importance of staying put and guarding his gate. Even the mushroom cloud billowing up across the desert didn't worry old Charlie. He had seen some strange test explosions out in the middle of the desert from time to time, probably just another one. He was committed to making sure that his entrance wasn't breached. He would stay put until he heard otherwise from one of his supervisors.

He was trying to think of a ten-letter word for "a 19th century orchestral bass instrument" that started with the letter O and ended with an E, when he noticed Casper's red Viper speeding at least eighty or ninety miles an hour out of the parking lot. Charlie put his puzzle down with the hope of getting some instructions as to what to do. Obviously today wasn't a normal working day.

Earlier he had wondered what was going on and had tried contacting his supervisors by phone and walkie-talkie, but never got a response. Casper coming was both good and bad news. Casper would give Charlie instructions, but no doubt with all that seemed to be going on today, he would most likely be in a bad mood. Charlie braced himself.

The Viper continued to speed down the road before it slammed on its brakes, just before hitting the row of speed bumps a few yards before the guard house. Smoke rose from its large racing tires, leaving long, wide skid marks on the road. Charlie stepped out of his air-conditioned room, just as the skidding Viper's low chassis bounced and bottomed out, banging against the concrete bumps. By time the car approached him it had slowed down to about ten miles an hour.

Both relief and panic came over Charlie when he saw that there were two people he'd never seen before driving Casper's car.

At least he wouldn't have to deal with Casper's bad mood. Instead he would have to determine if these people were authorized to be driving Casper's car. Charlie stepped into the road and when it became apparent that the drivers weren't going to stop, he reached for his sidearm. The Viper's horn blasted loudly, startling the guard, making him jump and drop his gun. With amazing agility for an old man, Charlie jumped back onto the sidewalk that circled the guardhouse.

As the Viper roared past, Charlie heard the driver yell, "Get out of here, you fool!" Then the red muscle car took off like a bullet. Charlie watched the car in awe and confusion. After a few seconds, the Viper was just a red dot and a distant rumble. Ethan turned and saw the confused guard look in horror as the massive mushroom cloud began engulfing the Eden, Inc. airbase. He clearly had no idea what to do, as he ran inside, back to the safety he thought would be provided by his guardhouse.

Patik had the Viper's V-10 engine wide open. Fortunately the road was straight and they were headed directly away from the blast, so they were able to maintain some distance from the growing mass. Far away in the sky, Ethan saw Casper's helicopter. It appeared that he was trying to get around the debris cloud and chase them, but the helicopter was being pushed in the opposite direction.

Ethan suddenly felt, the same way he had felt sitting in the escape pod praying to a God he didn't really believe in to get him safely back to Earth. He was a helpless passenger in a car. If Casper and The Crusher could maneuver past the bomb blast and reach them, there was nothing they could do. They were no match for a jet helicopter gunship.

The main road was just a few miles ahead and once they made it there, they would be with other cars and perhaps there would be safety in numbers, but Ethan seriously doubted that the fear of collateral damage would in any way make Casper hesitate. No, the Interstate highway would not be their sanctuary.

Dust, sand, and hot wind tore across the desert as the fallout cloud continued to build. What was left of the Eden, Inc. buildings was hit with scorching hot radioactive wind that vaporized everything in its path. Patik had the Viper in sixth gear, pedal still to the floor. They were going over one hundred and seventy miles an hour and getting faster. It was the fastest Patik had ever driven and every nerve was on edge. Despite their speed, the wind and sand were catching up to them. Patik's adrenaline was pumping hard, though Ethan watched the sky with growing relief. The helicopter seemed to be trapped behind the rapidly expanding cloud and continued to move away from them.

The Viper arrived at the Interstate freeway on-ramp. Patik only slowed down slightly and didn't bother to look to see which direction they were headed. His objective was to just stay in front of the expanding wall of death. The road was empty and smooth and the Viper growled as it sped away.

After a few minutes, they realized the cloud appeared to get smaller as they drove further and further away. Patik was cautious and wasn't ready to slow down yet; besides, as relief washed though him, he was having a good time setting a new personal speed record. Ethan continued to scan the sky for Casper's helicopter. It seemed that for the time being they were free from Casper's retaliation, but how long would that last?

After about ten minutes, the cloud was just an ugly grey mass in the distance. In front of them was a mini-van, the first car they had seen on the road since they'd hit the highway. Patik slowed down to a hundred miles an hour, passing the van at eighty. Patik looked at the speedometer and grinned; he was still driving fast but it felt like he was joyriding at five miles an hour through a parking lot. More cars were up ahead so Patik slowed down some more to match the traffic. Now it felt like he was stuck in molasses.

Ethan finally broke the silence. "So what do we do now?"

Patik shrugged. "Well, the car is certainly Lo-Jacked and not at all inconspicuous, so it won't be long until they find the car and us in it. Casper may put a news report to all the TV stations—two fugitives driving a stolen red Viper—and our names and faces would be broadcast all over the TV and internet," Patik said matter-of-factly in his lilting voice. "No doubt, in a few hours our identities will be known to everyone in the area. We will need to ditch the car and find a safe place to lay low."

"I was thinking more about what do we do now that Cameron, Simon, and M'buy are dead and Eden, Inc. is in ruins?"

"Listen, mate!" Patik's Indian accent got thicker anytime he got excited. "We stopped something catastrophic from happening and that was good, but Casper's not done. Despite all that we did, he still has lots of resources and there are dozens more scumbags like him out there."

The Viper passed a cluster of cars. Ethan felt a little bit like a celebrity as they received enthusiastic looks and waves from the passengers.

Patik continued. "All the things that we hold dear: freedom, liberty, openness, respect for mankind and the environment, are all constantly under attack by these greedy corporate predators."

"Yeah," agreed Ethan.

"Unfortunately most people don't know and don't care to know this fact. Our cause is never advertised, only spun by the corporate media to make us look bad. Just like no one is going to know that we just prevented twelve nuclear bombs from going off around the world, so the value of what we do is priceless, and we have to accept that this is our lot in life."

"So we're running from the law, doing what's right, and getting no credit?"

"That's about it!" said Patik.

"Damn. That kind of sucks, doesn't it?"

Patik nodded, then stepped on the gas, the G-force slamming the two of them back against their seats once again. "So let's enjoy the ride!"

Epilogue

Sipping her morning coffee, still in her pajamas and slippers, Senator Amanda Goldman went to her computer to open her e-mail. She scanned down the screen. There was the usual stuff, but then one caught her eye. The subject line read: "Leverage." The return address read Casper Degas. "Casper Degas?" She thought, and immediately got nervous. She hated that bastard and assumed, "He's going to try to bully or blackmail me."

"Well, bring it on!" she thought, so with clenched teeth she clicked on the email.

To her surprise it was an elaborate set of documents complete with video, photos, and audio clips detailing a laundry list of illegal acts by dozens of senators, members of Congress, lobbyists, and corporate big shots. These files could provide enough solid evidence to ruin careers, and in some cases put people in prison for years.

The senator scratched her head. "Why would he be sending me this?" Most of the senators on the list were the guys Casper helped put in office and who did his bidding.

She was trying to get support on a bill that would make it illegal to lobby Congress, so the senators and members of Congress could actually represent the people who voted for them, instead of being held hostage by the businesses that financed their campaigns. None of her colleagues were particularly interested, but as she looked through the email she got excited and thought: "This could be a game changer."

* * * *

Andrew Rosser, who lived in Florida, was hired to build an app that would help raise money for the World Wildlife Fund, a nonprofit group that did what it could to save animals and their habitat from extinction. The group had good intentions, but they weren't raising the kind of money that was going to make any kind of real difference. Andrew agreed with the World Wildlife Fund's cause and he really wanted to see them raise money, and often thought about what he could do to improve it. Andrew looked at the app every day, out of curiosity, to see what the daily tally of fundraising was. The last time he had checked the site, it had raised $10,198, an increase of $198 over the day before. He opened the site, expecting the usual. When he saw the number, he rubbed his eyes and did several double takes. It was now $100,010,198.00.

* * * *

In Argentina, Rodolfo Wabich, a graduate student at the University of Buenos Aries, was working on an idea for his master's thesis when he was interrupted by the ding of an arriving email. Not doing anything in particular, he gladly opened his messages. The subject line read: "Fwd: Not For Profit"

It looked like junk, but he opened it anyway. To his surprise, the message was comprised of detailed plans for a low-wattage electric engine that worked on magnetism. Years before when he was an undergraduate, he had thought about something similar, but his professors all told him it was impossible. Now there was a video of the engine working. There was some red-haired guy explaining it in detail while driving around in a car he had built. The video went on to show the engine being used as an electrical generator. A single solar panel powered the engine, which generated thousands of watts of electricity.

Rodolfo looked over at his water cooler. It was a present given to him by his older brother Fredrico, who had seen it at an international commerce convention and thought it was something that his younger bother would appreciate. The machine made filtered, water from condensation out of the air. It seemed more like a novelty than a practical tool for making large amounts of water, because it required so much electricity.

Rodolfo looked back at the engine on the screen. Then an idea for his thesis popped into his mind, how he could end drought and famine. The instructions in the email said:

"Use This Technology To Change The World For The Better. Not For Profit!"

He looked at the recipients of this e-mail. It had been forwarded over twenty times, and each time there were hundreds of names that it was sent to. Rodolfo had a sudden burst of inspiration and motivation. Pulling on his headphones, Rodolfo opened up a new document and began to type furiously. He wanted to get his project built before someone beat him to it.

* * * *

Ethan sat on the grass in front of an old oak tree at the Boyle Heights cemetery in East LA. Vince's body had been cremated, then held by the county for two years waiting to be claimed. When no one claimed the ashes, they were eventually dumped into a common unmarked grave along with 1,651 other people, mostly homeless and poor.

For the first time since he had arrived back on Earth, Ethan wasn't being chased and hunted like a rabbit. Eden Inc's desert air base was destroyed, the corporation's bank accounts had been emptied, and Casper Degas, for the time being, was in hiding. Finally Ethan had some relief.

Now his grief had suddenly hit him hard. Ethan missed his dad and had wanted more than anything to make his father proud. Vince had been such a muscle-head that being physically strong had meant everything to him. Ethan hadn't shared that same level of body builder enthusiasm, and had always felt he had let his dad down.

Ethan plucked at a blade of grass, accidentally yanking out a clump of dirt and grassy roots along with it. "How ironic that I would become the strongest man on the planet and Vince wouldn't be around to see it. And the accident that gave me my strength would also be the thing that got him killed." It just didn't seem fair.

When Ethan had left that morning to go onto the shuttle, he hadn't properly said goodbye. It didn't seem necessary—after all, it was just a summer job and he figured before he knew it he would be back at gym working alongside his dad, as if he had never left.

His mind turned to Casper Degas. That bald-headed psychopath had taken everything and everyone away from him. A dark rage seethed through Ethan's body and started to burn deep. Casper was still out there and he was going to continue to do all the things he had done to ruin Ethan's life, as well as countless other people's. Ethan clenched his jaw. When people like Casper get away with the crimes they commit, it just makes them more cynical, more confident and they come back even bolder.

Ethan wasn't going to let that happen. He rose to his feet and brushed the grass and dirt off his rear end. If Casper Degas was out there rebuilding, Ethan Stone was going to be there to stop him.

THE END